KNOT MY REALITY

Miranda May

Knot My Reality

Copyright © 2023 by Miranda May.

All rights reserved.

No part of this book may be used or reproduced in any manner without written permission from the author, except for the use of brief quotations in a book review.

This book is a work of fiction. All names, characters, events, and locations are the work of the author's imagination. Any resemblances to actual persons, living or dead, events or locations is entirely coincidental.

Published by Luna Moon Publishing 2023

Cover Design by EmCat Designs

Editing by Owlsome Author Services

To my fabulous reading teams!
Without y'all, this would not be nearly as good!

Foreword & Trigger Warnings

Hello readers!

Welcome to my first omegaverse! I've been super psyched to get this written and out for all of you to read. I currently have five planned standalones in this series and at least one novella, if not more.

Please be aware that this series is a reverse harem/why choose romance, meaning that our FMC won't have to choose between her men. There is explicit language and sexual encounters—including group sex. There is also M/M within the harem, so if this isn't something you read, then turn around now.

If you read this story and love it, make sure to review! It's what gets me the Zon to share my book more!

Just a few possible trigger warnings: discussion of mental health issues and past trauma revolving around abuse from family members/past partners. There is a moment that can be considered cheating from one of the suitors, but is followed by a discussion with the FMC. If any of this will be triggering for you, please don't read this story. Your mental health is what's important!

Happy reading!

The Event

March 5, 2033 was the day the world ended…

At least that's what the people who woke up that morning thought was happening.

It's the day the sun never rose and the day natural disaster after natural disaster bombarded the Earth. Earthquakes, tsunamis, hurricanes, blizzards, volcanic eruptions—anything one can think of, they ravaged the Earth.

Cities destroyed, and billions died.

Then came the sound. It started so quietly, no one noticed it over the chaos.

Louder and louder, it grew until no one could ignore it. Those still alive collapsed to their knees, hands to their ears, sure their eardrums were going to burst.

A blinding, bright white light lit up the sky and then every person fell unconscious.

When they awoke, they found a changed world where the sun rose in the west and set in the east. A world where humanity as they knew it changed. Anyone that survived what they dubbed the apocalypse—later named the Event—found themselves biologically changed.

It took years of research to discover what had changed, but those living it figured it out quickly. Humans had evolved and now had new designations—alpha, beta, and omega.

They learned to live with these new designations as they rebuilt the world they once knew. Nothing would ever be quite the same, but that didn't mean it couldn't be better.

Chapter One

Bree
Year: 2258

A glance in the mirror has me screwing up my face in disgust. "Remind me why I agreed to do this again?"

Tessa's laugh is loud, filling the room before she steps up behind me. My eyes meet hers in the mirror and she gives me a quick smile.

"Because you're a control freak?"

"I am not." I frown, turning to glare at her.

Tessa laughs again. "Yeah, keep telling yourself that lie. I know the truth."

Scrunching up my nose, I don't reply. It's not the first time that we've had this argument and I'm sure that it won't be the last. And no matter how many times I argue with her, we both know that she's right. I am one hundred percent a control freak—which generally works in our favor. Right now? Not so much.

Forcing my eyes back onto my reflection, I try to pretend that I'm someone else—anyone else—so that I can be objective.

Chestnut brown hair pulled up into a stylish twist that I would never have the patience for. Amber eyes lined in a way that makes them pop and pouty lips painted a bright red. The dress draped across my body matches my lips exactly, as do the shoes that aren't visible from beneath the hemline. For me, it's just too damn much, but for *Heated*? It's kind of perfect, and that's what matters.

"You look gorgeous, omega," Tessa says quietly, reaching over to grip my hand in hers.

My body relaxes not just at her words, but at her touch, even as my mind continues to race. Such is the way of omegas and alphas, which is why our partnership works so well. We balance one another in a way that two alphas, two betas, or an alpha/beta combination never could.

Tessa and I met at college orientation, and the pair of us hit it off immediately—something that our designations shouldn't have allowed. Tessa had been the first to tell me that my ideas weren't only good, but that they could change the world. Okay, maybe not change the world, but make it at least a little better.

Living as an omega who wanted to do something more with her life other than finding her pack and popping out babies, I was often laughed at. I was told to learn my place, to not try to change things—even from my own parents. Well, some of them, since I was born into a pack. But not Tessa. Tessa understood our designations weren't the end all, be all.

It had taken us a couple of years, but before we started our senior year, we'd managed to get our new company, Fated Industries, off the ground and even launched our very first app—*Knotted*.

Knotted allows for omegas like myself to find an alpha, or multiple alphas, to help them through their heats. No commitment, no shame. As much as society tries to force it upon us, we don't need packs to get through our heat and we should have a way to get through it that isn't just us spending days miserable, alone, and wishing to be filled with a knot.

Our second app, *Mated*, came three years after graduation. *Mated* allows those omegas looking for their forever pack to begin their search safely. No relying on our families to introduce us to packs that they approve of. No going to bars, hoping we'll meet the ones meant for us. Our teams thoroughly vet each alpha, beta, and pre-established pack. They each go through extensive background checks before being approved for the app. Personality tests match omegas and potential packs, or non-pack alphas and betas, that we believe are their best option, but they also have access to every available alpha, beta, and pack in the database. There are no limits on who they can speak to, meet, or even court. We don't want to limit anyone. Even though neither Tessa nor I have found our happily ever afters, we love hearing every success story of the packs formed with help from our app.

Now, seven years later, we're taking our brand even further. *Heated* is an experiment that we hope will be successful. A reality dating show where we match an omega with twenty suitors. The group of twenty suitors can comprise single alphas, single betas, or packs—bonded or unbonded.

Today begins the first day of our very first season—which, if it doesn't go well, will be on me. Not just because it was my idea, my baby. But because I volunteered to be our very first omega.

Tessa squeezes my hand and I meet her gaze once more. Her voice is soft when she speaks. "You're finally ready to focus on you and to find your pack now that you don't have to worry about the company. You want this, and I want it for you."

"Yeah, but why couldn't I pick out the suitors, so I could know what I was getting myself into?" Even I can hear the underlying whine in my voice.

Tessa's eyes roll skyward, her mouth moving but no sound coming out. Is she...

"Are you praying?"

Her head drops, a droll look on her face. "I am. I'm praying for patience with you. Why did we think you being the first omega was a good idea again?"

"I feel like you're trying to insult me, but I'm not sure how."

"As we already discussed, you're a fucking control freak, Bree, and you signed up to let me, your best friend, and the rest of the production team control your life for eight weeks. This was a terrible idea."

"Nah, it'll be fine."

She raises her eyebrow, giving me a pointed look before nodding to where I'm chewing on my thumbnail.

Fuck.

I drop my hand, shaking it out. I hadn't even realized I'd been doing it. Taking a deep breath, I close my eyes for a moment before nodding.

"I can't pick out the suitors because that's an unfair advantage that the other omegas wouldn't have. As with the future omega contestants, I could approve or veto scents only. I understand, and I'll try to be better about allowing you all to do your jobs."

"Good omega," she purrs, sending a shiver up my spine.

I let out a growl as soon as I realized what she's done. "Go take a flying leap off a tall building, alpha."

I fucking hate it when she does that, and she knows it. Shaking my head, I turn back to the mirror once more. I can't seem to stop looking at myself. I know it's because I almost don't recognize myself. And I hate it. We'd had the fitted, formal gown designed just for me, but it's not something that I would ever choose for myself. The hair and makeup? Not something I would bother spending so much time on. I feel like I'm being expected to sell a lie.

It's not the first time I've had to dress up like this since we regularly have to go to events, being the owners of Fated Industries, but this feels different. I am supposed to be myself, but not look like myself. That makes no sense to me. I wonder how much of this discomfort has to do with what's coming and my lack of control over it.

"Bree," Tessa sighs as she pulls me away from the mirror, waiting until I'm facing her before she continues, "we want to add a flair to the show. Pretty dresses on pretty omegas and tuxes on hot alphas and betas will draw eyes. If we don't have viewers, we don't have a show."

I kind of hate how easily she can read me, but it's also comforting. "I understand. I just wish that I could look more like myself. Also, hopefully one day we'll have handsome omegas in tuxes and gorgeous alphas and betas in pretty dresses."

"And you will look like yourself—sometimes. But sometimes you have to dress up, just like when we have to go to events. And yes, eventually, we'll have alphas and betas in dresses, and omegas in tuxes. If this season does well. If it doesn't, we'll never see that."

I wrinkle my nose, but understand what she's telling me. And I won't be the only one dressed up.

Tessa's phone rings, and she lifts it to her ear. "Tessa." She pauses, listening to the person on the other line. "Got it. Bree and I are on our way now."

My hands fly to my stomach as nerves threaten to overwhelm me. This is it. It's time to put my game face on. I don't think I would be so nervous if I didn't care as much as I do, because I want this to be a success—not just because it's my brand on the line, but because I want a pack. At thirty-two, I'm well past the age that most omegas find their pack. But I'd chosen to put my career first, and I've never regretted that—I won't ever regret that.

"C'mon, Bree. It's time for your introduction interview. The first car is about thirty minutes out."

I nod, remaining quiet as I follow her from the room that will be mine for the next eight weeks. Eight weeks—that's all the time that I have to decide which of my twenty suitors I want to be a part of my pack. Eight weeks before my heat begins.

Fates above. Will that be enough time? Can I do this?

If I can't, then the show will fail. Because if I can't do it, then no one can. I don't want the show to fail. I want omegas to have another way to find their pack. Unlike with *Mated*, which is really geared toward younger omegas, *Heated* is for omegas like me. Past the age that society considers our prime age to find a pack because we focused on our careers, or we weren't ready. It doesn't matter the reason. I want to show the world that there are other options for omegas. That's what *Heated* is really for.

Continuing to follow behind Tessa, I lose myself in my thoughts as she leads to the massive grand foyer and then outside. The house that we're using for the show is massive—it has to be for the amount of people that are on the show or working on the show. Though, it isn't just a house, but a compound. On the property surrounding the massive house are cottages to be used by the staff and their families.

We'd built it here in Rancho Mirage, just outside of Palm Springs, because of its relative closeness to Los Angeles. LA is where our company is based, while we live in Thousand Oaks. There are so many people in the greater Los Angeles area that we decided we needed to go further out to build the compound. Palm Springs is a vacation destination for many people who live in LA, but by choosing Rancho Mirage, we could get a larger lot to build what we wanted.

Tessa and I have been working on this idea for years, and we had this compound built two years ago when we first got the green light from the network. We figured that if the show didn't work out, we'd turn it into some kind of center for omega heats. It's another idea that we've had, but that's next on our list after *Heated* is a success—or a failure.

We walk down the stone walkway, turning off and heading to one of the many gazebos on the compound. My introduction interview will take place here, but the rest of my post-meeting interviews will take place at the end of the walkway, where I will meet each of the suitors. While I'm doing my interview, Tessa will interview the suitor, or suitors, at the gazebo where my first interview is taking place. These interviews are to find out what our initial thoughts are on meeting one another.

Unless we watch the show when it airs, neither party will be privy to these interviews—not even me. Because, yes, I'd already asked Tessa if she'd let me watch them, and she'd refused. And it makes sense why I can't watch them, but I'm definitely a control freak and the idea of not knowing is already driving me crazy.

This entire process is disconcerting, but I'm glad that I'd volunteered to be our first omega. It'll help me understand what our future omegas are going through. Even knowing that, my stomach is in knots.

Knots. Ha.

Tessa glances over her shoulder, eyes narrowed when I snicker. I shoot her a quick grin, shrugging. I'm fairly certain she doesn't need to hear my juvenile thoughts.

"Bree, darling," a smooth, joyful voice calls out to me, and I don't have to fake my smile when I turn to face him.

Reginald pulls me into his arms, hugging me close. He lets out a whistle when he pulls back. "Damn, girl. You sure clean up good, don't you?"

"Shut up. Asshole." I swat playfully at his arm as he easily dodges my blow, chuckling.

Reginald is a beta that I also met my freshman year of college. He, Tessa, and I used to do everything together. Until a talent scout "discovered" him and he starred in a blockbuster summer movie. Then he was a household name, but lucky for us, he never forgot us.

Though we didn't get to see him as often, he helped us in any way that he could while we were building our company. And when we'd needed a host for *Heated*, we considered no one else. He and his pack are staying on the compound in a cottage, and it's been nice to spend so much time with him for the first time in years.

"Are you ready for this?"

I shake my head, following him onto the gazebo, and settling into the comfy nestlike chair that I'd chosen. "Absolutely not. I'm terrified."

"You? Terrified? I've never known you to be afraid of anything, B." Reginald shakes his head before leaning forward to squeeze my hand. "You've got this. All of those men are going to love you, and so are the viewers. You've got nothing to worry about."

"Easy for you to say," I mumble before rolling my shoulders and sitting up straighter. "Let's do this."

Tessa grins as she bends down to attach the mic to my dress, handing me the small box that it's attached to. I take it with a frown.

"What do you want me to do with this?"

Tessa laughs. "Tuck it in your bra."

My eyebrows shot up. "You want me to what now?"

"If you can't figure it out, I'll be happy to help you." Reginald winks as I glare at him.

"I'm sure that your omega would love that."

"You know Tyler loves you."

I snort. "Yeah, Tyler loves me from a distance. And I promise you, he wouldn't like it if he found out you had your hands anywhere near my boobs."

Reginald smirks as he shrugs. "You're probably right. But what he doesn't know..."

"That's it. Someone get me a phone. I'm calling Tyler and telling him you're hitting on me."

"Like he would believe you."

I lift an eyebrow, saying nothing. I actually don't know if Tyler would believe me or not, but it's not like I'm serious—just like I know Reginald isn't. As long as we've been friends, there's never been a moment where either of us considered becoming more than friends.

Dropping my eyes, I pull the front of my dress away from me, considering how I'm going to do this. My eyes shoot up when Tessa and Reginald burst into laughter. I don't know exactly why they're laughing, but I'm absolutely sure that I'm the butt of the joke.

"Just hook it to the inside of the front of the dress, like this," Tessa says as she takes the small box back from me. Seconds later, she has it hooked to the inside of my dress and I realize you can't even tell it's there.

"The two of you are assholes."

"Now, is that the way a proper omega should talk?" Tessa snickers.

Instead of answering, I shut my eyes and remind myself that I love Tessa and that killing her isn't the answer. "I thought we were in a hurry?"

"Right, right. I'll leave the two of you to it, then."

My head snaps up. "You're leaving me?"

Tessa tilts her head to the side as she considers me. "I'm heading to the control room, so I can make sure that all the cameras are good before the first suitor arrives."

"Oh, okay." Glancing down, I chew on the inside of my lip—because fates forbid, I mess up my lipstick. I'll never hear the end of it. I hate that my nerves have made me sound so meek and quiet. It's so unlike me.

"C'mon, B. It's just you and me having a conversation. You don't need Tessa here for that," Reginald says as he leans back in his seat.

"You, me, and a thousand cameras." I purse my lips before forcing a smile. "You're right though. I'm good, Tessa. I'll see you later."

Tessa hesitates for a moment and I know that her alpha instincts have to be screaming at her for leaving a distressed omega. Eventually, she nods and forces herself to walk away.

Turning back to Reginald, I gesture to him. "Do your thing."

"My thing?" Reginald laughs, throwing his head back. "Relax, B."

I try to—I really do—but it's not like I have some magic relaxation switch. I make myself as comfortable in the chair as I can, wishing that I could lift my legs beneath me, but knowing that Tessa will kill me if I wrinkle my dress before the suitors have even arrived.

Giving myself a quick pep talk, all I can do is hope that once Reginald and I start talking, I'll be able to relax. "I'm as ready as I'll ever be."

Reginald glances over his shoulder at Lydia, one of our producers, who gives him a quick thumbs up, before turning to look at the camera just over my shoulder.

"Hello, I'm Reginald Williams, and welcome to *Heated*."

Reginald turns to a camera off to the side of the gazebo. "*Heated* is the first of its kind. For the next eight weeks, you'll watch as our omega chooses between twenty suitors to form her pack before her heat hits. Let's meet our first season's omega—Bree Timmons."

He turns back to me and it's like the cameras don't exist as he meets my eyes. "Welcome, Bree."

"Hey, Reginald." I snicker, shaking my head. "I'm sorry, I'm just a little nervous."

"Well, no one can blame you for that. After all, never before has anyone chosen their pack this way. But before I have you tell us how that makes you feel, why don't you tell our viewers a little about yourself?"

"As Reginald said, my name is Bree Timmons. Some of you might recognize my name. I'm the CEO of Fated Industries, which I run with my partner, Tessa Hanson, who is the COO."

"And why would Fated Industries sound familiar to our viewers?"

Now, this? This I can do. I lean forward slightly, making sure that I'm speaking directly to the camera behind Reginald.

"We're the creators of both the *Knotted* and *Mated* apps. And *Heated* is our newest venture."

"So, you're the first omega on your own show? Tell us more about that."

"Tessa and I have been dreaming about making *Heated* a reality for years. One of the biggest obstacles for us was what omega in their right mind would want to be a guinea pig for this kind of show? The only answer that I could think of was that I do it myself. How could I ask other omegas to go through this process if I've never gone through it myself?"

Reginald nods. "Obviously, you don't have a pack yet, or else you wouldn't be here." The two of us laugh together before he continues, "So, why now?"

"I'm thirty-two, which, as has been pointed out to me regularly, is well past the age when society expects omegas to find their packs. I spent the years that omegas usually spend finding their pack, making my company a success. And it is a success. So now, it's time to do something for me. It's time for me to find my pack.

"And if the process and, in turn, the show is a success, then we can offer this opportunity to other omegas who waited to find their packs like I did. I don't know if everyone is aware of the statistics, or not, but every year there are fewer and fewer females born. It's something that is becoming a serious problem in our society, because without women, we have no way of reproducing.

"Women now only make up thirty percent of the population, which is a dramatic decrease from years past. Of that thirty percent, only one percent is born an omega. It's the same percentage for female alphas. So, of the thirty percent of females born, ninety-eight percent are betas.

"The beta population has been increasing every year. Sixty percent of the population is born betas, thirty percent alphas, and only ten percent omegas. And no one can figure out *why* this is happening."

I take a deep breath, realizing that I've gotten completely off-track—which isn't all that uncommon when I discuss the problems within our society. It's something I feel strongly about, and I don't feel like enough people are talking about it.

"Sorry, Reginald." I shoot him a sheepish grin. "I tend to go off on tangents."

Reginald just grins at me. "It's understandable. It's something that affects all of us, but is so often ignored."

"It is, but the reason that I brought it up is that it's hard being a female now, but a female omega? Or even a female alpha? We're in high demand, and we don't all want to spend our life being nothing more than a human incubator." I pause, realizing how bad that sounds. "I respect those who want to have children as soon as possible, but I always knew that wasn't for me. And I know that I'm not the only omega who feels that way. So Tessa and I wanted to make this show about more than just an omega finding her pack. We wanted it to allow omegas like me to find their packs—even if we're considered past our primes."

Reginald chuckles. "I don't think that anyone would consider you past your prime."

"You might be surprised," I tell him as I cock an eyebrow. He doesn't get it, and there's no way that he could. I don't think there's any way that I could explain it to make anyone else understand. "But while you might not understand, *they* get it."

"Who?"

"The omegas who chose to not find their packs young. They're living it, just like I am. They understand what I'm talking about. They know the feeling of being a disappointment to their family, to society. No one else can understand it, because you haven't lived it. But that's why we need *Heated*."

Reginald meets my eyes, inclining his head in understanding. "Now, you're about to meet your very first suitor. How are you feeling about that?"

"Nervous as hell." I laugh, eyes widening because although it's true, I hadn't meant to blurt it out like that. I can almost hear Tessa fussing at me about cursing, and I'm sure she'll give me shit about it later. The network bigwigs requested we keep the cursing to a minimum, but I think they're sadly mistaken about what's going to be happening on this show.

"I know nothing about these men. I don't know their names or what they look like. The only thing that I know is that I approved their scents at some point—because we obviously don't want to allow someone onto the show whose scent is repulsive to the omega. I don't even know which of the scents I approved belong to the suitors."

"I can see how that would be nerve-wrecking. But just think, you'll be so busy meeting suitors you won't have time to be nervous."

I make a face at him before remembering that I'm still being filmed. Let's hope they don't decide to use that clip. I'm one hundred percent sure it wasn't an attractive look for me.

"I'm not sure that's how it works, but thanks."

Reginald chuckles before glancing to the side. He nods and turns back to face me. "It looks like your first suitor is only minutes away. Are you ready for this?"

"No," I sputter before forcing myself to take a deep breath. I force a smile and straighten my shoulders as I stand. "But what choice do I have?"

Reginald stands with me, reaching out to squeeze my hand. "You've got this, Bree. And the good news is that I'll be the one doing all of your interviews. Tessa will oversee the suitor interviews."

"Not fair. I'd rather have Tessa." I bite my lip to keep myself from smiling because I already knew this, as I watch him from the corner of my eye for his reaction.

"Bitch," Reginald cries out before grinning. "Whatever, I know I'm your favorite. Let's go meet your first suitor. You're going to rock this."

Chapter Two

Bree

I feel like an idiot standing here waiting for some random man to arrive in a limo. A glance to my left reveals Tessa and Reginald whispering as their eyes remain locked on me. I narrow my eyes for just a moment before remembering the cameras that are locked on me, recording my every action. That's something that's going to take a lot of getting used to.

The sound of tires on pavement causes me to jerk my attention back to the circular driveway. It takes a moment for the limo to come into view, as the entrance is quite long and shaded by trees on both sides. It looks beautiful and Tessa said that it adds more drama to the reveal—whatever the hell that's supposed to mean.

Nerves flutter in my stomach and it takes everything in me to not lift my hands to press down on it. Not only would it not help, but it would let everyone else see just how nervous I am. I know I admitted to being nervous out loud, but that differs from showing just how nervous I am. I might be an omega, but I hate showing my weakness to others. It's not how an omega is supposed to act, but let's be real—I've never been, and never will be, a typical omega.

Most people expect an omega to be mild, meek, and passive. To not have an opinion of their own. After all, that's why we need alphas, isn't it? I've never been that type of person, and it has nothing to do with what my designation is.

Let's just hope that these suitors of mine understand and appreciate that. Otherwise, *Heated* is going to crash and burn before it even begins. And I can't have that. I won't have that.

The limo slows to a stop in front of me, my eyes locking onto the door that my suitor will exit any time now. Will he be an alpha? A beta? Will I remember his scent? I'd approved close to one hundred scents, and from there, the team narrowed that down to twenty.

Will it be a single suitor? A bonded pack? An unbonded pack?

I grasp at the sides of my gown, trying to hide the way my hands are shaking. Why is he taking so long? Had they told him to sit in the limo for a certain amount of time? Does he not want to be here? Is he disappointed in me already?

No. I will not let my omega instincts take over right now. I'm a strong, independent woman. I am more than my omega instincts.

Finally, the door opens, and he steps out. Even without scenting him, I know that this man is an alpha. He's tall, well over six feet. With buzzed brown hair, scruff covering his face. He's burly, muscles bulging against his clothes even as he stands still.

Our eyes lock, his chocolate brown meeting my amber ones. Neither of us speaks or moves, and finally, his scent hits me—sandalwood with just a hint of sage. It makes me instantly relax, and I offer him a smile. He doesn't return the smile as he moves toward me. If I had to guess, I'd say that he's in his thirties.

I watch the way his tux moves against his body, his muscles even more apparent when he moves. His hand lifts, messing with the bow tie as he makes a face. It's obvious that he isn't comfortable in the tux. It makes me wish we hadn't decided on formalwear for the introductions. How can anyone be themselves when they're uncomfortable in the clothes that they're wearing?

"Hi." I offer him my hand as he stops in front of me. "I'm Bree."

He glances between my hand and my eyes for a moment before taking it in his. He squeezes lightly before letting it go, annoying me. I hate when men—especially alpha men—shake my hand as if I'm going to break, but I'll try not to hold that against him.

"Owen. Owen Reid."

I wait for him to say anything else, but he just stands there, glowering at me. He looks like he'd rather be anywhere but here. It makes me wonder why he's here. Biting back a sigh, I try again.

"So, what do you do, Owen?"

His eyes light up for the first time. "I'm a MMA fighter."

That explains the muscles.

"I love MMA," I tell him with a genuine smile. "I do Jiu Jitsu myself."

He nods. "It's a good choice for women, especially omegas. It's good for you to learn self defense."

Silence falls between us again, and I really hope that it isn't like this with all the suitors. There's no way I can do this repeatedly.

"Great," Tessa calls, and I can hear her shuffle around behind me. "Why don't we go do your interviews?"

Keeping my smile plastered on my face, I give Owen a quick wave as he follows Tessa down the pathway. My smile falls slightly as I turn back to Reginald.

"So, that was..."

"Awkward?" I snort.

"Yeah, it was definitely that." He grins, brushing his hand over my arm. "Do you want to do the interview now or chat for a minute? We have time. The initial meeting was supposed to last for ten minutes, and that only lasted for two. We're allotted ten minutes for the interviews, and then there's a ten-minute window to get everything reset before the next suitor arrives."

"Let's just get the interview over. It's going to be a short one."

Reginald nods his acceptance of my words. "Tell me about your meeting with your first suitor, Owen."

"Well, he was..." I shrug. "I have no idea what he was. How do you get to know someone who doesn't talk? I mean, I get that we only have a few minutes together, but there was no effort on his part. He only spoke when I spoke to him and never more words than he had to.

"Maybe he's as nervous as me, but he didn't smile the entire time either. And that handshake? What a joke? My first impression is not great, but I'll try not to hold that against him."

Taking a deep breath, I can't help but shrug. What more can I possibly say about Owen? I got nothing from him during that meeting. Here's to hoping he's a little more open to talking at our next meeting.

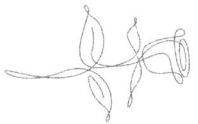

Owen

I settle into the chair, uncomfortable with all the cameras and this woman's attention on me. What was her name again? I think it started with a T. Tina? Tammie? Tessa! That's it.

"So, you met Bree. What are your initial thoughts?"

I hate interviews. I've always hated interviews. *Heated* hadn't been my idea. My manager had told me it was a great opportunity for me—mostly for my career. But he'd told me that if I were to get an omega and a pack out of it, it would be even better. I've been dreading coming here, knowing that they'll expect me to talk.

Talking isn't something that I excel at. Half the time, I say the wrong thing. The other half of the time, people are so intimidated by me they're not even listening to what I'm saying. And interviews are the worst of them. But I don't really have the option to remain quiet for this. Even knowing this, I could barely get myself to speak to Bree, and now they want me to talk about how much of an idiot I'm sure I looked like? Great.

"She… uh…" I flail my hands around, trying to find the right words.

Bree is gorgeous—there is no mistaking that. She'd tried to get me to talk, but I hadn't wanted to embarrass myself. Though, I'm fairly certain that I still had.

"She seems very nice," is what I settle on.

"Nice?" Tessa tilts her head. "Would you like to expand on that?"

I shake my head. I really don't know what they want me to say, but I know that I've already gotten it wrong.

Tessa sighs, rolling her eyes—though I don't think I'm supposed to see that. "Fine, Hector will show you to the house. You'll wait in the game room. We'll show each of the suitors there once they've finished with their interviews. It'll allow you all to get to know one another while Bree finishes meeting all the suitors. There's a bar, but don't get drunk, please.

"Once you have all arrived, Bree will join all of you in there and spend some time with all of you before we do our first rose ceremony. I'm sure you have questions about the rose ceremony since it wasn't in the packet. I won't be answering them as Bree will explain the ceremony to you and the viewers once we're in the ballroom." Tessa hesitates for a moment. "I understand that you're a man of few words, but try a little harder if you honestly want a chance with her. If you don't talk, she can't get to know you."

I sit there for another moment, blinking after her as she turns on her heel and walks away. I don't know why I'm so surprised by her words, but I am. Right on the heels of the surprise is anger. Who does this female alpha think she is, telling me what I need to do to win this omega? An omega I don't even want. Why had I let my manager convince me this was a good idea?

Fuck her.

"Owen?"

I turn to find a beta standing there. I crook an eyebrow in his direction and grunt.

Hector swallows, a panicky look rising in his eyes. "Umm, I'm Hector. I'm supposed to show you to the game room?"

I stand without a word, gesturing for him to lead on when he doesn't move right away. Coming on this show was a terrible idea.

Bree

I'm feeling better after chatting with Reginald and doing even better after Tessa stops by to chat with me. I can't let this first meeting sour me for the many others that I have coming. With nineteen suitors left to meet, my day is barely getting started.

I'm pulled from my thoughts when I hear the tires of the next limo coming up the drive. Here we go. There's no way that this meeting could go worse than the first one, right? It can only go up from here.

The limo pulls to a stop in front of me, and the door opens instantly, putting me a bit more at ease already. The man that steps out is just as tall as Owen, but he has more of a slender build. Not a strand of his silver streaked mocha hair is out of place, green eyes sparkling as they turn to me. He smirks and I can already tell that he's an alpha as he runs his hands over his tux before turning back to the limo as if waiting for someone.

A second man steps out, his deep, dark brown skin glistens in the sunlight. Another alpha. He closes the door behind him before straightening his tux in the same way as the first man. He is shorter than the first man, but only by a few inches and has the same slender build. He turns to me with a grin before they both make their way over to me.

"Hi, I'm Bree." I offer my hand once more, hoping that these two will actually shake it. Their alpha scents mingle together as they move toward me. I get hints of cedar, water, and moss. It's a pleasant combination. I wonder what their individual scents are, but know that I'll be able to tell once they're closer.

"Good evening, Bree," the first man steps up first, taking my hand in his and lifting it to his lips. A blush spreads across my cheeks at the light brush of his lips against my skin, causing his grin to grow. "I am Wren Dumont. It is a pleasure to meet you, omega."

There's a slight accent to his words, but I can't place it, though I really like it. I hope that he'll keep talking so I can hear more of it.

Wren releases my hand, stepping back to allow the other man to step forward. He takes my hand in his and shakes it firmly, bringing a smile to my face. "I'm Wilder Montgomery."

Wilder holds onto my hand for a moment longer before stepping back to stand beside Wren. I glance between the two of them for a moment, a little overwhelmed. Both men are extremely attractive, but that isn't what's throwing me off my game. It's the kiss on my hand, followed by the handshake. Both actions were respectful, but such polar opposites.

"You have different last names, so you're unbonded?" My statement ends up being more of a question.

"Yes," Wren says with a nod. "Wilder and I met a few years ago at a business conference. We got along well and knew that we were meant to be pack mates, but not lovers."

"Ahhh." I nod. With the lack of females in the population, there have been more and more packs that end up involved with one another—it's honestly the norm in this day and age—but there are still those that are nothing more than friends or brothers.

"A business conference, you say? What is it the two of you do?"

Wilder is the one that speaks up this time. "I run my own tech company, and Wren runs a communications company. We had worked on many projects together before we met at the conference—we just hadn't met in person."

I want to ask about their ages, as they both seem to be in their forties, but I don't know how to go about it without seeming rude. Screw it, I can't get to know them without asking questions, right?

"Please don't take this the wrong way, but how old were you all when you met?"

Wilder laughs. "You want to know how old we are, don't you? I'm forty-two, and Wren is forty-six."

"Like you, we chose to build our companies over finding packs. By the time I hit forty, I realized it might just be too late for me." Wren shrugs. "Then I met Wilder, who is only a few years younger than me, and realized that maybe I wasn't the only one who had decided to wait."

I grin. "Trust me, I understand. Tessa and I both wanted to make sure that we made Fated Industries a success before worrying about packs. There was less pressure put on her than there was on me. My mother told me I was a waste of an omega."

"She did not." Wilder steps into me, lifting his arms as if to pull me into him before hesitating.

I'm moving into arms before I have time to think about what a bad idea it could be. I lay my head on his chest, feeling the purr before I hear it and my body immediately relaxes. This is just one reason omegas need alphas—just another thing I've been missing out on.

"I am feeling left out," Wren says with a chuckle.

My face flushes as I step away from Wilder, head ducking. I feel Wren step closer before a finger is lifting my chin until I meet his eyes. "I am sorry if I embarrassed you, omega. It was a joke—a bad one, obviously. If you need comfort, seek it from whomever you'd like, and no one should make you feel wrong about doing so. I am the one who should be embarrassed."

"It's quite alright. I've just become accustomed to denying my omega urges so that others wouldn't look down on me." I shrug. "I guess that's harder to overcome than I thought it would be."

"The good news is that you're about to have twenty men here to help remind you there is nothing wrong with your omega urges," Wren smirks, winking as he steps away from me and his hand falls away.

My eyes lift, finding Tessa giving me a signal to wrap it up. "It's wonderful to meet you both, and I'm looking forward to getting to know you better."

"And you, Bree." Wren snags my hand in his once more before lifting it to press a kiss to the palm this time, and something about it feels a million times more personal.

Wilder nudges Wren out of the way, taking both of my hands in his before lifting them to his lips. He kisses the knuckles of both hands before lowering them between us without letting go. "It's our pleasure."

"Gentlemen, if you'll follow me," Tessa says as she steps up, gesturing for the two men to follow her.

I shoot her a grateful smile as I turn towards Reginald. I'm also grateful for the scent canceling panties I'm wearing, as I can feel slick slide from my suddenly overheated body. All they'd done was offer me comfort and kissed my hands. Am I truly that touch deprived as to get this turned on by their actions? Because it has to be more than just the fact that they're alphas.

"You okay, Bree?" Reginald's arm wraps around my waist, giving me a quick squeeze.

I nod, still trying to get my thoughts together. "Yeah, it's just... a lot. I didn't expect this to be so much, so quickly."

A quick squeeze of my hand and he's moving out of the camera's view. "Alright, Bree, you've now met another two alpha suitors. How are you feeling? What are your thoughts about Wren and Wilder?"

"They're... interesting. I don't know what I was expecting of my suitors, but it's nice to find alphas who put their lives on hold to establish and run their own companies. Though, I'm sure they likely didn't receive as much backlash as I did. Alphas don't have quite the same expectations put on them as omegas do, do they?"

I shrug, eyes unfocusing for a moment as I start to lose myself to my thoughts. I take a moment to shake myself from the thoughts as I lift my head to look at the camera and Reginald again.

"Wren seems to be very smooth. I'll need to keep an eye on him to see if he's more than the smooth operator he seems. Wilder seems genuine, which leads me to believe that Wren probably is too. And they're both extremely attractive, but I doubt Tessa would choose unattractive men."

Reginald and I laugh together. "But I'll have to wait and see. I understand the point of these meetings, but it's kind of hard to get to know someone with just a few minutes of conversation, isn't it?"

Wren

I settle into a chair with Wilder beside me, turning our attention to the female alpha standing beside the camera.

"Hello... Tessa, was it?" I ask, knowing that's her name, but not wanting to appear overconfident.

Tessa gives me a small smile and a nod. "That's correct. Now, this interview is for the two of you to discuss your initial meeting with Bree. So what did the two of you think of the omega you'll be wooing?"

"Wooing?" Wilder snorts, but straightens when he realizes neither me nor Tessa are laughing with him. "I'm sorry. It's just such an old-fashioned word. I wasn't expecting it. Is that what's expected of us? For us to woo Bree? I'm not against the idea... But I'm sure we're on the older end of the spectrum of men here to win a place in Bree's pack, and if I've never wooed a woman, then I can guarantee you the younger ones will have no clue what you're asking."

Tessa bristles slightly at his words, but quickly reins herself in. "It's what Bree wants. She wants to be wooed. She wants to be won over, so while it's not demanded of you, it would make the omega you're trying to win over very, very happy."

I nod, filing away her words for a later time.

"Then woo her, we shall. Though, I'm going to be honest," Wilder begins, glancing at me before turning his attention back to Tessa. "I didn't think Bree was the type to want someone to woo her. It's not the impression I got when we talked with her."

"But she is an omega used to having to hide away her omega tendencies—or at least that's what our conversation led me to believe. I'm not surprised that beneath that steel spine she's had to create, she wants something softer from the men courting her."

"Courting? You're sounding so much older than you are, old man." Wilder grins, slapping his hand on my back before once more turning his attention back to Tessa and the camera. "I think Bree is a strong omega, a strong woman who hasn't had the chance to be who she really is because of her goals and ambitions. Is it fair? Absolutely not, but I can hope that being around us and the other suitors will allow her to be that person. And she's fucking gorgeous."

"You were doing so well until the end, Wilder." I shake my head at my pack mate before focusing on Tessa. "But he's right. I agree with everything he said. Obviously, we'd received information on Bree before we arrived, but I think she will be different while here. I don't think she'll have much of an option being surrounded by so many alphas."

"I enjoyed speaking with her," Wilder adds. "Though it wasn't nearly enough time. So I look forward to spending more time with her. And apparently wooing her."

I nod. "I do not know exactly how this will work out, but I guess that is all part of being the first set of suitors on a show that is the first of its kind. But I'm looking forward to getting to know Bree and seeing if we could fit together in a pack."

"Was there anything else you'd like to add?" Tessa asks, waiting for both of us to shake our heads before smiling. Then she explains the next part of the process—waiting in the game room, time with Bree as a group, and then something about a rose ceremony that Bree will explain to us.

Wilder and I rise from our seats. I turn as I hear someone approach, finding a beta standing just off the gazebo with a smile. "You must be Hector."

"Yes, sir," he says. "If you'll just come with me, I'll show you to the game room."

Turning back to Tessa, I give her a nod. "Thank you, Tessa."

She seems surprised when Wilder echoes my words before she returns the nod. "Thank you both. I wish both of you the best of luck because Bree is a handful."

And with those words, she saunters off and leaves the two of us blinking after her. So Bree is a handful? I cannot say that I mind the idea of that. I have no doubt that Wilder and I can handle her.

Wilder grins as he jumps off the gazebo, landing gracefully next to Hector. "Thank you, as well, Hector."

Snorting, I shake my head at Wilder's antics, even though I am used to them. When he is at work, he is all business, but outside of work? He doesn't know how to act his age, and I would not want it any other way.

I follow behind Hector and Wilder as the beta leads us to the house while Wilder continues talking to Hector, not really allowing the beta to get in a word. Now we have to wait for the other suitors, a definite downside to being the second to arrive. I know it will test both mine and Wilder's patience, but for a chance to speak with Bree again, I think I would do just about anything.

Wilder

I chat with Hector as he leads us into the house and I'm honestly blown away by the inside of the house, even more than I was by the outside. It's obvious that whoever built this house put a lot of thought into it. The grand foyer that we've entered the house through is all black marble floors and white walls. Black and white photos line the walls, but I don't have time to linger and see what the subject of the photos is, as Hector is already moving up the split staircase.

He pauses on the landing where the stairs split in both directions to glance back at us. "Both sets of stairs will lead you to the second floor living area, just opposite sides. The second floor also houses the theater room, two pack suites, and four shared rooms."

I just nod as he moves to the staircase to the left, following quickly behind him with Wren right at my heels. We come out into the living room, which is filled with black leather couches and chairs, an enormous television mounted to the wall, and a small bar to the side. There's a short wall surrounding the area and when I glance over, I realize it overlooks the foyer with the stairs leading up, cutting into some of the open air.

"This hallway leads to the bedrooms and theater room. I don't know the room assignments, so you'll have to wait until later to find out." He starts up the stairs and we follow him once more. "The third floor houses two additional pack suites and six additional shared rooms. Instead of the living room, it has the game room."

We step onto the landing and directly into the game room, a hallway to our right. There are four televisions mounted to the wall and what seems to be every gaming system known to man. In the center of the room, there are three pool tables. There are a couple of foosball tables to the side, a ping-pong table, a pinball machine, and arcade games in another corner. There's four dartboards set up on one wall and a large bar dominates another. And even with all of that, there's still seating sporadically throughout the room. Tall bar style tables and stools, plus couches before the television screen.

"Wow," I murmur as I take it all in. This is every grown man's dream room right here. My eyes catch on a man slouched down on one of the couches. "Hey, man."

The man looks up at me and Wren, grunting before turning his attention back to the drink he holds in his hand. Turning back to Wren and Hector, I raise my eyebrows. "Well, then..."

"That's Owen. He doesn't seem to talk much," Hector supplies.

Wren's eyes narrow as he stares at Owen. "That's Owen Reid. He's a MMA fighter, and a damn good one at that."

I snicker at the joy on Wren's face. He might not seem like the type, but he has a huge obsession with MMA fighting. I've watched a few fights with him, but they're just not my thing. But Wren really gets into them. This is probably as close to fangirling as I'll ever see him as he saunters over to sit beside Owen, offering his hand.

"Hello, Owen. I'm Wren Dumont, and I'm a huge fan of your fighting."

Owen blinks up at him for a moment before sliding his hand into Wren's. "Thanks, man."

I have to fight back my laughter as Wren's brow wrinkles when Owen says nothing else. He looks so perplexed because Owen is back to staring at his drink.

Hector clears his throat, drawing my attention to him. "I need to head back. I'll be escorting each suitor or pack of suitors up here. You're welcome to anything in this room, but we ask that you not venture from the game room unless it's to use the bathroom. If you need to use the bathroom, you'll take this hallway," he points to the hallway on the stairs we just came up, "and it's the first door on the right. If there's anything else you need, just let me know when I bring the next suitor. As a reminder, there are cameras in this room, the hallways, and the bedrooms, as you agreed to when you signed your contract. The mic you're wearing is always recording and cannot be taken off unless you're showering or sleeping. Both are being monitored. If you leave this room, a member of security will escort you back. Don't do that."

"Sure, Hector. Thank you."

He heads back down the stairs. When I turn back to the room, I find Wren still trying to pull Owen into a conversation he obviously doesn't want to have. I don't bother fighting my grin as I head for the bar. The bar is well-stocked with anything I can think of, and none of the liquor is cheap. I grab the bottle of Macallan 18, adding ice to two glasses, and pour the Scotch into each glass before heading to the couch.

Wren turns to me, frustrated as he grabs the offered glass. He takes a sip, all the frustration melting off of him. "A Macallan 18? I didn't think they'd have such good Scotch here."

"The bar is well stocked and not a cheap liquor to be found." I gesture toward the bar.

Wren doesn't bother looking as he settles back into the couch, taking another sip from his drink. I follow suit, elbowing him in his side. "You can't force someone to talk to you... Which feels really weird to say to you, as it's usually you telling me that."

Wren lets out a long-suffering sigh but nods. "When you're right, you're right. I may have allowed myself to get a bit overexcited."

"A bit?" I smother my laughter when he pins me with a look of disdain. "Right, sure. Do you want to look around?"

"Let's enjoy our drinks first."

I nod, settling back further into the couch, loving how comfortable it is. I'll have to ask where they got it. I think I want one for our house. There's still seventeen more suitors to arrive, so I better get ready for a long wait until I get to see Bree again.

Chapter Three

Bree

Another interview completed, and now it's time to meet another suitor. I can't help but wipe my hands down my dress, anxiety rising in me. This really was a terrible idea. If I'm already feeling like this after just three suitors, how am I ever going to make it through twenty?

"Just keep breathing, Bree." Tessa's words are quiet from where she stands just off camera. A quick glance in her direction shows her smiling brightly at me, a thumbs up aimed in my direction. "You've got this. You're doing great."

The crunch of tires on gravel has me turning back to the driveway, wondering who I'll meet this time. Time speeds up for once and the next thing I know, the door to the limo is swinging open to reveal yet another tux-clad man.

He's not as tall as the others, probably only around five foot ten, but it's still very clear he's an alpha. Muscles ripple beneath the tux as he straightens it, his head lifting and his brown eyes catching mine. His hair is silver with hints of a darker color beneath it, though I can't tell if it's black or brown. A full beard graces his face, giving him a rugged look. Wide shoulders fill out the tux well and I have to fight to keep from rubbing my thighs together as his scent hits me—a dark amber and oak combination with just a hint of something spicy... pepper, maybe? Yes, that's what it is, but white pepper, not black.

He looks and smells delicious.

And then he smiles, and it's like my heart stops.

"Bree," he says as he moves forward, reaching for my hands. "I'm Roman Knight, and you're breathtaking."

"So are you," I squeak, internally rolling my eyes at how stupid I sound. A great first impression, I'm sure.

But Roman just chuckles, throwing his head back as the laughter spills from him. I can't help but grin up at him as he squeezes my hands. He doesn't release them as his laughter quiets.

"I think the two of us will get along just fine, omega." His voice is gruff, a bit of a growl to it that has me shivering.

"I certainly hope so," I purr, shocking myself. I don't think I've ever spoken to another person this way, let alone an alpha. It seems my omega instincts are coming to the forefront with meeting this many alphas at once. It should make for an interesting evening, that's for sure.

And on that note...

"Tell me a little about yourself, Roman."

"Obviously, I'm an alpha. I'm fifty-two and I work as a history professor at Hartfield University just outside of LA."

My eyebrows shoot up. "Oh, I know Hartfield U well. It's where Tessa and I attended college. But a history professor? That's so not what I was expecting you to say."

"Oh? And what were you expecting?"

"Ummm..." I nibble on my bottom lip before remembering my lipstick, stopping immediately. "A lumberjack?"

He laughs again, and it sends butterflies shooting through my body, slick bursting from me. There's no damn way I'm going to make it through this process if I don't stop slicking. Too much more and the scent canceling will not be working any longer.

I laugh with him this time. "Honestly, I don't know what I thought you'd say, but history professor wasn't it. You must love history."

"I do. Especially Greek history."

"Greek, really? I would've thought it would be Roman history."

And then we're laughing again, and I don't want to stop. How can I feel so comfortable with someone and so turned on at the same time? A throat clears—Tessa's way of telling me to wrap it up since I can't seem to look away from Roman.

"It was a true pleasure meeting you," Roman says, obviously understanding the hint. He squeezes my hands, hesitating for a moment before leaning forward to press his lips to my cheek. They linger there for a moment longer than necessary. "I look forward to the next time we meet."

"Me too."

"I think I'm going to watch from the control room for now, if that's alright with you, Bree?" Tessa asked, raising her eyebrow. "Unless you need me here to help you."

I shake my head. "No, that's fine. Thank you, Tessa."

She shoots me a quick smile before nodding for Roman to follow her.

Roman follows her down the pathway, and I can't stop myself from turning to watch him walk away—and I am not disappointed. His pants hug one of the nicest asses I've ever seen as he walks. He glances over his shoulder, catching me looking. He just raises an eyebrow and grins before facing forward once again.

I fan myself, trying to cool off when I feel Reginald stepping up behind me. "I'd totally call him daddy."

"Reginald!" I slap his arm, but can't say I'm entirely opposed to the idea. "He does kind of have a daddy vibe, doesn't he?"

He nods as he turns me to face the camera once more. "He really, really does."

I wait until he's returned to his spot beside the cameraman before speaking. "Roman is not what I was expecting—not just from an alpha, but based on what I saw. Which just goes to show that we shouldn't judge a book by its cover. One would think I'd have learned that by now."

I laugh. "But he's hot, there's no denying that. I loved the way he laughed with his whole body. It's like he doesn't take it too seriously, you know? You can't always find that quality in an alpha, and I kind of love it. I'm definitely looking forward to getting to know him better."

Roman

I shake my head as I walk away from the little omega.

Bree. Her name is Bree.

That I'm having to remind myself to call her by her name and not by her designation is uncommon for me. I know well that there is more to a person than their designation, but with Bree it's different. I've never responded to another person like this—especially not an omega.

And for the first time in many years, I think maybe my sister is right. Maybe it isn't too late to find myself an omega—even if she's twenty years my junior.

I wince at that because that's an enormous gap in our ages, but with the connection I felt to her, I won't allow it to become a burden. Age is just a number. Isn't that what people say? I've never been a firm believer in the idea, but I want to be. I want to think that there could be something between me and Bree.

"Roman?"

I startle at the feminine voice calling out my name. I'd been so lost in my thoughts I'd almost walked right past the gazebo. I grimace as I step up. "I'm sorry, Tessa. I was a little lost in thought."

"I can see that." She laughs. "Bree can have that effect on people."

"I bet she does." I chuckle as I sit in the chair across from Tessa. "So, how does this work?"

"This interview is to get your thoughts on your first meeting with Bree. We'll use clips of the interviews throughout the episodes. Then, once we've finished, Hector here will show you to the game room, where you and the other suitors will wait until you've all arrived." The beta standing beside Tessa waves, a tentative action on his part that I return.

"Then Bree will come spend a couple of hours with all of you before we move to the ballroom, where we'll hold the first rose ceremony."

I rack my mind, trying to recall anything from the packet they'd provided us that would explain what the rose ceremony is, but I come up blank. "Rose ceremony?"

"Don't worry, you'll learn about it with the other suitors tonight. It was Bree's idea, and we wanted to allow her to be the one to explain it to you." She shrugs one shoulder as if to say 'what can you do?'
"So, Roman, you just met Bree for the first time. What are your first impressions?"

"Hmmm," I murmur, not knowing where to start. "She's obviously breathtaking. I definitely forgot how to breathe for a moment there when I first saw her. She's not what I was expecting. Though I don't actually know what I was expecting."

I chuckle at my stupidity. "My sister is the one who signed me up for *Heated*. I just thought I'd be on my own for the rest of my life. I've dated betas before and while the experiences were fine, I didn't feel drawn to them. There's so few omegas that I didn't think I would ever find one for myself. I almost didn't come because I didn't want to get my hopes up.

"But I'm so glad that I did because Bree is everything I could have ever wished for and so much more. She brought out my alpha side in a way I've never felt. All I could think about was getting to know her better. Kissing her. Smelling her. Her scent is divine. Champagne and berries, but somehow so much better. I think I'm smitten."

Tessa laughs. "Smitten after just ten minutes? That might be a record for Bree."

A blush creeps up my neck as I realize what I've admitted, but I wouldn't take it back even if I could. It's absolutely true. I'm smitten with Bree.

"I can only hope that I made just as good of an impression on her as she did on me," I say with a shrug, keeping my eyes locked on Tessa. I won't show my embarrassment or make myself weak before this alpha.

"I would say, based on her words and her actions, that you did. She does still have sixteen more suitors to meet, so I can't honestly say what your chances are, but you did good, Roman."

"Thank you," I tell her.

Tessa clears her throat, waving her hand around in front of her. "Was there anything else you'd like to add?"

"No, I think I said enough for now."

Tessa tries to hide her smile, but I still catch it. "Then, if you follow Hector, he'll show you to the game room. Good luck, Roman."

"Thank you." With a last nod, I step off the gazebo and follow Hector as he leads me up the pathway.

I can't wait to see Bree again. I *need* to see her again. The next few hours are going to be torture, but I know once I see her again, it'll all be worth it.

Bree

Talking with Reginald, even with the cameras on us, has calmed me down some. I don't feel nearly as worked up when the next limo pulls to a stop in front of me; the door opens immediately.

The man that steps out isn't much taller than me, maybe five foot seven? His black hair is slightly shorter on the sides and longer on top, long enough to flop down into his eyes. He's obviously of Asian descent—maybe Korean? He's on the slender side, but I don't doubt there are muscles lying beneath his tux. He's young, definitely younger than me.

I would have guessed he was a beta even before his scent hits me, but as I breathe it in, it just confirms it. The combination of eucalyptus, lavender, and chamomile is relaxing, immediately setting me at ease. A smile lights up his face as he steps up to me, offering his hand.

"Hi, Bree. My name is Emmett Kwon." He inclines his head as I slide my hand in his.

"It's nice to meet you, Emmett." A quick shake of hands and we're both letting go. "So, tell me a little about yourself."

"Beta. Twenty-five and I'm a chef."

"A chef? I love to eat." I laugh. "Where do you work? Anywhere I might know?"

He flushes, even the tips of his ears turning red as he ducks his head, mumbling, "Lyrical."

"Seriously?" I breathe out.

Lyrical is *the* restaurant to be seen at in LA and the waiting list for reservations is at least a year long. I've yet to eat there, but it's been on the list of places I'd love to try.

"Fancy," I add with a grin. "So you're one of those hoity toity chefs?"

Emmett grins and it lights up his face, turning him from boyishly good looking to hot as hell. "Yeah, I guess I am."

"Does that mean I can expect you to cook for us while you're here?"

His smile grows even wider. "I'd love nothing more."

A comforting warmth grows in my belly and rises to my chest. I like this beta a lot. Omegas need alphas—there's no getting around that—but a pack is nothing without its betas. They are what hold a pack together and make sure that alphas and omegas remember that they're more than their instincts.

And Emmett? He's a good beta. I might not have spoken to him for long, but I can already tell that.

"I'm really glad you're here, Emmett, and I look forward to getting to know you better. And to taste your cooking. Don't think you're getting out of that, because I *will* remember."

"I can't wait." His voice is quiet as he smiles once more before heading down the path toward the gazebo. I know I shouldn't, but I can't help turning to watch him walk away as well—I'm already pretty sure this is going to be a thing I do with most of the suitors. At least if they all look like the five I've met so far. They're all so unfairly hot, but so different from one another.

"This is going to be hard as hell, isn't it?" I ask, not expecting an answer.

Laughter spills from Reginald's lips as I face him once more. "One hundred percent. Did you really think it would be easy?"

"I don't know." I shrug because I honestly don't know what I was thinking. "I just didn't realize how hard it would be. I've only met five of the suitors and there's still fifteen to go. Sure, Owen got off to a rough start, but the other four? What if they're all like that? I'll never be able to choose."

"Sure you will," Reginald consoles. "After you've gotten to know them better. Why don't we focus on them one at a time, yeah? Tell me your thoughts on Emmett."

I dip my head a little as the smile slides across my lips. "He seems sweet. His presence was calming—even his scent. I can't help but wonder if they chose him so he could be a calming influence for me. Which, let's be real, I could probably use on the regular. So maybe he was. Maybe Tessa chose him for that reason. Who knows?

"But he's a chef at Lyrical. I've heard amazing things about their food, so I look forward to him cooking for me. I love to eat. I don't know if you're supposed to say that as an omega, but I definitely have to work out more frequently because of my love of food. But good food is totally worth it. And I'll find out soon if Emmett is as well."

Emmett

I'd enjoyed getting to talk with Bree. I might have enjoyed it more than I should have. After all, I'm not an alpha. I can't offer her a knot like they can, or an alpha purr.

Even as those thoughts rush through me, I shake them off. No, I might not be able to offer her those things, but there are other things I can offer her that an alpha can't. I won't be sent into a rut when she goes into heat, which means I'll be able to keep my head. I can make sure that the pack has everything they need during the heat.

Betas are what hold together the pack during heats. Alphas and omegas are usually both too out of their minds to worry about things like eating or drinking during heats. It's the betas who make sure that the omega is taken care of, even bathing her when needed. Sometimes alphas are coherent enough to help deal with the necessities, but it can't be counted on.

That's not to say betas aren't involved in the heat. While I might not be part of a pack, I've helped packs during heats when they don't have a beta. There's been many occasions I've been requested through the *Knotted* app to help when omegas are having new alphas help them with their heats. Because it's easier to have someone who doesn't get lost in the heat in case someone tries to force an unwanted mating bond.

And yes, I've seen it happen. I've had to pull an alpha off an omega as she begged for his bite. They'd agreed beforehand that there would be no mating bites, but they were both too lost to their instincts.

But in all of those cases, I was the one to ready the omega for the alpha knots she'd be taking with both mouth and cock. But there's never been an omega that I've clicked with enough for either of us to want to make it permanent. It sucks, but I also enjoy being able to help any omega who doesn't have a beta to watch out for her—or him. I've even joined a few heats with male omegas. I'm attracted to both men and women, which is helpful since there are more men on the planet than women. I'm definitely of the why choose mentality.

As I step up to the gazebo, I shoot Tessa a quick smile before dropping into the chair, lounging in it more than sitting in it. Tessa grins back at me.

"Did you tell her?"

"What? That I'm a chef at Lyrical?" I nod. "Yes, she was very impressed, just like you said she would be."

"I know my best friend well," she says. "She loves food."

I laugh, throwing my head back. "I picked up on that. Though she called me a hoity toity chef before asking me if I would cook for her while I was here. I consider that a win."

"Yeah, I would call that a win for sure. So, besides her loving that you're a chef, what are your thoughts on your first meeting?"

"It certainly wasn't long enough. Ten minutes doesn't allow you to really get to know someone, ya know? But I like her. Obviously, she's beautiful, but it's more than that. She seems genuine, and I'd like to get to know her. I didn't even read the information on her you sent in the packet."

Tessa frowns. "No? Why not?"

"I didn't want it to bias our first meeting." I tap my chest, where the packet lays in the inside pocket of my jacket. "I brought it with me though, and now that I've met her, I'll read it. It's not information I'd have when I met someone out in the wild, so why should I have an advantage for that first impression? It wouldn't feel like a genuine first impression if I already knew information about her. Does that make sense?"

"Yeah. That actually makes sense. Though, it probably puts you at a disadvantage because I'm sure everyone else read it."

I shrug. "I don't mind. I think our first meeting went well, and I know there are nineteen other men here vying to be a part of her pack. The odds were never in my favor, but I'm glad I did it this way. I felt more comfortable, and it allowed me to get a better idea of the woman she is. It could've been that the two of us didn't gel and while that would have been disappointing, I would've accepted it. Because it would've been genuine."

"But you're going to read it now?" Tessa asks.

"Uhhhh, yeah. I know there could be something between us, so I'll read the information. It's no different from searching social media to find out more about the person you're seeing, right?"

Surprise has Tessa raising her eyebrow. "That's very... mature of you? I'm not sure that's the word I'm looking for, but I wouldn't have expected that from someone your age. You're how old, again?"

"Twenty-five, but my mom has always said I'm an old soul."

"I can see that." Tessa nods. "Was there anything else you'd like to add?"

When I shake my head, she explains how the rest of the evening will play out, even mentioning something about a rose ceremony that I assume I'll read about in the packet or it'll be explained at some point.

I stand, turning to find another beta standing there. "You must be Hector." At his nod, I grin, offering my hand. "It's nice to meet you. I'm Emmett."

Hector hesitates for a moment before shaking my hand. "It's nice to meet you as well. If you'll come with me, I'll show you to the game room."

I follow him down the pathway, staring up at the house—no, it's too large to call a house. Mansion? I'm not actually sure, but it's the place I will call home for the next eight weeks, or at least I hope I'll be here for the full eight weeks. I'd love for Bree to choose me for her pack, but only time will tell.

Bree

I think the waiting might be the worst part of this whole thing. I just want to get these initial meetings over with so I can really get to know these men. I'll have a short time with them before I'm expected to hold the first rose ceremony. When we'd come up with the guideline for the show, we hadn't known I'd be the omega, but I can't help but wonder what the hell we'd been thinking. How can we expect an omega to make choices about whom to send home or go on a date with after so little time?

The sound of tires on gravel has my head jerking up as I watch the next limo approach. Who will it be this time? I don't even know how many of the twenty will be alphas and how many will be betas. There's been the two unbonded alphas, but will there be more packs?

The man that steps from the limo takes my breath away. Not too tall, probably only five foot nine and utterly gorgeous with his dirty blonde hair and piercing ice-blue eyes. But that's not what has me gawking. I know who this man is!

"Sasha Rostova?" I gasp, moving to meet him in the middle. I have to fight to keep my hand by my side as I want to run it along the scruff on his face—not a full beard, but he obviously hasn't shaved recently.

"Ahhh, so you have heard of me before." His Russian accent has slick spilling from me and a full body shiver running through me. I'm barely able to hold back the moan threatening to fall from my lips. Apparently I have a thing for accents, but I don't know why that surprises me—I've always had a thing for accents. I think this entire process has my mind just a little addled.

"Of course I do. I'm a huge fan. I've seen you in *Don Quixote, The Nutcracker, Romeo and Juliet,* and *Swan Lake*. You're phenomenal." I grin, knowing that I'm totally fangirling over him right now and not caring. "An alpha—the only alpha ballet dancer in generations. Born in Moscow, but immigrated to America as a teenager. And you're close to my age, though I don't recall the exact number."

"Zirty-zree to your zirty-two, if I recall correctly?" Sasha smiles at me and all I can think is this man is the most beautiful man I've ever seen in my life. His scent finally hits my senses and my eyes roll back in my head—leather, sandalwood and vanilla. Amazing.

"I am also a fan of you," he continues, his accent making it slightly harder to follow his words. "Your apps have made life much easier for my omega sisters to find zeir mates. It is zey who demanded I come on *Heated*. How could I say no when I have a chance to meet such a beautiful omega?"

I wonder how well the camera picks up my flush because apparently this is the way I respond to alphas interested in becoming a part of my pack—blushing.

"Thank you, alpha," I whisper.

"It should be I who zanks you, omega, for zis chance."

I just stare up at him with a grin on my face, totally at a loss for words. "Ummm... you're welcome?"

He grins. "I will go, so zat you can meet your next suitor. You will find me later, *da*?"

"Yes. Absolutely."

Sasha sends me a wink as he walks backwards behind Tessa, who apparently came down to see how this meeting would go. He watches me as I watch him until he backs into her and she yells, "Stop staring at the omega and pay attention to where you're going, alpha."

Lifting my hand to my mouth, I stifle my giggle as Sasha shrugs at me with a raised eyebrow before following Tessa's command. At least now I know why Tessa reappeared so soon after saying she was going to watch from the control room. That little bitch wanted to see how I'd react to meeting an idol without realizing she was there. She's so lucky I love her.

I spin around, finding Reginald gawking after Sasha.

"That was Sasha Rostova!" I squeal, Reginald's attention snapping back to me. "I can't believe I just met Sasha Rostova! He's one of my suitors. How is this my life right now?"

Reginald laughs. "I know how much you love Sasha, but why don't you tell everyone else? Did meeting him live up to your expectations?"

"I did ballet growing up, but never had the right body type. That probably should've been my first clue that I would emerge as an omega." There were so many signs as I'd been growing up, but never had it occurred to me I'd be an omega. It's funny looking back on it now.

"I always loved ballet, even after I had to give it up. Now, I enjoy watching it. I try to go see a ballet at least every few months, but I go as often as I can. Sasha is the best dancer I've ever seen. The way he moves and the stories he tells with his dance? He's exceptional.

"And that man could never be disappointing. I might be a little obsessed and I've read most of the articles I can find on him. Everyone always says how down to earth he is, and he really seems to be. I'll have to wait to see if he remains that way, but it seemed genuine to me. I can't believe Sasha Rostova is one of my suitors."

Sasha

I follow behind the female alpha who had tried to put me in my place—which I had allowed her to believe happened. But really, I only followed her because I wanted to. Letting her think I had been following her orders does not hurt anyone, so I will allow her to continue to believe it. Plus, it had made Bree laugh, and damn, do I want to hear her laughter again.

I had seen a picture of her before, so I knew she was gorgeous before I had laid eyes on her. But no camera can do justice to her beauty. She is even more beautiful in person. That she had squealed after she thought I was out of earshot—though I was not—is adorable.

I love that she has an appreciation for ballet. There are many people in this world who do not and look down on me for making a career of it. The amount of times I have heard that being a ballet dancer is not what alphas do is astonishing. I do not know what makes people believe they have a right to judge me or my life, but I do not care what they think one bit. Let them think what they want if it will make them happy.

Just like I will continue to do what I love, which is dancing. That I am so popular is a disadvantage as far as keeping people out of my personal life, but it is worth it when I can spend my days and nights beneath the lights, losing myself in the dance. There is no other feeling like it—especially when there is an audience to feed off of.

"Right over here, Sasha," Tessa gestures toward the gazebo, and I lope along after her, settling into one of the waiting chairs with grace. "So, Sasha, as I'm sure you noticed, Bree is quite a fan."

I grin. "I might have picked up on zat."

"I'm sure you did, but what did you think of the first meeting?"

"It is hard to say. I zink she might have been awestruck at meeting me. I can only hope zat it does not remain zat way with each meeting because I do not believe zat will allow us to get to know one another. And I truly would like to get to know her. I zink zat we could have a connection if she can move past my celebrity status."

Tessa nods. "I could see how that would be hard, but I know Bree well, and I don't think that'll be a problem. She has no idea who any of her suitors will be before meeting you, so I think she was just surprised—pleasantly surprised, but still surprised."

"Ahhh, *da*. Zat makes sense. In zat case, I look forward to spending more time with her tonight. She is quite beautiful, and she has eyes zat are kind. Running a business as an omega—even if she is running it with an alpha—I am sure zat she is unable to often show zat side of herself. I am sure zat is hard on both of you, what with society's expectations of you. I have heard it time and again from my sisters. Because you are female, you are expected to procreate at the earliest possible opportunity. It does not matter if it is what you want or not. Zose cannot be easy burdens to bear for either of you as you grew your business."

Tessa's smile is a little bitter. "It wasn't easy—especially for Bree. But I think it made both of us stronger and made us work harder, so we could prove to others that we could do it."

"And you did. You should both be proud of yourselves."

"While I appreciate the sentiment, you're meant to be talking about your first meeting with Bree."

I shrug. "And I was. Zere is not much more I can say. It was a brief meeting."

Tessa nods, explaining how the evening will progress, explaining that the night will culminate in a rose ceremony that will be explained to us later. She is already walking away before I can open my mouth to thank her. I shrug to myself as I climb to my feet, finding a beta waiting for me at the bottom of the stairs—who, I am guessing, is Hector. "You are Hector?"

"I am."

"Well, zank you for showing me to ze game room. I appreciate it."

Hector just hums before turning to walk toward the house. I follow in earnest, counting down the moments until I will meet Bree again.

Emmett

I glance up when I hear Hector's voice filtering up the stairs. Another suitor has arrived, probably another alpha, seeing as I'm the only beta in the game room so far. Which is fine by me. Every pack needs at least one beta and if there's only a few of us, my chances are much higher that Bree will choose me.

Hector and an alpha appear at the top of the stairs and I grin because I'd been right—yet another alpha. I'm surprised that there has been no head-butting between the alphas already in the room. With this new arrival, that makes five alphas in one room. So far, Owen has kept to himself, not allowing anyone to pull him into a conversation. Wren and Wilder are playing a round of pool. They seem nice enough, though they're close to twice my age.

Roman *is* actually twice my age, but I enjoyed chatting with him. He seems really into history, but I won't hold that against him. I wonder who this newest alpha is. Like the others, he has an alpha's grace, but he's not built the same as any of the other alphas. That's not to say he's lacking in muscles, because he has plenty of those. He doesn't carry himself the same as most alphas I've met—his muscles distributed differently. And like the other four alphas, he's hot as hell. I have no idea how Bree is going to choose from these alphas if they're all this hot.

I pop out of my seat, grinning brightly as I approach the new alpha and Hector. "Hey! I'm Emmett. Emmett Kwon."

"Hello." The alpha doesn't smile as he offers me his hand, but it's not off-putting. He seems friendly enough, but maybe someone who doesn't smile often? An accent laces his words, though I'll need to hear him speak more to figure out where it's from. "I am Sasha Rostova."

I shake his hand, my grin growing. "Russian?"

"Very astute, you are."

"Thanks, Hector. I'll introduce him to everyone." Hector hesitates for a moment before shooting me a nod and taking off down the stairs. I chuckle, wondering why he's so uncomfortable around this many alphas.

I walk Sasha around the room, introducing him to Owen first. Owen straightens in his chair, eyeing Sasha for a moment before relaxing back into his seat with a grunt—surprise, surprise.

"He doesn't talk much," I tell Sasha with an eye roll. "We've all tried to talk to him and received a grunt for our troubles. Though, he apparently spoke two whole words to Wren."

Wren looks up at the sound of his name. He eyes Sasha, seeming to size him up as he steps forward and offers his hand. "I'm Wren Dumont."

"It is nice to meet you," Sasha says, and I decide I kind of love his accent.

Wilder steps up to introduce himself while Roman makes his way over to us. Once the introductions are over, I turn my focus back on Sasha. "What is it you do, Sasha? I'm a chef. Wilder and Wren run their own companies, and Roman is a history professor."

Sasha hesitates for a moment before lifting his head, all alpha arrogance as he speaks. "I am a professional ballet dancer."

Roman tilts his head to the side as he considers Sasha, before slapping his hands together with a grin. "You were in *Romeo and Juliet* last year, yeah?"

"*Da*. I take it you were zere for one of ze performances?"

Roman nods. "You were magnificent."

"Zank you."

Silence falls around us, and I want to beat my head against the wall. What is it with these alphas and not speaking? Wilder catches my eye with a grin, raising an eyebrow. Thank goodness, I'm not the only one who has noticed.

"Are you all just planning on sitting around in awkward silence until Bree arrives? Because I will literally die of boredom if I'm forced to do that."

Wilder's head falls back as his laughter booms throughout the room. "Emmett, I think you and I are going to be good friends. How about we leave these brooding fools to their silence and play a round of darts?"

"Yes, please. Thank you."

Wilder and I head toward the dart boards and a glance over my shoulder shows the other three alphas gaping after us. I snicker as I take the darts Wilder offers me.

"This is going to be an interesting experience." I shake my head. "I really hope they have some other outgoing people, or this is going to be so dull."

"Wren's usually more outgoing, but it's a new situation and it's got his back up. There's going to be who knows how many alphas all living under the same roof. That can cause some problems and he's trying to avoid that by holding back until he can get an idea of everyone's personalities."

I nod, understanding. "That makes sense. I wonder how many betas there will be. Based upon this group, I'd say that we'll be the minority here. Which makes sense, as Bree will want—no, she'll need multiple alphas."

Wilder nods. "She does, but I guess we'll find out soon enough. Now, shall we play?"

With a sigh, I move up to the line and toss my first dart. I know this will be an interesting couple of months. I just hope that they've planned for what it could mean having so many alphas together under one roof. I guess only time will tell.

Chapter Four

Bree

Trying to bring myself down after meeting one of my celebrity crushes is harder than I'd like to admit. I can only hope he didn't think I was too stupid or too much of a fan. I'd hate for the fact that I'm a fan to cause any issues between us. Even if he's not meant to be my alpha, I'd love to be friends with him and learn about the ins and outs of professional ballet.

But I also know that I can't focus on Sasha. After all, he's only one of twenty men here to... what? Woo me? I snicker at the idea, but straighten when the next limo arrives. The door doesn't immediately open, but when it does, it reveals a young, handsome alpha adjusting his suit jacket and... Did he just zip up his pants?

All I can do is blink as his eyes catch mine. He shoots me a smirk before turning back to the limo and holding his hand out to someone inside. A dark-skinned man steps from the limo, linking his hand with the alpha's as they step towards me.

The first man, the one I'm sure is an alpha, is young. He has to be in his twenties—maybe even in his early twenties. He's somewhere around six feet tall, his dark hair hangs in his dark brown eyes, and there's a bit of a swagger in his walk. Between that and the smirk he'd shot me when he'd caught me watching him zip up his pants, I'm certain he's going to be a cocky little shit.

Straightening my back, I ready myself to put him in his damn place. I've known alphas like that before and I won't allow anyone to push me around. It's best that he knows that now.

As my eyes find the other man, some of the tension leeches from me. He's older than the alpha, and I'm almost certain he's a beta, but I can't be sure until I scent him. He's attractive with his goatee, close cropped hair, and eyes even darker than his skin, almost black. He's slightly taller than the alpha, but doesn't have quite the bulk of the alpha—who is also on the slender side for an alpha.

"Bree," the beta says as they come to a stop in front of me, his scent confirming his designation—buttercream, prosecco & blackberries. It, and he, makes me want to lick my lips. "I'm Carter, and this is my alpha, Riley Woods."

The alpha's scent is sugar and nectarines, pairing well with his beta's. Because Carter didn't provide a surname, I'm certain they're a bonded pair, but it's best to not make assumptions. "It's wonderful to meet you both. Are you bonded?"

Riley grins as he reaches over to tip Carter's neck to the side, revealing his bonding mark. Carter knocks Riley's hands away and frowns. "You could've just said yes." There's a bit of a bite to Carter's words and it makes me wonder about their relationship.

"I could've, but where's the fun in that?"

I scoff, clenching my jaw in disbelief. "You know he isn't a prize or an object for you to show off, right? He's a person. Just because he's not an alpha, it doesn't make him less than you."

"He doesn't—" Carter begins, but Riley holds up a hand to cut him off.

"Did I say that's what I thought?" he asks, voice dangerously low. He certainly has the whole bad boy thing going for him. It's too bad for him I outgrew that stage years ago.

"You didn't have to. Your actions said it for you. If that's not how you feel, then maybe you shouldn't act that way."

"And maybe," Riley murmurs as he steps into my space, "you shouldn't make judgments about people you've just met."

I grind my teeth, fighting against the instinct to bare my neck to the alpha, who is trying to force his will on me.

"Damn it, Riley." Carter grabs the alpha by the neck and jerks him back. "You promised you'd give this a chance, but all you're doing is being an asshole."

I'm shocked that this beta felt comfortable speaking to his alpha like that when he is this angry. But as I watch, Riley melts. His anger is gone like it was never there as he reaches up to cup Carter's cheek with his hand. "I'm sorry, baby."

"It's not me you should apologize to. It's Bree. She's the one you're treating badly. It's her you're making think you're a possessive asshole."

Riley shrugs. "Well, I am." But he does turn to me. "I'm sorry."

"We've only been bonded for a few weeks," Carter explains. "We want to find an omega, but the bond is riding Riley even harder than it is me."

While I understand his words, I can't understand why they'd come on the show just weeks after bonding. It also means they weren't bonded when they applied for the show. Did they bond because Riley thought he could lose Carter? It's not like I can ask those questions—not so soon after meeting them.

"I won't hold it against you, alpha, so long as it doesn't happen again. I'm not a fan of alphas who treat betas and omegas as if they're possessions."

Riley's jaw clenches as he inclines his head, but says nothing. Carter's smile is soft as he leans in to kiss my cheek. "Thank you for that, Bree. I appreciate you giving us a chance and look forward to getting to know you better. And I'll do my best to keep him from acting a fool again."

"So, how old are the two of you? What do the two of you do for work? And if you don't mind my asking, how did you meet?"

"I just turned forty a month ago, and I work as an ADA." Carter turns to Riley, but the other man remains silent. A huff of air and a shake of his head later, Carter tells me, "Riley is twenty-four and works at his dad's pharmaceutical company. He'll be taking over as CEO once his dad retires in a few years. As far as how we met... Let's leave that for the next time we talk."

I nod. "Okay, yeah. Next time. It was nice chatting with you, Carter." I pause. "Riley."

Riley glances at me, eyes cold, before he pulls at Carter, leading him down the pathway. Carter tosses me a warm smile. "It was wonderful meeting you, Bree."

I make a face, one that I'm sure isn't attractive in the least, before I remember that this is being recorded. My eyes catch Reginald's, who is snickering. I stick my tongue out at him, hoping that this part gets cut. "Soooo, your face tells me a lot about how you're feeling, but why won't you tell us just in case Tessa cuts that out? Though I'm going to beg her not to."

"Carter was very nice and sweet. He's obviously done well for himself if he's an ADA. That's not an easy position for a beta to get. I like a man with a drive to do well." I hesitate, trying to figure out just how honest to be before deciding fuck it. I might as well be myself.

"Riley, on the other hand? His actions, the way he spoke to me, and his choice of words rub me the wrong way. If it weren't for Carter, I would dismiss him tonight. But because they're a pack, I can't have one without the other, so I'm willing to give Riley another chance. We'll see how the rest of the evening goes."

Riley

I'm aware I'm being an asshole, but I fucking hate being here. And it's not because I hate the idea of having an omega—it's something I want more than I know I've let on during this initial meeting with Bree. And I know Carter really wants us to have a bigger pack with an omega of our own. He wants children and knows that he isn't getting any younger.

I'd met Carter at a bar I regularly haunted, and he was there celebrating a big win. I don't even remember what it was he won, but as soon as our eyes met across the bar, I knew he was mine. We've been together since that night, which had been about six months ago. It had been Carter's idea to join *Heated* as he'd been planning to enter as a single beta before meeting me. I'd agreed because I want an omega, but also because it meant that he saw us as forever.

My alpha instincts had been riding me hard, almost immediately, to make him mine, but I hadn't wanted to rush him. Okay, maybe I did, since I suggested it barely a month after we'd met. But we were already living together, so I'm not sure why he'd been so shocked by the idea. He'd informed me he wanted that, but he wasn't ready yet.

Then we'd found out we were to be two of the twenty suitors on *Heated*, and my instincts went on high alert. I *needed* to make him mine before we arrived. Two weeks ago, he'd agreed, and it had been the best two weeks of my life. But all I can think about is being inside of him, my alpha side demanding it every moment I'm with him. Which is why I'd rather be anywhere but here at the moment.

I feel bad about the way I treated the omega, but it's like I'm fighting against my instincts being here. Maybe it would have been better if I'd waited to give him my mark. It might have made this process easier—though who knows? It might have made it harder.

"Riley, I swear to everything holy—if you don't knock it off, we're going to have a problem." Carter tugs on my hand until I turn to face him. "Do you even want to be here?"

"Yes." I sigh. "I do, and I know you do, too. But it's so hard being around other people right now. All I want to do is lay you on the nearest surface and rut into you for hours. I'm trying—I know you don't believe me, but I am."

Carter's face softens. "I get it, I do. And I know it's harder for you as an alpha, but I *really* want this, Riles. Please, don't ruin this for us before we've even had a chance."

"I will try harder," I agree, reaching up to cup his cheek. "You know I'd do anything for you."

"I do, and thank you."

"Gentlemen?" a sharp feminine voice cuts off anything else we might have said.

We both turn to the gazebo to find the female alpha standing there, and she looks *pissed*.

"Tessa," Carter says, a smile lighting up his face. "I am so sorry for what just happened. Riley and I have had a talk, and he will be better. I promise. He isn't always like this."

I hate that my beta is apologizing for me. I don't like it one bit.

"It's not Carter's fault," I tell her, grimacing. "I'm having a harder time than I thought I would fighting my alpha instincts."

She sighs. "You are awfully young and you've only been bonded for a few weeks. While I might not know exactly what you're feeling, I can imagine it. But you can't speak to or treat Bree like that. She won't allow it and neither will I. If you both truly want a chance at being a part of her pack, you're going to need to get your alpha side under control. I won't hesitate to have you removed if you continue to act like that."

"Thank you for understanding, Tessa. I will do better."

"Good. Then get your asses over here so we can get this interview underway."

Feeling properly chastised, I hurry up the steps to the gazebo, pulling Carter along with me. We settle into two chairs side by side. When Carter tries to pull his hand away from me, I squeeze tighter and shake my head.

"It keeps me grounded, if you don't mind."

"Sure, Riles. I don't mind at all." Carter shuffles in his chair until he finds a more comfortable position while allowing me to cling to him. Then we're facing Tessa and the camera at her side. "So... what now?"

"We'd like to hear both of your thoughts on your initial meeting with Bree."

Carter snickers, turning his head away as if I wouldn't know he was laughing.

"Your shoulders are shaking, Carter. I know you're laughing, so why bother hiding it?"

Carter turns to me as he laughs loudly, body shaking with the sound. A smile spreads across my lips at the sight. This is my favorite side of Carter. His job is so stressful that he doesn't always get to have these carefree moments, but that just makes me crave them even more.

Finally, he gets the laughter under control and turns back to Tessa, who is grinning. "It wasn't a great first meeting."

"And why was that?"

I clear my throat. "That would be my fault. Carter and I made the decision to bond a couple of weeks ago, and I'm feeling a little... possessive at the moment. Which isn't an excuse for the way I treated Bree. I can only hope that she'll give us another chance. I'm well aware I'm a bit of a cocky asshole normally, but this is a little extreme, even for me."

"Because of him being an asshole," Carter swings his free hand in my direction, "we didn't get a lot of time with Bree. She said she would give us another chance, so I'm feeling okay about it. Riley might be an asshole, but when he cares about you? That's it. He'd destroy the entire world to keep you safe and happy. So I just need to make sure Bree gets to see beyond his asshole tendencies."

"You know we're going to have to bleep out every time the two of you say asshole, right? The network will never allow that much 'strong language' on a prime time show." Tessa does the whole finger quotes thing around strong language. "I get the feeling we'll be using that bleeping a lot for this show."

I shrug. "This is me, and I need to make sure Bree knows what she's getting into, so I won't change how I act because it causes you more work."

"Damn, you really are an asshole, aren't you?" Tessa scoffs.

"Yup," I say, popping the p. "It usually means you either love me or you hate me. But I won't be fake to make people like me. If they don't like me, then fuck them."

"Seriously, Riley?" Carter squeezes my hand as he shoots me a glare. "I thought you said you were going to try."

"I am, and I will. But this is me, Carter. You fell in love with me, asshole-ness and all."

Carter just shakes his head as he stares at me, but the corners of his mouth turn up, telling me he doesn't disagree with my statement. "Maybe, but I'm fairly sure saying... duck with an f is worse than what Tessa already said she will have to bleep out. Maybe rein in the cursing?"

"Fine," I groan, turning my attention back to Tessa. "Look, here's what you need to know about me. I'm an only child of a billionaire. Growing up, no wasn't a part of my vocabulary. I know that I'm privileged and a bit spoiled. But I'm not afraid to work hard for the things I want. And Carter and I both want to find an omega. Bree might not be the omega for us, but there's no way of knowing that unless we try, so that's what we're going to do."

"I appreciate your honesty and authenticity," Tessa reluctantly admits. "Is there anything else either of you would like to add?"

I glance at Carter and shake my head. "Nope."

"Me neither."

Tessa nods, explaining how the rest of the evening will proceed before walking away without so much as a goodbye.

As I stand, keeping my hold on Carter's hand, I turn my attention to Hector. "I'm not saying this to be mean, but if you don't mind, we'll follow slightly behind you? I don't especially feel like allowing anyone near my beta at the moment."

"Of course, alpha. I understand that you've just bonded, and I remember what it was like so soon after I bonded with my alpha." Hector's smile is hesitant as he steps back onto the pathway. "Just call out if you need to stop for any reason, so I don't lose you."

"Thank you for being so understanding, Hector." Carter gives him a soft smile that pulls a low growl from my throat. "Seriously, Riley?"

I hold up my hands in surrender, letting go of his hand and for the first time since we'd stepped out of the limo, I don't feel the need to grab it back immediately. "That just slipped out. I know you were just being nice to the beta, who is being understanding, but my alpha side did not approve."

"Obviously," Carter says with an edge of annoyance. I don't think he's actually angry with me, but I know he doesn't approve of this possessiveness that I can't seem to fight back. "Let's just follow Hector and see how badly you react to a roomful of other alphas and betas."

I groan at the thought as Carter starts down the steps. I dart after him, wrapping my arm around his waist. "Mine."

"Riley." There's a bit of a whine to Carter's tone, making me grin—which probably isn't the correct response. He glances down at me, shaking his head. He pulls me in for a kiss.

My tongue darts out to run along the seam of his lips, wanting to deepen the kiss, but Carter breaks away before I can.

"Yes, I'm yours, Riley. But I don't want it to just be the two of us. You agreed you wanted a big pack, so you're going to have to learn to share me."

"I know that, and it *is* what I want. I swear I'm trying."

Carter's smile is a little sad. "Then that's all I can ask of you."

"I love you, Carter."

"I love you, too, Riley. Now let's scope out the competition." This time it's Carter that reaches for my hand and pulls me down the pathway. I'm going to try to do this, not just for Carter's sake, but for mine, too.

Bree

It's hard to not allow the prior meeting to affect the next one, but I do try to tamp down on my annoyance with Riley as the next limo pulls up. It's not my next suitor's fault that Riley is an asshole and I don't want to take it out on them.

As soon as the door opens, I know that won't be a problem. The man that steps out is massive—a Viking of a man. He's well over six feet tall and has a build that goes along with it. Unlike the previous suitors, he doesn't wear a full tuxedo. He wears the pants and the white button down, but has left the top three buttons open, and in place of the tux jacket, he's wearing a leather jacket. The sides of his dirty blonde hair are shaved, but the top is long and parted on the side. It falls almost to a chin that's covered in a full, almost bushy beard.

He smiles when his eyes lock on me, laughter dancing in his clear green eyes. I get a small peek of a tattoo from his open shirt and I can't help but wonder what it is and how many others he might have. I easily return his smile.

"Finnegan Abernathy at yer service." There's a Scottish lilt to his voice that lends a sense of charm to him as he bows at the waist. His bourbon and bonfire scent rushes through me and I love the unusual combination.

"Bree Timmons," I choke out between my giggles. "It's wonderful to meet you, Finnegan. Do you prefer Finnegan? Or Finn? Or something else?"

"It all depends oan where I am. Finnegan is a fine name, after all, so A'll never discourage such a pretty lady from using it. My parents called me Finn as a child, so it's something A'm used tae hearing, if ye would prefer it." He grins conspiratorially as he leans in. "But if ye were tae call me alpha, I would nae complain in th' least."

Heat rushes through me, straight to my core, and I once again feel slick spilling from me. My hand is up and fanning myself before I can stop it. When Finnegan catches sight of it, his grin grows.

All I can do is laugh. "I think I could listen to you read the dictionary to me and be happy." I hesitate. "Alpha."

Finnegan's eyes flash with desire, causing me to bite down on my bottom lip. His hand comes up and pulls it from between my teeth. "Nae need tae abuse that pouty lip. It could nae have done anything wrong."

"Umm... yeah. So, Finnegan." I'm flustered, there's no if's, and's, or but's about it. "Tell me a bit about yourself?"

"A'm forty-two an' a psychologist. Originally from Scotland, but moved here about ten years ago. I love my motorcycle an' my wee Luna more than anything else oan this earth."

"Little Luna?" I ask. Does he have a daughter? Not that I have a problem with that, and given his age, it wouldn't be unheard of. Though a daughter is a rarity.

"Ahhh, Luna is my Scottish Terrier. A'd show ye a photo, but they made us give up our phones."

"I love dogs. I'm sure you'll be able to show me a picture sometime soon. In fact, I'll insist on it."

We chat for a few more minutes before I catch Reginald waving at me. "It was wonderful chatting with you, Finnegan, and I look forward to talking some more tonight."

"Th' pleasure is mine, Miss Bree." Another bow at the waist and a quick brush of his lips against my knuckles, and then he's gone.

I end up fanning myself with my hand again. "Is it hot out here, or is it just these alphas?"

Reginald chuckles. "Pretty sure it's the alphas—and the betas. Tessa has done well for you."

"She has... And I obviously have a thing for accents. Finnegan is very different from the other alphas. It felt like he was genuinely himself and he didn't care what anyone else thought. Choosing to wear at least part of the tux, but making it his own, was a smart move. It set him apart, but it also told me so much about him even before he opened his mouth. There's something sexy about a man who is comfortable with who they are."

Finnegan

I can't say for sure how this first meeting with Bree went, but I think it went well. She didn't mention that I wore only part of the tuxedo that we were told to wear. I wouldn't have felt comfortable wearing it. I'm not a tuxedo wearing kind of guy, and I didn't want to come to Bree as anyone but myself.

She's a pretty wee thing, but I can tell that she's no pushover—which is something I look for in a woman. I need more than those ten minutes with her to get any actual idea of the type of person she is, but I'm looking forward to that chance.

"Right over here, Finnegan."

I lift my head to find Tessa waving me over to the gazebo. I'm not usually the type to forget about my surroundings, but that wee omega has me a bit out of sorts.

"Good day, Tessa." I stop at the bottom of the stairs, bowing at my waist. It's something that both my mom and dad taught me from a young age. You show respect to women at all times, and that respect never goes out of style. Am I over the top with it? Absolutely, but that's just who I am.

A giggle spills from Tessa's lips before she clears her throat to hide it. "Why don't you come on up so we can get this interview going?"

I straighten up, moving up the stairs, and dropping into a chair. "Do yer worst."

Tessa shakes her head, fighting a smile. "Tell me, Finnegan. How do you think your first meeting with Bree went? What do you think of her now that you've met her?"

"I believe it went well. A'm sure my Scottish brogue helped because women love accents, aye?" I wiggle my eyebrows up and down until Tessa is grinning back at me. "Bree seems lek a nice lass. An' she didnae frown upon my choice of attire. I knew she was beautiful from th' pictures A've seen, but I still was nae prepared for how much more beautiful she is in person. I look forward tae getting tae know her better."

Tessa's grin drops when I mention my attire, and now she's staring at me with narrowed eyes. "In the future, when you're given a dress code, I expect you to adhere to it."

"Maybe. It just depends oan what it is. A'm nae making any promises."

"I'll be keeping my eye on you, Mr. Abernathy."

I wince. "If ye feel th' need tae use my last name, please do not tack oan th' Mister. That's my da. If ye must tack something oan, use Doctor please."

"Was there anything else you wanted to add?" At the shake of my head, she gestures to the stairs where a beta is now standing. "This is Hector."

She gives a quick rundown of how the rest of the evening is going to go, but gives me no time to voice any questions as she hurries away. I can only imagine the amount of work she's having to do to produce this show. Standing, I turn to Hector with a grin. "Hello, Hector. A'm Finnegan an' I appreciate ye escorting me tae th' game room."

"It's my pleasure, Finnegan." Hector nods his head before gesturing up the path to the enormous house. "Shall we?"

"We shall."

Now I get to deal with a roomful of alphas and betas before I get to see the lovely omega again. Let's hope it doesn't take too long.

Carter

Riley has me pinned against a wall when I hear Hector arrive with another suitor. I push against his chest, trying to get him to back off and to stop kissing the mate mark on my neck. He can't seem to help himself, but every time he touches it, my cock is instantly hard. That wouldn't be so bad if we weren't surrounded by others.

Which is probably why he won't stop touching me.

As a beta, the mark doesn't ride me as hard as it does my alpha. Sure, I'm still horny as hell and would love nothing more than to have Riley rail me into the closest surface, but that can't happen right now.

Every time I've attempted to speak to any of the other suitors, Riley has growled and pulled me away. This will not work if I can't get him to rein in his alpha side. There's no way Bree will choose us if Riley can't play well with the others. She's looking for a pack, not a single alpha and beta. I know Riley wants this just as much as I do, but if he keeps allowing his instincts to ride him, we don't stand a chance.

"Riley." My exasperation is clear in my tone as I try to push him away once again. "You need to get yourself under control. Both of us need to talk to the other suitors, or we're going to be out on our asses before we've even gotten a chance. Bree needs a pack and if you won't let me be near any other alphas or betas, then she's going to think you can't share. Do you think that will endear us to her?"

Riley nips at my mark one more time before forcing himself to take a step back. "I'm fucking trying, Carter. You don't understand how hard my alpha side is riding me."

"I can see it, Riles. Hell, I can feel it through the bond. But if this is how you're going to be the entire time, we should just leave now. Maybe now isn't our time." I hate the words even as I say them, but seeing and feeling my alpha this torn apart—I hate it more.

"No." Riley shakes his head. "I'll figure out a way to rein it in. I don't want to be the reason this doesn't work out."

I feel the turmoil through our link as he tries to push away his alpha instincts. He's so young and I think that might be part of the reason he's struggling with this so much. I don't care that he's so much younger than me. I love him and I know he loves me. While I don't regret allowing him to mark me, I can see why it might have been better to wait.

"Do you think you can come with me to meet the others now—without growling and baring your teeth at them?"

"I can try."

I actually appreciate that he doesn't try to lie about it. Would I prefer it if he was positive he could do this? Of course, but I know that isn't an option right now. I slide my hand into his, not bothering to attempt to speak to the silent, brooding alpha sitting on the couch. I think his name is Owen. The adorable beta, Emmett, had tried to introduce us to everyone when we'd arrived, but Riley hadn't allowed it.

Instead, I walk over to Emmett and the other alphas who are greeting the newcomer. Emmett must hear us coming as he glances over his shoulder, raising an eyebrow, but says nothing.

"I'm sorry about earlier," I tell him, glancing around the group. "Riley and I are newly mated, and his alpha instincts are riding him hard with so many alphas here."

"That's alright." Emmett grins and I can already hear the growl rising in Riley's chest.

I drop his hand and slam my palm flat against his chest. "No, alpha. What did we just talk about?"

Riley squeezes his eyes shut, shaking his head before blinking back at me. He doesn't apologize for his reaction—nor did I expect him to. It's not his way, which can put a lot of people off of wanting to get to know him. Might as well let everyone see he's a possessive asshole, even without the bond riding him. That way, everyone knows what they're getting into, I guess.

I turn back to the group with a smile. "I'm Carter Woods and this is my alpha, Riley."

"Introductions are taking longer and longer," Emmett says with a grin. "This is Wren and Wilder. They're an unbonded pair, both run their own companies. Roman is a history professor. Sasha is a professional ballet dancer and, according to Roman, he's one of the best and the only alpha in his profession. And the newcomer is Finnegan. He's a psychologist."

That's a lot of information at once, but I think I'll be able to keep all the names straight, though I know Riley will struggle. "I'm an ADA and Riley is training with his father to take over the family company in the next few years. Emmett, I didn't catch what you do for a living. And does anyone know about Owen?"

"Owen is a MMA fighter." Wilder grins. "Not that he told us that. We only know because Wren here is a big fan."

"Of his fighting—not the man," Wren says, eyes darting over to the man in question, a frown marring his face. "The man seems to be a bit of a douche."

Owen's head turns slowly to glower at the group of us, telling me he'd heard Wren's words. Emmett lifts his hand, but Owen just turns back to face the blackened televisions.

"Well..." I trail off, not sure what to say, but I absolutely agree with Wren—Owen is a douche.

Emmett shakes his head as he turns back to me. "I'm a chef."

"Oh? Anywhere we might know? We're from Los Angeles, so if it's anywhere around the city, we might know it."

"Lyrical."

My eyes go wide as I slap a hand against Riley's stomach. "Holy shit, you're not just a chef—you're *the* chef. That's mine and Riley's favorite place to eat."

Emmett flushes, his head ducking. It's freaking adorable. "Thanks."

"No, thank you. I'm not joking. We have a standing reservation there every week... Except for the next couple of months."

Riley clears his throat. "Your food is amazing, Emmett. The combinations aren't something I would ever think of putting together, and I never leave disappointed."

I grin at Riley, hoping he can read how proud I am of him right now.

"So you can speak." Emmett perks up, a smile lighting up his face once more. "It's nice to meet you, Riley."

And then something strange happens—my alpha blushes. I've never seen this man blush. I didn't think he was capable of it. But here he is, bright red and seemingly unable to form words as the gorgeous beta smiles up at him.

I should be jealous, and I can feel a bit of the bond pushing at me, but it's easy enough to shove aside. Emmett is hot and I would not be opposed to getting to know him better. And for my alpha to get to know him better. There's just something about Emmett that seems to draw people to him—except Owen, who is obviously very antisocial.

Maybe Riley and I can do this. He'd allowed me to speak to Emmett and be in the presence of other alphas. Now, we'll just have to wait and see if he can keep it up. Because I want this for us. The chance at having an omega in our pack? It's everything I could ever want. Adding more alphas and betas? Well, I'm not averse to the idea. I've always wanted to be a part of a bigger pack, and maybe this will be our chance to get everything we want.

Chapter Five

Bree

Reginald and I talk a bit as we wait for the next limo, though I'm not actually sure what we talk about. My mind is already on the next suitor I'll meet. I haven't even met half of the suitors yet. I still have eleven men to meet. My mind keeps wandering to how I'll ever decide on who will be a part of my pack. I'm already beginning to feel overwhelmed and there's still so many suitors left to meet.

I'm so lost in thought, I don't hear the limo pull up. It's not until I hear someone's foot hitting the ground that I look up, and holy shit. I can only stare at the beautiful man before me. There's no doubting his Native American ancestry with his light brown skin and prominent features. He's well over six feet, his black hair is straight and longer than my own, falling to his waist. A broad, proud nose and full lips grace a face that is beautiful in its masculinity. Two others step out of the limo behind him, but I can't seem to break away from this man's stare. His deep brown eyes seem to reach deep inside of me and I need to know him—need to know why I feel this drawn to him without him ever speaking a word.

All three scents drift to me, though they're quite intermingled. Crisp air and driftwood with a bite of green apple. Smoldering wood, toasted marshmallows, and fire roasted vanilla. Lavender, pear, and driftwood. They're scents I wouldn't think would go together, but the combination sets off a yearning inside of me.

"Hi," one of the others says with a laugh.

My eyes drift away from the first man, finding the other two to be just as breathtaking. The man who'd spoken stands slightly shorter than the first man with light golden brown hair slicked to the side, the sides shorter than the top. His gray eyes are sharp behind a set of black-framed glasses. Tattoos peek out from the neck of his tux and when he lifts his hand in a wave, I discover that tattoos cover his hands as well. There's a piercing in his eyebrow and gauges in his ears. He has the hot nerd verb on lockdown.

The third man is probably right at six feet tall and wider built than the other two. His dirty blonde hair is wavy and long enough to be pulled up into a man bun. A scowl sits on his bearded face, but I don't see any animosity in his bright, electric blue eyes. One corner of his mouth lifts in a half smile as I continue to just stare at them.

It's that movement that shakes me back to myself as I laugh. "Shit. I'm sorry. The three of you together is a lot. That many hot men should not be allowed to ambush an omega at once."

The first man grins. "I mean, I could make them get back in the limo if you'd like."

"No, we're good. I'm Bree, obviously. Apparently, meeting a whole slew of hot men back to back has made my brain go offline, so I apologize. I'm not usually like this."

"I'm Onyx Holt," the first man says, still grinning as he offers me his hand.

The man with the glasses takes my hand as soon as Onyx releases it. "I'm Hudson Kennedy. It's a pleasure to meet you. And I certainly don't mind that we've flustered you."

The third man groans, knocking Hudson away with his shoulder. "I apologize for him. It's hard to get him to take much of anything too seriously. I'm Maddox Pierce."

He holds my hand for a moment longer than he needs to, but I can't say that I overly mind. I grin as I look from one man to another. "Unbonded pack?"

Onyx nods. "We've known one another since we were in diapers. We knew from the time that we were kids that we were meant to be a pack, but we always wanted to wait to bond until we met our omega."

"That's sweet. I assume that means you're all the same age?"

"Yup," Hudson pops the p as he grins down at me. "We're all thirty-four. We've been inseparable our whole lives. We even run a tattoo shop together—Infinite Ink."

"Oh," I squeak. "You three own Infinite Ink? It's almost impossible to get an appointment there. Tessa tried for like a year before she gave up."

Maddox nods. "She told us during our interview. I thought she was going to reject us just for that."

"She would never!" I shoot him a mock glare.

His smile grows. "That's what she told us... Well, she said she'd try not to hold it against us."

"That sounds like her." I laugh because it really does. It's just one of the many reasons I love her. "What's it like to be friends with someone for your entire life? The longest I've been friends with someone is Tessa and Reginald, and we've only known each other since college."

Hudson grins. "It's awesome because I have these two guys who know everything about me and still accept me—who still want me around."

"Most of the time," Onyx grumbles, making me grin.

"Whatever, Onyx. You love me." Hudson wraps his arm around the other man's neck and it leads to the two of them tussling.

"Can't take them anywhere," Maddox murmurs as he moves to stand next to me, both watching the other two men.

I shrug. "They're having fun, and it's nice."

Glancing up at Maddox, I hesitate to ask the question currently sitting on the tip of my tongue. I know I project confidence, and I usually am very confident, but it's different when I know these men are all here for me. Maddox turns his head, focusing his attention on me instead of his pack mates.

"You should just ask whatever question is on your mind. After all, isn't that why we're here? To get to know one another?"

"Sure, but how do you know when is the right time to ask the big questions? I literally just met you all moments ago. Maybe I should wait."

Maddox tilts his head as he watches me. "Nah... I feel like in this situation, everything is up for grabs, or whatever."

"Fine," I agree. "Are the three of you... together?"

"We are." He smirks. "Now, was that so hard? It's not like it's a secret. It's one of the things we had to answer when we applied. Tessa said that wouldn't be a problem for you."

"Oh, it's not," I assure him. And it's really, really not. My tongue darts out to wet my suddenly dry lips as I imagine these three incredibly gorgeous men together—but it's the only thing that's dry right now as I feel slick gush from me once more.

Damn.

"What did you say to put that look on her face?" Hudson asks, startling me, as I hadn't heard him and Onyx move back to us.

My eyes widen, face flushing as I look anywhere but at the three of them.

Maddox chuckles, but doesn't answer the question. "I think Reginald is trying to tell us our time is up."

A quick look at Reginald tells me he's correct. My face is still bright red as I lift my head to stare at the three of them. "It was really nice to meet the three of you."

"I think I can honestly say that the pleasure is all ours, Bree." Hudson lifts my hand to his lips and I can feel my blush darkening. He just grins as Onyx and then Maddox repeat the gesture.

"We'll see you soon." Onyx leans over to whisper his words in my ear, and it sends a shiver down my spine.

It takes all of my self restraint to not lift my hand to fan myself because *holy shit*. I shake my head, forcing myself to not watch them walk away. I'd been right—this decision is going to be next to impossible.

"I'd ask you what you thought of them, but I think it's fairly obvious." Reginald smirks, and I kind of want to smack him. Instead, I take a deep breath and pretend like he didn't speak.

"I can't believe they own Infinite Ink," I breathe out. "I wonder if they'll give me a tattoo."

"Since when do you want a tattoo?"

I shrug. "I mean, I've always kind of wanted one, but I didn't know what to get."

"Mmm hmmm... sure." Reginald makes a face, though I'm not sure why he's so surprised by it. "So tell me what you think of the guys?"

"Obviously they're hot—" I frown when Reginald makes a face while moving his mouth with my words, seemingly to mock me. "Do you want me to answer your question or not?"

I wait for him to gesture for me to continue. "They're all so different, but the bond between the three of them is so obvious. It reminds me of me and Tessa, but they've known one another since they were babies. That's crazy to me. I really enjoyed the bit of conversation we had, though. I definitely want to get to know them better." I laugh. "Plus, they're hot."

Because I don't think I can state that enough.

Onyx

"So, seriously, Mad, what did you say to put that look on her face?" Hudson asks, digging his elbow into Maddox's stomach when he doesn't answer right away.

Maddox smirks as he glances between the two of us. "She wanted to know if the three of us were together, and I told her we were. I'm assuming she was imagining it, and that's what caused the look."

I hum my agreement. That definitely explains the look and the blush that overtook her when Hudson and I arrived back at the conversation.

I'm a little irked that I missed out on chatting with Bree for longer, but it's good that she understands our dynamics from the start.

I reach down to adjust my hard cock, not trying to hide it from my two best friends and lovers. I hadn't been able to scent Bree's arousal, which makes sense. She's probably wearing scent canceling panties, so we wouldn't all go wild at the scent of her perfuming. But the look on her face, along with the blush that swept over not only her face, but her chest, had my cock hard as a rock in seconds.

"I like her," I murmur.

Hudson smirks, eyes flashing down to my cock. "You mean your dick likes her?"

"You barely spoke to her," Maddox says with a frown.

"That doesn't change the fact that I like her. A lot can be said without words." And Bree's eyes had spoken to me, drawing me in. I veer off to the gazebo where Tessa is waiting for us. "Hello, Tessa."

"Onyx. Hudson. Maddox. It's wonderful to see the three of you again." Tessa gestures for us to take a seat in the chairs across from the camera that she moves to stand next to. "We're looking for your thoughts on your first meeting with Bree."

The three of us sit, glancing between one another before Hudson shrugs, turning his attention to Tessa and the camera. "She was very nice and didn't hold back saying what she was thinking—something I appreciate in a person."

"She didn't get mad when these two knuckleheads started horsing around." Maddox points at Hudson and me. "She wasn't upset when she found out that the three of us were involved with one another, even though we're not currently bonded."

"Nope," Hudson says, popping his p—something he knows me and Maddox hate. "In fact, she seemed to like that idea, which is always a plus in my book."

"Will you please just stop talking for a minute?" I ask him, raising my eyebrows. He just smirks at me, but nods. Facing the camera, I shake my head. "She genuinely seemed like she wanted to get to know us. That's something I'd really like to get the chance to do—us getting to know her.

It's easy to tell if you're physically attracted to someone in that short of a meeting, but you can't actually get to know someone in ten minutes. So I'm hoping that we'll have the time to speak with her and really get to know her."

Maddox nods. "I agree. My first impression is that she's open minded and kind, though I believe she's not someone you'd want to mess with. There's just something about the way she holds herself and the look in her eyes that tells me she has a spine of steel. I'd love to see that in action."

"You say that now," Tessa murmurs, and I don't think I was supposed to hear it, but I do. I shoot her a smirk, telling her that not only had I heard her, but I see it as a challenge. Because I want to see it. I want to see all parts of her.

"Was there anything else the three of you would like to add?"

Hudson leans forward, his hands draped over his legs. "Bree is sexy as hell—especially when she blushes. I think I'll try to make that happen more."

Maddox lets out a heavy sigh, swiping his hand over his face. "No, I think that's it."

"Good." Tessa fights back a smile as she speaks. She goes over the schedule for the evening—the game room with the suitors until we all arrive, and then Bree will join us. Then something about a rose ceremony that will be explained to us. I don't recall reading anything about it in the information provided, so it must be something they added last minute.

Then Tessa is gone, leaving us looking for Hector. I stand, turning toward the stairs leading down from the gazebo and find a beta man standing there. "Hector?"

"That's me."

Hudson jumps out of his chair and bounds down the stairs to throw an arm around Hector's shoulders. "I need the scoop, Hector. I'm sure you've seen all kinds of things already. Tell me everything."

Maddox moves to stand beside me, shaking his head. "He's a menace."

"Yeah, but he's our menace," I say with a grin, wrapping my arm around Maddox's waist as we watch Hudson drag Hector up the pathway. The beta looks a little panicked as he glances over his shoulder at us. "We should go save the poor beta from him."

"Yeah, he's done nothing to be punished by having to deal with Hudson when he's like this." Maddox takes my hand in his as we hurry to catch up with Hudson and Hector.

While Maddox sounds annoyed with Hudson, I know the truth. Both of us love to see Hudson happy. He deals with debilitating depression that can be hard on all of us. It's something he's dealt with since childhood, so we know the signs. I'd been worried that he was slipping into another episode just before we received the phone call from Tessa telling us we'd been selected as suitors on *Heated*. But the news seemed to pull him from the hole before he'd sunk too far.

I wonder if having an omega will help with his episodes. Which brings my mind back to Bree. I want her to be ours. Now, I just need to figure out how to make that happen.

Bree

Twelve down, eight to go. Why had I thought that twenty suitors was a good idea again? I don't know how I'm going to be around twenty attractive men for eight weeks. The amount of slick I've spilled already tonight is ridiculous—and I'm not even done!

I remind myself to smile as the next limo pulls up. The door opens and out steps—you guessed it—another hot alpha. Over six feet with wide shoulders, honey brown hair, and sky-blue eyes. Yup, I want to lick him.

He grins and my knees go weak. I'm going to need my omega side to get herself under control. A pretty face and a pleasant smile should not be enough to make my knees go weak, and yet… here we are.

"Hi, you must be Bree. I'm Gabriel. Gabriel Ramirez." He offers me his hand and I take it as I try to remember how to make my mouth work.

I'm not this woman. I'm better than this. I need to get it together.

"It's nice to meet you, Gabriel."

"And you." He leans back on his heels as his hands slip into his pockets. There's a moment of silence before he purses his lips, leaning towards me with a grin. His scent drifts to me—slate rocks, cool water, and something woodsy. "So, this is weird, right? It's not just me?"

I burst out laughing. "It's totally weird. Honestly, I've been trying to figure out between meetings why I thought this was a good idea."

"Right, because you and your partner came up with the idea for *Heated?*"

I nod. "I came up with the original concept, and then we figured out how to make it work together. I, obviously, didn't think it through too well, though. I'm so in over my head, but I'm glad I decided to be the first omega. Because I can't imagine having someone else being the first one to do this."

"It'll definitely make it easier to help omegas in future seasons."

"If there are future seasons," I scoff, waving my hands around. "Who in their right mind would want to watch me awkwardly carrying on a conversation with way too many attractive men?"

A smirk slides across his lips. "Does that mean you think I'm hot?"

My eyes go wide, a sigh of exasperation spilling from me. "See? Awkward."

"I don't know. I kind of like it." His hand brushes back a piece of hair, tucking it behind my ear. "It shows that you're being real. No one wants someone who's on twenty-four seven, right?"

"Yeah, I guess." I drop my eyes, nibbling on my bottom lip. "Enough about my awkwardness. You know what I do for a living, but how about you?"

"I'm a kindergarten teacher."

"No shit?" I ask, giggling when he nods. "I bet all the moms hit on you."

Now it's his turn to blush. "I mean, yeah, I guess I get hit on sometimes. I honestly don't pay attention to it. I'm there for the kids."

"That's really sweet. Adorable, actually."

"Adorable?" He raises an eyebrow as he shakes his head. "Just what all men want to be called."

I swat at his arm, but he dodges the half-hearted blow with a laugh. "I happen to like adorable, but I'll try to not call you adorable again. How long have you been teaching?"

"This is my fifth year. I was lucky enough to get a placement right out of college. One upside to your mom being the principal, I guess."

"Nepotism at its best, am I right?" We laugh together, chatting for a few more moments before he's walking away from me down the pathway, and I find myself staring at a smirking Reginald again—probably because he caught me checking out Gabriel's ass. I can't really help myself. These men are just so freaking attractive.

"Are you going to stare at me with that shit-eating grin the entire time?" I ask, hand on my hip as I stare him down.

He shrugs, nodding. "Probably."

"Awesome. Let's get on with this. Gabriel is sweet. I can't believe he blushed when I called him adorable—which, by the way, just made me think he was even more adorable. And what's with men not enjoying being called adorable? It's not an insult—it's a compliment. It's not like I don't think he's hot. I absolutely still want to bang him."

I stop, realizing what I've just said. It's not like I can take it back, so I guess I'll just roll with it.

"I said what I said, I guess. I love that he's a teacher, and for kindergarten at that! I could never. That many young children all at once? I do not have the patience for that. I have nothing but the utmost respect for that man, knowing what he does for work. My heart melts at the idea of seeing him with all those kids. Ugh, I'm getting all mushy. Bring on the next one!"

Gabriel

I can't stop grinning as I head toward the gazebo. Sure, she called me adorable, but it didn't sound so bad coming from her lips. Her plump lips that I wanted to kiss more than anything else, but I held myself back. We'd only known one another for ten minutes. That's not enough time for her to be comfortable with me kissing her.

But I *do* want to kiss her.

I climb the steps to the gazebo, shooting Tessa a smile as I sit. "Hey, Tessa."

"Hello, Gabriel. It looks like your first meeting with Bree went well. Why don't you tell me your thoughts?"

"It felt so easy talking with her. I mean, don't get me wrong, I don't struggle with talking with people. But with Bree, it felt like this wasn't the first time we'd met. It was like talking to an old friend, and I kind of dig it."

I rub my hand over my chin as I consider what to say next. "I love that she was awkward and called herself out on it. Few people would do that. She called me adorable—which most men know is usually the kiss of death. But she didn't make it feel like that. She even said she liked adorable, so maybe that increases my odds? Who knows? I can tell you that ten minutes with her was not enough."

"That's sweet," Tessa gushes, holding up her hand before I can speak. "I know. Sweet is like adorable to men. It's not an insult. It's a compliment, and it's something that Bree likes in men. So it's definitely not a bad thing."

I sit back in my seat with a nod. I'm not upset about being called sweet, but I had planned on giving her a hard time about it.

Tessa waves her hand dismissively, which would normally annoy me, but I think that's just the way she is. "Was there anything else you'd like to add?"

"No, I don't think so."

"Perfect. Hector will show you to the game room." She gives me a synopsis of what to expect for the rest of the night, which will end with a rose ceremony, and apparently Bree will explain it to us. I'm not sure if I should be scared or not.

"Thanks, Tessa," I call out to her even as she's walking away. She raises her hand in acknowledgement, causing me to chuckle.

Someone clears their throat and I turn to find a beta male standing at the base of the stairs. He gives me a quick smile. "I'm Hector. If you'll come with me, I'll show you to the game room."

"Excellent." I slap my hands down on my thighs, which causes Hector to jump, before standing and making my way down to him. "Sorry about that."

"It's no problem. I'm just a little jumpy today," he says as he leads me up the path. "There are a lot of alphas all in one place. Things are a little... tense in the game room—just a warning."

His words have me straightening and my senses on high alert. "It's difficult to bring so many unknown alphas together. We'll work it out, and I'm sure none of them will hurt you."

"Logically, I know that, but I can't seem to get my body to understand that." He laughs and I return his smile.

My thoughts are already on the game room and what I'll be walking in on. Hopefully, we don't have a room full of posturing alphas. That isn't what I signed up for. No, I signed up for a chance with a beautiful omega, and I will not blow that by going all alpha male. It doesn't matter how the others act. All I can control is my actions and reactions.

Fuck. I really hope we're almost all here so Bree can join us. The sooner the better.

Hudson

We've been up here for about a half an hour when I hear footsteps on the stairs once more. I've been chatting with Emmett, who is adorably attractive, for the last few minutes while Onyx and Maddox have wandered the room, chatting with the other alphas.

Emmett leans forward, eyeing the landing as Hector appears with yet another alpha. I don't have a problem with alphas—hell, I'm in love with two of them—and I'd been fairly certain the alphas would heavily outweigh the number of betas. But damn. Did they all have to be so attractive? I'm sure that was a deciding factor in who was chosen to appear on the show since it's the premiere season, but still…

And this new alpha? He's hot as hell, and I'm guessing he's younger than me and my pack.

Emmett grins up at me. "I'm going to go say hi. You wanna come?"

"Why the hell not?"

Which is how I find myself trailing the adorable beta. I nod to Hector, shooting him a quick smile. I know he hasn't been having the easiest time with all the alphas—apparently Riley and Carter are newly bonded, and the alpha isn't dealing with it well. Emmett said it was worst when they first arrived, so I can only guess how that might have gone for poor Hector.

"Hey, I'm Emmett. Beta, obviously. And you are?"

I stifle the laughter threatening to spill from my lips. No one could ever call Emmett shy, that's for sure. His presence makes me feel comfortable, which is the main reason I'd followed him over to greet the new alpha.

"Gabriel." He grins at Emmett before turning his piercing blue eyes on me, lifting his eyebrows. "But you can both call me Gabe, if you'd like. It's what my friends call me."

I offer my hand. "I'm Hudson." When he drops my hand, I reach up to press my glasses further up my face, watching as Gabriel assesses both of us.

"Are the two of you?" Gabriel gestures between Emmett and I.

Emmett laughs. "No, we just met. He and the other alphas in his pack arrived just before you. But he's nice to talk to... and look at."

"I do have eyes and certainly noticed that," Gabriel says with a laugh, and I can feel myself flush. I know they'll see it. Damn being so pale, even with a tan. Now I understand how Bree must have felt. It's not nearly as much fun on this side.

"Why don't we introduce you to everyone?" I spin on my heel and head towards the others, hoping this blushing thing stops before Onyx and Maddox notice. They'll never let me live it down.

There's a chuckle behind me and if I had to guess, I'd say it was Gabriel, but there's no way I'm turning around to check. I suck on my teeth as I head toward where Roman, Maddox, and Finnegan are talking.

Maddox glances up as I approach, eyes narrowing as he takes me in. I don't doubt that he's noticed the blush, but it's too late to change course now. I force a smile as I come to a stop.

"We have new meat," I announce, gesturing behind me as Emmett stops beside me and I can feel Gabriel's presence at my back. He's about my height, maybe slightly broader, but he shouldn't feel like such an imposing figure. "This is Gabriel. Gabriel, this is Roman, Finnegan, and Maddox. Maddox is one of my pack mates."

"It's nice to meet all of you." I can't help but glance back at Gabriel while he speaks. His eyes are on the other alphas, but they drop to meet mine and I have to fight the urge to gulp.

I'm here with my pack to win over an omega—not to add another alpha or beta to my existing pack. I've got to get my shit together. Deciding to put some space between Gabriel, Emmett, and me, I move to Maddox's side.

"What's wrong?" Maddox murmurs, his hand moving to squeeze the back of my neck.

I just shake my head, eyes shooting up to look at Emmett and Gabriel once more. Both men are staring at me with matching smirks.

Shit.

"What do you do for a living?" Roman asks, seemingly oblivious to the tension in the air.

Gabriel keeps his eyes locked on me for a moment longer before turning to look at Roman. "I'm a kindergarten teacher."

Roman grins. "I'm a college professor—not quite the same as being a kindergarten teacher. Your job requires a lot more patience than mine does."

"Yeah, I'm fairly certain college students are about as much work as my kids." Gabriel laughs and I can't tear my eyes away from him.

"That might be true, but I can kick them out of my class. An option I'm assuming you don't have."

"That's true." Gabriel's eyes move back to the rest of the group. "What do the rest of you do?"

"I'm the head chef over at Lyrical," Emmett chimes in.

Gabriel pauses. "That sounds familiar, but I've definitely not been there before."

"A'm a psychologist," Finnegan offers in his Scottish brogue.

Maddox answers for us. "Hudson, myself, and our third pack mate, Onyx, own a tattoo parlor, Infinite Ink."

Gabriel nods slowly, eyes focusing on me again. "That makes sense. I might not be able to see all of your tattoos, but they're peeking out. I can't wait to see them all."

That sounds awfully suggestive to me. Is he hitting on me? A glance at Maddox, who's frowning at Gabriel with narrowed eyes, tells me Gabriel is *absolutely* hitting on me.

I suck in a deep breath, forcing myself to smile. This damn alpha is throwing me off my game. I need to get it together.

Emmett seems to take pity on me as he grins up at Gabriel. "Why don't I introduce you to the others?"

Gabriel shoots me a wink before turning his attention back to Emmett. "I'd like that. Thank you."

I watch the pair of them head toward Onyx and Sasha, who are leaning against the wall, watching the room. They don't seem to be talking, but neither man looks uncomfortable.

Maddox grabs my arm and steers me towards the bar. "We're going to grab drinks. Do either of you need one?"

They both decline and I allow Maddox to drag me across the room. "What the hell is going on, Hudson?"

"I wish I could tell you." I shake my head, grabbing a beer from the fridge and offering it to Maddox. He shakes his head, so I pop it open and take a long drink from it. I hadn't planned to drink, but I need something to get my head back on straight.

"Gabriel was hitting on you. Why?"

"Because he finds me attractive? It shouldn't be too hard for you to understand, seeing as you're sleeping with me."

Maddox sighs. "That's not what I meant, Hud. He's not the first person to hit on you, and I'm sure he won't be the last. But you weren't flirting back. You were blushing and stuttering. That's not like you."

"Between him and Emmett flirting with me, it just threw me, I guess?" I down the rest of the beer. "I don't know what came over me."

"You like them."

I shrug, ducking my head. I've never kept anything from Maddox and Onyx, and I don't plan on starting now. "I don't know them. Sure, they're attractive and I felt completely comfortable when it was just me and Emmett. I don't know."

"It's okay if you like them, or if you're just attracted to them." Maddox ducks down until I meet his eyes, giving me a soft smile. It makes me melt because it's rare that he looks at anyone like this. He's usually all stoic and serious. I love seeing this side of him.

"Neither me nor Onyx will be angry with you. You know that. The only rule, as you well know, is that you have to talk to us."

I laugh. "I know. Like I said, I don't know what all that was about. I've never reacted to anyone like that before. It freaked me out a bit, I guess."

"Well, then I think the three of us will need to talk about this. Maybe before bed or in the morning? We don't—"

"*Mine.* He's mine. You don't touch him. I will fucking end you." An angry voice resonates throughout the room, causing both mine and Maddox's heads to spin in the direction Emmett and Gabriel had set off in.

Now what?

Chapter Six

Bree

I'm exhausted. Having to be "on" time and time again as I meet man after man is harder than I thought it would be. There's got to be a better way to do this, though I can't think of one yet. I'll have to work on that. Don't want to wear out the omegas on day one, now do we?

I just have to remind myself that it won't be much longer as the next limo comes to a stop. Out steps a young man—holy shit, how old is he? Shaggy red brown hair hangs in his bright blue eyes that he quickly shakes away as he grins, revealing two dimples. He's about five ten and on the slender side. I'm fairly certain he's a beta—something his river slate and moss scent confirms for me as he comes to a stop in front of me.

"Hi! I'm Brody Sullivan. Twenty-two. An EMT. And you're Bree. Which, can I say, how much more beautiful you are in person? Like, you were gorgeous in the photos, but they don't do you justice at all. I mean, wow."

There's nothing I can do to stop the blush that rises along my cheeks, my head ducking for a moment before I force myself to lift it up again, and give him a shy smile. "Thank you. I wish I could say the same, but I never got to see pictures of you all."

Somehow, his grin grows, and he's so freaking gorgeous, but way too young for me. "That's all right. As long as I haven't disappointed you."

"Not in the least." I laugh, shaking my head. "You're so young. You do know how old I am, right?"

"I do. You're thirty-two, but I'm a firm believer that age is just a number. Not to mention, you don't look your age at all. I would've guessed mid-twenties if I met you at a bar or something."

He's absolutely too young for me, but there's just something so uplifting about him. I want to be around him more, so I'm going to do my best to not let his age affect my decision.

"You're very quick with the compliments, aren't you?" My nose wrinkles as I grin up at him. "You're very good for my self-esteem. I agree, age is just a number, but I think you're the youngest one here—at least, so far—that doesn't bother you?"

"Why should it? It makes me different from most of the others vying for your hand." He reaches down to grab my hand, lifting it to his lips. He doesn't let go of my hand as he lowers it. "I bet I'm also one of the few betas, which also makes me different. I think that's an advantage, not a disadvantage."

A glance at Reginald tells me that our time is almost up. Deciding to be brave, I step closer to Brody as I tilt my head to keep my eyes locked with his. "I do appreciate confidence in a man."

"Well, then you're going to love me. I have plenty of confidence." Brody's head ducks down until his lips are just inches from mine. "May I kiss you?"

I should say no because I'd just met this man a few minutes ago, but everything in me is telling me to say yes. And I should listen to my instincts, right?

"Since you asked so nicely..." I trail off and then his lips are on mine. It's a nice kiss as his lips move against mine. I appreciate that he doesn't try to deepen the kiss, but it leaves me craving more.

We're both grinning as we break apart, just staring at one another for a moment before I notice Reginald gesturing for me to wrap it up. "It was very nice to meet you Brody, and I look forward to talking to you more in the future."

"The pleasure was all mine." He glances at Reginald as he bites his lip. "Fuck it."

He leans back down to capture my lips with his, pulling me flush against his body. This time, I feel his tongue skim across my bottom lip, but then he's pulling away and stepping back. "I'll see you later, after you've met the rest of your suitors."

He's walking away before I can even form any words. All I can do is blink after him. He turns around and when he notices that I'm watching him; he shoots me a wink before continuing down the path.

"Wow," Reginald murmurs, pulling my attention back to him.

"Wow, is right. How does someone that age have that much confidence? I definitely didn't when I was twenty-two."

Reginald chuckles. "Yeah, I don't think any of us did."

I can't help casting another glance down the path, but Brody is already gone. A sigh escapes me as I focus my attention on Reginald once more. "He's too young for me."

"Didn't you agree that age is just a number?"

"What was I supposed to do?" I shake my head. "But I like him. I'm going to try to not let his age factor into my decision. He's like a literal ray of sunshine. Who wouldn't want that?"

Reginald snickers. "Well, I hope you plan on giving him a chance, since you already let him kiss you."

I flush, wrinkling my nose and forcing myself to keep my head raised. "He asked so nicely. How could I say no?"

"Easy. It's just two letters. N. O. No."

"Fine." I chew on the inside of my mouth, considering the real reason I didn't tell him no. "I didn't want to tell him no."

"Was that so hard?"

"Yes," I whine. "You're an asshole. Why did we hire you for this?"

Reginald grins as he stares down at me. "Because you love me and you thought it would be easier to have someone you're comfortable with as the host since you'll be doing interviews with me on the regular."

"Hmph."

"You better admit you love me and that I was the only person for this job, or I'm going to start calling you a cougar."

I gasp, my mouth dropping open. "You wouldn't. I'm not even old enough to be called a cougar."

"Cougar," he teases.

"Fine, fine. I love you and there's no one else I'd want to host *Heated*."

He grins when I continue to scowl at him. "Anything else you'd like to add about Brody?"

"I'm looking forward to getting to know him. And I definitely would like to keep him around. I don't think I've ever met someone who makes me want to smile so much."

"And you deserve to have someone like that in your life, Bree."

I grin as Reginald comes over to wrap his arm around my waist. I lean my head against him. He isn't wrong—we did choose him to be the host because I was comfortable with him. But he's also someone who is easy to talk to and is good at soothing people, so he'll be good for the future omegas as well.

"Thanks, Reginald."

"Anything for you, Bree."

His hold on me helps me settle from meeting Brody, which is why I stay there for longer than I should as we wait for the next suitor to arrive.

Brody

As I make my way to the gazebo, I'm fairly certain I have a goofy smile on my lips. I don't know what made me ask Bree if I could kiss her, but I'm glad I did. I'd wanted to beat my own ass as soon as the words slipped from my lips, but when she'd said yes? I wanted to shout my excitement to the skies.

And what a kiss it was. Which is why I couldn't help but kiss her one last time before I walked away. Betas aren't as affected as alphas by an omega's presence, but that doesn't mean we aren't affected at all. She smells amazing and all I want to do is go back and kiss her again, but I know that isn't an option.

I hurry up the steps to the gazebo, sitting in a chair and turning my grin on Tessa. "Hi, Tessa!"

"Hi yourself." Tessa returns my grin. "So how does it feel to be the first one to kiss Bree?"

My eyes are wide, but my smile goes nowhere. "No one else tried to kiss her? I don't know if that makes me an asshole or the luckiest man here."

Tessa laughs. "I don't think anyone would ever call you an asshole. A puppy, maybe, but never an asshole."

"A puppy?" My brow wrinkles, my smile slipping but not gone as I try to figure out what she's talking about.

"It's a thing in romance books. It's a character that reminds you of a puppy. Cute, happy, and you just want to hug them. Also known as a golden retriever."

"And is that a good thing?"

Tessa shrugs. "That depends on who you ask. If you were to ask Bree, she'd say it's a good thing."

"Well, that's all that matters then." I shrug.

"Okay, puppy. Tell me about your first meeting with Bree. What are your thoughts on her? And the kiss? We wanna know it all."

I can't help the dreamy expression I'm sure to be wearing as I think of Bree. "She's amazing. Sweet and kind. Beautiful. And a damn good kisser. I'd definitely say the meeting went well since she agreed to allow me to kiss her. I don't even know where that came from. I just kind of blurted it out because I couldn't stop looking at her lips."

I can feel myself flushing, something I hate, but know there's nothing I can do to stop it. "That could've gone very badly. I'm glad it didn't. I would've hated to be sent home on day one. I can't wait to talk to her again, and I definitely want to kiss her again."

"Okay. Down, puppy." Tessa laughs. "Was there anything you wanted to add?"

"Is this puppy thing going to stick?"

"Oh, for sure. You're stuck with it now."

I wrinkle my nose. "Fine, I'll learn to live with it. And no, I don't think there's anything else to say."

"Excellent. In that case, please follow Hector." She gestures to a beta male who waves before proceeding to go over the plan for the evening, which will end in some kind of rose ceremony that Bree will explain to us.

"Awesome. Thanks, Tessa." I bounce to my feet, hurrying down the stairs until I reach Hector. I grin as I offer him my hand. "Hi, Hector. I'm Brody."

Hector shakes my hand and then we're heading up the path to the house I'll be staying in. "It's nice to meet you, Brody. Just know that there's a *lot* of alpha energy in the game room right now. There's a newly bonded alpha/beta pairing, and the alpha is having a hard time keeping himself under control."

"How newly bonded are we talking?"

"A few weeks?"

My eyes go wide as I shake my head. "I'll bet he's having a hard time keeping himself under control. When my sister bonded with a pack—she's also a beta—we didn't see her for over a month, though she talked to us every few days. Her alphas were feeling extra possessive. She told me they barely left the house that entire time. She had to take the time off work because one of them kept insisting they go with her, and then they proceeded to threaten anyone who dared speak to her."

"Yikes. I mean, my alpha and I had a rough few weeks when we bonded. Thank goodness Tessa and Bree are so understanding."

"Bree is pretty awesome, isn't she?" I ask, my smile growing once more.

Hector nods. "She's one of the best people I've ever met, let alone worked for."

After that, we fall into a comfortable silence that allows me to think about the pretty omega. I know I'm only a beta, but I don't think that'll mean anything to Bree. She's so kind and accepting. I wonder how many other betas will be here. But what I really want to know is what I have to do to get Bree to choose me to be a part of her pack.

Bree

I'm feeling restless as I wait for the next suitor. I think back, counting how many I've met, and realize that I only have six left to meet. Hopefully, at least a few of those are part of a pack because then I'd be almost done. I tried to ask Reginald to tell me more about the next few suitors, but he was as tight-lipped as ever, refusing to give me any information.

That's probably the most frustrating part of this entire process. It's driving me crazy not knowing who I'm meeting. This is hard for my inner control freak. It's made slightly easier because it's Tessa who chose these alpha and beta men for me, but it's definitely making me twitchy.

The sound of wheels on gravel has me perking up just before the next limo turns into view. I bite the inside of my cheek as I try to hold back my anxiety and excitement. One would think I'd be less excited at this point, considering how many men I've met in the last few hours, but any of these men could be future members of my pack. While it's anxiety-inducing, it's also really freaking exciting.

The limo comes to a stop, and the door swings open quickly. The man that steps from the limo takes my breath away. He's gathered his long dark brown hair, which is a lighter caramel color at the ends, at the crown of his head in a bun. I wonder if the coloring is natural, from the sun, or if he gets it done. A thick beard covers his face, a beard that has my mind wandering to what it would feel like against the inside of my thighs.

My whole body flushes at the idea, slick spilling from me. I'm ever so grateful for these scent canceling panties. How embarrassing would it be for this man—no, this alpha, I realize as his scent hits my nose—to know just how turned on I am by his appearance?

My eyes dart to meet his dark brown eyes as I try to bring myself back under control. He's absolutely gorgeous—not that any of the men I've met today are unattractive—but add in his scent and I want to melt into a pile of goo at his feet. It's heavy on leather with a touch of sandalwood, and I want to crawl into his arms and cover myself in the scent.

"Hi," I squeak out, internally grimacing at the sound.

"Hello, Bree." He smirks as he makes his way over to me. He obviously likes the effect he's having on me. "I'm Maverick. Maverick Kelley."

"It's very nice to meet you." I'm proud of myself for how strong my voice sounds. Even though I've had to suppress my omega side for years to make it in the business world, I've always been a proud omega. With that being said, there are times it's very frustrating to be an omega. Times like now, when a scent rushes through me and makes me forget how to act like a normal person. Luckily, it doesn't happen often—excluding today. I wonder if it's from meeting so many alphas in such a short period of time.

I offer Maverick my hand, which he shakes with a good grip—another point for him—but he doesn't release it right away. "Obviously, you're an alpha, but why don't you tell me a bit more about yourself?"

"Sure." Maverick's big hand engulfs mine as he runs his thumb up and down my palm, and I have to fight back a full-body shiver. "I'm thirty-seven, and the oldest of five—all alphas. I'm an architect and I love my job."

"Your poor mother," I murmur, eyes locked on where his thumb continues to stroke along my palm. Between that and his deep voice, I'm more on edge than I'd like, and slick is definitely filling my panties. "Five alpha children? I bet you all were a handful."

"Mama is an omega," Maverick says, thumb pausing its movement until my eyes lift to meet his. "She's fierce and takes no shit from anyone. I know others see omegas as weak, but she's the strongest person I've ever met. It's because of her I know what it truly means to be an omega. You're fierce when you need to be, and you're not to be fucked with when it comes to someone you love or something you feel passionately about. And you're far from weak, which I would've known about you even if I hadn't been raised by an omega. You can't be weak to run a Fortune 500 company—especially alongside an alpha."

"I'm glad that I don't have to educate you on omegas then. That's at least one less person to worry about," I say with a laugh. "But you're right, it wasn't always easy to get our company to where it is. Most people view not just omegas as weak, but also female alphas. You don't even want to know the amount of alphas and betas I've had to deal with who thought they could walk all over me."

"I'm sure you set them straight on what a mistake that was."

I shrug. "For the most part. Some are just idiots, and don't want to admit when they're wrong. But enough about me. You're an architect? I don't think I've ever met anyone who was an architect. Tell me about it?"

"You might regret asking that," he says with a grin. "I can talk about architecture for hours. I love being an architect. Designing is probably my favorite part. But there's nothing better than seeing something you created being built. I love being able to point out buildings that I designed. It drives my siblings crazy."

And he wasn't lying—he really can talk about it for hours. But I'm not complaining, as I love seeing him talk about something he's so passionate about, and it gives me time to just watch him. He lights up when he's talking about being an architect, making him even more attractive. That he obviously loves it means I could sit here and listen to him talk about it for hours and not be bored. But Reginald can't allow that, a fact that I'm reminded of when he gestures for me to wrap it up.

"I'm sorry to cut you off, Maverick, because if I'm honest, I could listen to you talk about this forever, but I'm being told our time is up." I wrinkle my nose, letting him know how annoyed I am over this.

"I'm sorry for dominating the conversation," he says with a wince, but I'm shaking my head before he's even finished speaking.

"No, please don't be sorry. I enjoyed listening to you. It's obvious that you're passionate about it and I learned a ton. Hopefully, we can finish this conversation at a later time."

Maverick nods. "I'd love that. It was nice meeting you, Bree. I look forward to our next interaction."

Maverick leans over and kisses my cheek. My eyes fall shut as his scent rushes over me. As weird as it sounds, I could sit here for hours drowning in his scent. It makes me feel safe, almost like coming home.

"Me too," I manage to squeak out before he shoots me another smirk and heads up the path.

"Fuck," I mutter as I turn to watch him walk away. I bite my lip as I watch the way the black dress pants hug his ass.

Damn.

"Here," Reginald says a second before a handkerchief appears in front of me, cutting off my view of the alpha.

Turning around, I frown. "What's that for?"

"To wipe off the drool."

"Fuck you!" I shriek as I launch myself at him, punching him in his chest repeatedly.

"Ow, ow. Okay, okay. I'm sorry. Please stop punching me. You hit hard for an omega." Reginald drops the handkerchief as he gathers my wrists in his hand. "Damn, Bree. You're going to have to explain the bruises to Tyler?"

"Oh, you can tell him to call me and I'll explain to him about what an asshole you were being. I'll make sure to tell him how you told me I hit hard for an omega. I'm sure he'll love that."

Reginald's eyes are wide as he drops his hold on me. "Damn, Bree. Don't be like that. Why would you want to get me in trouble?"

"I don't know. Why do you have to be an asshole?" I ask with a raised brow.

"Touche." He sighs. "You know I didn't mean it, right?"

I nod. "I do, but that doesn't make it alright to say it. While you might not mean it, there are a ton of people out there who do believe it. And if they heard you say it—a movie star—it would just reinforce their bigoted beliefs."

"You're right. I'm sorry."

"And I forgive you, but just remember that your words can hurt someone even when you don't mean for them to." I squeeze his hand, giving him a small smile. I know he was joking with me, but it's a habit I've tried to break all of my friends of. While I might not take his words seriously, there are many out there that would. I'd hate for him to unintentionally hurt another omega or make someone else think that their bigoted opinion is okay.

"So what did you think of Maverick?" he asks me, a twinkle in his eye.

I narrow my eyes at him, wanting to hit him again. "I think he was a hot, intelligent, passionate man—who smelled divine."

"Oh, we could definitely tell you thought he was hot," Reginald snickers, dodging my hand as it shoots out to slap his stomach.

"Keep it up, Reginald, and you're going to get your ass beat. We still have a long night ahead of us. Are you sure you want to piss me off right now?"

Reginald pulls me into his arms, squeezing me to him. "I never *want* to piss you off. It's just so easy to do."

I yank out of his hold as I shake my head. "Such an asshole."

I shift from side to side. My slick-filled panties are beginning to feel uncomfortable and I don't think I can stand here much longer without taking care of it. Not to mention, I don't know how much more slick they can hold. "Do we have time for me to go to the bathroom?"

"Absolutely, sweetheart. I'll walk with you, just in case any of the suitors are out and about." He wraps his arm around my shoulders, leading me down the path toward the house. "We don't have time for you to take care of yourself, though. We don't want to leave the next suitor waiting while you get yourself off. Oof."

I grin when my elbow meets his stomach, cutting off his words. He's so lucky I love him. I wouldn't put up with this shit from just anyone. He's also lucky I'm in dire need of a new set of panties as I hurry us along. It means I don't have time to make him properly regret his words.

Maverick

Walking away from Bree is one of the hardest things I've ever had to do. I've had no one ask me to talk about my career—my passion—and mean it. Her eyes didn't glaze over when I started talking about what I loved about architecture. No, instead she was actively listening and asking questions. It made me feel good.

Which I guess is the entire point of an omega. They're calming to alphas. They're what keeps us centered. I've never really felt like I was missing out on anything by not having a pack or an omega, but meeting Bree has informed me on just what I'm missing out on.

I'd always figured I'd find my pack and my omega at some point, but then the years kept slipping by. Three of my younger siblings have already found their packs—one of them has even bonded with an omega. My youngest sister is a female alpha and only sixteen. I know it will be harder for her, especially since she has four older brothers who will be happy to threaten anyone who thinks they can hurt her or mistreat her. I'm fairly certain that my mom has completely given up on me ever mating with anyone. Hopefully, I can prove her wrong.

I push aside the thoughts of my family as I approach the gazebo, loping up the stairs with ease before taking a seat.

"Well, Maverick, you and Bree ran a little over your time. It seems you were in a very engrossing conversation." Tessa grins at me.

Heat rises to my face, and I know there will be a faint blush if anyone looks close enough. Between my olive-colored skin and my tan, I rarely have to worry about blushing, as it's usually not enough to show. But right now? If I was any paler, there would be no question that I'm blushing.

"I might have gotten a little carried away talking about architecture." I shrug sheepishly. "Bree is just so easy to talk to, and she seems genuinely interested. Most people ask to be polite, but she really wanted to know."

"She doesn't tend to ask questions she doesn't want answered. You haven't known her for long, but you'll figure that out on your own." Tessa tilts her to the side as she considers me. "But I do think you would've noticed, eventually. You seem observant. But enough of my thoughts. Tell me what you thought of Bree and your first meeting."

I smile as I think back to our meeting. "I mean, there's the obvious—she's gorgeous. But it's more than that. She's genuine and easy to talk to. She definitely has opinions on alphas' and betas' treatment of omegas, which I agree with, mind you. She's strong and independent. The independent part might be hard for some alphas to handle, as it's ingrained in our DNA to want to care for our omega. Not that I think she won't allow her alphas to take care of her, but I think at some point it might drive her crazy."

Tessa laughs. "And you learned all of that in less than fifteen minutes during a conversation that was mainly you talking about architecture. Are you part psychic?"

"No, definitely not. Though that might be helpful." I laugh. "I'm just very good at reading people—at least in broad strokes. I want to know all of Bre's strokes, though, not just the broad ones. I want to know all the little parts that make up the whole."

Tessa bobs her head, a small smile on her lips. "And with an attitude like that, I think you have a good chance of that. But since you ran over, we need to wrap this up quickly. Was there anything else you wanted to say?"

"Just that I can't wait to talk to her again—about something other than architecture this time."

The two of us laugh together before she introduces me to Hector, letting me know he'd be taking me to the game room. After that, we'll spend some time with Bree as a group before some kind of rose ceremony that Bree will explain to us. A little weird, but it's a new show. Who knows what kinds of things we'll be doing over the next eight weeks.

Standing, I start to thank Tessa before realizing she's already gone. Damn, she moves fast. Shaking my head, I turn to find Hector standing at the bottom of the stairs. He's a beta, and he seems mildly uncomfortable.

"Are you alright, Hector? You seemed stressed."

Hector laughs, but doesn't sound amused at all. "You'll find out once we make it to the game room. Come on."

I stand there for a moment longer before catching up to the smaller man with a shrug. If he doesn't want to tell me, then that's fine. He says I'll figure it out once we make it to the game room, so I'm guessing I'll find out soon.

And then, I should be able to see Bree again in a little over an hour. That thought puts a bit of a bounce in my step.

Brody

When the next suitor arrives, I glance up to take in the alpha before turning my attention back to Emmett, Carter, and his alpha, Riley. When I first arrived in the game room, it looked like a fight was about to break out. Riley had shoved Carter behind him, baring his teeth at Gabriel—whose names I learned after everyone had calmed down. Owen had been moving toward the snarling alpha from behind, and I'd known that there was no way it was going to end well if I didn't intervene.

I'd scurried over, putting myself between Gabriel and Riley, finding Emmett already there. A smile and some soft words as Gabriel had backed away had calmed Riley—until he'd felt Owen's presence. It took me, Emmett, and Carter to drag Riley away from the others and to an empty couch.

"How are you doing now, Riley?" I ask kindly. This isn't my first rodeo with a new bond mark. As a paramedic, we have to deal with them more often than not. "There's a new alpha in the room. I don't want you to freak out, okay?"

Emmett, Carter, and I are all crowded around Riley, each touching him and offering him our calming scents. As soon as I'd realized what was happening, I'd asked Emmett if he wouldn't mind helping me and Carter calm the alpha. He'd agreed with no hesitation.

"I think I'm alright." Riley shakes his head. "I'm sorry, Carter. He touched you and I snapped."

"Riley, he was just shaking my hand."

"I know! Fuck, I know that. I knew that then, but I couldn't stop myself. I know I messed up—again. I'm trying."

"You are, alpha," I say quietly, my smile never leaving my face. "Sometimes it's hard to fight those instincts riding you. We'll just need to make sure no one else touches Carter without making sure you're alright first."

Carter presses a kiss to Riley's cheek before turning back to me. "Thank you. You're really good at this."

"It's all part of the job." I shrug, not minding the compliment, but I'm used to this and they're not, which is why they don't know how to deal with it. It's obvious that Riley's education on the mating bond is lacking, or he would have a better grasp on his instincts. It's not surprising, as most alphas don't know half of what they need to know about mating. But that's fine. I'll be sure that this group knows what they need to know.

That may not be why I'm here, but it won't hurt anyone to learn more about mating—especially if they intend on taking an omega mate like Bree.

"Why don't we go meet the new alpha before the others? That way, you can ease your alpha's mind. Then I can actually meet the others." I stand, offering my hand to Riley. "How does that sound?"

Riley turns to Carter before nodding. "Yes, I think that's a good idea. Thank you."

"You're welcome. Later, I'll go over some coping mechanisms with you to make this easier on you."

Which is how I find myself approaching the new alpha alongside two other betas and a slightly feral alpha. Emmett waves to the alpha before ducking around him to speak with Hector. I can't hear any of their hushed conversation, but I assume he's explaining the tension in the room to the other man.

"Hi, I'm Brody. This is Carter and his newly bonded alpha, Riley. Please don't reach out to any of us to shake hands or anything. Riley is feeling a bit feral with all these alphas around his mate, so we're taking things slowly." I can practically feel Riley vibrating with tension behind me.

The alpha nods slowly, keeping his eyes on Riley. "I'm Maverick. It's nice to meet all of you. Riley, what do you need from me?"

I'm practically beaming up at Maverick—not that he notices, since his eyes never waver from Riley. Now here's an alpha who has been trained right. And with his words, I feel the alpha at my back relax.

"If you could avoid touching Carter, I believe I'll be fine. Thank you."

Maverick grins as Emmett appears beside him. "I'm the oldest of five alphas. Three of them are male and have found their packs. So, this isn't my first rodeo in dealing with territorial alphas who have just bonded. One of my brothers even has an omega in his pack. It's good that you've bonded a beta before an omega. It means you'll be able to handle it better when you find your omega."

"I'm glad you've dealt with it before," I tell him. "Because I don't think anyone else in this room has. It's been... interesting. I arrived just before you and I thought there was going to be a fistfight."

"Which totally wouldn't have been hot." Emmett smirks and I can't help but laugh at him. "I'm Emmett, by the way."

"It's nice to meet you, Emmett." Maverick's eyes sweep over the room before focusing on us once more. "The three of you are the only betas? It was smart to surround the two of them—an alpha's instincts don't consider betas as much of a threat."

"I think I take offense to that?" Emmett frowns.

I laugh. "I've seen some betas who were definite threats, but for an alpha, they only see other alphas as threats usually. The man might see a beta as a threat, but the inner alpha? He just sees someone weaker." I pause when I see them all gaping at me. "Before we get certified, paramedics are required to take alpha, beta, and omega psychology classes. We have to know how to deal with each designation."

"And what if someone identifies as another designation than the one they were born to?" Emmett asks.

"There are some who identify differently and that's something that is covered in our classes. When we show up, we're not to assume anyone's designation. We ask. We wait until they tell us what their designation is and then we interact with them as we would anyone who'd been born to the designation."

"That's so cool." Emmett grins at me, his awe very clear.

Should I let him know I'm not into men? Nah, it seems too early for that conversation. Instead, I turn back to Carter and Riley. "Did you want to come with us while Maverick and I meet the others?"

Riley shakes his head quickly. "I think I need a few more minutes."

"Then we'll go have a seat on the couches—away from Owen." Carter takes his alpha's hand and leads him away.

"I've pretty much been walking everyone through and introducing them as they arrive." Emmett shrugs. "Might as well keep doing it. Come along."

"This is going to be interesting, isn't it?" Maverick asks, voice low as we follow Emmett.

"That's for certain." I laugh, wondering what I've gotten myself into. "But at least it won't be boring, right?"

Maverick laughs with me as we approach the first group. I'm thankful that my training could prevent a fight, but wonder what would've happened if I hadn't been here. I make a note to ask someone about that. I'd like to find out what measures they have in place with this much testosterone in one place—with this many alphas in one place. They have to have a plan in place to keep the omegas safe.

As Emmett introduces us to a pair of alphas, I push those thoughts away. That's a problem for later.

Chapter Seven

Bree

Within fifteen minutes, I find myself waiting for the next arrival with fresh panties—still scent canceling, thank the fates. I've just made it to my mark when I hear the squeal of tires as the next limo makes its way up the driveway. I love the fact that I haven't had time to psych myself up about meeting my next suitor.

The limo comes to a stop, but the door doesn't immediately open. I chew on the inside of my lip, not wanting to mess up my lipstick yet, but freaking out the longer it takes for the door to open. What's taking so long?

The door suddenly opens, and a man pops out, grinning as he moves toward me. He ignores the calls coming from the limo, which informs me that this meeting will be with more than one alpha or beta.

"Hi, Bree." The man continues to grin down at me as he comes to a stop in front of me. He runs a hand through his red hair, causing it to stand straight up, and I can't help but return his smile as he bounces from foot to foot.

His woody scent drifts to my nose, informing me he's a beta. I'm momentarily distracted as I try to separate the wood smells—sandalwood and cedar are obvious, but there's another there that I'm struggling to identify.

"Teakwood!" I exclaim and the man laughs. "Sorry, I couldn't figure out what the last wood was in your scent."

"I'm glad you figured it out," he says as he offers me his hand. I can hear others exiting the limo behind him, but I can't tear my attention from him as I slide my hand into his. He's extremely attractive with his full red beard and piercing green eyes. He's probably just under six feet tall, so he still towers over me. "I'm Levi Astor, pack beta."

"It's nice to meet you, Levi." I finally pull my attention from him as someone clears their throat. I find three men standing behind the beta, all alphas based upon their scents.

"Levi, you should have waited for us," one of the alphas says. He seems to be the oldest of the four, maybe in his early fifties? There are threads of gray through his perfectly styled brown hair, but his beard is almost completely gray. I get a whiff of his fascinating scent, a blend of black raspberry, vanilla, and plum, as his gray eyes turn to me. "I apologize for our beta. He can be... enthusiastic at times."

I smile, turning my attention back to Levi as I speak. "I didn't mind."

"Regardless, it was rude and I don't stand for that with my pack mates," the man says, a growl to his voice that has my smile falling as he steps up beside Levi. "Apologize, beta."

Levi winces at the alpha growl behind the man's words. "I'm sorry, Bree. Dominic is right, that was rude of me."

I bite down on my tongue, teeth grinding as I remind myself that their pack dynamics aren't for me to interfere with—yet. "Dominic? I take it you're the head alpha."

Dominic shoots me a charming smile as Levi steps back, his head bowed, and the other two alphas step forward to stand just behind Dominic—essentially cutting off my view of the beta. "Yes, I'm Dominic Astor, and I am the head alpha."

"It's nice to meet you," I say, not really meaning it as I turn my attention to the other two alphas. "And you are?"

Dominic growls quietly, telling me he doesn't appreciate being dismissed, but he can go fuck himself. I don't like the way he treated Levi, and that doesn't speak well for this pack's chances with me.

One of the men steps forward, offering me his hand. His face sits in a scowl, which sets me on edge—and not in a good way—as I take his hand. He's attractive with his black hair spiked to perfection, rich brown eyes, and neatly trimmed beard. It's too bad that this entire pack, except Levi, seems to set me on edge. "I'm Cillian Astor. Alpha."

He drops my hand and steps back before even shaking it—which pisses me off. His scent of fresh air, spruce, and cedarwood brushes against my senses for a moment before the last man steps forward. His dirty blond hair is cut close to his head on the sides, with the top long enough to be spiked up. His hazel eyes draw me in as he extends his hand toward me. "Hi, I'm Brayden Astor. The newest alpha to join the Astor pack."

Though he doesn't smile, his tone is kind and I find myself smiling up at him as he actually shakes my hand. His scent of ozone, amber, and sage drifts to my nose and I feel my shoulders drop as I relax for the first time since Dominic spoke.

"It's nice to meet you as well, Brayden. Will the four of you tell me your ages and what you do for a living? Maybe how you met?"

Brayden steps away, letting his hand slide across mine as he does so. He turns his attention to Dominic, so I do the same.

Dominic's smile looks a little forced as he speaks. "I'm fifty-four and a surgeon. Cillian is thirty-six and works in banking. Brayden is twenty-four and is a model who's trying to make his way into acting. Levi is thirty-one. He's a fitness model and a personal trainer. It's actually because of him that we all met."

I don't really like the way Dominic is dominating the conversation, so I turn my attention to Levi. "Oh? And how did you end up bringing your pack together?"

I hear Dominic mumble something under his breath—somehow I don't think it's complementary—but I just keep my attention on the beta. He blushes under my attention and it makes me smile.

"Dominic and Cillian were two of my first personal training clients. They both asked me out, and I didn't see a reason to say no. I'd informed them both that I was seeing other people, but when things started turning more serious, I decided it was time for the two of them to meet. They hit it off and the Astor pack was born." Levi ducks his head, glancing at Brayden from the corner of his eye. "I met Brayden at a shoot, and I knew from the first word he was meant to be a part of our pack."

"I like that," I tell him before turning my attention to encompass all four of them. "It was very nice meeting your pack. I look forward to speaking at a later time, but our time is up."

Dominic nods, already moving toward the path Reginald indicates to them. He doesn't say anything to me, nor does Cillian as he follows his head alpha. The two of them pause when they realize Levi and Brayden aren't with them.

"You heard the lady. Our time is up. Let's go." There's a bit of a bark to Dominic's word, but Brayden and Levi still hesitate.

"It was really nice to meet you, Bree," Levi murmurs, lifting my hand to his lips as he smiles. "I hope we can talk more later."

Levi passes my hand to Brayden, who also presses his lips to my skin. "You're lovely, Bree, and I look forward to getting to know you better."

"Levi. Brayden." Dominic has gone full alpha as he barks out their names. The two of them shoot me apologetic smiles before they scurry after their head alpha.

I'm sure my eyes are blazing as I turn my attention to Reginald. "I hate alphas like that."

"I know you do." Reginald's smile is sad. "Why don't you tell us why and what you thought of the other three members of the Astor pack?"

I fist my hands at my side, trying to calm down so I won't say anything I regret. You know what? Fuck it. The viewers should see the real me—even the part that tends to speak without thinking.

"There are so few omegas in this world that we're often looked down on. We're thought to be weaker, less than alphas and betas. I'm not less than anyone, and especially not because I'm an omega. Alpha barks should only be used in the most dire of situations. They're not meant to be used just because the alpha doesn't like what's being said or done." I shake my head as memories of my childhood rush through me. "I was raised in a pack. There was one alpha, three betas, and my omega mother. My alpha father liked to use his alpha bark anytime he wasn't getting his way. He used it to beat down my beta fathers and my omega mother. And once I got old enough to have opinions of my own, he used it on me. I never saw him use it on my younger alpha brothers, but that doesn't mean he didn't."

Forcing myself to take a couple of deep breaths, I try to reign in my anger. "Alphas who use their barks as a weapon are a disgrace to their designation and to the human race. I have no use for them, and this first meeting has not endeared this pack to me because of Dominic's use of his bark. I really liked Levi and Brayden. I don't like how Dominic expected the attention to be solely on him—it makes me think he might be a bit of a narcissist, especially since he's a surgeon. Cillian didn't say much, but the little he did makes me think he's more like Dominic than Brayden."

"Will you still give them a chance?" Reginald asks, voice quiet and subdued. I know he also hates alphas who act like Dominic, but I know it doesn't make him as angry as it does me.

"Of course I'll give them a chance. Maybe they were nervous, and it was making them act like assholes. Who knows? If I don't try to get to know them, I'll never know. And I don't want to be that person."

Reginald beams at me. "You really are too good of a person, Bree."

"I'm really, really not." Shaking my head, I realize I only have one more suitor to meet. Thank the fates. "So just one more, right?"

"Yeah, just one more. Do you need anything?"

Shaking my head, I allow myself to get lost in my thoughts of the Astor pack. I truly hope that Dominic isn't as abusive as he seems, because that's exactly what using an alpha bark unnecessarily is. Based on Levi's response to his reprimand, I don't hold out too much hope. I would hate to see Levi's and Brayden's brilliant personalities be smothered by an overbearing alpha.

"Bree?" Reginald's hand lands on my arm and as I glance up at him, I realize he's called out to me more than once. "Are you really okay?"

I nod, forcing myself to smile. "I'm fine, or at least I will be. It's just that talking about my childhood brings up a lot of feelings that I'd rather not deal with. But I'll be fine. And I'm excited because I only have one more suitor to meet. Then we can get on with the next part of the night and then I can finally go to sleep."

"I can get Tessa if you need her..." he trails off when I shake my head. "Okay, if you're sure."

"I'm sure. Thank you."

Am I okay? Mostly. But I will be fine and I don't need Reginald and Tessa fussing over me when I should be focusing on the last suitor that I'll be meeting. And focusing on that is much better than focusing on my childhood. Or on the alphas that came later.

No, I can't let my mind go there.

I straighten my dress and decide to take a few moments to meditate while I wait for the last suitor.

Dominic

I'm pissed as I stalk to the gazebo. First, my damn beta didn't bother following proper procedures. He should've been the last one to meet the omega, not the first. He knows better. He knows how much I need control over unknown situations. I already don't do well in them because of my OCD, but to have my damn pack mates making it worse?

Yes, Bree is beautiful. Yes, she smells amazing. But that doesn't mean they can just forget everything else but her. First, it was Levi and then it was Brayden. I can cut Brayden a bit more slack as he's still new to our pack and doesn't fully understand just how bad the OCD is. And that's my fault. I hate feeling weak.

I'm the damn head alpha and I can't even control my pack. My hands are already shaking as I try to calm myself by moving my thumb from finger to finger, trying to ground myself.

"I'm sorry, Dom."

My nose flares as I turn to glare at Levi. "It's a little late for sorry, isn't it, beta?"

Am I being an asshole? Absolutely one hundred percent. But he knows fucking better. And now I have to go give an interview while I'm losing my shit. This will go over really well.

"C'mon, Dom. Levi just got overexcited. He didn't mean to make you feel out of control. He would never do anything to hurt you on purpose. Neither would Brayden. We love you, you know that." Cillian grabs my arm, pulling me to a stop and forcing me to face him. His hands land on my face. "You've got this, Dom. You won't let the OCD defeat you."

Brayden moves to stand beside Cillian, reaching down to grab my clenched fist in his hand and giving it a squeeze. I feel Levi's weight against my back and I let my eyes fall shut at the feeling of being surrounded by my pack.

I know they love me, and they wouldn't do anything to hurt me. Cillian isn't saying those things because I don't know, he's saying it so I can remember—so I can ground myself. I don't know where I'd be without them.

"I know you didn't mean to, Levi. You too, Brayden. I need you to be more conscious of your actions when we're going into new situations. This is not the place for me to have a breakdown. I need your support with this." It's so hard to admit to the last part. To admit that I'm weak and I need their help isn't something an alpha should do. My father would have beaten my ass if he saw me right now. It's a good thing the asshole is already dead.

Maybe he's rolling over in his grave, I think to myself with a grin.

"There's my guy," Cillian murmurs before brushing his lips over mine. "You okay now?"

I nod slowly. The attack isn't completely over, but I'm under control enough to do this interview. "I need the three of you to let me do the talking. It's the only way I'm going to make it through this."

"Of course, Dom," Brayden says as he leans in to kiss me. "Whatever you need."

I turn around to face Levi, raising my eyebrows as I await his answer. "I promise, Dom. I really am sorry. I just got too excited."

"Shhh," I whisper as I lean down to kiss him. I pull back, cupping his cheek. When he leans into my touch, I smile. "I know you didn't. I'm okay, I promise."

"Okay." Levi's smile is sad, something that I hate.

I brush another kiss across his lips before pulling away from the three of them. "In formation, please."

Brayden and Cillian stand side by side, with Levi behind them. When I turn around, Cillian will be on my right and Brayden on the left. A sharp nod and then I spin on my heel and the four of us march up the stairs to the gazebo.

The alpha female is waiting for us with her lips curled up in a sneer. Fates only know what she's thinking right now. I know how I came off while speaking to Bree, and while I'm sorry for it, there's no other way I could've handled it as everything spun out of control around me.

Tessa can just deal with it. She's not the one I need to impress. Though I will need to make it up to Bree once I see her again. Great.

"Pack Astor," Tessa spits out as I take the center seat with Cillian sitting on my right side and Brayden on my left. Levi takes a seat on Brayden's other side and I catch a glimpse of Brayden reaching for Levi's hand. I let out a sigh of relief, knowing that Brayden will be sure that Levi follows my instructions—even if he gets excited.

"Good evening, Tessa," I say with a smile. "It's good to see you again."

"Mm-hmm," the woman murmurs, and I know there's so much she wants to say that she's holding back. "Why don't the four of you tell me your thoughts about your first meeting with Bree?"

I incline my head slightly. "It did not quite go as planned."

"Would you like to expand on that statement?"

I really don't, but what choice do I have?

"We're a bit of an old-fashioned pack, as is my preference. That means that as the head alpha, I should have been the first to greet the omega." I hesitate as Tessa glares at me. "I'm sorry—Bree. Then it would have been Cillian, Brayden, and finally, Levi. I don't like it when the procedures we have in place aren't followed."

"That's not old-fashioned—that's archaic," Tessa spits out. "Alphas aren't better than betas. And they're certainly not better than omegas. We're more than our designations."

"I agree. I said none of what you just accused me of. You read into the words I said and twisted them to fit your biased opinion of me and my pack."

Tessa still looks pissed as she turns to Levi. "How can you be a part of a pack that thinks you're lesser than?"

Levi grinds his teeth, but keeps his mouth shut as he turns to look at me.

I clear my throat, waiting until Tessa turns her attention back to me. "If you have any questions for my pack, you will direct them to me."

"You're a fucking dictator. I don't know how that slipped by in the interviews, but I won't stand for this. I won't allow you to treat Bree like she's less than. I won't allow you to belittle her. I think your pack should leave now."

I feel a weight bearing down on my chest, making it hard to breathe. My hands begin to shake, but my alphas each take one in their hand to remind me they're there.

"Once again, you're putting words into my mouth that I haven't said. I believe that you hold a bias against the old traditions that my pack follows, but that is not an acceptable reason to ask us to leave. We have in no way harmed anyone, especially not the ome—Bree." I'm proud of how steady my voice comes out even as I'm losing it. "We will not be leaving until Bree asks us to leave."

I rise to my feet, my pack following suit. "I believe this interview is over. I would appreciate it if you could tell me where our room is so we can have some time to regroup."

"No, you will join the other suitors in the game room. Hector will show you the way," Tessa bites out before stalking away in a huff.

"Who the hell is Hector?" Cillian asks.

"Umm... that would be me." A timid beta male stands at the base of the stairs and gives us an awkward wave.

"Hello, Hector. I would appreciate it if you could please show us to our room. I need a moment with my pack before we're forced to endure the other suitors." I move to the bottom of the stairs, coming to a stop in front of the man and towering over him.

Hector pales, visibly swallowing. "I'm very sorry, alpha, but I can't do that. Tessa is the boss, and if she says to bring you to the game room, then that's where I'll be taking you."

"Please?" Brayden asks as he moves to my side. "We just need a moment after those cruel words that Tessa threw at our pack."

Hector hesitates before shaking his head once more. "I can't. Come with me."

Then he's scurrying down the path, expecting us to follow. I force myself to take a deep breath. "It's fine. I'll be fine. Let's just get this over with. The sooner we can get back to our room, the better."

I force myself to follow the beta, even as my mind is running off in a thousand different directions. Maybe coming on *Heated* was a bad idea. I'm not sure I can handle the lack of control I have over everything.

Bree

"I'm sorry, Bree," Reginald says, for what has to be the hundredth time.

I fight to keep the grimace off my face and turn to face him. "It's fine. You didn't give the limo a flat tire, did you? And you've done everything you can to make this go faster. You already sent another limo to pick up the suitor and sure, it's put us about thirty minutes behind, but it's fine. And not your fault, so you can stop apologizing, yeah?"

"Right." Reginald nods and I'm grateful when I hear the tires on the driveway. "Oh, good. They're here. You're almost done, Bree."

I don't respond, keeping my attention on the limo as it pulls to a stop in front of me. The door flies open and a hulking body climbs out. He has to be close to a foot taller than me and covered in muscles that I can see rippling, even beneath the tux he wears. His blond hair is messy, as if he'd been dragging his hands through it again and again. He doesn't have a full beard, more of a scruffy look, and the hair on his face is much darker. His crystal blue eyes draw me in.

When he grins, I melt. There's a dimple in his cheek that I want to lick. Slick gushes from me at the sight, but when his scent hits me I'm practically panting. Clove and cedarwood, with just a hint of orange, assaults my nose and I find myself wanting to climb into his arms so his scent can surround me. What a yummy smelling alpha he is.

"Hey there, darlin'," he drawls, a thick southern accent apparent in his words. "You must be Bree. I'm Dalton Cole and it's so nice to meet you."

"It's nice to meet you, too." My voice is breathy and I berate myself once more for allowing these alphas and betas to get to me like this.

He stops mere inches from me before leaning closer and taking a whiff of my scent. "I suddenly have a hankering for some champagne, darlin'. Well, I'll be. Your scent is so appetizing."

I blush at not only his words, but at the hungry look in his eyes.

You can't climb the alpha that you just met, Bree, I remind myself.

"Dalton, why don't you tell me a bit about yourself?"

"I might could do that for you, but I'd rather listen to you talk than do all the talking."

I laugh. "Unless you didn't read the packet provided to you, you already know the basics about me, while I know nothing about you."

"Oh, I for sure read that—more than once. But it's not the same as talking to someone." Dalton shrugs. "But I guess it's only fair if I share about myself. Though don't be surprised if I try to get you to tell me more about yourself. If I'm honest, I'm plumb obsessed with you and your scent."

And I'm blushing again as I suck my bottom lip between my teeth before remembering my lipstick and letting it go quickly. Dalton's eyes follow the movement, that hungry look still in his eyes.

And now I want to climb him like a tree again.

Dalton shakes his head as if trying to clear it. "I'm thirty-eight. I run my own construction company that I inherited from my old man. I'm the baby of three. My older brother and sister are betas like my mama. We're all still close and try to have Sunday night dinners. It makes mama happy, which in turn makes the old man happy."

"Did you just call your dad an old man?" I giggle.

"It's a southern thing darlin'." He shrugs. "I'm sure my accent gave it away, but I was born and raised in the south. I'm just a good ole southern boy."

"I like your accent, and the way you say things," I tell him, and it's true. I haven't been around many people who are from the south since I was born and raised in California. "How are you liking California so far?"

"The weather is amazing," Dalton says with a grin. "It's a lot different from back home, but I think I could get used to it."

We chat for a few minutes before I once again see Reginald gesturing for me to wrap it up. I barely refrain from rolling my eyes. At least this is the last suitor.

"It seems our time is up." Disappointment seeps into my voice. "But on the upside, you're the last suitor to arrive. So you'll see me again very soon."

"Darlin', it was a pleasure talking to you and getting to know you. I'll be seeing you soon." Dalton grabs my hand, squeezing it as he leans in to press a soft kiss to my cheek. "And I can't wait to talk to you more."

I flush, not even knowing why, as I watch him walk away. Turning back to Reginald, I find him wearing a knowing smirk. "What is that look for?"

"You're so screwed, B." He laughs. "How the hell are you going to choose your pack from twenty insanely attractive men?"

He makes a good point, but I won't be admitting that to him. Instead, I give a shrug as I try to keep an air of nonchalance. "I'm sure that they were all on their best behavior... or at least *most* of them were. They'll show their true colors soon, and I'll see if their first meetings are actually an indication of their true selves."

"That's true. Luckily, you don't have to make that decision yet. So, tell me what you thought of Dalton."

"He was a sweetheart. You always see the character in the movies who is a southern gentleman, and that's what he reminded me of—with a bit of mischievousness behind it. Which I really like. And I love his accent. I've always been a sucker for a good accent. In case that wasn't made abundantly clear today."

"Same, B. Same." Reginald grins. "Anything else to add?"

I think about it before shrugging. "Not that I can think of. Though, you can verify that the order of events is what I came up with, and that Tessa and the other producers didn't change them on me."

Reginald shakes his head. "Nope. I've been given very firm instructions to not tell you anything and that if you asked, I'm to remind you that you're not working on the show. You're this season's omega and that's all you should be focused on."

I grind my teeth, trying to fight back the grimace that wants to break free. I'm going to have a very loud, spirited conversation when I see Tessa next. And by very loud and spirited, I mean I'm going to yell at her until she concedes to the fact that it isn't fair to keep details from me. I can't work like that.

I'll go crazy, not knowing what's happening—a fact that she is well aware of. We, and everyone who works with us, know that I'm a control freak. Yes, I wanted to be on the show, but I did not agree to having everything kept from me. And I'm not going to allow it. This is not the agreement we came to. If I was any other omega, I would expect to know what the schedule was for the day. Tessa's in for a rude awakening if she thinks I will let this slide.

Dalton

Well, that little lady was a surprise—and not one I hated. Beautiful and unafraid to speak her mind. She's no southern belle, but that's just fine with me. I never wanted any of those women that my mama was constantly trying to set me up with. Though Bree was as sweet as my mama's sweet tea. I definitely would like to get to know her better.

Telling her I'd enjoyed my visit to California had only been a bit of a white lie. It's not what I'm used to, and not everyone here is kind. I've heard many people making fun of my accent when they think I can't hear them. Then there are the ones that mock me to my face. Honestly, I prefer them. At least they're being genuine in their hate. Saying I sound uneducated and that I must be stupid. It has sucked.

But there's no hate in that omega. She likes the way I talk, and since she's the reason I'm here, that's all that matters. I do hate that my limo got a flat tire. I'd offered to change it, but the driver had been a little snooty about that. So I didn't change the tire. I just sat in the back of the limo and sulked like a child. Not my finest moment.

The driver of the limo that picked me up was much nicer, and he hurried as much as he could to get me here. But based on the schedule I'd been provided, we were still thirty minutes late and I don't doubt that they kept Bree waiting for me the whole time.

I heave a sigh in my annoyance as I climb up the steps to the gazebo. Tessa is waiting there for me, a bottle of water in her hand. She offers it to me. "I'm sorry about the delay. No one considered that a tire might go flat on the drive over. I've already spoken to the company owner and let him know how unacceptable it was for you to have to sit on the side of the road for thirty minutes to wait for another limo. You would think that the drivers would know how to change a damn tire."

"I offered to do it for the driver and he told me that wasn't my job. Then he told me to get back in the limo and wait for someone else to pick me up." I grab the bottle of water, taking a long drink before turning my attention back to Tessa. "He was rather rude, if I'm being honest. I know things are done a bit differently than they are back home, but there was no reason for him to respond that way."

Tessa's eyes narrow. "I guess I will be calling the owner again. That's unacceptable behavior. I'm sorry that you had to deal with that."

I drop down into one of the chairs and shrug. "It's fine. He didn't hurt my feelings any, but if he'd been driving someone else, who knows how they would've reacted, ya know?"

"I do know. But since we're running behind, let's go ahead and get this interview done. I want to check on Bree before she heads up to the game room to spend time with you and the other suitors."

"Sure. Sure. I'm sorry to have inconvenienced Bree."

Tessa shakes her head. "*You* did nothing wrong. Tell me about your first meeting with Bree. What are your thoughts on both the meeting and Bree?"

"She's a sweetheart, that little lady. My mama would love her—even if she ain't southern." I laugh, thinking about Bree meeting my mama. That would be a sight to see. "She was very gracious, even with as late as I was. I'm sure she's been standing around waiting for me to arrive, but she acted like we had all the time in the world. Talking to her was easy. I can't wait to get to know her better."

"And I'm sure she can't wait to get to know you better, either, Dalton. Thank you for your patience with everything and for being such a good sport. Hector will show you to the game room, and I'll bring Bree up as soon as she's ready. Then she'll spend time with all of you before the rose ceremony, which she will explain later."

She's gone before I can even rise from my chair. I shrug, turning to find a beta waiting for me. I guess it's a good thing I didn't have any questions. "Hector?"

"That's me." He gestures for me to follow him as he starts up the pathway. I try to catch up with him and he just speeds up, causing me to frown.

I guess today just isn't a day for me to get along with people. Except Bree. And again, she's the only one that matters. And maybe the other men she chooses to be a part of her pack as well, but who knows who that'll be. There's twenty of us here and they haven't given us any information as to how big of a pack Bree wants. I guess that's something I can ask her about when I see her next.

Levi

Things are not going well. Dominic is on edge—something we knew was going to happen, but it's worse than we expected. When we'd arrived in the game room, he'd almost gotten into a fight with three different alphas. I don't even know their names because we had to tear Dominic away and to the other side of the room.

We tried to find a quiet room so he could decompress, but security was there before we could even open a door to any of the rooms on this floor. So, our pack is now on the opposite side of the game room while the rest of the room glares at us. Just fucking great.

I don't blame Dominic. He has a medical condition, though I don't believe he disclosed that to Tessa or anyone involved with the show. So he's coming off as a controlling, possessive asshole. Not the impression I want my pack to be making, but what choice do I have?

"Dom, did you tell anyone about your OCD so they could make arrangements for you?" I ask quietly, making sure my back is to the room so no one can read my lips.

Dominic sneers at me. "Of course I didn't. Why would I expose my weakness to them? So they can exploit it? I don't think so."

"Or maybe," Brayden begins, glancing at me before continuing, "they would have allowed us to go to our room before coming up here if they knew you had a medical condition."

Cillian glances from Dominic to Brayden before his eyes fall on me. I beg him with my eyes. He tends to side with Dominic on everything, but I can only hope that this one time he'll choose me and Brayden's side.

"Maybe they're right, Dom…"

"No, absolutely not. I will not allow this disease to be what defines me on this show. I'll get it under control." Dominic leans back, arms crossing over his chest—his signal that he's done with this conversation.

His stubbornness is going to get us kicked off this show. He's going to ruin this for us. Why did he even bother to sign us up for it, knowing he wouldn't be able to handle the loss of control? I don't want this show to be what drives our pack apart, but I don't know if I can forgive him if he doesn't listen to us. We're his pack. He should care what we have to say. He should listen to us.

I'm too pissed off to remain sitting here, so I clamor to my feet.

"Where are you going, Levi?" Dominic demands as he leans forward, placing his palms on his thighs.

"I'm going to meet the other suitors and get the hell away from you before I say something we both might regret." I shoot one last look of disappointment at my head alpha before spinning on my heel.

"Levi, get your ass back here!" Dominic barks at me, causing my body to lock up at the command in his voice.

I turn around and sneer at him. "Is this how it's going to be? You're going to bark at me when you don't get your way? Is that how you're going to treat your pack? The people you love most in the world? If you do this, I will grow to resent you. That resentment will grow into hate and before you know it, we'll be four strangers living under the same roof, torn apart by your own stubbornness and refusal to listen to the three people who love you more than life itself. Choose carefully, Dom, or this will be the beginning of our end."

I'm breathing hard, the anger slowly building to a rage that I can't seem to push back. The tears gleaming in Dominic's eyes tampers it for a moment, but the longer he holds me there, the more the rage grows. It won't be long until it's all I feel. No one in my pack has seen me lose my temper because it's dangerous when I do. I've worked hard to make sure I have the longest fuse possible because bad things happen when I lose myself to the rage.

Am I sorry I hurt him? A little. Do I regret the words I said? Not in the least.

Finally, Dominic's face crumbles. "Fine, I'll speak with them. And you can... you can go and speak to the other suitors. I'm sorry."

The hold of his bark falls away, but I move toward him instead of following my intended path. Dropping to my knees before him, I grip his face in my hands. "I love you, Dominic. Hector should be bringing up the last suitor soon—honestly, I think he should've already gotten here. Let's go wait near the stairs and we'll ask Hector to bring us to Tessa. Or have her come to us."

I stand, hands moving to grip his, pulling him to his feet. "We'll do this together."

"Together," Dominic murmurs before leaning forward to press a lingering kiss to my lips.

When we break apart, I step aside to allow Dominic through, but he stops me by taking my hand and pulling me to his side. "No, I need you by my side."

I duck my head, smiling as I lean into him. We make our way to the stairs, veering away from the other suitors. Just before we arrive, Hector steps off the stairs with another alpha beside him. I feel Dominic tense, so I squeeze his hand to remind him we're there for him.

Out of the corner of my eye, I can see Cillian and Brayden have both laid a comforting hand on our head alpha. Turning back to Hector, his eyes are wide as he stares at the four of us.

"Hector, we need to speak to Tessa. It's extremely important. Can you please take us to her? Or bring her to us?"

Hector's mouth opens and closes a few times before he shakes his head. "I can't take you to her, but I'll call her and let her know you need to speak to her? She's going to ask me why you need to speak with her. What should I tell her?"

I glance at Dominic, not sure how he wants to handle this. His jaw clenches, eyes on the floor. He hates this. "Can you please tell her we need to discuss a medical condition that wasn't disclosed?" he finally manages to get out.

"Yes, I can do that. If you'll remain here, I'll step downstairs to make the call." Hector nods and scurries down the stairs.

"Are you the reason that man was so terrified to speak with me?" the alpha who'd just arrived asks, a heavy southern accent in his words.

My eyes narrow as I take a step toward the alpha. "Why don't you back off?"

He holds up his hands in surrender. "I'm sorry. I'm Dalton. You told Hector there was an undisclosed medical condition. I just wanted to make sure y'all are alright? Is there anything I can do to help?"

My shoulders slump and I feel like an asshole as I step back. "I'm sorry for assuming."

"I can see how my choice of words could be misconstrued."

Dominic clears his throat. "Unfortunately, there isn't anything you can do, but I appreciate you asking."

A throat clears behind us and we turn to see one of the betas standing there. "Hi, I'm Emmett. I'm sorry to interrupt. I just wanted to see if I could introduce you to the others?" His eyes dart between us and Dalton.

"I would greatly appreciate that, Emmett," Dalton drawls. "But I believe the... I'm sorry, I didn't get your pack name?"

"Pack Astor," Brayden supplies. "I'm Brayden. Levi is our beta. The grouchy looking one—oh, both of them look grouchy. The young one is Cillian, and Dominic is our head alpha."

I snicker as I glance at Cillian and Dominic, who both look affronted at Brayden's words as he grins back at them.

"Well, it's nice to meet you, Pack Astor." Dalton turns his attention back to Emmett. "They're waiting for Hector, but I would appreciate you introducing me."

All four of us breathe a sigh of relief as they walk away, leaving us to wait for Hector. Tessa will understand, right? I really hope so.

Chapter Eight

Bree

The sound of heels on the path has me turning so I can watch as Tessa approaches. I wonder if she'll keep the footage of the verbal ass whooping I'm about to give her in the show. Probably not. It won't make either of us look good—not that I care.

"Oh, look, it's the boss," I sneer, shaking my head. "You told Reginald he wasn't allowed to tell me the order of events? Even if I wasn't a huge part of the reason that this show is even happening, as an outside omega, I would expect to know what was going to be happening throughout the days. I know that I'm a control freak, but do you think it's going to help anyone if I'm off the rails, because no one would tell me what the hell is going on?"

Tessa's lips pull back from her teeth, a growl falling from her lips as she turns to Reginald. "You really do enjoy pitting the two of us against one another, don't you? Asshole."

Those words take the wind from my sails as I turn on Reginald. "Please tell me you weren't lying to me."

Reginald shrugs. "The two of you just make it so easy."

"Asshole," Tessa and I mutter together. We glance at each other before bursting out into laughter. Our giggles last for a few moments as we try to get ourselves under control.

Finally straightening, I turn to face Tessa. "I want to watch the feed of the game room."

"What? No, absolutely not."

Knowing this was going to be her answer, I already have an argument ready. "I think it's something we should incorporate into the show, assuming it works when we try it. The omega meets twenty suitors and is now overwhelmed with the many intense smells. They're overwhelmed because while they've had a surface level conversation with the suitors, they don't know anything about them. The suitors could have been putting their best—or worst—foot forward.

"They're more likely to be acting like themselves in the game room with the other suitors. They won't feel the need to impress someone, so they can be themselves. They're all aware they're being recorded, so why not allow the omega a chance to see the suitors without being in the room?"

Tessa considers me as she works through the idea in her head. "I like the idea, but we can't have footage of the control room on the show. That needs to remain a mystery."

"I'm aware," I say with a triumphant smile. "But you *can* pull the game room footage and show it. And if you bring one camera into the control room, you can have it focused on the omega to record their reactions. Maybe two cameras with one focused on the omega's face and another focused on their hands on the screen, in case they're pointing something out. They can be kept stationary so the viewers can't see the control room."

"That could work." I can see Tessa working out the different angles inside her head, but I already know I'm going to win this one. Because it's a brilliant idea and I really want to get a glimpse of the suitors while they won't know I'm watching.

Finally, Tessa nods. "Alright, let's do this. Head to the basement and use the bathroom if you need to. I'll have your makeup artist meet you down there for touch-ups. I'm going to grab two cameramen to the control room and we'll get it set up, so I'm sure it'll work. Then you'll get your peek at the suitors, you sneaky bitch. Don't think I don't know what you're doing."

I hold up my hands in surrender. "I have no idea what you're talking about."

But even as I say the words, the smirk on my face gives me away. At least it's a good idea that we can make work for all the seasons. And I really do think it'll be helpful not just to me, but to the future omegas.

Tessa lets out a heavy sigh, obviously not amused with me as she flips me off. I try to hide my giggles with a cough, but I'm not fooling anyone as Reginald falls into step with me as we head for the house.

"You're a brat."

I just shrug because he isn't wrong. At least when it comes to Tessa and Reginald. The rest of the world has never been allowed to see this part of me because I had to be stronger than everyone else with ovaries of brass to get anyone to take me seriously in the business world.

Appearing on *Heated* could end up being a setback with the old, crotchety men I have to deal with regularly, but I'm doing this for me. For the first time in my life, I don't care how my actions make me appear. I'm an omega and I'm damn proud of it. It's kind of nice to get to be myself all the time and not have to hide my feelings behind a wall of ice.

"On a more serious note, how are you doing?"

I glance at Reginald out of the corner of my eye, but his eyes are on the path in front of us and not on me. His face is blank, but I know he's left playful Reginald behind and brought out protector Reginald.

"I'm doing good," I tell him softly. "It's a lot—meeting that many alphas in such a short period is overwhelming. Especially since they, and the betas, are all so fucking hot."

That pulls a smile from him as he glances down at me before I continue, "And I'm used to dealing with strange alphas regularly. The other omegas might not, so I think viewing the suitors in the game room will give them—us, really—time to unwind and center ourselves before we're shoved into a room with all twenty of them at once."

"It's a good idea. I'm not overly surprised that the control freak wants to watch them without them knowing."

I jab him in the side with my elbow and he dances out of my reach as we make it to the house. Instead of heading to the stairs that lead upstairs, we veer off to the hallway on the right. When we hit the next hallway, we veer right again. At the end of the short hallway, between the kitchen and dining area, is a door that leads to the stairs that will take us to the basement.

Designing the compound had been one of my favorite parts of the entire process. The house is massive—it has to be since it will house twenty suitors, some in packs. Not to mention a demanding omega. And since no one will leave the house except for show sanctioned dates, we needed to make sure it had everything we could need.

The basement might be my favorite place besides my suite. There's the massive control room that will remain locked at all times. Anyone who is allowed in there has a badge that they must scan to get access, or they can be let in by the security guard. It might seem like overkill to have a security guard inside the room, watching the cameras at all times, but we want to make sure no one gets access to the control room that shouldn't.

Not that the control room is my favorite part of the basement. There's a gym that takes up about a third of the space with every kind of equipment imaginable. There's an Olympic sized indoor pool and a hot tub that could easily seat forty people. There's a simple bathroom with multiple stalls, but my favorite part is the steam room. There are also showers in the room, but if you walk to the back, there's a steam room built to hold close to a hundred people. Overkill? Probably, but it allows for people to have space for themselves even if all the suitors are in there at once.

I wish I could go soak in the hot tub and follow it up with a long steam, but that's not on the agenda right now. Instead, I duck into the bathroom and take care of business before making my way back to the hallway, where I find Tessa waiting alongside Reginald and Allison.

Allison immediately pulls out a brush and powder, doing a quick touch-up as Tessa talks. "I think we can make this work, Bree. Thanks for your suggestion—even if it was partially selfish."

I grin as she leads us to the control room. "When do I get my badge back?"

"When you've finished your heat with your new pack." Tessa raises her eyebrows, waiting for me to protest.

"Fiiiiine." If only she realized I know where she hid it and if I really want to get into the control room, I can just steal it back. But for now, I'll allow her to think she's in control.

Tessa squints her eyes at me, probably trying to figure out my angle, before scanning her badge and opening the door. She gestures for me and Reginald to go inside. I rush in and bang my hand against the window separating me from Leo, our security guard who's on duty right now. We actually have three guards who rotate, one on the day shift and one on the night shift every day.

"Hi, Leo! How's Astell? And the kids?"

Leo chuckles. "They're all good. Somehow, I'm not surprised that you found a way into the control room."

I grin, shrugging my shoulders. "What can I say? I get what I want."

"Yes, you do. As an omega should." He laughs, eyes narrowing on a screen. "Well, you better get on with this segment so you can see your suitors again."

Something about the way he's looking at the screen makes me think something is going down and I desperately want to see it, so I rush ahead and make my way to the terminal surrounded by cameras.

Glancing down, I see the terminal already has the game room camera pulled up. I force myself not to look yet, turning my attention to Tessa. "Just let me know when I can look."

Tessa glances over my shoulder at the cameramen before giving me a sharp nod. She and Reginald move to stand between the two cameras as I let my eyes fall to the screen before me. Counting the bodies, I only see nineteen of the suitors. I'm surprised that Dalton hasn't made it up there yet.

Pushing away the thought, I focus on the screen and I already don't like what I'm seeing. Even through the screen, the tension is palpable between the suitors. Pack Astor sits together on the far side of the room, while many of the other suitors shoot them glares. What the fuck had they done?

"Sound?" I ask, eyes shooting up to Tessa, who shakes her head. I frown, knowing this is my own fault for not thinking of it. I hadn't thought to ask for sound because I'd assumed it would be provided. But you know what they say about assuming.

My eyebrows shoot up in the air as I watch Levi begin to stalk away from his pack, only to stop suddenly. Eyes narrowed, I realize Dominic must have used his bark on his pack mate. "That fucker. Shit, sorry. I can't believe he just used his freaking bark on Levi—again. I don't want that kind of alpha anywhere near this show. They're done."

I'm shaking, I'm so angry. I hate that there's nothing I can do for Levi, but he'd chosen his pack, and he's going to have to live with that choice. Unless he wants out, then I'll help him. I don't know how, but I'll figure it out. I just need to get him alone.

I'm shocked when Levi falls to his knees before his head alpha, holding his face. What the fuck is being said? If I'm not mistaken, there are tears in Dominic's eyes. "I'm missing something. I wouldn't be if I had sound."

"Well, I guess you should've thought of that, huh?"

I glare at Tessa for a moment before turning my attention back to the screen. The Astor pack is now on the move and I'm almost afraid of what's going to come next. The other suitors are shifting, but no one makes a move. Hector and Dalton make it to the landing just as the pack arrives.

"Why is Hector cowering away from them? What did they do? Tessa, you better find out. I will not have anyone terrorizing our staff."

Tessa nods when my eyes flicker to her before returning to the screen once more. This is driving me insane. Levi and Dominic say something to Hector and then he's darting down the stairs. I jump when Tessa's phone rings, but I refuse to take my eyes off the screen as Dalton speaks to the pack.

My back goes ramrod straight as Levi moves aggressively toward the alpha. Maybe Levi doesn't need saving after all. Maybe he's just as bad as Dominic. Fates above, I wish I had sound, so I knew what was happening.

"Bree." Tessa's sharp tone pulls my attention from the screen. She looks pissed, but worried. Who'd called her and what had they said to leave that look on her face? "That was Hector. Pack Astor has requested to meet with me. Apparently there's a medical condition that wasn't disclosed in the interview and vetting process."

"What? Well, shit. This could be bad. I want to be there for the meeting." She better not fight me on this, because I don't intend on standing down.

Tessa runs a hand over her face. "Of course you'll be there. This impacts not just the show, but the company. Both of which you're involved in. I asked Hector to escort them to the dining room. It has lockable doors, so it's the best place to use as a conference room. Hopefully, we won't need it again this season, but it's something to keep in mind."

I nod as my eyes fall back to the screen. Hector is speaking to Pack Astor and they all look relieved at what he's telling them. Whatever this is, it's pretty damn serious.

"Alright, let's go then. Hector's already leading them downstairs. I'd prefer to be in the room when they arrive." I'm already moving toward the door, not bothering to wait for Tessa.

Leo has already buzzed me out when Tessa catches up. Neither of us speaks as we hurry down the hall to the stairs. When we push into the dining room, I'm relieved to see that we're the first ones there.

Turning to Tessa, I sigh. "What do you think this is all about?"

"I have no idea, but I'm pissed that they waited until now to disclose the information to us."

I don't have time to reply before the other door opens, revealing Hector and Pack Astor. "Pack Astor to speak with you," he says before stepping back into the hallway and pulling the door shut behind him.

"Gentlemen, why don't we have a seat?" Tessa gestures to the table before nodding for me to take the seat at the head of the table. She turns the chair beside me so that we're both facing the men in question before dropping into it gracefully.

Levi hesitates, glancing over his shoulder at Dominic. "We weren't aware that Bree would be joining us."

"Whatever the four of you have to say affects her not only as the omega of the season, but as CEO of Fated Industries. She has every right to be here." Tessa's words leave no room for argument.

"Of course she does," Dominic agrees as he moves to sit opposite me and his pack file into the chairs to his right and left. "First and foremost, thank you for taking the time to meet with us. I'm sorry for keeping this information from you, but I did not expect it to hit me as hard as it has."

Tessa and I remain silent, waiting for him to continue. Neither of us will say a word until we've heard what he has to say.

"I was diagnosed with obsessive-compulsive disorder as a child. I've tried every medication out there that's supposed to help, but none of it did. I tried therapy, but it didn't help curb the obsession as it should have. I was able to come up with ways to cope with my disorder, but being on *Heated* has left me feeling out of control—something that sends me spiraling into my disorder."

Dominic steeples his hands on the table, staring off into space as he continues, "When this happens, I lash out at everyone as I try to regain control. I'm well aware that I'm generally an asshole, but how I acted was unacceptable. The way I treated my pack was unacceptable. I know that neither of you approve of the old-fashioned way I run my pack, and I completely understand that. But they agreed to it so that I never felt out of control over our pack dynamics."

He lets forth a heavy sigh before meeting my eyes. "I didn't disclose the information, and I now realize why that was a mistake, but it was because I didn't want that to be the focus on the show. And I maybe didn't want the entire world to know that I'm broken."

"Having OCD doesn't make you broken," I tell him softly, feeling for him. I understand the need for control, even if I don't have OCD. "It's a medical condition that you can't control. There's no reason to be ashamed of having to work around your condition."

Tessa sighs beside me, running a hand over her face. "This is why you asked to be shown to your room before heading to the game room. If I'd been aware of the situation, I would've made it happen. This is why it's so important that you disclose this kind of information. I just thought you all were being dicks."

"Levi has made me aware of the mistakes I made." Dominic smiles as he reaches over to take his beta's hand, my heart clenching at the show of love. This is what I want for myself. But Pack Astor aren't the ones who will be able to give me that.

"There's another reason you should have disclosed your diagnosis," I say hesitantly. "Tessa regularly refers to me as a control freak and it's true. Because of my past, I can't date men who are controlling. Tessa wouldn't have selected you for my season if she'd known. Your disorder butting up against my stubbornness will leave all of us miserable."

Dominic nods slowly, eyes falling to the table. "So it's my fault that we'll be sent home. Of course."

I'm up and out of my seat before he even finishes talking. I skirt around the table until I'm standing beside him. I take his face into my hands, heart breaking as I watch a tear fall down his cheek. I hate that I'm hurting him—them—this way.

"It's not your fault that this won't work. It's kind of mine. I wish I could allow you to stay and give you a chance, but I have to think of myself. I can't put myself through that again. Don't blame yourself—blame me. Don't beat yourself up for something that isn't your fault." I hesitate, glancing between his pack mates. "What you have with these three men is something I want for myself, and I have to be honest if I want that to happen."

"The four of you will need to return to the game room and interact as if this meeting didn't happen. It would be best if you revealed your OCD diagnosis while speaking to Bree." Tessa hesitates, but I don't look away from Dominic as she speaks. "Knowing Bree, she had no intention of sending anyone home on the first night, but it'll allow her to open up to the viewers and suitors alike about her past relationship. Whether she chooses to share all of it with you or not is up to her."

I nod slowly. "And just because this didn't work out for us doesn't mean that we can't bring you back. As long as this first season does well, we have plans to help as many omegas as we can to find their packs. It might not be next season or the one after that, but we'll bring you back. When we have an omega that will work with your pack, we'll bring you back. I want the four of you to find your omega, and I'll do everything I can to make that happen."

"Thank you, Bree. Whoever you choose for your pack, they'll be the luckiest men in the world." Dominic reaches up to lay his hand on mine. "I won't forget this, and we'll do whatever you need us to do to make this as easy as possible."

And now it's my turn to fight back tears. Fates above. Who knew that rejecting men I barely know would be so freaking hard?

Trying to get my emotions under control, I step back so I can look between the other three members of the Astor pack. "The fact that you support your head alpha in what he needs to keep his disorder under control tells me more than any ten-minute conversation ever could. You're all good men and you love each other—it's plain to see. Keep doing that and one day, if you haven't found one on your own, we'll help you find your omega."

Shaking my head, I make my way back to my chair. Tessa reaches over and squeezes my hand as I sit. I can't hold back the tears anymore as they begin to fall down my cheeks. "Fates, it's times like this that I hate being an omega."

They all laugh with me and I'm finally able to get the tears under control. "Guess we're going to need Allison to come fix my makeup again."

Tessa chuckles. "Okay, so we'll get your makeup fixed while Pack Astor returns to the game room. You'll have two hours to speak with the suitors. It's up to you and them to decide if it's one-on-one or in groups. At some point, you'll need to sit with Pack Astor so they can reveal the diagnosis. Share as much or as little of your story as you want, Bree. I will not push you on this. The last thing we need is you spiraling."

"I know, Tess. I won't know how much I'll feel like sharing until I'm in the situation, but I'd like you all to know why I have to ask you all to leave."

Levi shakes his head. "You don't need to explain anything to us. We understand it wouldn't work. I'm sad about that, of course, but I understand. We all do. Please don't feel you have to explain yourself."

"I don't feel like I have to. I want to."

"I'd probably wait until close to the end to have this conversation. It's going to be long and painful." Tessa sighs, still holding onto my hand. Showing her support of me, as she always does. "Then you all will head to the ballroom for the rose ceremony. Bree will explain the importance of each of the roses before she announces that she'll be letting you go tonight."

"You're lucky," I say with a laugh. "You actually get a heads up that it's happening and won't be shocked."

Brayden laughs. "That's a good point, Bree. Thank you both for being so understanding."

"Of course." Tessa directs her attention to Dominic. "Are you okay to go back to the game room now, or do you need a little more time?"

"I'm good," he says as he rises. "Let's get this over with, yeah?"

I nod. "Yeah. Well, I guess I'll see the four of you up there."

Tessa and I watch the four of them leave the room, looking more hopeful than dejected, and I'm glad I could give that to them. This situation sucks, but I did what I could to make it better.

"I'm almost sad to see them go," I tell Tessa.

She laughs. "Of course you are. My little sensitive omega bestie. But it's for the best—for you and them."

"I know that, but it still hurts. And I'm going to have to do this time and time again, aren't I?"

"You are, and while I don't think it'll get any easier, you'll be fine. You're stronger than anyone knows and you'll do what's right for you. I believe in you."

I pull Tessa into a hug. "Thank you for always believing in me. I love you, best birch."

I can practically hear Tessa grinding her teeth. "I still don't know how you got your hands on a copy of not just one book from that long ago, but a whole series. I almost wish you hadn't. We're not angels who gain smut when we curse."

"No, but I love annoying you by calling you my best birch. That Merri Bright was really onto something with that series. I want to be Feather. She was a badass."

"I guess you're feeling better then." Tessa pushes me away from her as I try to cling to her. "Get off me, brat. I need to get Allison in here to fix your makeup."

Grinning, I let her go. I feel a lot better after that intense conversation, and I know that's what Tessa was going for. I don't know what I'd do without her. Let's hope I never have to find out.

Chapter Nine

Bree

Climbing the stairs to the game room, dread fills my stomach. As much as I don't want to have this conversation with Pack Astor, I know it needs to happen. And if my family didn't hate me before, they sure will after this. Not that I care what they think. I stopped caring about what they thought a long time ago. Tessa and Reginald are my family now.

I pause halfway up the stairs, pushing away those unhappy thoughts. They don't deserve my thoughts. They deserve nothing from me, and I have twenty men upstairs who all want to get to know me. With that thought, excitement fills me and overwhelms the dread.

Though I don't know who they are yet, my pack is up there waiting for me to choose them. And it's about time I get started on getting to know them.

Lifting my head, I find Emmett and Brody standing on the landing, grinning down at me. A laugh escapes me as I continue my path up the stairs. "How long have the two of you been standing there?"

Emmett makes a face. "Right here? Only a few seconds. Standing just beside the landing, waiting to hear your footsteps? Since Pack Astor came back."

I love his honesty. Reaching out to squeeze both of their arms as I make it to the landing. "Excited to see me again?"

"Hell yes." Brody's eyes widen as he realizes what he said, but he just shrugs as his smile turns a bit sheepish. "I'm fairly certain everyone in this room feels that way. Well, most of them. But we all thought it would be less overwhelming if Emmett and I greeted you versus all twenty of us swarming you at once."

"That's probably a good call," I say with a laugh, linking my arms through each of theirs. "Well, then I guess the two of you will be my escorts for the evening. That is, if you want to be."

"Ummm, duh." Emmett makes a face as if it was ever up for debate.

It warms me, my stomach flipping with butterflies. These two betas do something to me and I kind of love it. No, they're not alphas and they can't give me the knots I need for my heats. But they can give me something I crave almost as much—comfort.

"Who shall we chat with first, m'lady?" Brody asks as the three of us step into the room, eighteen sets of eyes zeroing in on us.

"Why don't you choose first? You've probably gotten to know them better than I have so far, and can probably choose better than I can."

Emmett nods slowly, meeting Brody's eyes over mine before leading me further into the room. It takes me a moment for our destination to become clear. They lead me over to where Roman, Finnegan, Gabriel, and Hudson stand chatting.

"Hello, alphas," I say with a slight inclination of my head as we come to a stop before them. "The betas have chosen the four of you for my first chat this evening. They'll be joining us as they're my escorts for the evening, but would you mind terribly if we sat down? These heels are killing my feet."

"Of course, Bree." Gabriel rushes forward, sweeping me into his arms and pulling a squeak from my lips as I find myself being carried across the room.

"That's not exactly what I meant." I grin up at him. He shoots me a wink as he returns the smile. "But I guess I won't complain about the ride."

"Seriously, Gabriel?" Emmett grouches from behind us and I lean up so I can peer over Gabriel's broad shoulders and grin down at him. Both Emmett and Brody are right behind him, grinning up at me. They don't actually seem put out by Gabriel stealing me away. They must like Gabriel—which is good because I also like him.

Gabriel sets me down on the couch, stepping back, and gesturing for the betas to sit beside me. He sits down in the center of the couch across from us as the other alphas catch up with us. Roman and Finnegan pull the two armchairs so they're beside the couch Gabriel sits on while Hudson looks torn.

Gabriel grins at the other alpha, patting the couch beside him. "You can sit by me, Hudson. I don't bite—unless you ask me to."

My eyes widen as I glance between the two alphas, wiggling between the two betas as slick spills from me.

Holy shit. Why is that so hot?

"It is, isn't it?" Emmett says with a grin, and I turn to him in surprise. "Oh, yeah, baby girl, you definitely said that out loud."

I squeeze my eyes shut as I flush. A quick shake of my head and I turn back to the alphas, finding a blushing Hudson sitting beside Gabriel. It looks like he tried to sit as far away from Gabriel as possible, but the other alpha had scooted over until there was no room left between them.

I lick my lips because the two of them together? Holy shit. But... wait a second...

"Where are Onyx and Maddox?" I ask Hudson, curious as to why he's not with his pack while another man hits on him.

Hudson lifts his head, nodding behind us. I turn to find Onyx standing with Sasha, both their eyes scanning the room before turning their attention to me. I give them a shy smile and a quick wave. They both nod and offer me their own smiles in return.

I duck my head and I'm sure if I didn't have on the scent canceling panties, I'd be perfuming for the entire room right now. I find Maddox standing with a large group that surprisingly contains Riley and Carter. Maverick and Dalton seem to be in an intense conversation while Maddox's, Riley's, and Carter's attention seem to be split between the other two men and me.

Neither Maddox nor Onyx seem bothered by the attention Hudson is currently receiving from Gabriel. With a shrug. I turn back to the alphas. "Your pack is the only one that doesn't seem to be grouping together."

"We all have varying levels of desire to socialize. Onyx has a tendency to find someone who is content to sit in silence and people watch with him. Honestly, if Owen wasn't such a jerk, he'd probably be sitting with him." Hudson winces. "Sorry, that wasn't nice. Maddox tends to find a group of people that don't expect him to be overly chatty, but who he likes well enough to throw in an occasional comment."

I love that I'm getting to know his pack mates through him. "And what does that make you?"

"The one who wants to be the center of attention," Emmett says with a grin. "He's like me, Brody, and Gabriel. We like talking to everyone. Social butterflies, if you will."

"Okay, I can see that." I swing my attention to Finnegan and Roman. "But the two of you don't seem like social butterflies."

Roman sputters. "Most definitely not. Finnegan and I were having a conversation about our careers when these two crashed into our conversation." He offers Gabriel and Hudson a smile. "But I'll admit, they do liven things up."

"We most certainly do," Gabriel says, winking at Roman.

I can't help but laugh before asking questions of each of the alphas and the two betas at my side. After about twenty minutes, I stand and give each of them a warm smile.

"I've enjoyed our conversation, but I need to meet with everyone tonight. Please, make yourselves at home. While temporary, this is your home. Once I'm done with each group, we'll head to the ballroom together for the rose ceremony. Don't worry if you have questions about it, as I will explain how the ceremony works then. Thank you for your time and candor."

Emmett and Brody both offer their arms and I'm quick to take them. Deciding to get what I expect to be a brief conversation over with, I steer them toward Owen. He's still seated on one of the couches that sits across from the wall of televisions and gaming systems. I give him a warm smile as we come to a stop in front of him.

"Hi, Owen. I'm not sure if you've met Emmett and Brody yet, but they've been kind enough to escort me from group to group tonight so I can spend some time with each of you."

Owen glances between the three of us and shrugs before lifting his drink to his lips once more. I bite the inside of my cheek as I fight to keep my smile in place. I drop my arms from the betas and move to sit next to Owen.

The betas settle on the coffee table, facing us, as I turn my focus on Owen. "So, you're an MMA fighter? It's not my go-to event to watch, but I've enjoyed the few matches I've seen."

Owen stares at me before grunting.

I turn my head to Brody and Emmett, eyes pleading. How the hell am I supposed to get to know Owen if he refuses to speak?

"What brings you onto *Heated*, Owen?" Brody asks, all smiles as usual.

Owen glances at him, making a face as he turns back to face me—obviously dismissing the beta and pissing me off.

"Brody asked you a question, Owen. It's exceptionally rude to not only ignore his question, but to dismiss him like that. You seem to have no desire to speak to me, so why are you even here?" I stand from the couch, hands going to my hips as I tap my foot, and impatiently await his answer.

"I'm here because my manager wants me here. I have no desire to be a part of a pack, and I don't need an omega." Owen wrinkles his nose at me and I'm practically seething at this point. "Why should I put in effort for something I don't want?"

I shake my head, trying to rein in my irritation. "Then you should've never applied for the show. You took a spot from someone who actually wants to be a part of a pack and to have an omega. You don't want to be here? Great, then I don't want you here."

Brody and Emmett have already moved to stand at my side, so I slide my arms through theirs once more. "Let's go find someone who actually wants to speak to us, yeah?"

Emmett's eyes narrow as he glares at Owen, daring him to say another word. Owen doesn't seem to care, already having gone back to his drink.

"That sounds like a great idea, Bree," Brody says as he leads us toward Wilder and Wren.

"Bree," Wilder greets me as we approach. "And Brody and Emmett. Hello again."

"Hello, Wilder. Wren. Brody and Emmett have agreed to be my escorts this evening."

"Lucky men." Wren smiles at all three of us. "And not an opportunity any of us would pass up, I don't think."

"Except Owen," Emmett hisses, eyes glancing over his shoulder at the man in question.

Wren hums. "And what did Owen do this time?"

"He told me he didn't want to be here. He has no desire to be a part of a pack or to have an omega."

"Then what is he doing here?" Wilder asks, eyes narrowing in on the back of Owen's head.

I laugh, though there's no humor to the sound. "Apparently, his manager told him to do it."

Wren shrugs. "Good. That's one less person you have to worry about. Now your selection has gone down to nineteen."

I smile, thankful for him ending the conversation about Owen. Anger is still lapping at me, but beneath that, the hurt is trying to creep in. No one enjoys being rejected. I also have to bite my lip to keep from correcting his statement because, technically, my choices have narrowed down to fifteen. But I can't share that yet, nor do I want to think about Pack Astor yet. I need to focus on the here and now until it's time to talk to them.

As with the previous group, I ask questions about the two of them. Emmett and Brody will occasionally throw in comments or answers to my questions, even when they're not directed at them. Wilder and Wren take it all in stride, never growing annoyed that the two betas are taking up their time. These two alphas are sure of themselves and what they can offer me, and I kind of love it.

I don't know how much of it is because they're alphas—I've met many insecure alphas in my life—and how much is just their personalities, but their reactions actually help shape my opinion of them better than their words do. They're both good men and good alphas. They would be a good choice. Not to mention they're both extremely attractive and smell amazing.

Brody squeezes my hand, drawing my attention from the alphas. He's still smiling, but it has an apologetic tinge to it. "Sorry to interrupt, but it's been a little over twenty minutes, and I know you need to spend time with everyone."

"Thank you, Brody." I give his hand a squeeze before darting forward and pressing a kiss to his cheek.

"What do I have to do to get that treatment?" Emmett asks. I turn to find him pouting, arms crossed over his chest. I laugh as I reach out to grasp his arm and pull him over, so I press a kiss to his cheek, too.

Turning back to Wren and Wilder, I grin up at them. "Thank you, alphas, for the chat. I look forward to speaking with you both more over the coming days."

"It was our pleasure, omega." Wilder returns my grin.

I wrap my free hand in Emmett's, as I haven't released Brody's, deciding that I'd rather hold their hands than their arms. I have to fight back a shiver as they both squeeze my hands, standing closer to me as we walk across the room.

They begin to lead me toward Pack Astor, but I pull them to where Onyx and Sasha are leaning against the wall, their eyes locked on the three of us.

"Hello, Onyx. Sasha."

"It is good to see you again, *Zaychik*." Sasha leans down to place a kiss on my cheek.

"*Zaychik*," I repeat, sure I'm butchering the pronunciation. "What does that mean?"

Sasha smirks. "It means bunny. It is a term of endearment in Russia."

A shiver runs down my spine that I can't hide from them. Sasha's smirk turns into a full-blown smile and I'm a puddle. If Emmett and Brody weren't holding me up right now, I'd be a puddle on the floor. This man is smooth.

"If I had known as a child that speaking foreign languages would be so well received by women, I might have paid more attention when my grandparents tried to teach me the language of our people." Onyx smiles as he shakes his head.

"I didn't get to ask earlier, but what tribe is your family from?"

"We're Navajo."

I nod slowly, trying to recall anything I can remember from school about the Navajo. "I know absolutely nothing about the Navajo."

Onyx laughs. "That's alright. I don't mind teaching you."

And for the next twenty minutes, Onyx speaks of the Navajo and what it means to him, and Sasha talks about growing up in Russia. They're both so proud of where they come from and I have to fight back the sadness that wants to overwhelm me. I wish I had pride in where I came from.

"*Gongjunim,*" Emmett whispers in my ear.

I turn to him with a frown, not even *trying* to repeat whatever Korean word he'd just said. "What does that mean?"

"Princess." Emmett wiggles his eyebrows at me, pulling a laugh from me. "My family didn't speak Korean unless my grandmother was around, so I never really learned it. I only remember a few things, but that's what my dad always called my mom. So I remember it well."

"This is really unfair to those of us who only speak one language." Brody's eyes are dancing with laughter. "But I think Emmett was trying to let you know we should move onto the next group."

"I *was,*" Emmett says with a pointed look at Brody, but he's laughing when he continues, "And now you've ruined it."

Rolling my eyes at their banter, I turn back to Sasha and Onyx. "Thank you, alphas. I really loved learning about where you come from.

I can't wait to get to know both of you better. Remember to make yourselves at home."

Emmett and Brody have already grabbed my hands, telling me they have no intention of going back to offering me their arms. Which is fine with me, because I like the feel of my hand in theirs.

I make a beeline for the last group besides Pack Astor. I both love and hate the bigger groups. I love it because it means I can speak with every one of the suitors without having to run from person to person, but I hate it because there's only so much anyone can speak when there's four or more other people in the conversation.

"Hello everyone," I call out as we approach. The conversation immediately dies out as five heads turn in my direction.

"Bree," Dalton draws. "I'm glad you've made your way to us."

"I don't know. It looked like you and Maverick were having a very heated conversation earlier." I smile to let them know I don't think they were arguing or anything.

Maverick laughs. "As I'm sure you know, Dalton runs a construction company and I'm an architect, so we have much to discuss—especially about which job is harder."

"And what conclusion have the two of you come to?"

"That they're never going to agree on that answer." Carter laughs. "I swear, these two are more stubborn than Riley."

"I don't believe that for a second," I say with a laugh as I turn my attention back to Riley. "You seem to be handling all of this better."

Riley tries to smile, but ends up grimacing. "I'm trying. Maverick and Dalton have been kind to us and shown that they understand what we're going through. They invited us to remain with the two of them so we can get to know other suitors."

"And Maddox has been good company," Carter adds. "He doesn't take any offense to Riley's sour face or random growls."

I stare at the beta for a moment before bursting out into laughter. "I'm sorry," I say, holding up my hands. "I don't know why I found that so funny."

I'm laughing so hard, tears are forming in my eyes. Not wanting to ruin my makeup—again—I turn my head to the ceiling to stare at the lights as I get my laughter under control. I dab at the corner of my eyes before dropping my head once more.

"I'm so sorry, Riley. I don't find the situation you and Carter are in funny at all. I can tell this is hard on you and that you're trying, but I just kept getting this image in my head of you growling and snarling like a dog while Carter held you back. It was hilarious in my brain, but that was rude of me, and I'm sorry."

Riley's jaw clenches, but he nods in acknowledgement while Carter lets out a bark of laughter. "I can see that. It would be hilarious. Especially if he was on all fours, like an actual dog."

"Beta," Riley growls, but there's amusement clear in his tone.

"So, new topic. Dalton, why don't you tell me more about... I don't even know what state you're from."

"Georgia born and bred, ma'am." Dalton winks when I startle at his calling me ma'am. "I'd love to tell you more."

And for the next twenty or so minutes, I listen to Dalton, Maverick, Carter, and Maddox speak about where they're from and their families. I just wish I could hear from Riley as well, but it's obvious he isn't holding it together as well as he wants us to believe. I will admit, he's definitely trying, but I'm just not sure that them being here is going to work out. But that's a problem for another day.

Now, I have to deal with Pack Astor and tear open wounds that have long since scabbed over. It's not that I don't want to talk about it. It's just going to be hard. Forcing a smile, I look between the men currently surrounding me.

"I appreciate all you letting me get to know you a little better, but I have one more group before we can begin the rose ceremony." With a sigh, I turn back to Emmett and Brody. "And I appreciate the pair of you escorting me this evening, but based upon their previous actions, I think it would be best if I speak with Pack Astor on my own."

Emmett looks unsure as he glances at the pack in question over my shoulder. "Are you sure? They can just suck it up and deal with it if you want us there."

"I'm sure. I think it'll make everyone a little more at ease if I go over there myself." I squeeze Emmett's arm before leaning up to kiss his cheek and then Brody's. Stepping back, I take in the entire group again. "Not too much longer and we'll be able to head to the ballroom. After the rose ceremony is done and over with, you'll all be shown to your rooms and then I'll give you a tour of the house."

They all call out their goodbyes as I make my way over to Pack Astor, taking a deep breath before letting it out as I ready myself for this conversation. It will not be easy for any of us, but it needs to happen.

Chapter Ten

Cillian

I lean back in the chair as Bree makes her way over to us. My pack mates and I sit at two of the tall bar tables while we wait for it to be our turn with Bree. We've been quiet as we all readied ourselves for what we know is coming. I hate that Dominic has to out himself about his diagnosis—not because I think it's a bad thing, but because I know it's hurting him.

I'd appreciated the way Bree had comforted him when he was on the verge of falling apart. She's a good woman—a good omega. But she's not meant to be ours. A fact that hurts more than I'll ever admit to my pack mates. Dominic doesn't need any more guilt. He's already beating himself up for losing this chance for us. What he doesn't realize is that he's more important than finding an omega.

Do I want an omega? Yes.

Will it make the pack feel more complete? Again, yes. But never at his expense.

I can only hope that Bree and Tessa will keep their word and bring us back for a future season. Or that we'll meet an omega on our own in the meantime. Dominic sees our pack as a failure so long as we go without an omega. Not that he thinks we're failures. No, he thinks he's a failure. And none of us can convince him he's wrong. That we'd love an omega, but we're happy with just the four of us.

Our pack needs a very special omega who can accept Dominic just as he is. As beautiful and kind as Bree is, she's already told us she can't accept Dominic as her alpha. And hopefully, we'll be able to find out why now. I'm hoping that once she explains her reasoning, Dominic will stop blaming himself.

"Pack Astor," Bree greets as she comes to a stop in front of our tables, but her eyes are on Dominic. "Alpha, would you be alright if I sat and spoke with you and your pack for a bit?"

I bite the inside of my lip as tears gather in my eyes at the look on Dominic's face. He knows this is the end, but having the omega address him directly makes him puff up and forget the hurt for now. Bree has allowed him the control he's been lacking.

"We would like nothing more, omega." Dominic gestures to Brayden, who quickly pulls a chair out for Bree and helps her to sit in it directly across from Dominic.

"Obviously, I'm making my way around to speak with each of the suitors. I saved your pack for last because I didn't feel like our initial meeting went well, and I was afraid this one wouldn't go any better."

Dominic ducks his head. "And for that, I apologize. There's no excuse for my earlier behavior, but there is an explanation I'd like to share. I hope you'll allow me to shed some light on why I acted the way I did."

"I would love that," Bree says as she gestures for him to continue.

I reach over to grasp Dominic's hand in mine as Levi does the same on his other side. This will be hard for our head alpha and we'll share our strength with him. He doesn't need it—I know that, but Dominic doesn't. He sees his illness as a weakness. He thinks he's lacking, which he certainly is not.

It feels kind of weird to be going over this again, when Dominic had just told Bree, but I understand why they need it to be on camera. Bree can't keep us on the show, so there needs to be a reason why. So all we have to do is pretend like this is the first time we've had this conversation—it shouldn't be too hard. Though I don't know where the cameras are in this room; I know they're there.

"As a child, I was prone to anxiety. Especially when going into new situations. But it was extreme, and I didn't understand why I reacted that way. My parents took me to see a psychologist hoping they could shed some light on why I didn't behave as other children did." Dominic takes a deep breath. "It took time, but I was finally diagnosed with obsessive-compulsive disorder—or OCD. My mother wanted me to continue to see the psychologist, but my father thought it was a better choice to try to beat it out of me."

Bree gasps, hands going to her mouth as she gapes at Dominic. He hadn't shared this part with her and Tessa. I'm honestly surprised that he's choosing to do so now. In for a penny, in for a pound, I guess. I squeeze his hand gently, letting him know I'm there. He shoots me a grateful smile before turning his attention back to Bree.

"My mother couldn't do anything to keep my father from me—or at least that's what she told me—but she did sneak me in to see the psychologist once a week for years. We tried medications and therapy. Nothing worked. The day I turned eighteen, I left my parents' home and I haven't returned since. I went to college and then got into med school. It was hard, especially with my OCD, but I fell in love with the preciseness needed to be a surgeon. So I did what I had to do to get through my schooling and my residency until I could finally be a surgeon. And it truly is the best career choice I could've made.

"But my personal life hasn't been as easy when it comes to dealing with my OCD. I know I should've disclosed it when applying for *Heated*, but I was sure it would mean we'd be rejected. We want to find the right omega for us, but I didn't realize how out of control I would feel here. Being in a new place, surrounded by so many new people. So I tried to take back my control in the only way I could. That's one of my biggest struggles with OCD—the need to control everything." Dominic shakes his head. "I hurt my pack mates while trying to fix myself, and that's not something I ever wanted to do. And I didn't mean to hurt you, so if I did, you have my sincerest apologies."

Bree stares at Dominic as she chews on her bottom lip. I want to rip it from between her teeth and soothe it, but I don't have that right. Instead, I squeeze Dominic's hand harder as I try to bring my alpha under control.

Finally, she gives a sharp nod. She releases her lip and lays her hands on the table, eyes scanning over the four of us. "Thank you, Dominic. I appreciate you being honest. I know that couldn't have been easy for you. If you had disclosed your diagnosis, you're correct, your pack wouldn't have been chosen for this season. It's not the diagnosis that would've kept you from being chosen, but your need to control. That's a trigger for me, and since you were so honest with me, I'd like to be honest with you."

"The reason I reacted as I did to your father beating you is that it reminds me very much of my own childhood." She shakes her head and seems to be trying to decide where to start. "As we all know, designations don't reveal until puberty, and there was no reason to believe that I would be an omega. The chances of a female omega were slim to none."

Bree looks so distressed that I want to tell her she doesn't have to tell us, but I think we all need to hear what she has to say—just as much as she seems to need to say it. Brayden slides his hand across the table, palm up. He stops just shy of her, offering it to her. Her smile is grateful as she lays her hand on his.

"Thank you, Brayden."

Before he can respond, Dominic leans forward. "Whatever you're trying to tell us is obviously difficult for you. Please don't feel you have to stress yourself by telling us."

"No, I need to do this. For myself and so you'll understand." She takes a deep breath, but doesn't let go of Brayden's hand as she continues. "I was raised in a pack. I had three wonderful beta dads who loved me unconditionally. My alpha father and omega mother, on the other hand... My alpha father liked to use his alpha bark on my beta dads and my mother when he wasn't getting his way. He abused them all, but they stayed because of me and because my mother refused to leave my father.

"Then my two younger brothers came along—twin alphas. That was fun. But by the time they came, I was already seven and had learned to form opinions of my own. My father didn't approve, so he started using his bark on me as well. Then my mother would berate me for angering my father. I tried to be the perfect daughter, but nothing was ever good enough for the two of them. If it hadn't been for my dads, I don't know what would've happened to me."

Bree swipes her hand across her cheeks, trying to wipe away the tears that have begun to fall. "I was fifteen when I revealed—a late bloomer. All of my friends had revealed when they were thirteen or fourteen—I even had one friend who revealed at eleven—though they were all betas. We were the only six girls in our year, so we stuck together.

"Omegas are meant to be cherished, so when I revealed, I was sure that my mother and father would stop treating me the way they had for most of my life. I was sadly mistaken in that assumption. If anything, it grew worse. So, I studied hard, determined to go to college and leave their house. They were having none of it. They expected me to marry an alpha as soon as I turned eighteen, well before my first heat.

"My dads helped me apply to colleges in secret and swore to me they'd find a way for me to attend. And they did. I was able to attain a full-ride to Hartfield University, which is where I met Tessa. I haven't been back to that house since the day I left. My dads come and visit me at least once a year, but I haven't seen my mother or father in fourteen years. Though, my mother regularly calls me to tell me what a disappointment I am since I haven't found a pack yet. But I know I'll never make her happy. She has my younger brothers for that. The sun shines from their asses in her eyes. It sucks, but I learned to live with it a long time ago."

"Fates above. I'm so sorry you had to grow up like that," Brayden says as he gives her hand a squeeze.

She shakes her head. "It's not your fault, but I appreciate the sentiment. I wish that was the end of the story, but it's not. I didn't date while I was in college. I was too busy learning everything I could while Tessa and I worked on starting Fated Industries. I didn't have the time or the desire to date. I was so sure that every alpha out there was just like my father and the man they wanted me to marry—we won't even go into the story of him.

"I was twenty-four when I met Theo. He was so unlike my father. He treated me like I was his entire reason for living—which apparently I was. He asked me to move in after we'd been dating for a month, and I said no. I wasn't ready for that and there were signs I was beginning to see that told me he wasn't the alpha for me. He was possessive and absolutely obsessed with me. After another few months, I realized it had grown worse. He begged me to move in with him, told me he couldn't stand being away from me. It would've been sweet if not for the look in his eyes. It scared me, but I ignored it.

"I refused to move in with him, telling him I wanted us to look for others to join our pack. That I didn't want to move in until our pack was complete. That was the first time he used his alpha bark on me, when he told me we wouldn't be forming a pack. It was only going to be the two of us. He told me only whores needed a pack. and I wasn't a whore—I was his.

"I tried to leave him after that. I wanted a pack and if he didn't want to be a part of a pack, then we were over. That's when he started stalking me. There's a lot to the story that I don't want to go into, but he kidnapped me on more than one occasion before I could convince the cops to do anything about it. Then he killed himself while he was in jail."

I can't believe this strong omega has been through all of this, but I still somehow don't believe she's done with her story. My stomach churns, understanding why she can't have an alpha like Dominic—though I know he would cherish her. It's obvious she isn't the omega for us.

"Fuck, Bree." Levi is up and around the table, pulling her into his arms as sobs escape her. "I'm glad he's dead, or I'd go take care of him right now. Please tell me there isn't more."

Bree laughs against his chest before pulling back to stare up at him. "I wish I could." She wipes away her tears and pulls herself together. "Thank you, Levi, but there's definitely more, and I need to get it out while I can."

Levi says nothing as he moves back to his seat, but I can see how angry he is—he's practically vibrating with it. I wish I could soothe him right now. He needs it. He's the one I'm most worried about in this situation. He really seems to like Bree, even though he only spoke to her once, and

I know he doesn't want to leave. He's too much of an empath. He has big feelings that he can't always keep under control.

"It took me a few years to get over the whole thing. I barely went on dates, and when I did, they were always a disaster as I searched for signs in them I missed in Theo. When I was twenty-eight, I met Jack. He was the CEO of one of the companies we were working with at the time, and he didn't treat me like the other alphas and betas did. He didn't look down on me for being an unmated omega at twenty-eight. He didn't make condescending remarks about how cute it was that Tessa let me think I was running things. Or rude comments about Tessa and I—about how we must be involved with one another." She shrugs.

"He was just different, and I liked that. I had Tessa and a few other friends join us for our first date, making it a group thing. I needed their opinions to make sure he wasn't another Theo—that he wasn't a leopard trying to hide his spots. Everyone loved Jack, so I agreed to a second date. He brought his three alpha friends, who he intended to form a pack with. He wanted to be sure that the five of us were a good match.

"I liked them all, and they were all very attractive. So I began dating all of them. Sometimes it was group dates, and sometimes it was one-on-one. Any time I wasn't at work, I was with them. I didn't realize they were slowly distancing me from my friends—even Tessa. It was at the six-month mark they stopped wanting to go out with my friends at all. They didn't want to share me, that's the excuse they gave me. It reminded me of Theo, but not enough to turn me off.

"So I went out with my friends and left them at home. They didn't like it. They demanded that I choose. Obviously, I didn't want to, but besides Reginald and Tessa, they weren't close friends. Reginald was rarely around because he had his own pack by then. Not to mention he's a freaking movie star. And I could see Tessa at work. So I agreed to give up my other friends, but told them I'd never give up my relationship with Tessa. We own a business together. It's not like I could just not see her—not that I wanted to. They agreed and asked me to move in with them. I didn't hesitate to agree. They'd been so amicable about my refusal to give up Tessa, and I loved them."

Bree clears her throat, fidgeting with her nails as she takes a moment. "It wasn't a week after I moved in that the abuse began. At first it was just verbal and mental, tearing down my self-esteem to make me think I couldn't make it without them in my life. Then they began to use their barks on me, tearing me down even more. Eventually, it became physical. I was so ashamed that I couldn't tell anyone. Not even Tessa. I hid it from her for over a year, pulling away from her a little at a time. I thought this was what I deserved, and I really thought I loved them. I disappointed them, and this was their way of showing their displeasure. That was the first time I understood why my mother never left my father.

"Then they beat me so badly that I was sure I was going to die. They left me alone at home so they could go get drunk at the bar. It took me over an hour to crawl across the room to my phone. I knew I should call 911, but I needed to say goodbye to Tessa in case that was it. I needed to apologize to her for the way I'd been treating her, for being a good friend. For letting it get so bad that I was going to die."

Tears are streaming down her cheeks, her eyes unfocused and far away. A glance at my pack mates tells me they're fighting themselves from reaching out to her just like I am. I want to take this pain away from her, but I know I can't. None of us can.

"When Tessa answered the phone, I couldn't do anything but cry in her ears. She demanded to know what was going on, where I was. But I couldn't answer her. I could feel myself slipping away, unconsciousness calling to me. I managed to choke out that I loved her and that I was sorry." She blinks a few times before glancing back at us, a sad smile on her lips. "I thought that was the end, but I'm here, so obviously I didn't die. I woke up in the hospital to the sight of Tessa single handedly fighting off my four alpha lovers who were trying to push past her to get into my room. I did not know how I'd gotten there or how I'd survived, but I knew I needed to get away from the men who I thought were my forever. Because next time? Next time they'd kill me for real.

"I pressed the call button as I cowered in my bed. They had to call security to have the four of them removed from the hospital. I spilled the story to Tessa, and she wanted me to report it to the cops, but I knew it wouldn't do any good. All four of them have families that have more connections than anyone could imagine. Once I was released, I moved in with Tessa. She took some alphas that she trusted and collected all of my stuff from their house. They tried to call over and over, but I blocked their numbers. I buried myself in my work for months on end, barely living. They kept dropping by and pounding on Tessa's door. They'd show up at our offices, causing a scene when security had them removed from the building. Then one day, it all stopped. I never saw them again, but I was always looking around the corner, wondering when they'd come for me. I don't know why they gave up, because they swore they never would. I was so grateful I didn't even question it.

"Shortly after, we finally got the green light to start working on *Heated*. Building all of this," she gestures around her, "is what saved me from losing myself. It's what helped me heal. But I swore I would never put myself in a situation like that again. My control freak tendencies got even worse. The only way I feel safe is if I'm in control."

She laughs. "Though Tessa hasn't exactly allowed me much control for *Heated* since I'm the omega, but she lets me have as much control as she can. But that's why I don't think we'd be well-suited as a pack. You need control and I need control. It won't work. So I hope you understand when I ask that you return home during the rose ceremony tonight."

"And you'll be explaining this rose ceremony, when?" I ask because it's driving me crazy, not knowing what it is.

Bree laughs. "At the beginning of the ceremony."

"Of course, Bree. I wouldn't want to remain here if it made you uncomfortable," Dominic says earnestly as he shoots me a glare.

"Does it suck to go home on the first night?" Levi asks with a laugh. "Sure, but we understand."

I grind my teeth together as Brayden says the same thing, just using different words. I can't help but make it clear the reason I'm okay with leaving—which is apparently not the same as my pack mates.

"Leaving is what's best for Dominic. He's my number one priority in this situation."

I expect anger at my words, but Bree just gives me a soft smile. "As he should be. What the four of you seem to have is special. I'm sorry that I'm not the omega for your pack, but I'm sure there's one out there just waiting to meet you. And while you're leaving here today, that doesn't have to mean the end of your *Heated* journey. If you'll allow it, I would love to keep your pack application—with the added information about your OCD, Dominic—for future seasons. I'd like to help you find your omega if I can."

"You don't have to do that," Dominic says softly, "but I won't turn you down if that's what you want. I'll see a therapist again to come up with better ways to cope with this next time. Now that I know what to expect, it'll be easier. And we wish you the best in finding your pack."

"They'll be lucky to have you," Levi offers.

Bree wipes at her face once again, trying to dry her face of the tears that have finally stopped falling. "Thank you for understanding. You really will make an omega very happy one day."

With one last smile, she waves goodbye and heads for the center of the room. "Thank you, everyone, for your patience. Our two hours are just about up. Tessa should be up here soon to show us to the ballroom, so if you need to use the bathroom or want another drink, this is your last chance until we're done with the rose ceremony."

I pull Dominic in for a kiss, leaning my forehead against his when I pull back. "I'm so proud of you for sharing all of that. I know it's hard for you, but you need to learn that it's nothing to be ashamed of. It doesn't make you weak to need help from time to time, but no one knows you need help if they don't know the situation. If you want, we'll join you for therapy so we can learn how to help you better."

"Thank you, Cillian. It means a lot to me to have all of you supporting me. I love you all."

We share a group hug before breaking up when Tessa calls out, "Attention, suitors! If you'll follow me and Bree, we'll lead you to the ballroom where we'll hold our first rose ceremony."

With a sigh, my pack and I follow behind the other suitors. This is our end, but I'm alright with that. We'll take care of each other and come back stronger than ever.

Chapter Eleven

Bree

Tessa reaches out for my hand as we lead the suitors down the stairs. "Are you okay?"

"I assume you were listening to everything?" I glance at her, seeing her nod before I sigh. "It was hard. It was a lot to talk about, especially all at once. But it also felt right. They deserved to know why it couldn't work between us, and it made me feel better to talk about it. Though I could've done without the tears."

Tessa laughs. "Allison is already waiting outside the ballroom. She'll give you another touch up, though it's not nearly as bad as it would've been if we weren't using stage makeup."

I shoot her a quick smile, but don't say anything else. I need another minute to myself and my thoughts. This is not how I saw the night going. Tessa was correct earlier. I really hadn't planned on sending anyone home tonight. But if Owen doesn't want to be here, I don't want him here. And Pack Astor and I will never work. Not to mention, I don't think Dominic needs to be here any longer. He's relaxed immensely since his conversation with me and Tessa, but it's clear he isn't comfortable.

We sweep down the stairs to the first floor, and I swing to the left. It doesn't take long to arrive at the ballroom and, sure enough, Allison is standing there with her makeup kit in hand. I turn back and wait for the suitors to crowd closer.

"Just through these doors is the ballroom. Tessa will show you inside while I get a touch up on my makeup. I'll be quick and then I'll come in and explain the rose ceremony to you. I appreciate all of you and the patience you've shown tonight. It means the world to me that you're all here."

I step to the side, allowing Tessa to lead the suitors into the ballroom before turning back to Allison. "I bet you didn't think you'd have to fix my makeup this many times tonight, did you?"

"No, but that's because I've never seen you cry before. I thought you were one of those rare people who can lock away their emotions." She shrugs. "I like you better like this."

"Like what?" I laugh. "A mess?"

"No, like you're one of us."

I smile, and she gets to work. Less than five minutes later, I'm throwing open the doors to the ballroom. I stop in the doorway, in awe of how they've transformed the ballroom for the rose ceremony. The curtains are open, leaving a view of the night and backyard for us. Hundreds of fairy lights give the room a warm glow that I love, along with hundreds of LED candles flickering. I know it'll be brighter once they turn on the lights needed for the cameras, but I enjoy the peace the space provides me for just a moment before I step into the room fully.

Tessa makes her way over to me. "Good as new, I see."

"Yes," I agree. "Allison is amazing at what she does."

"Which is why we stole her for the show." She laughs, glancing over her shoulder at the suitors. "I told them that once the ceremony was over, we'll show everyone to their rooms and they'll have free rein for the night. I know you offered a tour tonight, but don't feel you have to. Any member of our staff can do that if you're too tired."

"I want to, Tessa. I want to show them what we've built for the show and I want to spend more time with them. I am feeling a little worn down from spilling out my emotions, and this ceremony is going to be hard. I promise that if it gets to be too much, I'll let someone else do the tour."

Tessa assesses me for a moment before moving to my side with a nod. "Alright, everyone. Places, please. Let's get this done, so you can all get on with your night."

The suitors shuffle around while the crew turns the lights and cameras on. I move to the stage set up before the suitors, Reginald helping me up and moving to stand next to me behind the table. The table holds six vases filled with colored roses.

"How are you, babe?" Reginald squeezes my hand, worry written all over him, as he stares down at me.

"I'm okay, Reginald. It's been a lot, but I'm handling it just fine."

A smile morphs Reginald's face as he nods. "Of course you are. You're one of the strongest people I know."

Turning to face Tessa and the cameras, we wait for her signal that they're ready. When she points to Reginald, he straightens and that host's smile takes over his face.

"Welcome back, viewers and suitors alike. We've gathered in the ballroom for our first ever rose ceremony. Are you wondering what in the world a rose ceremony is? Well, don't you worry for a moment. Our very own omega, Bree, will explain it to all of you right now. Bree?"

"Thanks, Reginald." I turn to focus on the suitors, ignoring the cameras. Sure, we want the viewers to be interested in the show, but this is about me and the suitors—not the viewers.

"During the rose ceremony, I'll be handing out a rose to each suitor. Each color has its own meaning that I will explain to you. We won't hold another rose ceremony until a week from now to allow time for us to get to know one another. During that week, I may present some of you with roses, and you'll see why once I explain their meanings. After this week, we will hold a rose ceremony nightly. But before we get into that, let me explain the meaning behind each of the colors of roses."

I reach for a yellow rose, lifting it for the suitors and cameras to see. "The yellow rose is what most of you will receive tonight. It means I want you to remain so that I may get to know you better, but no date is being requested."

"The peach rose means I'd like you to join me on a one-on-one date. I won't be handing out any peach roses tonight because I will hand those and the lavender roses out during the week as I get to know each of you." I set the peach rose back in its vase, plucking a lavender one to show them. "The lavender rose is an invitation for a group date. I want to have enough time to get to know you all a little better before I decide on the dates. Over the course of the next week, there will probably only be group dates. This will allow me time with all of you."

Setting aside the lavender rose, I pluck both a white and a red rose from their vases as I will myself not to blush. "I will also not be handing out any red or white roses tonight. I don't know when I will hand any of these out, but I will eventually. The white rose is a request to spend the night with me in my suite. The red rose means I've chosen you to be a part of my pack."

Taking a deep breath, I set both roses aside and reach for a black rose. "The black rose is the hardest one for me because if you receive it, you'll be leaving the show. As much as I don't want to say goodbye to anyone—it isn't feasible for me to have a twenty-member pack."

I laugh and the suitors chuckle along with me. "And tonight, while I hadn't planned to hand out any of these roses, I will be." I take a deep breath as my eyes scan the suitors, smiling as I meet their eyes. "Reginald will call you forward individually—unless you're part of a pack. He will call all members of a pack up together. I don't want to keep you in suspense, so we'll get this started."

"The easiest way to do this tonight is to do it in the order of arrivals. In the future, your name will be called at random. I will announce the person or pack and you'll step forward and make your way to the stage where Bree will meet you on the steps with a rose. Are there any questions?" Reginald asks as he steps to the side of the stage.

When no one says anything, he shoots me another smile before stepping off the pedestal so he's out of sight of the cameras.

"First up, we have Owen Reid—designation: alpha; age: thirty-five; occupation: MMA fighter."

"Owen, I wish I could say it was wonderful getting to know you, but I was unable to do so, as you refused to speak with me. Your disdain for the show and me was made very clear in our conversation." I pull the rose from behind my back, offering it to him. "I'm sure it will come as no surprise that we'll be telling you goodbye tonight."

I don't stick around to listen to anything he has to say, or to see the look on his face. I've had enough of this alpha's negativity for the night. By the time I make it back to the table, Owen has made his way back to the other suitors. A sigh of relief spills from my lips as I relax. Part of me had thought he'd make a scene, but I'm glad to have been wrong.

We make our way through the suitors with Reginald announcing them and me presenting them with a yellow rose until it's Pack Astor's turn.

"Our last pack of the night is Pack Astor. Head alpha Dominic—designation: alpha; age: fifty-four; occupation: neurosurgeon. Cillian—designation: alpha; age: thirty-six; occupation: vice-president of investment banking. Brayden—designation: alpha; age: twenty-four; occupation: actor and model. Levi—designation: beta; age: thirty-one; occupation: fitness model and personal trainer."

Even though Pack Astor and I know what my choice will be, it still hurts. I wish things were different, but no amount of wishing will change what I can and cannot deal with. I take the four black roses and slide them behind my back as I make my way down the steps to them.

"Dominic, Cillian, Brayden, and Levi... While I didn't have the best first impression of your pack, I believe that our second meeting went much better. Unfortunately, Dominic revealed a medical condition that impacts your pack being eligible to remain on the show. Not because of the condition itself, but because of me and what I can deal with."

My eyes fall to Dominic. "Do you mind if I speak on your condition so the others are aware?"

He gives a quick nod and I give him a sad smile, tears pooling in my eyes once more. I look away from Pack Astor and turn my attention to the suitors.

"Pack Astor's head alpha was very brave tonight when he revealed he has obsessive-compulsive disorder. OCD manifests differently in each person diagnosed with it. Dominic's manifests in a way that he requires control over everything, including his pack. And there's nothing wrong with that... if I was a different omega."

Taking another deep breath, I bring the roses from behind my back. "I've had many alphas in my life who have attempted—and some have succeeded—to control my life. I can't allow that to happen again, so I've become a bit of a control freak myself." I laugh, a bitter sound, as I shake my head. "I can no longer allow anyone to control me like that, so we'll be saying goodbye to Pack Astor tonight. It breaks my heart to send them home, but I have to do what's best for me."

Dominic leans over to take a rose from me, but I hold on to it until he looks up to meet my eyes. "You're more than your diagnosis, and I'm sorry I can't be the omega for your pack. Don't let this bring you down. You'll find an omega for your pack, and I'm going to do everything I can to make sure that happens."

"Thank you, Bree." There are tears glistening in Dominic's eyes as he smiles—not a forced or sad smile, but one filled with hope.

I lean forward, pressing my lips to his cheek. "Lean on your pack. They love you." With those whispered words, I allow him to take the rose and step back. When Cillian steps forward, I offer him his rose and a kiss to his cheek. "Be strong for him when he can't. Love him and treasure him."

Cillian just nods before stepping back and taking Dominic's hand in his. Brayden steps forward, a sad smile gracing his lips. "I understand why we're leaving, but I wish we could've gotten to know you better."

"Same," I murmur before placing a kiss on his cheek. "But you have an amazing pack. Keep taking care of one another."

Then it's Levi's turn, and he grins at me. "I get a kiss too, right?" He wiggles his eyebrows at me, pulling a snort of laughter from me.

"Oh, Levi," I say with a sigh as I lean forward to give him exactly what he's asking for. "Never change. Your pack needs your humor and your ridiculousness. One day, the four of you are going to make an omega so very happy."

Before I grab the last rose, I have to blink a few times to push back the tears I've been fighting for the last few minutes. I'm glad to end the night on a happier note than saying goodbye to Pack Astor. I don't have it in me to give a long speech, so I hope Dalton won't mind.

"Our last suitor of the night is Dalton Cole—designation: alpha; age: thirty-eight; occupation: owner of Cole Constructions."

I step down, not bothering to hide the rose. I'm just ready for this to be over. I meet Dalton at the bottom of the steps and his smile lights up his face. "Dalton, I enjoyed both of my conversations with you and I'm looking forward to getting to know you better."

Dalton takes his yellow rose with a nod, seeming to understand that I need some time for myself before returning to his spot amongst the suitors. Reginald appears at my side, leading me back onto the stage.

"And so completes our very first rose ceremony. We began the night with twenty suitors and now there are only fifteen. With eight weeks to go, who knows how everything will turn out? Tune in next week to see how things progress between Bree and her suitors."

We all remain motionless until we hear Tessa call out, "And we're clear."

Tessa climbs onto the stage with us, staring out at the suitors. "Owen and Pack Astor, you're with me. I'll show you to cottages that you'll use until the morning when we'll have a car bring you home. Members of security are currently grabbing your bags and will meet us at the cottages. Please make your way over to the door and we'll get going."

Tessa grabs my hand, giving it a quick squeeze before hurrying away.

"Lydia has the rest of your room assignments." I gesture to the producer, who waves her arm in the air. "If you will all line up for her to hand them out, Hector and I will show each of you to your room. He'll be taking the third floor occupants while I take the second floor occupants. Thank you all."

I hurry off the stage, Reginald right on my heels. When I pause at the door, he pulls me out into the hallway and pulls me into his arms. "Are you okay, B?"

"I'll be fine. There was just a lot of shit that came up with Pack Astor and Owen today." I sigh against his chest, wrapping my arms around him. "I'm tired and a bit sad, but I'm also happy. There are fifteen men in there who could be a part of my future pack. I just can't wait, you know?"

"And there's not another omega who deserves that more," he tells me before pulling away. "You'll let me or Tessa know if anything becomes too much, yeah?"

I nod. "I will. I promise. Thank you."

"For what?" he asks with a laugh.

"For being a good friend."

He boops my nose. "Anytime, Bree. Anytime."

I grin because I know he means those words. He's one of two people I've always known I could count on, even if he is busy being a movie star half the time.

"I've got to get back in there. Hector is still nervous being around all the alphas after the way some of them treated him. I don't want him to feel overwhelmed."

Reginald nods. "And I should get back to the cottage before my pack thinks I've abandoned them."

He gives me one last hug and then he's gone, leaving me alone in the hallway. I take a deep breath before heading back into the ballroom. Half the suitors are already standing around the doorway and Hector is looking a little frazzled. I run a hand down his back and give him a smile before turning back to the suitors.

"If you're on the second floor, please line up against the wall on this side of the door." I gesture to my left, waiting until they've wandered away before gesturing to my right. "Third floor occupants, line up on this side against the wall."

It doesn't take long until everyone has their room assignments and Lydia is walking over to hand Hector and me a copy of the room assignments. "I've crossed out Owen and Pack Astor, so that's one less for each of you to show to rooms."

"Thanks, Lydia." I turn to Hector. "You good?"

He nods. "I am. I'm sorry I got so freaked out. You're the omega. You should be the one freaking out, not me."

"I'm also used to dealing with large groups of alphas at once. Don't stress about it, Hector. This is just day one. By the end of the season, you'll be a pro at wrangling alphas."

"Yeah, right," he mutters as he heads for his group.

Glancing at the sheet as I walk to my group, I realize no one outside of the packs is sharing rooms—and they get suites, so I know none of them will be complaining. "Looks like you all got the best of everything this season. No one has to share a room."

"Yeah, except us." Hudson wrinkles his nose as he looks at his pack mates.

"If you have an issue with sharing a suite—which has three separate bedrooms, I might add—then it sucks to be you." I lift an eyebrow at him, but he just grins at me.

He shrugs, glancing at Maddox and Onyx again. "I have to keep them on their toes. If they always think I want them around, then they'll stop trying. Obviously."

I can't help but laugh as I shake my head at him. It's apparent in his tone he's joking, so I guess I'll just play along. "I'm fairly certain that's not how it works, but if that's what you want to do, then who am I to rain on your parade?"

"Now, if you'll follow me, we'll head up to the second floor and get your rooms all sorted out." I don't bother waiting to see if they'll follow me—I know they will—as I start out of the ballroom. I want to get my group out of there as quickly as possible, so Hector has fewer people to stress about.

At the first landing, I take the staircase to the right. There's more of them staying on that side. Plus, it's the side that has the entrance to the theater room, so I can show them that too. We step out into the living room and I pause.

"This living room is for use by all suitors, not just those of you on this floor. Same for the theater room, which I'll show you as well. The game room on the third floor is also for all of you to use at your leisure. There will be times when you'll have downtime while others are out on dates." I hesitate for a moment. "And remember that you're always on camera—everything you say and do is being recorded. That's in every room of the house, including the bedrooms. The only rooms that don't have cameras are the bathrooms, the control room—which none of us are allowed in—and my nest."

"I'm assuming this means you hired voyeurs to work in the control room, then?" Emmett asks with a grin.

I return his smile because how can I not? "I don't know. It wasn't part of our pre-employment questions, but they knew what they'd be watching, so maybe?"

Gesturing for them to follow me, I head down the hallway. "The crew has already placed your bags in your room. We're going to head to the end of this hallway first so I can show you the theater room."

I can hear some of them murmuring behind me, but I don't bother trying to figure out what they're saying. I throw open the door to the theater room and step inside. There are rows of couches on different levels like in a movie theater, and there's more than enough room for all twenty suitors and the omega.

"There's two bathrooms off to the left. We keep the remote here in the back and you'll select which movie you'd like to watch on this screen. There are even a few tv shows, but we have a massive library of movies."

When I go to turn back to them, I realize how close they've gathered around. I swallow audibly as my eyes move from face to face, and I can feel my body warming. Once again, I curse myself for doing this. It's a damn good thing I made sure that scent canceling panties were on the budget. At this rate, I'm going to be going through multiple sets a day.

I clear my throat and push through them to get back to the door. I ignore my body's reaction to their scents and as I step back into the hallway, my mind clears slightly as I'm no longer surrounded by their scents.

"On this side, there are two rooms and one pack suite. Gabriel," I turn to the alpha in question with a smile, "you're here in the room across from the theater room. You have your keycard?"

"I do." Gabriel holds up the card in question, handing it to me.

"You should keep your keycard on you at all times. It won't open any room but your own. The only way someone can get access to your room is if you let them in or if they get hold of your keycard." I scan the keycard, hearing the lock disengage. Pushing it open slightly, I turn back to Gabriel. "Do you mind if everyone comes inside so they can see what the shared rooms that aren't being shared look like?"

Gabriel shrugs as he takes back the keycard. "I don't mind."

I push open the door, stepping inside and holding open the door until they all pile inside. "As you can see, the rooms are big. Each of the shared rooms has two queen beds, two dressers and nightstands, its own bathroom, and a closet. None of you are sharing, so we don't need to have a conversation about sharing space."

"This is bigger than my room in my apartment, that's for sure," Gabriel says with a laugh as he looks around before he turns back to me. "I'm not going to want to go home like ever."

I laugh. "I'm glad you find the accommodations to your liking, but eventually you'll have to return home, one way or another."

I have to bite my tongue to not blurt out that I'm hopeful it'll be with me. It's much too soon to be making those kinds of declarations. Not only is Gabriel hot, but he seems to have a great personality—a bit of a flirt, which I most definitely don't hate. Plus, he works with kids.

Swoon.

I clear my throat. "You're welcome to remain in your room if you'd like to get settled, Gabriel, or you can join us while I show everyone else to their rooms. The choice is yours."

"I think I'll join you all. Wouldn't want to accidentally knock on the wrong door in the middle of the night, after all."

Oh, this man has no shame. And the reactions of the other men are almost too much to handle. I beeline for the door, calling after me. "Well, come along then."

We reach the door to Emmett's room first, just beside the theater room. "Emmett, this one is your room, if I can borrow your keycard."

When he hands it over, his fingers brush against mine, and a glance at his face reveals a smirk, telling me he'd done it on purpose. He's also a flirt. Though, I don't know why I'm surprised. These men are here to win a spot in my pack. Of course, they're going to be flirting with me.

Feeling flustered, I scan the keycard and push open the door. Emmett follows me inside, but I stop the others from joining us. "All the shared rooms are exactly the same, though because of the differing sizes, they might have slightly different layouts. Emmett, you don't need to worry about anyone being in the theater room keeping you awake at night. All the rooms are soundproofed, including the bedrooms. We thought it would be better to keep things as private as they can be for you while there are cameras on you all the time."

"Good to know," I hear someone mutter, but when I glance at them, I can't figure out who it was.

"Emmett, you're welcome to join us or stay in your room."

Emmett moves to stand beside me, his hand going to my lower back. "As if I'd give up any time spent with you."

I let him lead me from the room, annoyed with my body as I feel a flush spread across my cheekbones and down my neck. I'm so tired of blushing around these men. I lead them to the door at the end of the hallway. It faces another hallway that connects to the other side of the floor.

"This is Hudson, Maddox, and Onyx's pack suite." Onyx hands me his keycard before I even have to ask for it. "Thank you, Onyx. Do the three of you mind if the others come in to see your room?"

This is the other reason I started with this side of the floor. I knew Riley wouldn't want the others in his and Carter's suite. As I expected, Hudson, Maddox, and Onyx all nod their agreement. I scan the keycard and when I push open the door, we're in the living area of the suite.

"Obviously, the pack suites are going to be set up differently than the shared rooms. This is the living area, so if you need time with just your pack, you have the space to do so. As I said before, there are three bedrooms and one bathroom in each suite. You can choose to use one room or all three of them—that's up to you all to decide.

"There are no kitchens in any of the suites or rooms as we're all expected to share meals in the dining room. The only time you'll be excused from group meals is if you're on a date with me. If you have a special diet or any allergies, you should have shared them in the application process. Just to be on the safe side, I would check with Lydia as she's the one who is keeping track of all of that."

I lead them down a short hallway to the bathroom. "All the bathrooms include soaking tubs, stand up showers, and the usuals you find in a bathroom. We chose to make everything on the higher end. I might have gone a little overboard trying to make sure we could meet everyone's needs."

With a laugh, I turn to the other door and throw it open. "This is the smallest of the three bedrooms. It still holds a queen-size bed and the other necessities. You'll also find a telephone in each of the bedrooms—both in the suites and in the shared rooms. You can't dial any outside numbers, but each phone has its own extension. You can share your extension with whomever you want—though I have access to everyone's extensions. I won't be sharing mine with anyone just yet."

I walk over to the nightstand that holds the phone and a sheet of paper. "This lists the extensions for anyone you might need to contact. Tessa's extension will send you to her cell phone. As will Lydia's and Hector's. There's an extension for the kitchen and the security room. It's housed in the control room, but if you need a member of security, they can route them to you.

"Let me just show you the other two bedrooms and then we'll get the rest of you sorted out in your rooms." Spinning on my heel, I feel a little bad that I'm not waiting to see if any of them have questions, but the longer I'm with them, the more overwhelmed I'm feeling. Today has taken a larger toll on me than I'd thought.

"The other two rooms are off the living room." I open the first door, revealing a room that is set up similar to the shared rooms. "Two queen beds and the necessities in this one. The other room is the largest of all three. It actually has a custom made bed that will allow up to a seven member pack to sleep all in one place if that's what they want."

I lead them over to the other room, allowing myself a moment to feel pride as they gape at the room. The bed is massive and close to the floor, with curtains of material hanging down from the ceiling. It's identical to the bed I have in my suite.

"We wanted packs to have a place to be together," I tell them before heading back to the hallway. "Let's show the rest of you to your rooms. I'm about to crash. I know I told some of you I'd give you a tour of the house tonight, but let's reschedule that for tomorrow after breakfast. You're welcome to tour the house on your own, but I just can't do the tour tonight."

"That's perfectly understandable," Emmett says as he takes my hand in his. "I'm sure that today has been overwhelming. Let's just get everyone to their rooms and then you can decompress on your own."

I give him a quick smile and squeeze his hand. "Riley and Carter, you're in the other pack suite on this floor."

It surprises no one when they decide to end their tour, now that I have shown them to their room. Riley heads inside without another word, but Carter hesitates in the doorway. "Thank you, Bree. For showing us to our rooms and for giving me and Riley another chance. He's not usually this bad."

"Spend some time with your alpha, Carter. Hopefully, tomorrow he'll be more himself."

Once the door shuts behind him, we continue down the next hallway. I point out the door on the right. "This is another shared room. It was where Owen would've been staying if he hadn't been such an ass."

I hear the others snicker behind me, but don't bother turning around. "There's only one other room off this hallway as there's only one entrance to the theater room. Sasha, this is your room," I tell him as we come to a stop outside the last door in the hallway. "Your bathroom is on the wall that belongs to the Woods' suite, but as I said, all the rooms are soundproofed, so you shouldn't hear anything they're getting up to."

"Zank ze saints for zat," he mutters as he scans his keycard. "Get some rest, Bree. I look forward to seeing you in ze morning after you've rested." He dips into his room, and I turn back to the others.

"Would you like me to walk you to your room, Bree?" Emmett asks quietly and I'm shaking my head before he's even finished asking.

"I just need some time alone and some sleep. But I'll see you all at breakfast. It begins at nine, but if you're hungry between now and then, you can call the kitchen and let them know what you'd like. You'll need to eat in the dining room or on the back deck. We want to keep the house as clean as possible by keeping the food in certain places only."

Maddox steps forward, pressing a kiss to my cheek. "Don't worry about us, Bree. We'll be fine. If we have questions, we'll call Lydia, Hector, or Tessa. You need to go rest. We're grown men. We can figure it out on our own, I promise."

I nod, already feeling myself relax as I start back down the hallway. Glancing over my shoulder, I shoot them a smile. "Thank you for understanding. Will you let the others know about the tour? I feel bad, but—"

"Go to bed, omega," Gabriel growls, but there's no bark to his command. Thank the fates, because I don't have the energy to chew anyone out right now.

"Fine, alpha," I sass as I head for the stairs. I almost want to see how he's responding to my sass, but I really need to get to my room. It doesn't take long for me to make my way back to the first floor and to my room.

Somehow, I avoid seeing anyone else, but as I swipe my door open, I find out why. Tessa sits on the couch in my sitting room. She stands as soon as she sees me, hurrying across the room to pull me into her arms.

"What do you need, Bree?"

"A bubble bath with a good book and a daiquiri?" It comes out as more of a question than I'd meant it to be, but I'm too tired to care.

"Done," Tessa says as she leads me to my bedroom. "Grab your Kindle and I'll get the bath started. Then I'll go make your daiquiri and bring it to you. Is there anything else you need or want? Like some food?"

I'm not feeling especially hungry, but I know better than to tell Tessa that. "How about a charcuterie board?" Should I feel bad that I just got done telling the suitors they can't eat anywhere besides the dining room and the back deck, and I'm having Tessa bring me food? Probably, but I don't.

"I'll have the kitchen make it up while I'm making your drink," she calls from my en suite. I can hear the water filling as I kick off my heels before grabbing my Kindle and heading towards her. She meets me in the doorway. "You did so well today, omega. I know it was hard on you, so spend the night relaxing. Don't worry about *Heated* or the suitors. I'll have Lydia give them a tour or something."

I shake my head. "No, I'm going to give them a tour after breakfast tomorrow. At least to those who'd like to join me. I'm proud of what we've done here and I want to show it to them."

"Fine," Tessa agrees, but I can tell she wants to argue. "But for tonight, you will not worry about anything else but yourself. Do you understand?"

It takes everything in me to not roll my eyes at her. I know she's just trying to take care of me, but damn, it can be annoying. "I got it, Tessa, and thank you."

She just nods before heading for the door as I make my way into my en suite. I set my Kindle on the side of the tub before stripping myself from the dress I've been wearing for too long. I step into the jetted tub that's big enough to hold at least four other people and slip beneath the bubbles as the water continues to fill.

And for the first time all day, I allow myself to relax.

Chapter Twelve

Maddox

Stepping from the shower, I grab a towel and wrap it loosely around my hips. I grab a second one and work on drying my long curly hair as I head back to the room that Onyx, Hudson, and I are sharing while we're on *Heated*. The large, nest-like bed is larger than the one we share at home, but it was the only bed that would hold all three of us comfortably. And I have no intention of sleeping alone during this process.

I'm surprised to see both Onyx and Hudson in the living room. Neither of them are early risers, and to them any time before noon is early.

"I thought I would have to drag the two of you out of bed for breakfast." Their heads jerk in my direction, telling me they hadn't heard me approach because they're both still half asleep.

"Hmmmm," Onyx murmurs, licking his lips as his eyes trail over me. "Are you breakfast?"

I snort, shaking my head. "No, Onyx. We're meeting Bree and the other suitors for breakfast. And we don't have time for me to be your breakfast."

"Shit," Hudson curses as he glances at the time. "We have to be downstairs in like twenty minutes."

I head toward the bedroom so I can get dressed, calling back to them, "And if you want showers, you better hurry, or we'll be late."

"Wanna save some water and shower with me, O?" Hudson asks, a bit of a growl to his voice. Turning back to look through the door into the living room, I see Hudson prowling across the room toward Onyx.

"No time for hanky panky," I remind them. Both men's heads turn to me as I drop my towel, eyes flaring with hunger. Shaking my head, I move to the closet to pick out my clothes for the day.

Onyx heaves a heavy sigh. "Maddox is right. We don't have time and I showered last night. So get that cute little ass in the shower so we aren't late meeting the little omega."

I bite my lip to keep from laughing as I hear Hudson bitching and complaining the entire way to the bathroom. He's so damn cute when he's forced to wake up this early. I pull on my pants, buttoning them as I feel someone step in behind me. I lean back into Onyx's hold, turning my head so I can kiss him.

"Morning, handsome."

Onyx's lips brush against mine once more. "It's definitely morning. I hate mornings."

"Oh, trust me, I know." I laugh, grabbing a shirt and pulling it over my head before stepping away so Onyx can get into the closet. "Neither you nor Hudson do well with mornings. Which should make the next few months interesting."

Onyx just grunts, and I bite my lip again to prevent the laughter from spilling from me. All that will accomplish is annoying Onyx, and I don't need him any grumpier. I pull on my socks and shoes before making my way back to the living room.

While Onyx and Hudson are night owls, I'm more of an early bird. Usually, by this time of day, I've already gotten in my morning workout, had breakfast, and am on my way to our shop. I'll spend the morning catching up on paperwork, doing the orders, and any other admin work that's needed. The shop opens at noon and I'm usually there by myself for an hour before some of the artists and piercers we have start strolling in. Onyx and Hudson usually make it there sometime between one and two. I usually stay until seven or eight, while my two pack mates will stay until we close at midnight.

We're only open Tuesday through Saturday, and sometimes one of us will be away at a conference or a show. This is the first time all three of us have been away from the shop at the same time for an extended period. But I trust our manager, Val, to keep things running while we're gone. She's been with us since the beginning, when we took her on as an apprentice. She's a fabulous artist, but she's the only one I trust with the shop.

Hudson stumbles into the room, naked as the day he was born, pulling me away from my thoughts of Infinite Ink. "Where's your damn towel?"

He waves in the general direction of the bathroom, but just keeps moving into our room—giving me a superb view of his dick. My own is now rock hard and I want to spank him for turning me on when we have somewhere to be in... fuck. We have eight minutes to get downstairs.

"Hurry the fuck up, you two. We've got less than ten minutes," I call out, as I reach up and squeeze my cock, willing it to go down.

Onyx chuckles as he drops beside me. "Enjoyed Hudson's show, did you?"

"Shut up, asshole. It's not my fault the two of you are so damn hot." A thought hits me, pulling a laugh from me. "Think we should remind Hudson that there are cameras everywhere and that he just showed his ass to everyone?"

"Like he cares." Onyx turns his attention to the bedroom, where we watch Hudson struggling to get dressed. "Honestly? I think if you mention it, he'll start walking around naked all the time. That man has no shame."

I nod my agreement because he's probably right. Looking at the time again, I growl. Hudson is taking too long. We're so going to be late. "Hud, if you don't get your ass—"

"I'm ready. Let's go. Gotta go see our future omega," Hudson says as he darts for the door.

"Sure, it's just the omega you want to see," Onyx teases. "There's not another alpha and beta you're hoping to talk to, is there?"

Hudson glares at Onyx over his shoulder as he throws the door open, but says nothing. He's already moving to the stairs, leaving us behind. I barely catch the door before it swings shut.

"I love that we were waiting for him and he just left us behind." Shaking my head, I hold the door open for Onyx as we head for the stairs ourselves.

"He's crushing hard on Gabriel and Emmett, not to mention Bree," Onyx says. "It's cute."

It really is.

Before we'd gone to bed last night, the three of us had a serious talk. We've always said we wouldn't mind a bigger pack and that if we met someone we were interested in, we just needed to be upfront about it. We're all stuck together for the next eight weeks, if we're lucky, so after Hudson admitted that he's drawn to not just Bree, but Gabriel and Emmett, Onyx and I promised we'd get to know the alpha and beta.

While we know we can't expect every member of our pack would be involved with everyone else, we'd like that to be the case. We hadn't spoken as much with Gabriel and Emmett as Hudson has, so we plan to get to know them to see if we also click with them.

I had warned Hudson that it could end in disaster if he gets attached to these two men, and then Bree doesn't choose all of us. He'd looked devastated at the prospect, which broke my heart. I just want him to be happy—for all of us to be happy.

"Step one, we get to know Gabriel and Emmett. If we agree that they're a good fit, then we make a plan between the five of us to win Bree over. If Hudson wants them to be a part of our pack, and we agree, we need to make sure that we all get chosen," I say as we walk down the stairs.

"Or none of us," Onyx agrees. "Though I like your plan the best."

I laugh. "Of course you do. Because in my scenario, we have an omega."

"Not just any omega—*the* omega." Onyx chews on his lip before glancing at me. "She's meant to be mine—ours. I can feel it in my gut."

I nod, but say nothing. I want to agree with him, but it's not our decision to make. Only Bree can decide who she wants to be in her pack.

We can do our best to convince her it should be us, but we can't force her to choose us.

Finally, making it to the dining room, I'm surprised to see we're the last of the suitors to arrive. Bree still isn't here, but everyone else has already found their seats. Emmett and the other beta, Brody, sit on each side of the head of the table that's being saved for Bree. Somehow, there's still a seat between Emmett and Hudson. On Hudson's other side is Gabriel, a seat next to him open as well.

My eyes narrow on Hudson, who just shoots me a smirk and shrugs. I don't know how he managed it, but he's making sure that Onyx and I do what we told him we would. "I'll take the beta, you take the alpha?"

"Yeah, probably a good plan. We need to see if he can handle both me and Hud in the morning." Onyx trails behind me as we make our way around the table. I nod to the other alphas as I pass them by, pressing a kiss to the top of Hudson's head before dropping into my seat.

"Good morning, Emmett," I murmur as the clock chimes at the top of the hour.

"Hey there, big boy." Emmett offers me a grin as he wiggles his eyebrows. "I think Hudson wants me to get to know his pack mates."

I chuckle. "That, he definitely does."

Before either of us can say anything else, Bree steps into the room. She's wearing jeans that look painted on and a flowy shirt that plasters itself to her curves as she walks. I lift my hand to bite down on it to prevent myself from groaning out loud. She is so fucking beautiful.

"Good morning, everyone," she calls out cheerfully as she drops into her seat. "I'm glad to see you've all made it on time. Sorry for my late entrance. Apparently, I'm meant to have a dramatic entrance once you were all here. Something about it being good television or something."

"Well, you certainly made an entrance," Gabriel calls out, pulling a laugh from Bree.

"They'll be bringing the food in any minute now, but I wanted to let you all know, in case you hadn't heard, that I'll be giving a tour of the house and grounds after breakfast for anyone who would like to join."

Bree pauses as a few betas step into the room, pushing carts overfilled with breakfast foods.

It smells amazing and I must be hungrier than I thought as my stomach gives a very vocal growl. As all heads turn to me, I want to beat my head on the table. How embarrassing.

"I'm so glad I'm not the only one who's starving," Bree says with a grin. "I usually eat breakfast by seven at the latest. I keep trying to tell my stomach we're on vacation and will therefore be eating later, but it doesn't care."

I return her smile as I incline my head. "It's the same for me. It's a bit of a change sleeping in later than six."

The crew sets the food before us and all conversation dies off as we fill our plates. Breakfast passes quickly and I'm able to speak a little with both Bree and Emmett. I can already see why Hudson likes Emmett. He's funny, flirty, and doesn't stop talking. Not that we need another talker in our pack—that's what we have Hudson for—but I could see Emmett fitting in well with us. And Bree seems to enjoy both him and Brody—damn betas, stealing the spotlight.

"Okay, who's up for a tour?" Bree asks after we've finished eating.

Most of the table calls out their agreement, except for the newly mated alpha and beta—Riley and Carter. Carter sighs, leaning on his elbows as he turns to Bree.

"As much as we'd like to join, I think Riley and I will sit this one out. Too many people all at once in small spaces just don't seem like a good idea."

Bree looks disappointed, but nods her agreement. "I was thinking after the tour, we could spend some time out back and have lunch out there. There's a pool and hot tub and plenty of space so the two of you can hang out with the rest of us, so Riley doesn't feel the need to fight all the alphas."

"Thank you for understanding, Bree," Riley says, head bowed. "I do want to get to know you and the other suitors. It's just not easy right now."

"Which is why you don't mate two weeks before coming on a dating show," someone mumbles. I don't know if they meant to be heard or if they thought they'd spoken quieter, but the entire table definitely heard their words.

"Wren," Bree hisses as she stands, hands banging down on the table, "that is rude and uncalled for. I think maybe you should sit out the tour as well."

Wren gapes at Bree. The first time I've seen him be anything but cool and collected since we'd arrived. Wilder glances between Wren and Bree before speaking, his disappointment threading through his every word. "I'll stay with Wren, and I apologize for his comment, Bree. Riley and Carter, I'm sorry."

"It's not you who should apologize," Bree bites out. "Nor will I punish you, because Wren let everyone know his feelings in such an inappropriate fashion. You'll join us for the tour. Wren, you need to apologize to Riley and Carter, and make sure you have yourself under control when you meet us on the back deck. If another comment like that makes its way from you, you'll be gone."

Wren continues to stare at her, his jaw clenched in anger or annoyance. I can't really say which. But he says nothing as he continues the stare down with Bree.

"That's how it's going to be?" she asks with a snort. "You have until we're done with the tour to apologize. If you don't, you will not be joining us for the rest of the day. No. Until you apologize, you'll not be joining us for anything at all—including meals."

This poor man is letting his alpha stubbornness keep him from apologizing. Or is he always like this? I guess it could be a personality trait of his.

"Seriously, Wren?" Wilder hisses, as the rest of us stand to follow Bree from the room.

She pauses beside Riley and Carter, squeezing both of their shoulders before leaning down to whisper something in their ears. I do not know what she says, but Riley's body immediately relaxes as she steps away from them.

"We'll start in the basement," she tells us, stepping through the other set of doors that leads to a hallway I haven't been down yet. We hadn't explored the house last night, wanting to wait until we could take the tour with Bree.

I find myself walking beside Emmett, so I turn to him. "Did you explore at all last night?"

Emmett shakes his head. "No. I stayed in my room and watched a movie until I fell asleep after eating. I figured I needed a good night's sleep if I was going to be getting up early."

"Not an early riser?"

"Nah. I used to be, but being the head chef at a popular restaurant means I need to be there for the dinner rush." Emmett laughs. "The restaurant closes at ten, thank the fates, and I don't have to stay past closing. One of my sous chefs takes care of everything after closing, so I'm usually out by nine. But I'm there at noon every day to prep for the day."

"Seven days a week?" I ask with a frown.

Emmett laughs. "Absolutely not. I could never. I usually only work four days a week, Wednesday through Saturday. There's another chef that I trained to be a mini-me. She covers my off days. She's been working with one of the sous chefs to get them up to par so he could take over her role while she covers mine while I'm here. Hopefully, they're not destroying my reputation while I'm gone."

I chuckle as he makes a face. I know the feeling. We have guest artists filling in for us while we're gone. We're paying big bucks to have some of the best artists come in for a week at a time to make up for the fact we're not there.

"Alright." Bree claps her hands to get our attention as the last suitor steps out of the stairwell. "The basement houses the control room that none of us have access to, but it also has all the other fun stuff down here."

She walks over to a door, pushing it open to reveal the biggest home gym I've ever seen. "For those of you who like to work out or those of you who are like me and force themselves to work out, we have pretty much every piece of equipment you can think of."

I let my eyes scan the room, practically drooling over the state-of-the-art equipment. Damn, I wish I'd known about this so I could've gotten my workout in this morning. Not that taking a couple of days off is going to hurt me. I just really like working out.

"You have something there on your lip." Emmett nudges me with raised eyebrows. "Oh, it's definitely drool. I should've known you'd be one of those fitness fanatics with a body like that."

I narrow my eyes as I stare at him. "And what's wrong with liking to work out?"

"Not a damn thing. Especially not with results like that." Emmett's hand waves up and down to indicate my body, and I realize he's flirting with me.

Huh. Has he been flirting with me this whole time and I hadn't noticed? That actually seems on brand for me.

"Thanks?" It ends up coming out as more of a question than I intended, but I'm not really sure how to respond. Is he flirting because he'll flirt with anyone? Or is it because he thinks it'll help him with Hudson? Or is he actually interested?

Fates above. This is why I hate dating. I'm terrible at it. That's why I'm here with my pack and not on my own. Both Onyx and Hudson are much better at this than me. Not to mention, I came here intending to win a spot in an omega's pack, not start something with a beta—not that I'm against starting something with this beta.

"If my flirting is making you uncomfortable, I can stop," Emmett says, head dropping. "You're a very attractive man and I... I'm sorry."

"No." I reach out to grab his hand when he turns to leave. "I'm just... not good at all of this. And I'd only expected to have to overcome that for Bree. I didn't know we'd meet other suitors who might draw our interest as well. I'm enjoying getting to know you—including the flirting. I'm just not good at it myself, nor do I know how to respond to someone who's flirting with me."

Emmett grins. "That makes me like you even more, Maddox," he purrs as he steps closer. "I like when a man can admit his flaws and communicate when he's struggling. I think getting to know you is going to be a lot of fun."

This time, when he turns to leave, he grabs my hand and pulls me along. We end up standing next to Bree, who turns to us with a grin. "I saw you drooling all over the equipment, Maddox. I'm guessing you'll be using it while we're here."

"Absolutely. If I'd known it was here, I would've gotten up earlier so I could get a workout in before breakfast."

"Morning workouts are my favorite. We should set up a time to meet down here, so neither of us has to work out alone."

"Really?" Did Bree just make a daily workout date with me? Who knew my workout addiction would let me have time with her?

She grins at me. "Absolutely. I'm sure others will join us when they find out, but we'll see how serious they are about it." She claps her hands together. "Come on, let me show you all my favorite parts of the basement."

We all trail the omega as she shows us the shower room with the massive steam room that I will also make use of daily. Then she shows us the indoor pool, hot tub, and the two bathrooms.

On the first floor, she points out where her suite is and shows us the living room before leading us up to our floor to show off the living room and theater room. We don't bother going to the third floor, as we're all aware of the game room that's there.

Then we get a tour of the grounds, which are massive. There have to be at least fifty cottages spread out and Bree tells us she and Tessa wanted to make sure there are plenty of places for the crew and their families to stay while we're filming. Then she leads us into a beautiful garden that backs up to the back deck area. There are tall hedges that cut off the deck area from the rest of the property.

The pool out here is slightly larger than the one in the basement, but it's set up to mimic a natural spring with a waterfall and everything. Lounge chairs circle the pool, and the hot tub can easily hold all the suitors and Bree all at once. There's a seating area with tables and chairs and another massive bar.

Bree turns to smile at us, making eye contact with the twelve of us that joined her on the tour. "And that's the end of our tour. If everyone would like to change into their swimsuits, we'll all meet out here. We can spend a lazy day in the sun, drink a few drinks, and have lunch. I'll be spending this time getting to know all of you, just like last night. I will tell you, I plan to hand out roses throughout the day. There will be a group dinner date tonight, so you should all be on your best behavior."

She pauses for a moment, eyes finding Wilder. "And on that note, Wilder, will you join me? We need to find your pack mate and find out if he's bothered apologizing or not."

Wilder winces, but makes his way over to Bree, the two of them heading inside. Hudson bumps against me, pulling my attention away from the omega. "We should go get changed."

"Where's Onyx?" I scan the deck before finding him leaning against the bar as he chats with Gabriel. The two are leaning close to one another as they talk, smiles on both their faces. "That seems to be going well."

"It does." Hudson's voice sounds a little dreamy. "I saw you and Emmett earlier. That seemed to go well, too."

I nod slowly. "It did. I can see why you're drawn to him. So is Bree. I think any damn one he sets his sights on will feel drawn to him. He's good with people."

Hudson hums his agreement. I grab his hand and lead him over to Onyx. "Hey, O. You ready to get changed?"

"Yeah, I guess." Onyx's smile slips slightly as he pulls away from Gabriel. "You'll come find us later, won't you, Gabriel?"

Gabriel's eyes move from Onyx to me and Hudson before he nods. "Absolutely."

"We look forward to it," I tell him as I grab Onyx's hand and drag my two pack mates along behind me. It seems both of them are smitten. This should make things interesting.

Chapter Thirteen

Bree

"What if he hasn't apologized?" Wilder asks as we climb the stairs to the third floor.

"Then he won't be joining us for group activities or dates, including meals. He'll be able to socialize with any suitors while I'm out on a date, or any down time that you all might have." I shake my head, still pissed off that Wren had refused to apologize.

Who does that?

He'd been unnecessarily cruel to Riley and Carter—who have already realized that mating just before coming on *Heated* was a bad idea. They don't need it rubbed in their face. We're all human, and therefore, not perfect. We all make mistakes, and the smart ones learn from those mistakes.

Now, we just need to see if Wren has learned from his.

Wilder stops just outside the door, clearing his throat as he runs a hand over his hair. "I get that part, but if he is a stubborn ass and won't apologize? How long do you allow that to go on? And is there really a point of me spending time with you if he refuses? When he leaves, I leave. And I'm sure at some point, you'd send him home."

And now I understand better. He doesn't want to be sent home, but he doesn't think his pack mate will apologize. I wish there was something I could say to assure him that wouldn't happen, but if Wren refuses to apologize, that's exactly what will happen.

"Why don't we check in with him and see if he's apologized like I asked him to? Then we can go from there, yeah?"

Wilder nods, pulling out his keycard and scanning us inside. He pushes open the door to reveal a very drunk Wren sitting on the couch, a bottle of Scotch in his hand.

"Wren, Bree's here to see you."

Wren's eyes turn to take us in. Instead of saying anything, he just lifts a brow. I clench my jaw, already knowing he hasn't apologized. Stubborn fucking alpha.

"I'm going to take a stab in the dark and guess you didn't apologize to Riley and Carter?"

"Why would I?" Wren scoffs. "It's not like I wasn't telling the truth. I did nothing wrong."

Now it's my turn to scoff. "You were cruel for no reason. Do you believe that the two of them haven't already realized they made a mistake? What good does it do anyone for you to point it out? All that accomplishes is hurting them. That's why you need to apologize.

"But you have no intention of apologizing, do you? I will not drag this out. If you don't apologize, the two of you are going home. Period. Wilder, I'm sorry. I'll give you the night to convince him to apologize. If he hasn't apologized by breakfast, the two of you will be leaving *Heated*. I wouldn't put up with this as a producer, but I especially won't put up with this from someone who wants to be in my pack.

"I won't have someone who's too stubborn to admit when they've done something wrong in my pack. Don't let your stubbornness ruin this, not just for you, but for your pack mate. Your decision could take this opportunity from him as well." Shaking my head, I turn back to Wilder. "I think you need to spend the day with your pack mate, trying to convince him to do what's right. If you convince him to apologize today, then the two of you can join us. Otherwise, neither of you is welcome."

Wilder nods. "I understand, Bree."

Turning to look at Wren, my anger slides into disgust. I don't know if I can ever look at him the same, even if he apologizes. This isn't what I want from an alpha, and it might just be best to cut the cord now before I find myself attached to Wilder.

Wren doesn't look at me as he takes another drink straight from the bottle. Afraid of what I might say, I hastily make my way to the door. Sadly, slamming the door to their suite doesn't make me feel any better.

Fates, why is this so hard? It's only day two and I've already sent home five people. At this rate, I'll be sending home another two more on day three. I hadn't been planning to send anyone home until the second rose ceremony at the end of the week, but maybe this is better.

I head back downstairs, running into Roman on the second floor.

"Hey, Bree," Roman calls out with a smile.

I force my anger and disappointment away, returning his smile. "Heading out back?"

"I am." He pauses for a second. "I'm going to guess, based on your body language, that Wren didn't apologize?"

I sigh, annoyed with myself that I hadn't covered up what I was feeling better. "No, he didn't. I've asked him and Wilder to remain in their suite. If he doesn't apologize by breakfast tomorrow, then I'm going to have to send them home."

"That's probably for the best," he says with a shrug. "And I'm not just saying that because it means two fewer people competing for a spot in your pack. You don't seem like the type to do well with an alpha who refuses to listen to you."

"I don't expect everyone to bow at my feet, Roman," I tell him with a smile to let him know I'm teasing. "And I don't even mind some stubbornness—I don't need someone who always agrees with me. I'll be the first to admit, I'm not always right. But I need someone who will listen to me when I tell them they're being cruel. I've been beaten down enough in my life that I don't want to watch my pack doing it to others. I won't allow that, and I honestly don't think it's asking too much to want that."

"It's not asking too much and you shouldn't put up with it. That's why we're all here, right? To figure out if we're the men you're looking for in your pack. Not all of us are going to fit what you're looking for. If someone isn't what you're looking for, I think it's better to send them home as soon as possible. The longer we're all here, the harder it'll be to say goodbye."

I nod, understanding what he's saying, and he's right. Keeping anyone who is unsuitable for me won't help anyone. I'll need to remember that.

"Thank you, Roman. I needed to hear that." I pause as we reach the bottom of the stairs. "I still need to get changed, but I'd like to talk with you some more, if you wouldn't mind."

"Mind?" he scoffs. "I'd be honored."

"Excellent. I'll see you out there shortly." Waving to Roman, I head toward my suite, already mentally going through my wardrobe in my head.

Tessa and I had gone shopping before heading out here to Rancho Mirage, and we may have gone a bit overboard on buying me new clothes. We bought way too many swimsuits and I'm not even sure I remember what they all look like. Shaking my head, I push my way into my suite to once again find Tessa waiting for me.

"How are you doing, hon?" she asks as she stands.

"I'm going to need you to stop showing up in my suite all the time. What if I wasn't alone?"

Tessa taps the earpiece that's barely noticeable. "I have eyes and ears everywhere, Bree. Someone would've warned me if you were heading here with someone else. Plus, what are the chances of you bringing someone to your suite in the first two days?"

"Slim to none," I grumble. "But that could change at any time, so maybe wait outside my suite next time."

"If that's what you want. I don't want to make this any harder on you than it already is. I just thought you might like to see a familiar face." She hesitates for a moment before continuing, "We also want to do an interview with you about the situation at breakfast. Preferably before you head out to the deck."

I grin at her. "So what you're saying is, you're *really* here to drag the poor, emotional omega off to prod at her wounds."

Tessa smacks my arm. "That is not at all what we're going to do, brat. If I recall correctly, you're the one who came up with the business plan for the show—which includes interviews any time there are major conflicts."

"Yeah, yeah, yeah. I got it, birch. This was my idea." I grin as I head for the dresser. "Well, since you're here, you can help me pick out a swimsuit."

"I can't wait to watch this," Tessa says as she follows me over and we pull out the options. "You're going to be perfuming all over the place and driving the suitors crazy."

I shrug. "Not much I can do about it since no one has come up with a way to make a swimsuit scent canceling." I pause, head tilting as I think about it. "We should work on that. We can afford to hire a research and development division. We can have them work on making more scent canceling clothes because sometimes we just can't wear panties."

"Slow your roll, Bree. I actually love that idea and I'll look into it, but you're not working right now. Right now, you're focusing on being an omega who's searching for her pack. You are *not* to worry about the company. Or come up with new ideas." She laughs, shaking her head.

"Yeah, the chances of that are slim to none, but if you want your interview, you better help me pick out a swimsuit, or I'm going to be here forever trying to decide."

Tessa says nothing as she looks over the choices before leaning over and grabbing one. As soon as I see it, I know she's right. That's definitely the one. It's a black bikini of sorts. The bottoms are high-waisted with a thick strip that criss-crosses along the front, revealing a sliver of my hips and lower back. The top is a halter with under wire that will keep the girls where they're supposed to be, but will reveal just the right amount of cleavage. The sexiest part is the eight thin straps that start at the bottom of the bikini top and end at the halter. It makes it appear like I've caged my boobs and it'll give the guys peeks of skin between them.

I grab it from her with a smile. "You're the best at knowing what I want when I can't even figure it out," I tell her as I strip.

It's not the first, nor will it be the last time Tessa has seen me naked. While I'm not attracted to women, and Tessa is, there's just no attraction between us on her part. We're more like sisters, best friends forever.

Once I've pulled the swimsuit on, Tessa is handing me a white almost sheer cover up. I pull it on, loving the way you can see hints of the swimsuit and my skin beneath it. Tessa laughs.

"Those suitors are going to lose their minds when they see you."

"Good." I grin. I'm looking forward to seeing their faces when I walk out. "So where are we going to do the interview? I'd recommend the deck, but I think I'd be a little distracted by all the gorgeous skin that's going to be on display."

"True enough." Tessa taps a finger against her chin. "That means the living room is off limits too, since they'll need to walk through there to get outside. Oh! Let's do it out front. We'll use the gazebo we used the night of the arrivals."

I consider the idea and it's really our best option. "And it's so nice out today. Are you going to do the interview, or Reginald?"

"We'll have Reggie do it. That's what we're paying him the big bucks for, after all."

I giggle. "Don't let him hear you calling him Reggie. He'll have a fit. You know he hates that."

"Why do you think I do it?" Tessa gives a short laugh, eyes scanning the floor of my room. "Where the hell did you put your mic?"

I dig through the pile of clothes I'd placed on my bed, holding up the mic in triumph when I find it. "Where the hell am I supposed to put it on this thing?"

Tessa grabs it from me, lifting my cover up so she can tuck the box into the back of my bottoms before bringing the mic to my front, tucking it into my top. "That'll do. Remember, we got the top of the line ones so they're fully submersible. You don't need to worry about it while in the water. Though, if someone messes with your top, you'll need to be careful that you don't lose it."

"No one is going to be undressing me in broad daylight with all the suitors with us."

Tessa raises a brow. "Are you sure about that?"

I open my mouth to assure her I would do no such thing, but then I snap my mouth closed. I really can't promise that, and Tessa knows that. She shoots me a knowing grin.

"I'm going to call Reginald and get some cameras set up. Meet us out front in like fifteen minutes?"

I nod. She heads out and I throw myself down onto the bed, deciding that now is as good of a time as any to think about getting a research and development division going at Fated Industries. Tessa should know better than to tell me to not worry about the company—it's my baby. I'm always going to worry about it or be thinking of ways to improve it. What she doesn't know won't hurt her.

Thirty minutes later, I'm finally sitting on the gazebo with a frozen daiquiri in hand. Apparently, Reginald had been "tied up" and unable to come out any sooner. Based on the indentations on his wrists, I'm willing to bet he was literally tied up. Good for him and his pack, I guess, but I'm definitely not going to ask any questions.

"Good afternoon, Bree." Reginald smiles that million-dollar smile of his. "There's been a bit of tension in the house today. Why don't you tell me about it?"

Taking a long sip from my daiquiri, I shake my head. "There's been tension in the house since the arrivals, Reginald. Some of it seems to have released after Owen and Pack Astor's departure, but Pack Woods is still causing some issues. Riley is having problems with Carter being around anyone, but especially the other alphas. He's actually done really well with the betas, Emmett and Brody, being around them. After the initial meeting, he's been fine with me being around them as well.

"Riley and Carter have realized that bonding two weeks before coming onto *Heated* wasn't their best decision. I'm still hoping that Riley can get his alpha instincts under control, as I need to be sure that whoever is a part of my pack can get along with all the members of the pack, you know?"

Reginald nods. "It's no fun when pack mates don't get along. It causes a lot of tension, and I can only imagine what that would do to an omega."

"Yeah, it wouldn't be pretty. I'm even having problems with the tension in the house, and I'm used to high tension situations." I tap the nails of my free hand against the arm of the chair. "This morning we had our first breakfast together—even Riley and Carter were there. It went well, but when I offered to give a tour, Carter and Riley declined joining, wanting to give Riley a break—something I admire. They admitted he needed some downtime away from the others.

"Then Wren made a comment about the fact that they'd bonded only two weeks ago. The words themselves weren't overly bad, but it was the condescending tone of voice he used. I didn't like it, so I demanded that he apologize to Pack Woods and he refused. I told him he was no longer welcome to join us for the tour and if he didn't apologize, he wouldn't be able to join us for any other group activities today.

"When we got back from the tour, Wilder and I went upstairs to see if he'd done what I asked—he hadn't. On top of that, he was drunk off his ass." I shake my head, annoyance rising within me again. "I don't need an alpha that can't admit when he's wrong. So I told Wilder he has until tomorrow at breakfast to convince Wren to apologize. If he doesn't, then they're gone. I hate to punish Wilder for Wren's stubbornness, but they're a pack. If I take one, I take both of them.

"Even though I gave them that time for Wren to apologize, I don't know that I want them to stay, even if he does. If this is the way Wren behaves, I don't need or want him as part of my pack. A part of me hopes he won't apologize, so I don't have to feel bad for sending them home."

"Wow," Reginald says, eyes wide. "That's tough. But you need to remember, you're in charge here. You're the omega and you get to choose who you want or don't want as part of your pack. You shouldn't feel bad about making those decisions. They all knew what they were getting into when they signed up for *Heated*."

This right here is why we'd wanted Reginald to be the host. Yes, it allows me to have the support system I need between him and Tessa, but more than that, we know Reginald will be like this with any omega.

"Thanks, Reginald. I needed to hear that." Lifting my drink to my lips, I consider my next words. "I think I may not wait until tomorrow. I might ask them to leave tonight. Do you think we should put together another rose ceremony? I'd like the others to hear what I have to say."

"We'll do whatever you want us to do, Bree. You're the one running the show... kind of." He snorts. "For now, why don't you enjoy your afternoon with the suitors in the pool? Decide who you want to invite on your group date. After your date, we'll take care of this, yeah?"

Nodding slowly, I know I'm going to need to push this away for now. Compartmentalize. I can do that. Because I need this afternoon to get to know all of them better, to allow them to get to know me better. Maybe I'll even get more kisses. An omega can hope.

"That sounds like a brilliant idea, Reginald. Thank you."

With that, I stand and make my way back to the house. By now, I expect all the suitors will be outside, waiting for me. I guess I'll be giving Tessa another dramatic entrance.

Reaching the doors that lead to the back deck, I take a moment to watch the suitors before they know I'm there. Hudson, Maddox, Onyx, Gabriel, and Emmett are hanging out on the lounge chairs, drinks in hand as they talk animatedly. I'm curious about how Gabriel and Emmett seem to join the three pack mates more often than not. I watch as Gabriel places his hand on Hudson's thigh, leaning in to whisper something to him, and warmth creeps over me. I have no doubt that I'm perfuming as I watch Hudson blush, ducking his head.

Emmett leans over to Onyx, pressing his smaller body against the larger man, and pulls him into a kiss. A whimper falls from my lips as I suck in a deep breath. There's definitely something brewing between the five of them and I wouldn't mind being in the middle of that group.

Forcing my eyes to take in the other suitors, I find Riley and Carter in the pool with Brody, Maverick, and Dalton. Riley seems relaxed as the five of them talk, occasionally one of them breaks off to dunk under the water. My thighs clench when Riley stands from his dunk, water running down his perfectly sculpted body.

This might have been a bad idea.

I tear my eyes away from Riley to find Finnegan, Roman, and Sasha leaning against the bar as they talk. Not a single damn suitor is wearing a shirt, and I would love to make it a rule that they have to walk around shirtless at all times. I also know that would be bad for my sanity.

I really want to lick them all.

Squeezing my eyes shut, I take a few deep breaths to calm down. The last thing I need to do is walk out there wafting around my perfume. While I'm aware it's going to happen, I'd hoped I could prevent it from happening as soon as I walked on the deck. Guess I was wrong... kind of. Technically, I'm not on the deck yet.

I roll my neck and give up on trying to hide my arousal. Sliding open the door, I step onto the back deck and all conversation comes to a stop. A blush creeps up my neck as my eyes dart from one man to another, all of them looking at me with desire in their eyes.

It's going to be a long afternoon. How the hell am I supposed to choose who to take on my group date?

Chapter Fourteen

Bree

I see some of the suitors' noses twitching, telling me I'm still perfuming. I know I shouldn't be ashamed of it—after all, it's a part of an omega's biology. It's hard for me to remember I'm supposed to let my omega out to have free rein here when I've held it locked up for so long.

A healthy way to handle things? Definitely not.

The suitors seem to be incapable of speaking and I don't want to continue standing here like an idiot, so I sashay my way to the loungers, setting my drink down before sliding the almost sheer coverup down my arms, and laying it on a free lounger.

"Wow," Emmett finally says, jumping off his lounger and hurrying over to me. "You look amazing, Bree."

Emmett grabs my hands, lifting them to his lips as he grins at me. "And I can't imagine what the alphas are feeling if your perfume is hitting me this hard."

"An omega's perfume doesn't affect betas, Emmett." I giggle.

"I don't know who stated that as fact, because I guarantee you, I'm being affected. I feel a little punch drunk. And I've only had one drink, so I know it's not that."

I don't know what to say to that because I've always been taught that omegas don't affect betas like they do alphas. I don't think Emmett is lying or exaggerating, so it's making me question what I think I know about the designations and packs. I already know some parts of our curriculum are wrong, so what's to say this isn't too?

"Thank you... I think?" I laugh, realizing Emmett is still holding onto my hands. As much as I don't want to break away from the contact between us, I can't just stand here staring at Emmett all day. I tug on my hands and Emmett looks down, eyes slightly glazed over.

"Oh, oops." Emmett releases my hands and steps back, a slight blush on his cheeks. "Sorry about that."

Picking up my drink, I take a long sip, hoping it'll cool me off. It does not. "No need to apologize. I like it when you touch me." My eyes go wide as I realize what I've said. I feel the need to facepalm right now—but thankfully, I don't actually do it.

Emmett just grins in response, eyes sliding to my drink. "What are you drinking? I can make you a new one."

"It's a banana daiquiri. Do you know how to make it?" I ask, eyebrows raised. Most people don't know how to make my drink of choice, but I should've known better than to doubt Emmett.

"I've filled in for the bartender at work when they need a break. The drinks I can make would surprise you. Do you want a light hand or a heavy hand with the rum?"

Tessa made the daiquiri I'm currently drinking, meaning it's light on the rum. Not to mention, I'll probably be out here for hours, so I should be fine with a heavy hand. Plus, alcohol helps in awkward situations, right?

"Heavy," I decide. "Thank you, Emmett."

He hurries away to the bar, so I turn back to the four alphas on the loungers. "It looks like you all have been enjoying yourselves."

Maddox's eyes narrow on me. "Were you being a bad omega and spying on us?"

I shrug, watching him from beneath my eyelashes. "Maybe, maybe not. But you should know I'm very good at being a bad omega."

"I'm sure you are," Gabriel says before patting the chair between his legs. "Why don't you come sit and chat with us for a bit? I promise not to bite—unless you beg me to."

And there goes the slick rushing from me already. Not even five minutes out here and I'm soaked. Great.

"You can't say things like that, Gabriel," I scold him as I make my way over. "They don't make scent canceling swimsuits yet. The last thing we need is for all of you to go into rut."

"I have much better control over my alpha side than that, little omega," he purrs as I sit between his legs. He wraps his arms around me, pulling me back until I'm leaning back against his chest, our bodies touching from the top of my head to the bottom of my butt.

I wiggle a bit, feeling his thick cock hardening between my ass cheeks. A smirk slides over my lips, as I'm sure that all the suitors out here are dealing with hard dicks right now.

"Be careful, little omega, before you start something you aren't ready for." Gabriel's breath is hot against my neck as he speaks.

I feel him stiffen as I perfume once more. This really is going to be a long fucking afternoon, but I somehow manage to not sass him about him not knowing what I'm ready for and what I'm not. This really doesn't need to turn into a giant fuckfest on day two of the show. Tessa might kill me. Maybe.

Instead, I just settle more firmly against him and finish my drink. "Why aren't you guys in the pool?"

"Honestly?" Onyx asks, continuing at my nod. "We wanted to give Riley some space. He seems to do best with the betas, Dalton, and Maverick. We didn't want to overwhelm him."

"That's sweet of you to think of him and do what you can to make him comfortable—unlike some alphas," I say with an eye roll. I know I'm not supposed to be thinking about Wren right now, but seeing how easily these alphas are dealing with Riley's alpha riding him so hard makes me realize just how much I hate the way Wren is behaving.

"Some alphas are too stubborn for their own good," Maddox offers. "I may be stubborn, but I know how to listen to others. Not all alphas can—especially to someone they believe to be 'weaker' than themselves."

I giggle at Maddox's use of air quotes. "And those are the kind of alphas I don't want."

Hudson leans over, his hand on Gabriel's arm as he tells me, "The good news is you'll find that none of us are that kind of alpha."

"And I'm not an alpha," Emmett adds, offering me the drink he made before dropping onto the lounge chair beside me and Gabriel. He has a drink in his other hand that looks like a banana daiquiri.

"Did you make yourself one too?" I ask, trying to hold back my giggle.

Emmett shrugs. "I'm comfortable enough in my masculinity to drink a frozen daiquiri." As if to prove his point, he takes a long sip before humming. "Damn, that's a good drink."

I take a sip from the glass he'd brought to me, moaning as I swallow the frozen drink down. "Holy shit. That's the best banana daiquiri I've ever had."

"I bet you don't doubt me again."

I take another sip, a satisfied sigh falling from my lips. "I definitely won't. You're officially in charge of my drinks while we're here."

Onyx laughs. "Did you just make Emmett your cabana boy?"

"I don't mind, *gongjunim*. Trust me. I'll be your cabana boy any time you want me to." Emmett shoots me a wink and my mouth falls open at the suggestiveness of his words.

And I perfume again.

"You missed the conversation because you were making me a drink, but you can't say things like that. No scent canceling swimsuits. I'm going to perfume every time you make a suggestive comment."

"Challenge accepted." Emmett smirks, one eyebrow quirked.

"You're going to be the death of me."

Gabriel chuckles behind me and I feel it from his chest before I hear it. "In French, the word for orgasm is *la petite mort*, or the little death. I don't think your words are nearly as discouraging as you think they are."

Swiping my hand over my face, I laugh and can't seem to stop. I'm not one hundred percent sure what's come over me, but I just think that's hilarious.

"I guess I'm in for a good time then, aren't I?" I gasp out between laughs. "I need to get in the pool. It's much too hot out here."

Without waiting for a response, I climb to my feet and head for the stairs that lead into the pool. Glancing over my shoulder at Roman,

Sasha, and Finnegan and then Onyx, Maddox, Hudson, Gabriel, and Emmett, I raise my eyebrows. "It's pool time, boys. You coming?"

Lowering myself into the pool, I keep my drink well above the pool line as the suitors hurry to climb into the pool. Some of them jump right in, while others use the stairs as I did. I make my way over to where Riley and Carter stand with Brody, Maverick, and Dalton.

"Hello, gentlemen." I'm trying to tread water while keeping my drink out of the water. It's not going well.

Maverick's arm snakes around my waist as he pulls me against his rock hard body. "Let me help you out," he murmurs.

Is anyone surprised that I perfume again? Because I'm not.

"Your scent is extra potent today." Carter hums as his eyes rake over me. "Don't you think so, Riley?"

"You smell fucking divine," Riley growls, causing my eyes to widen.

This is the first time I've seen him focused so fully on someone other than Carter.

"I've invited everyone into the pool, so I wanted to make sure you were going to be alright." I choose to ignore Riley's words, as I don't know how to respond to them, or why they send a shiver down my spine.

Sure, I love an alpha growl just as much as any omega, but I'm still unsure about Riley. He's obviously hot as hell, but I'm not sure he can share. Which is another thing I'm not looking for in an alpha. Not all alphas want to share and while that might be okay with other omegas, it's not okay with me. I've always wanted a big pack. Call me greedy, but me and my omega? We want all the cock we can get.

Carter elbows Riley when he doesn't respond, as he's too busy staring at me. Riley shakes his head a few times before smirking. "Yeah, I think my alpha side and I have come to some kind of agreement."

"Good, because you and Carter need to spend more time with the other alphas. I want a bigger pack, but I don't want one where there's discord between pack mates. I need everyone to get along."

Riley gives a sharp nod, reaching out to wrap his arm around Carter's waist. "In that case, it looks like we have some alphas to speak to."

I chew on my lip as I watch the two of them walk away. While I appreciate what he's doing, part of me wonders if he can do it. I really don't want to break up any fights.

"It's alright, darlin'," Dalton says as he moves to block my view of Pack Woods. "Give him a chance to prove to you, Carter, and himself that he can do this. He doesn't need anyone hoverin'. He can either do it, or he can't. Ain't no way to know unless we let him try."

I nod, snuggling into Maverick's side more firmly. "I know. I'm just not good at not controlling everything going on around me."

"The two of us will be happy to distract you, if that's what you need, omega," Maverick murmurs, ducking his head to nose at my neck. "In fact, I think we should insist on it. You seem to need a distraction."

I let out a squeak as Maverick easily lifts me, settling me between him and Dalton. "Oh... ummm..." I stutter, barely keeping hold of my drink as they press me between their hard bodies. I can feel every muscle as they shift, their hard cocks pressing into my body. My thighs clench as I lift my drink to my lips and gulp down half the drink in one go.

"Relax, darlin'." Dalton's lips brush against the skin at the nape of my neck, and I can't hide the shiver that runs through me. It's been much too long since anyone has touched me like this outside of my heat. A decision that had felt right at the time, but now my touch-starved self has apparently turned into a horny little omega.

Maverick's hands run along my sides, down my ribs to my hips and then back again. "May I kiss you, omega?"

"Yes, please." The words come out breathy as I plead with him to do just that. "Kiss me, alpha."

Maverick swoops down, pressing his lips to mine as I thread my hands through his thick, dark hair that's hanging loose for the first time. His lips brush against mine time and time again, but it's not enough. I pull him closer, running my tongue along the seam of his lips.

I need more, a fact that Maverick seems to pick up on. He opens to me, and our tongues dance as we both fight for dominance. Whimpers and moans fall from my lips as I undulate between the two alphas. I want more—so much more.

When Maverick breaks the kiss, I whine at the loss. But then Dalton's lips are there to take Maverick's place. I wrap an arm behind me, around Dalton's neck, opening to him.

His kiss is so different from Maverick's. He doesn't fight me to dominate the kiss. No, he kisses like he's making love to my mouth and I love it. When he pulls away, I'm already pulling Maverick back to take his place.

Dalton's hands slide around my waist to lie flat on my stomach, close to where I wish he'd touch me. Maverick's hands now rest on my hips, squeezing harder the longer the kiss continues.

"Can I touch you, darlin'?" Dalton's voice is gruff as he grinds against my ass.

"Yes," I whine against Maverick's lips, unwilling to break the kiss to answer Dalton. "Please. Please, touch me."

Maverick growls before deepening our kiss once more.

Dalton's hands move up and away from where I want him to touch me. My pussy is drenched, slick spilling into the pool. I want his fingers there—or his cock. Definitely his cock. I want to feel his knot brushing against me as he fucks me into oblivion. I know that's my omega side begging for all the cock. It's too soon. I don't know these men well enough to have them rail me, do I?

On the other hand, does it matter how long I've known them?

That's the omega in me talking, for sure. But maybe she's right.

All thoughts fly from my head as Dalton palms my boobs, lifting them as if weighing them as he sucks on my neck. As nice as it feels to have him touching me, I need more. He's obviously a mind reader as his thumbs move up, brushing lightly over my nipples again and again until they're pebbled and begging for more.

Maverick breaks our kiss to watch Dalton work his magic before ducking down to take one of my nipples in his mouth. Even with the fabric between us, I'm panting as he sucks and licks at my nipple.

Meanwhile, one of Dalton's hands is making its way back down my body. He hesitates for a moment with his fingers playing with the fabric of my bottoms. "Yes or no?" he rumbles against my ear.

"Yes," I cry out, louder than I mean to as Maverick bites down on my nipple, causing my back to bow out of the water. "Please, alpha."

For a moment, I allow myself to wonder what the others are doing—are they watching? Are they touching themselves? Or each other?

That sends a spike of heat through me as Dalton's hand slides beneath my bottoms. He doesn't take the time to tease me, his fingers moving straight to my wet slit, and running one finger along it.

"You're soaking wet, darlin'," he pants in my ear as he continues to stroke over my center. His cock is so hard, I almost beg him to fuck me with it. It's fucking massive and I can just imagine what it would feel like as he fucked me.

Somehow, I keep the words from spilling from my lips as I dig my nails into the back of his neck and into Maverick's scalp. "I need your fingers inside me. Please, alpha. Fuck me with your fingers."

Both men chuckle, seeming to enjoy my desperation. If I wasn't so turned on, I'd give them a piece of my mind—maybe. No, probably not. They can be amused all they want as long as they're taking care of me.

Dalton thrusts one finger inside of me, but that's not nearly enough. I need so much more.

"More. I need more. Now." What starts out as a plea turns into an order. I want to come. No, I *need* to come.

"Whatever you need, darlin'. Ask and you shall receive." Dalton adds a second finger, and it's still not enough. A whine falls from my lips and he adds a third finger. There's a slight burn as I try to adjust to the size of those thick fingers, but it's just what I need.

Maverick switches his attention to my other nipple, his hand moving up to continue working over the one he's just abandoned. Their hold on me changes until they're each grasping one of my hips.

The sounds falling from my lips are a mess of panted demands, whimpers, and moans as Dalton fucks me on his fingers. It doesn't take him long to find the perfect rhythm as he grinds the palm of his hand on my clit.

Pleasure rolls through my belly with each stroke of his fingers and grind of his palm—not to mention the attention Maverick is lavishing on my nipples. My hips move of their own accord, meeting each thrust of Dalton's fingers. I'm climbing higher and higher, so close to exploding.

Dalton's lips crash down on mine as he curls his fingers to hit that spot inside of me that has me seeing stars at the same time Maverick bites down on my nipple, and I explode. The orgasm rushes through me, my whole body shaking as I grind against Dalton's hand, biting down on his lip as my back arches. My walls pulse around his fingers, trying to pull him in deeper as he continues to fuck me through my orgasm.

With a sigh, I collapse against Dalton to find Maverick grinning down at me. "I think we both deserve a taste, don't you, omega?"

I whine, barely nodding before Dalton is lifting me from the water. Maverick's hands moving to my ass to help him.

"Put your legs over his shoulders, darlin'. Let him get a good smell and look before he tastes you."

I flush at Dalton's words, but do what he says. I hook my legs over Maverick's shoulders as the alpha pushes my bottoms to the side. His eyes fall shut as he takes a deep inhale of my scent.

Another squeak falls from my lips as he buries his head between my thighs, nose running up my slit. "Fuck, Bree. You smell amazing. I can't wait to see how you taste."

That's all the warning I get before his tongue glides inside of me, lapping up my slick. My head falls back onto Dalton's shoulder as another moan slides from my lips, harmonizing with Maverick's groans as he devours me.

"Darlin', I'm not going to lie. That's really fuckin' hot," Dalton drawls, and when I lift my head to look at him, his eyes are locked on Maverick's head between my thighs.

Maverick slides two fingers inside of me, fucking me on them as he sucks my clit between his lips. I buck against his face without meaning to. Another whine falls from me as Maverick's fingers slide out of me before he... is he offering them to Dalton?

"Have a taste, man. She tastes better than she smells." Maverick only lifts his head long enough to speak before he's devouring me once again.

Dalton glances at me, raising his eyebrows as he leans over to suck Maverick's fingers into his mouth. His groan has me grinding against Maverick's face. I pant as I watch Dalton lick and suck Maverick's fingers until they're clean of my slick.

"That's so fucking hot. Why is that so hot?" I ask, not expecting an answer as my head falls back to Dalton's shoulder again.

Dalton chuckles. "I think it's because you enjoy seein' two men together."

He's absolutely right. I really do—assuming it's what they want and are okay with me watching.

"You should know, neither Maverick and I swing that way, but working together to please you? I'm sure Maverick will agree that we have no problem with that."

Maverick hums his agreement, causing my back to bow again as the vibrations hit my clit. My head falls back enough to see the rest of the suitors watching the three of us, a hungry glint in all of their eyes.

I cry out as another orgasm hits me. I convulse around Maverick's tongue as slick gushes from me.

I hadn't realized I was an exhibitionist, but seeing all those hungry eyes watching me is what sent me over the edge. My entire body goes lax. If it weren't for Dalton and Maverick holding me aloft, I'd probably be drowning right now.

Maverick's head pops up from behind my thighs as he lowers my legs to wrap around his waist instead. He grins, his face soaked in my slick. And honestly? I'm not sure I've seen anything hotter.

"I'm going to let your juices dry in my beard so I can remember this moment all night long."

Another rush of slick spills from me, sure to be soaking the front of Maverick's swim trunks at his words. He doesn't seem to mind, so I don't worry about it. I realize then that I'd lost my drink at some point; the cup floating around us.

I pout as the two alphas lower me back into the water.

"Why are you poutin', darlin'?" Dalton asks.

I point to the cup floating in the water. "My drink."

Emmett appears from out of nowhere, causing me to jump. "Don't worry, Bree. I made you another one when I saw the first one go down—though it wasn't the only thing going down, was it?"

If I wasn't already flushed from back-to-back orgasms, I knew I'd be blushing as I throw myself into his arms, smacking a kiss on his lips as I cling to him. "You're the best cabana boy an omega could ask for."

Emmett hands me the drink with a chuckle. "If this is the response I get for bringing you drinks, I'll happily be your cabana boy."

I take a long sip of the drink, realizing that I'd just let two alphas get me off in front of all the suitors—not to mention all the cameras—before I threw myself at Emmett. Definitely not how a "proper" omega should behave, so I guess it's a good thing I'm not a proper omega.

I knew the cameras would catch me having sex or in some kind of compromising position eventually, but I didn't think it would be on day two. Damn horny omega.

"To the shallow end, cabana boy!"

Emmett just laughs as he carries me until my feet can easily touch the bottom. No part of this pool is overly deep. We wanted to make it so that people could easily walk around the entire pool and not have to worry about drowning their drinks. I struggle in certain areas, but that's because I'm short.

Emmett helps me stand on my own before I turn to the other suitors. All their eyes are on me and I know I should feel embarrassed or overwhelmed, but I don't feel either of those things. I feel like I could leap tall buildings right now.

"So that happened," I say with a shrug.

"It certainly did." Gabriel shoots me a wink. "And can I say that I'll watch you come any damn time you want? Even better if I'm the one making you come, but I don't mind watching."

I flush slightly, but I will not feel ashamed of what I just did with Dalton and Maverick. I have no reason to be ashamed. I smirk, heading for the stairs. I don't want to get out just yet, but I'd like to sit. The stairs will allow me to do both.

It's not until I'm sitting that I realize Riley and Carter are nowhere to be found. I turn to the others with the question on my lips, but they seem to already know what I'm going to ask.

"Riley and Carter decided that they should go back to their suite," Roman offers.

"Oh, no! Did I set off his alpha?"

Finnegan laughs. "Not in th' way ye're thinking."

"Riley was about to start railing Carter in the pool," Gabriel offers bluntly. "Carter convinced him it would be best if they took it inside."

"Oh. Ohhhh." I bite back a whimper, choosing to take a long sip of my daiquiri. "I hope we didn't make anyone uncomfortable?"

Maddox snorts. "I don't think that's something you need to worry about, Bree. We all know why we're here. This is part of you figuring out who you want to be a part of your pack. And if we're a part of your pack, it's something we'll be seeing regularly."

"Right." I take another long sip, trying to figure out how the hell I'm going to decide who to ask to join me for the group date tonight. Should I invite Dalton and Maverick because they'd taken the time to get me off? Or should I not include them because they'd gotten that time with me? Ugh…

"Whatever you're thinking right now, Bree, just turn it off." Roman drops to sit beside me.

I bite my lip, watching him from the corner of my eye. Roman might be in his fifties, but he damn well takes care of his body. "I have to figure out who to invite to the group date tonight."

"No, don't worry about that right now. Just worry about having a good time. You'll know who to invite when it comes time." He moves to sit behind me, his hands moving to my shoulders.

I have to bite back a moan when he digs his thumbs into my tense muscles. I hear him chuckle behind me as he continues to massage my shoulders and back.

"You're worrying too much and it's making you tense. You've got so many knots back here—and not the good kind of knots." We laugh together and I allow myself to fully relax into his touch.

"Okay, Roman, what should we talk about then?"

Chapter Fifteen

Roman

Glancing in the mirror again, I shake my head. I feel like a teenager again. When I'd told Bree to relax and that she'd know who to invite to the group date tonight, I'd never expected her to choose me. Imagine my surprise when she handed me a lavender rose after we'd finished a lunch of sandwiches and various salads and fruits.

I'm proud that I was the first she invited, but I'm still not sure about the others coming with us. Brody is so young and he's a nice kid, but that's exactly what he is—a kid. I'm old enough to be his father. Hell, I'm old enough to be Bree's dad, but I'm trying to ignore that fact. Dalton and Maverick are older, which helps. But they're also the two that brought Bree to orgasm in front of all of us.

Am I jealous? A little. But I can guarantee that all of us were a little jealous. We all wanted to be the ones making her fall apart. I squeeze my cock through my pants. I've been rock hard since Bree's first whimper. Never mind that it's been hours since then. I can't seem to get the sight of her coming out of my brain.

Looking down at my watch, I realize I have enough time to take care of my not so insignificant problem. I probably should, so maybe I won't spend the entire date with an erection.

Grabbing a hand towel, I throw myself down onto my bed and release my throbbing cock from my pants. I sigh in relief as I circle my shaft, working my hand up and down my length. With my free hand, I push my pants down my hips before lifting my shirt higher on my chest. The last thing I need is to come all over my clothes.

Closing my eyes, I cup my knot, squeezing in time with my strokes. I recall the sounds Bree made as she came around Dalton's fingers and then on Maverick's face. In just a few strokes, I'm already on the edge—which I know should embarrass me, but it's hard to be embarrassed while thinking about how beautifully Bree falls apart.

I squeeze my knot, riding the line between pain and pleasure as the sound of my hand against my cock sounds throughout the room.

"Fuck," I curse, picking up the pace as I thrust into my hands. There's no way I'm going to last. Two strokes later, I'm coming across my stomach as I pant for breath. The hand around my knot palpates, poorly imitating an omega squeezing down on it. I continue to stroke my length through my orgasm that seems to go on forever as I drain my knot.

I fall back onto the bed, happily spent. I won't lay here for long. I don't want the cum to dry on my skin, but I just need a moment. A moment to enjoy the bliss of a much needed orgasm.

A knock on the door startles me, just barely keeping myself from sitting up. I grab the hand towel and quickly wipe the remnants of my cum off my stomach as I call out, "Just a minute."

Not that they can hear me, since the rooms are soundproofed. Shaking my head, I toss the towel onto the nightstand before tucking my cock back into my pants. Hurrying into the bathroom, I wash my hands. Another knock sounds as I straighten my clothes, hoping that whoever's at the door can't tell that I was just masturbating like a fucking teenager.

I throw open the door to find Brody, Dalton, and Maverick standing there. "What's up?" I ask with a frown.

"We just thought we could all go down together." Brody smiles and I swear this kid's default is smiling, which annoys me.

And that makes me sound like a grumpy old man. Great.

"Good idea." Turning back to my room, I check to make sure I haven't forgotten anything. But what is there to forget? We have no phones and we have no use for a wallet while we're here. "I guess I'm ready."

The four of us head for the stairs, hearing voices from the game room. I pause for a moment to check who's here and realize that all the suitors except Wren and Wilder have gathered there.

"Oh, look, it's the lucky assholes!" Hudson yells from across the room, pulling laughs from all of us.

"Enjoy dinner. Don't do anything I wouldn't do," Emmett offers with a smirk.

"Why do I get the feeling there isn't much you wouldn't do?" I lift an eyebrow at the beta who just shrugs.

With a laugh, Maverick slaps a hand on my back, leading me toward the stairs. I hear Dalton and Brody talking as they follow behind us, but I have no idea what they're talking about.

"What's wrong, Roman?" Maverick nudges me with his elbow.

"I'm just wondering why I'm here. I'm fucking old as shit compared to most of the suitors. Half the suitors, not to mention Bree, are young enough to be my kids. I don't know what to talk about with most of them. That's why I've mostly been sticking to hanging out with Finnegan—and he's still ten years younger than me."

"I'm only a few years younger than Finnegan. Same with Dalton. Now, Brody? He's the baby. He makes all of us feel old as shit."

"It's not my fault that I make you doubt yourself," Brody offers with a laugh. "I'm a catch."

I snort. "You're right. You're a catch, kid. But what am I? What do I have to offer?"

Dalton's hand lands on my shoulder. "You offer years of experience. There's a reason some people are into the whole daddy thing."

"Oh, Daddy Roman. That has a good ring to it." Maverick's tone is teasing, but I can't help but blush. I don't think I'd mind Bree calling me daddy, if that was her thing.

Maverick snorts. "You're into that, aren't you, old man?"

"Shut up." I shove Maverick into the wall before hurrying down the remaining steps. Turning back, I find the other three laughing as they follow at a slower pace. "Where were we supposed to meet her? I don't think she told us?"

"Lucky for you, I thought to call Tessa and ask." Maverick grins as he steps off the stairs beside me. "She said the four of us are to pick Bree up from her room."

I scoff. "Like a proper date?"

"This is a proper date—just a group date," Brody points out.

"I know it is. I'm sorry. I'm just up in my head." I shake my head, forcing myself to push away the thoughts of inadequacy. I know they chose me for *Heated* for a reason, and Bree seems to like me well enough. I just need to get out of my head and be myself. That's all I can do. After that, it's up to Bree.

Dalton's hand lands on my shoulder, squeezing. "The upside to group dates is there's always someone to take over if you need a minute."

Maverick sends a thumbs up my way. "You've got this Roman. She wants to get to know you better. That's why you're here tonight. So let her get to know you."

Then we're heading to Bree's suite. Maverick's the first one to arrive, knocking lightly. I think I hear a noise from behind the doors, but it's hard to tell with these damn soundproofed rooms. It takes a few minutes, but finally the door opens to reveal Bree.

My jaw drops as I scan her from head to toe. Her chestnut hair is down, flowing in loose waves over her shoulders. She's wearing make-up, but just enough to enhance her natural beauty—nothing like the previous day's makeup. I prefer her like this.

She's wearing another dress, but this one is much more casual. It's black and strapless, hugging her breasts before flowing down to the top of her hips. It tightens there before flaring out and ending at mid-thigh. She wears sandals that wrap up her calf, tying just below her knee.

"I think you could wear a trash bag and still take my breath away," I say as I continue to stare at her in awe.

Bree's head ducks as she flushes, but she watches me from beneath her eyelashes. "Thank you, Roman. You look wonderful—all of you do."

Brody steps forward and takes her hand before having her spin. I have to bite the inside of my cheek to keep from groaning as the skirt flares up, giving us peeks of her panties.

"You're the prettiest omega I've ever seen," Brody says before kissing her hand. He passes her to Dalton, who just stares down at her for a moment.

"Ravishin'. Gorgeous. Darlin', I can't think of a word to describe just how amazing you look right now." He ducks his head to kiss her before spinning her to Maverick.

Bree giggles as she lands against Maverick's chest. "A girl could get used to this."

"And she should." Maverick swoops in and kisses her. Then she's in my arms.

Do I kiss her? I've already told her how beautiful she is. Why has my mind just shut off?

Bree is smiling up at me. "Will you kiss me, Roman? You're the only one here I haven't kissed."

My eyes dart up to Brody, who just shrugs his shoulders, a smirk playing on his lips. I'll definitely be asking him about that later. I turn back to the omega in my arms and nod. "It would be my pleasure."

Bree splays her hands across my chest as she goes up on her tiptoes and I lean down to meet her lips. It's just a brush of my lips against hers, but it leaves me craving more.

"Well, now that we have that part of the evening out of the way," Brody says with a grin, offering his arm to Bree. "What are the plans for this group date?"

Bree's hands drop away from me as she slides her arm into Brody's and we head to the grand foyer. "We'll be eating on the back deck. We've got a surf and turf menu. Don't worry, Roman." She turns to look at me over her shoulder. "I know you don't eat meat, so they'll be making you some shish kabobs."

"Thank you." I return her smile, loving that she remembers I don't eat meat—something we'd discussed beside the pool earlier today. I would've been fine just having a salad, as it's what I usually do when I'm out with others, but that she thought about it and made arrangements for me? It warms my heart.

Brody and Bree lead the way through the living room and out onto the deck. Fairy lights brighten the area that's beginning to darken. The sun is dipping beneath the horizon, and I can't wait to see what it looks like once the sun is completely set.

"Roman, will you sit by me?" Bree's voice pulls me away from staring at the setting sun.

"Of course." I move over to her, pulling out a chair for her. Once she's settled, I drop into the seat beside her. Brody takes the seat at her other side. Dalton sits on Brody's other side while Maverick sits beside me.

"I don't know if the three of you eat seafood as I haven't seen your files. Tessa won't let me, no matter how hard I beg." She laughs. "But the kitchen has your preferences."

"I love me some seafood." Dalton grins, Maverick and Brody agreeing.

Bree turns to face me. "Do you mind if I ask you why you became a vegetarian?"

"Sure, it's nothing special. It's not because I'm opposed to eating meat. After I graduated from college, I spent a few years traveling all over Europe. They have so many meatless dishes and I felt better when I didn't eat meat. I tested the theory when I came back, going out for some barbeque. Honestly? It just didn't taste as good and it left me feeling heavy. So I started a vegetarian diet and haven't looked back since."

"But that's a good reason to become a vegetarian. I know some people have to give up meat and/or dairy because of health issues. Those are the ones I feel sorry for because most of them don't *want* to give it up." Bree glances around the table. "No one's getting me to give up meat. I should warn you now, don't take food from my plate. It makes me stabby."

"And you'll have a knife. Let's not test that, boys," I say with a grin.

We laugh, talking amongst ourselves. Each of us shares a little about ourselves and it's nice to learn something about the guys and Bree. After all, we're all in this together until Bree decides it's time for us to leave. We should get to know one another.

By the time the food comes out, we've all had a drink and have moved onto a second. Instead of daiquiris, Bree is drinking wine and I've joined her. It's a nice pinot noir. The others are having beers like the heathens they are.

"You were born and raised in California, weren't you?" I ask Bree.

She nods. "I was."

"Have you visited any of the vineyards? Like this one?" I nod towards the bottle we're drinking. It's a vineyard I've visited before, not too far north of LA.

"My grandparents actually owned a small vineyard. I visited often when I was a child." There's a faraway look in her eyes, and I can't help but wonder what she's thinking about.

"Not as an adult?"

She shakes her head. "No. It's my father's parents and since I don't speak with him, they stopped speaking with me."

"That's terrible." I take her hand in mine, squeezing it. "They're still your grandparents. They shouldn't take sides like that."

"His whole family is that way. So is my mom's. Now my beta dads? Their parents still adore me and understand why I keep a distance from my family. Once or twice a year we'll meet at one of their parents' houses and I'll get to see all of their families. It's nice, but also sucks that I can't just visit when I want. They actually live in San Diego—my parents, that is."

"They're so close. That must be hard."

"It used to be." Bree sighs. "But it's gotten easier and easier as the years have passed. My mom and father didn't even know about the troubles I've had with those alphas since I left home. My dads do, but they're not allowed to speak about me in the house. They're all supposed to act as if I don't exist."

Maverick leans forward, looking around me to see Bree. His brows are drawn, and I can practically taste his rage in the air. "Why do they stay? It doesn't sound like a happy life in your childhood home."

"I've asked. They say they love my mom. She's different with them than she is with me. To her, I'm just a disappointment. If I'd married young and had a slew of kids by now—which is what she expected of me—I'm sure she'd still find something to complain about. She's not what you'd call motherly."

Brody takes her other hand. "Unfortunately, not all women who have babies were meant to be mothers."

"Don't I know it." Bree scoffs. "Let's talk about something happier. Like that food."

Bree practically bounces in her chair as she points to the crew members currently bringing the food to the table. The kabobs they place before me look and smell divine. Glancing at Bree's plate, I see she and the others have a steak, lobster tail, and shrimp—which also smells amazing. I might not eat meat, but that doesn't mean I can't appreciate the smell.

A large bowl of salad, a bowl of corn, and a bowl of mashed potatoes sit in the center of the table and then the staff is gone before any of us can thank them.

"Y'all's staff is very efficient, darlin'," Dalton says with a grin. "Though I wish they'd hang around long enough for us to thank 'em."

"I'll be sure to pass along the compliment and the complaint to Tessa." Bree laughs before lifting a shrimp to her lips. She moans as she bites down on it. The sound is so sensual, my cock hardens.

Maverick laughs. "Be careful about those noises you're making, Bree. We might think you're hungry for something not on your plate."

Bree's eyes pop open, cheek flushing as she looks between us. "What do you mean?"

"He means you just moaned like you were when he was between your legs." Brody shrugs when I turn to him with furrowed brows. He is not the one I would've expected to hear say something like that. "And you did."

Bree laughs, taking a long drink of her wine. "I will attempt to keep my moans to myself? Obviously, I wasn't aware of the sounds coming from my mouth."

I just shake my head and reach for the potatoes and salad, heaping them on my plate. I'll have to come back for the corn later. The first bite of my kabobs has me moaning sinfully. I don't know what they did to these kabobs, but damn, they're good.

"If I'm not allowed to moan over the food, then neither are you."

We all laugh because it's only fair, but it's also hilarious.

We remain outside for about an hour after we've eaten when Bree turns to me. "What time is it?"

"Fifteen after eight."

"Damn," she curses. "We need to head inside. We're having an emergency rose ceremony."

I tilt my head, trying to figure out why we'd be having a rose ceremony on day two when she'd told us there wouldn't be another until the end of the week.

Bree sighs. "I've decided to send Wren and Wilder home. Even if he apologizes, I don't want an alpha like that as part of my pack. It's better we do this now than drag it out."

"That's smart." Maverick nods. "Should we head to the ballroom, then?"

"We're meeting there at nine, but I'd like a few moments with Roman, if you don't mind?"

Dalton's the first on his feet. "Of course, darlin'. Like I told you earlier, ask and you shall receive." He walks around the table, kissing her sweetly. Maverick and Brody follow suit while I try to figure out why she wants to speak with me. She doesn't want to send me home, does she?

I can't think of anything I'd done wrong. Is it my age? If it is, then why would she ask me on a date? Fuck. I'm not ready to go home.

"Are you alright, Roman?" Bree asks as she slides her chair out.

"Umm... I think so? I might be freaking out a bit about why you wanted to talk to me."

Bree laughs, a throaty sound that goes straight to my cock. "It's not anything bad, I promise. I just feel like I've been picking up on something from you. Are you uncomfortable being here?"

My first reaction is to tell her no. Instead, I take a moment to think about what she's really asking. "It's not the show. I actually love the concept and the guys are mostly nice. And you? Well, you're amazing."

"So what is it?"

I chew on my lip, wondering if I really want to admit it to her or not. "I'm just so much older than the other suitors. I've got thirty years on Brody, twenty on you. I just don't know why I'm here. I get Dominic was older, so obviously they wanted a variety of men. But why choose me when you could choose someone younger?"

"Age isn't even on my list of things to consider when choosing my pack. If it was, I'd probably be booting both Emmett and Brody. Not to mention Riley. They're all in their twenties. I've never dated someone younger than me before, but I've definitely dated men older than me. I once went out with a beta thirty years older than me." Bree laughs at whatever face I make. "What I'm trying to say is age doesn't matter to me. It's you, the person, that matters. It definitely doesn't hurt that you're hot as hell."

"What?" I sputter. "I'm not..."

"Oh, yes, you are. The first moment I saw you, I knew you were what people meant when they said silver fox." Bree leans forward, revealing a bit of cleavage that I can't help but glance down at. "Will you turn your chair for me, Roman?"

Confused, I do what she asks until I'm sitting facing her. Her palms land on my thighs, nails digging in slightly. "You might not think you're sexy, but trust me, I do. If I wasn't wearing my scent canceling panties, you'd know, too. Instead, why don't I show you?"

It's not until she's on her knees before me, small hands undoing my pants, that I realize what she was really saying. My hands land on hers, stopping her. "You don't have to do this, Bree."

"I know I don't *have* to. I don't have to do anything, but I want to suck your cock so bad. Will you let me?" Bree pouts for a moment before smirking. "Daddy?"

My cock jumps in my pants, and I know Bree noticed when her smile grows, looking almost predatory.

"You like that too? Good. Now, let me suck your cock, alpha."

There's a command to her voice that I wouldn't expect from an omega, but considering it's Bree, I'm not too surprised. She certainly has no problems voicing what she wants, and why the hell am I fighting this so hard? Of course, I want her mouth on my cock. I'm not an idiot.

Finally, I lift my hands from hers, moving to grab at the arms of the chair. Bree shoots me a triumphant grin before she makes quick work of undoing my pants and pulling my cock out.

"Oh, daddy," she whines, clenching her thighs together. "What a pretty cock you have."

Then she's licking a stripe up my length before she presses kitten licks all over the head of my cock, her eyes locked on mine the entire time. "You're so big and you taste so good."

She takes me into her mouth, bobbing up and down my length as her hands move to roll my balls between her fingers. As much as I enjoy watching her, I can't keep my head up as I let out a long, loud groan.

Bree pops off my cock after a few more bobs of her head and then she's licking and kissing up and down the sides. Her tongue traces a thick vein and it's taking everything in me to keep from shoving it back into her mouth and fucking her face.

"Mmmmm. Will you fuck my face?"

My head jerks up quickly, wondering for a moment if I'd spoken out loud.

Bree ducks her head bashfully. "You don't have to if you don't want to. I just prefer when my partner is in charge, taking what they want from me."

"Oh, sweet girl, you should be careful who you admit that to." Standing, I glance around until I see a seating area that has some pillows.

Bree whines when I step away. "Don't worry, sweet girl. I just want to make you as comfortable as I can."

I hurry over and grab a pillow, bringing it back and dropping it before her. "Kneel on this. It'll protect your knees."

She doesn't argue, just moves forward until she's kneeling on the pillow. Her hands sit on her thighs and she looks fucking gorgeous. Taking my cock in hand, I stroke along its length slowly. I'm not sure if Bree is conscious of it, but she's leaning towards me—practically begging to take my cock in her mouth.

I wrap my hand in her hair before bringing my cock to her lips, rubbing it over them for a moment. "Open for me, sweet girl."

Bree opens her mouth, sticking her tongue out. I run my cock head across her tongue, painting it with my precum. I have to bite back a groan at how hot she looks right now.

"If you need me to stop at any time, just tap my thigh, okay?" When she nods, I tut. "I need your words, sweet girl."

"Yes, alpha. I'll tap your thigh if I need you to stop. Now, fuck my face."

I don't have to be told twice as I slide my cock between her lips. I thrust shallowly at first, but I can see her twitching, fighting herself from trying to take control. If she wants more, I'll give her more.

On my next thrust, I hit the back of her throat. When I start to pull back out, she whines before forcing her head further down my cock. I slide down her throat, and then she swallows.

"Fuck, sweet girl. Your mouth is heaven." It's obvious that she either lacks a gag reflex, or that she's trained herself to not gag. "Do you want it rough?"

Her mouth is full of cock, but she still tries to use her words like I told her to. I ease back out and finally I can understand the word she'd been chanting over and over—just one simple word. "Yes."

Taking her at her word, I wrap both hands in her hair and fuck her face in earnest. I force my dick into her throat with each thrust. I'm not gentle with my thrusts or the way I'm pulling her hair. One would think with the orgasm I'd given myself that I'd be able to last longer this time around, but nope.

Bree truly makes me feel like a teenager again. I feel warmth building in my lower back, telling me I'm close. I look down to tell her when I realize her hips are shifting. I keep pounding into her mouth as I follow the line of her body to see that she has spread her legs until her knees have hit the ground again and she's rocking her pussy against the pillow for relief.

"You like this, don't you, sweet girl?" I ask, grinning when she nods frantically. "Good girl. I'm going to come and you're going to swallow it all down. Then I'm going to watch you ride that pillow until you come. Do you understand me?"

Bree whines around my cock, pulling me that much closer to the edge.

"Fuck, yes." My head falls back, hips moving in quick, short bursts until I'm coming in her mouth. I make sure not to touch my knot, not wanting to drown her in my cum—at least not tonight.

My hips roll forward as I ride out the orgasm before pulling my cock free. Bree swallows, and I smile again. "Let me see, sweet girl."

Bree's mouth drops open and I see that she's swallowed it all.

"What a good girl. Now, I want you to get yourself off with that pillow. You want that, don't you?"

"Yes, alpha," she cries, hips already moving. She lifts on her knees for a moment, making the pillow more compact before she's riding it again. It's honestly one of the hottest things I've ever seen.

Bree's hands move up to her breasts, squeezing and pinching her nipples through the dress, her hips never losing their rapid rhythm. Less than a minute later, she's moaning out my name as she comes.

I tuck away my cock before dropping to my knees before her. "You're such a good girl," I tell her as I push back the damp hair from her face.

"Would you like a taste, alpha?" Before I can process what she's asking me, she reaches between her legs and then lifts her soaked fingers to my lips.

I open my mouth, tongue running the length of her finger before growling and sucking them into my mouth. "That's the best damn thing I've ever tasted, omega," I purr.

Bree collapses forward, leaning her head on my chest. I continue to purr for her, loving how she relaxes into my arms. A few minutes later, she pulls back with sleepy eyes. "As much as I'd like to stay right here with you, I'm going to need to change my panties before the ceremony."

I throw back my head, laughing. I climb to my feet, helping her up. I lean down to press a simple kiss to her lips, but her tongue darts out and I allow her to deepen it. It makes me realize that her tongue had been on my cock before it had been in my mouth.

Finally, she breaks the kiss with a sigh. "I hope that showed you I want you around, and that you're not too old."

"Thank you, Bree."

She snorts. "Did you just thank me for a blowjob?"

"Kind of. In a roundabout way, I guess." I shrug. "But that's not what I meant. Thank you for noticing that I was uncomfortable and asking about it. I'm not always good at talking about what I'm feeling."

"It was my pleasure." She pauses. "And yours."

Shaking my head, I press my lips to her forehead. "You better get inside and change those panties. Don't want to be late for the ceremony."

She nods, turning to hurry inside. My hand comes down on her ass as she passes me and she lets out a squeak. She turns to me with narrowed eyes. "Don't start something we don't have time to finish, alpha."

Before I can form a response, she's darting inside, leaving me to stare after her. Bree is going to be a handful, that's for sure. But I'm no longer worried about how my age will factor into her decision. Could that be because she'd just given me the best blowjob I've had in fifty-two years? Maybe, but I'm alright with that.

Chapter Sixteen

Bree

I'm grinning from ear to ear as I hurry back to my suite, barely believing what had just gone down. I'd enjoyed the group date, but I could tell something was bothering Roman. I'm glad I decided to ask him about it because while I understood his worries, our difference in ages doesn't bother me.

Which is a little funny considering the gap between me and Brody is a much smaller gap, and I'm still having issues accepting that it's okay for me to date someone ten years my junior. Intellectually, I know that it's society that has deemed it unacceptable for women—no matter their designation—to date men younger than they are. It's a carryover from the time before our world changed so drastically—before there were alphas, betas, or omegas. It's a stigma that I've never thought about much, but one I'm having more trouble overcoming than I thought I would.

But Roman? Reginald was right in calling him daddy—he embodies daddy energy. I'm definitely not against calling him daddy, and it turned me on. It's definitely something to be explored.

I can't believe that I gave him a blowjob right there on the deck with the cameras recording and where anyone passing through the living room could have seen. And then humping a pillow to get off? I'm turning into a very horny omega, and I'm not sure if it's because I'm finally allowing my omega side to the forefront or if it's being around this many alphas, but I'm definitely not complaining.

I quickly change into new panties, knowing that Tessa will be here any minute to bring me to the ballroom. Not even a minute after I've tossed my soaked panties into the hamper, there's a knock on my door. When I open the door, Tessa is standing there with a knowing grin on her face.

"It seems your date went well."

"There will be no slut-shaming in my suite." There's no heat to my words because I know Tessa is over the moon for me. But we wouldn't be friends if we didn't mess with one another.

Tessa steps into my sitting room, shutting the door behind her. She gestures for me to follow her to the couch. Once we're both settled, her face turns serious. "I just want to make sure you're one hundred percent sure about the ceremony tonight?"

"I am. There's no reason for me to drag it out and get anyone's hopes up. Wren isn't the alpha for me, so it's time for him and Wilder to go home." I glance down at my clenched hands. "The suitors need to realize when I say something, I'm serious. I won't have this kind of behavior in my pack, so I won't allow it in my suitors. It's best that they all know that now."

"I'm not questioning your decision, Bree." Tessa grabs my hands, uncurling them until she can link our fingers together. "I want you to make decisions that make you happy. I know you didn't want to send anyone home in the first week, and now you're going to have sent seven people home in the first two days."

I shrug. "Maybe that was unfair of me to assume. Planning *Heated* and being on *Heated* are two very different things. I didn't realize how hard it would be. You picked out some unfairly attractive men for me to choose from. I'm physically attracted to every single one of them, but choosing a pack isn't just about attractiveness. This is forever, so I need to follow my gut when making these decisions."

"I'm proud of you." Tessa pulls me in for a hug and I melt against her. Though I act like a hardass most times, I'm a sucker for a good hug or cuddle.

"Thanks, I guess? But why?"

"You're letting your omega side help you choose what you both need for your pack. You've had to suppress your omega time and time again, and it's nice to see you so in sync with that part of yourself."

I say nothing as I burrow further into her. Best friend cuddles are always needed and appreciated.

"If you'd like to talk about what went down with Roman, I'm totally here for it—I mean, you. I'm totally here for you."

My hand slaps down on her back and she lets out a less than ladylike groan as she pushes me away from her. But she's grinning at me when she says, "Brat. I don't know why I put up with you."

"Because you love me. Duh."

Tessa wrinkles her nose. "I guess." She hesitates for a moment. "You seem happy, Bree, and that's all I've ever wanted for you. After everything you've been through, I didn't know if this would be too much for you. I'm glad it's not and I can't wait to see who you choose for your pack."

Tears prickle behind my eyes and I jump up from the couch, waving my hands in front of my eyes. "Nope. I will not cry before the ceremony. No more mushy talk."

"We should probably get to the ballroom, anyway."

I take a deep breath, letting my eyes fall closed for a moment as I try to center myself. I don't know if the rose ceremonies will become easier as time passes, but I'm not a fan of them right now—that much I can tell you.

"Alright, I'm ready. Let's do this."

The two of us head for the ballroom to find Reginald waiting for us. "The suitors are understandably confused that there's another rose ceremony when you said there wouldn't be another until the end of the first week. Me and the crew have just been ignoring their questions, telling them you would explain."

"Thank you, Reginald."

Reginald and I walk in side by side when Tessa opens the door for us. The room falls silent as we make our way to the stage. Reginald helps me up the stairs and we move to the center of the stage to the table that holds only one vase this time. There are fifteen roses: two black, two lavender, and eleven yellow.

"I'm sure all of you are wondering why we're hosting another rose ceremony when you were told there wouldn't be another for a week. With it only being day two, I can understand the confusion." Reginald straightens his jacket as he speaks not only to the suitors, but to the cameras. "Bree decided that this ceremony couldn't wait until the end of the week. Bree?"

"Thank you, as always, Reginald. I didn't want to hold another ceremony today, but I needed to. I won't keep anyone here that doesn't have a chance at being a part of my future pack." I grab the fifteen roses from the vase and make my way to the suitors. "There are some things I just won't let stand. Lying is one of those. Being cruel to the other suitors is another."

I pluck the two black roses from the bundle and move to stand in front of Wren and Wilder. "I also won't draw this out. Wren, you acted inappropriately towards Riley and Carter. Then you refused to admit that you were in the wrong and apologize. Wilder, I'm sorry. I know I told you that you could have until the morning, but I realized that even if Wren apologized, I don't want him in my pack. As the two of you are part of an unbonded pack, that means if one of you goes, both of you go."

"This is bullshit," Wren roars, knocking the rose from my hand when I try to offer it to him, and I can't stop myself from flinching. "I'm being punished for saying what we were all thinking." He gestures to him and the other suitors. "I did nothing wrong."

I sense security shuffling behind me, ready to end this. "This is why you're going home. You've proven to be stubborn to a fault. I don't want someone who won't listen to what I'm saying and consider my thoughts and feelings. You're not the alpha for me."

Without another word, I turn my attention to Wilder. "I'm sorry to have to say goodbye to you." I hand him the black rose, rising to my tiptoes so I can press a kiss to his cheek.

Wilder purses his lips and tries to force a smile, but it's obvious that he's pissed—whether that's at me, Wren, or himself, I can't say. "I don't blame you for sending us home. If I were in your shoes, I would've too. It sucks, but I'm glad you're advocating for yourself and refusing to accept anyone that could end up hurting you."

He turns his gaze to Wren, eyes flashing with ire. "Bree is correct. You acted unacceptably. I've never seen you act this way before and I don't like it. This is not my friend and pack mate." Facing me once more, he asks, "Would it be okay if I go now?"

I want to say yes, but that's not really my call. I turn to find Tessa and she gives me a small nod of agreement. "Of course, Wilder. Thank you for taking this as well as you have. Wren, if you'd like to be excused now, you can go too."

Wren snarls in my face before slamming into my shoulder and knocking me off balance as he storms from the room. Snarls and growls fill the room, but I'm not sure who they're coming from. The roses I'm holding go flying in the air and my arms pinwheel as I try to catch my balance. I already know it's a lost cause and I'm going to hit the floor, but strong arms wrap around me and haul me back to my feet.

"Are you alright, darlin'?"

I force a smile as I turn my attention to Dalton, nodding once. "I'll be fine. Thank you for the save."

"Any time." Dalton grins, making sure that I'm steady on my feet before releasing me and stepping back.

"I'm sorry," Wilder whispers as he hands me the roses that he's obviously picked up for me. Turning his attention to the suitors, he smiles grimly. "Take care of her. She only deserves the best, so be the best."

And with that, he hurries from the room, leaving me nearly in tears at his words. "Well, that didn't go quite as I expected." My voice is shaky with unshed tears, but I refuse to cry over Wren's behavior. He's obviously used to getting his way and is throwing a tantrum because I stood up to him—as bullies usually do. I'm glad he's gone. I'm just sorry that Wilder got taken down with him.

"As you can see, I have a lot of yellow roses and just two lavender roses. I'll be having a group date with two lucky suitors tomorrow." I decide to just hand out the roses to those in front of me before moving to the other groups.

Yellow roses go to Dalton, Finnegan, Brody, and Emmett. Then it's Riley's and Carter's turn. "I know things have been a struggle for the two of you because of the mating bond riding you, so I'd like to have a date with just the three of us. I think it'll be a good chance to get to know both of you better."

I offer the first lavender rose to Carter before handing the second to Riley.

"Thank you, Bree, for being so understanding," Carter says with a smile while his alpha remains silent. He lets out an exasperated sigh before continuing, "Riley is grateful too, he's just an asshole."

I snort, though I try to cover it with a cough. I must not do a good job as Carter's eyes glimmer with stifled laughter. Moving on, I hand out the rest of the yellow roses before moving back to the stage.

Reginald clears his throat. "I want to make it clear that violence is not acceptable on *Heated*—especially when it's directed towards an omega. Physical altercations between the suitors won't result in immediate departure, but it won't help your case any. But if *any* of you are violent towards Bree—intentional or not—you won't wait until the rose ceremony to be sent home. You will be immediately escorted off the property.

"With that being said, we appreciate you for joining us for this unscheduled rose ceremony. With any luck, there won't be any other unscheduled ceremonies before the week is up. Have a great night, gentlemen."

Reginald steps in front of me, his back to the suitors, and Tessa rushes up the steps to join us. "Are you okay, Bree?"

"I can't believe that happened. I'm so sorry, Bree. There was no record of Wren being a violent person. This is totally on me."

I place a hand on both of their arms. "I'm fine. The worst that could've happened was I busted my ass, but Dalton saved me from a bruised tailbone. Tessa, this isn't your fault. I never would've guessed Wren would react this way. Hell, Wilder was shocked at his behavior. There's no way you could've predicted this."

A throat clears, pulling my attention from my friends. I find Emmett standing at the bottom of the steps. "Yes, Emmett?"

"We were all worried about you and wanted to make sure you were okay."

I glance up to find the suitors grouped together, their eyes flashing from me to Emmett and back again. A smile lights up my face at their concern. "I'm fine, Emmett. I promise. I would appreciate you letting the others know. Tessa and Reginald are going to walk me to my suite, and then I'm going to get a good night's sleep. I'll see all of you tomorrow at breakfast."

Emmett returns my smile before hurrying back to the others.

"Walk me to my suite, friends?" I tilt my head, staring at both of them when they don't answer right away.

"Of course!" Tessa's response is way too upbeat, telling me she's still worried and beating herself up. Nothing I say will make her believe otherwise. Like me, she can be a bit stubborn, so I don't try to placate her any further as the three of us head toward my suite.

I tell them both goodnight before shutting the door. Now that I'm alone, I allow myself to fall apart. Tears spill down my cheeks as my body shakes, the adrenaline rushes away, leaving me feeling empty. I hadn't lied to everyone exactly. I will be fine, but I also knew I needed to be alone to let myself fall apart.

Wren had scared me, but I'd been able to hide that. I would never let another alpha think I fear them, and I was able to keep my fear under lock and key until I was alone. Could I have admitted to everyone that I wasn't okay? Absolutely, but what would that have helped?

It would have made Tessa beat herself up even worse than she already is. She'd probably have assigned a member of security to be with me at all times, which is not something I want. Reginald would've insisted that he pamper me, something I neither want nor need. As for the suitors, I didn't want to show them my weakness.

Not that I believe any of them would've used it against me, but Wren's behavior has made it abundantly clear that there's no way to really know someone after two days. I couldn't chance it.

I drag myself through the sitting room, bedroom, and into the massive closet. Pushing aside the clothes on the far wall, I run my hand blindly down the wall until I find the thumb scanner. Within seconds, the door to my nest is opening and I fall inside.

I shuffle around until I find the switch for the fairy lights before closing the door. I'd spent a week making sure my nest had everything I could need. This is where I'll spend my heat in less than eight weeks. When I choose someone to be a part of my pack, it's here that they'll mark me. Where I'll mark them.

Curling up around a body pillow, I pull a few blankets around me, building a small wall before I pull another over me. The padded flooring of the nest feels like heaven against my tense muscles. A few deep breaths and I feel my body relaxed.

My nest is my happy place.

With that thought, I succumb to sleep.

Emmett

"I don't think she's as okay as she's trying to get us to believe," I tell Gabriel as we make our way up the stairs to our floor. "I think she's freaking out, but doesn't want us to know that."

"What makes you say that?" he asks, frowning. I don't know if he believes me or not, but I appreciate that he's willing to listen to what I have to say.

"I know you don't know what it's like to be a beta, obviously, but one of the things we're good at is sensing what people are feeling. Just a glimpse. I think it's because we're meant to be the caretakers." I shake my head. "Something was just off about her energy."

Gabriel is quiet for a moment. "Maybe she's just feeling a little overwhelmed?"

"Are you talking about Bree?" Brody's head suddenly pops up between me and Gabriel.

I nod. "You sensed it too, didn't you?"

"Yeah, something was definitely off. If she'd just been tense, I would agree with Gabriel, but it's more than that. Her hand was shaking when she handed out the roses. It wasn't much, but it was enough for me to notice."

We make it to the second floor and step into the living room, where the other suitors have gathered. Everyone is murmuring amongst themselves. I know everyone is freaking out over what happened with Wren. I know I never expected him to react that way. I sensed nothing violent about him. We can only guess what caused his reaction, as there will be no answers coming our way now that he's gone.

I'm glad he's gone.

Brody sighs. "Knowing that something is off doesn't mean we can bother her, though. If she was hiding it from everyone, then she obviously didn't want to lean on any of us."

"True. She has only known us for two days. Of course, she isn't ready to let us in yet. But I hate that she felt the need to hide it not just from us, but from her friends."

Someone's hand comes down on my shoulder, startling me. Turning, I find Onyx with a sad smile on his beautiful face. "I overheard your conversation. You need to remember, Bree is used to pushing down her omega side, so she doesn't appear weak to her business associates. That isn't an easy habit to break. Not to mention, if we didn't see Wren being the type to react this way, then neither did she. She's hurt and probably doubting her judgment."

"You might not say a lot, but you're always paying attention, aren't you?" I ask him.

He nods. "I speak when I have something to say. You'll learn, beta." He runs a hand down my cheek, my eyes falling shut of their own accord as I fight back a shiver. "It's okay to worry about Bree, but don't let it eat you up inside. She will learn to trust us, of that I have no doubt."

Onyx brushes his thumb over my lip as he nods to the other two men, and then he's walking away. I just gape after him, wondering what the hell just happened.

"I'm not even into men, but that was hot." Brody laughs.

"I *am* into men, and that was really fucking hot." Gabriel moves to my side to stare down at me. "You alright, Emmett?"

I blink up at him for a moment before grinning. "Hell, yes, I'm alright. There's just too many hot men here. You're all a little overwhelming at times."

Gabriel grins down at me before the three of us burst into laughter. I know I won't be able to just forget about Bree and the pain she's going through, but it's nice to enjoy the company of the other suitors. We might not be doing anything special, but we're all together.

Technically, we should view one another as competitors, but I'm glad we're not. I'm glad we're all forming a kind of brotherhood as we all try our hardest to win over Bree's heart. Who knows how big of a pack she'll decide on? I don't think she'll choose all thirteen of us, but technically she could. That's a lot of dicks and a whole lot of alpha energy, but that's her prerogative.

I wasn't sure what it would be like being on *Heated* since I had nothing to base my opinions on, but I'm finding that I enjoy spending time with both the suitors and Bree. Obviously, I'm outgoing, and I've never had a problem making friends. But this is so different. We're all here for one reason—to try to win a place in Bree's pack.

But I've already found new friendships that I'd like to continue once we leave here, whether I'm chosen for the pack or not. Looking at Gabriel from the corner of my eyes, I let my eyes roam around the room until I find Onyx, Maddox, and Hudson, realizing that I might have found even more than that. Making romantic connections amongst the other suitors might be a bad idea, but I can't make myself believe that right now.

I'll just keep playing it by ear and hope that Bree is the right omega for me, and that I'm the right beta for her.

Chapter Seventeen

Bree

After spending the night in my nest, I feel much better. A night away from the cameras, surrounded by my favorite things, is exactly what I needed. I'm sure Tessa checked the cameras after I didn't want her or Reginald staying with me and she would have seen I'd spent the night in my nest. Depending on her mood, she might or might not mention it when she sees me next.

One of the hardest things about being an omega is how overwhelming everything can be. I feel everything intensely, which I don't think is a bad thing. It does mean I often feel overwhelmed, but I've learned over the years to bury it down deep until I'm alone. I'm well aware it's not the best of coping mechanisms, but sometimes we just have to do what we have to do to get by.

Though, I'm hopeful I won't need to do this for much longer. Soon, I will have a pack I can rely on. I may not be used to relying on others besides Tessa and occasionally Reginald, but I want to. I want to choose a pack I can rely on, who will make me feel safe with them at all times. It's the omega dream, isn't it?

My dream differs from many omegas, because I can't always rely on my pack. I have a business to run, which is something my pack will need to understand. That's the entire point of *Heated*—to find packs for omegas who don't just want to pop out babies and run the household. I don't know how it'll work once I have babies, but I hope that my pack and I will work it out so I can keep working.

Opening the door to my nest, I'm surprised to find Tessa sitting inside my closet. My eyes narrow as I take her in. "How long have you been there?"

Tessa gives me a tired smile as she shrugs, telling me she's probably been there most of the night. "I wanted to be here in case you needed me."

"Stubborn ass alpha." I shake my head as I make my way out of my nest and move across the room to sit next to her.

She drops her head to my shoulder with a sigh. "I knew you weren't okay, so I made sure I was available in case you ended up needing me. It's what besties do."

"Yeah, yeah, yeah." I lean my head against hers. "That's also what leads to exhaustion."

"Shut up, brat, and just thank me." Tessa grabs my hand in hers. "Are you doing better this morning? Did a night in your nest help?"

"It did. A lot, actually. I was just having a few moments of self doubt and was feeling overwhelmed. There's been a lot of changes for me in just a few days. Not to mention Wren turned out to be so different from the man I thought I was getting to know." I let out a deep sigh. "It makes me wonder if any of the other suitors are hiding their true self from me."

"Don't worry," I cut her off when she opens her mouth to argue with me. "I'm not thinking that anymore. Like I said, self doubts and being overwhelmed. I don't feel that way this morning."

"In that case, get dressed before you're late for breakfast." Tessa climbs to her feet before helping me stand. "We have your date all set up for this afternoon."

I nod. "Good. I'm hoping that getting away from everyone will help Riley. If not, then this just might not be their time. Will you let the suitors know I'll be a few minutes late for breakfast? I need a shower. I'm sure I smell like stressed out omega."

"Well, now that you mention it..." Tessa wrinkles her nose as she takes a deep whiff of my scent. "You're smelling a little burnt."

I grab the closest thing at hand, a tennis shoe, and start after Tessa as she tries to hightail it from the closet. It's too much effort to catch up to her, so I launch the shoe and it bounces off her ass.

Tessa lets out a yelp, coming to a stop and rubbing a hand over her cheek the shoe had hit. "That hurt, brat."

"That's what you get for being a brat. Go get some coffee so you don't come off as a complete hardass to the suitors. And don't forget to tell them I'm going to be late."

"I am a hardass," I hear her grumble just before I shut the bathroom door, already stripping as I make my way over to the shower.

I won't let yesterday's doubts become a problem today. I get to eat breakfast with all the suitors before setting off for my date with Riley and Carter. Then we'll come back and hang out with the rest of the suitors.

I love that we made the first week a fairly stress-free week. It's just about getting to know the suitors. I plan to have a group date each day for the rest of the week. On the day of the rose ceremony, I'll spend the day with all the suitors before making some decisions. I can only hope that's enough time to get to know them better than I do right now. I still have seven and a half weeks, but I know it'll be easier if I can narrow the field some.

While I want a bigger pack, I don't have a need for thirteen men in my pack. I'm not sure how many I'll choose, I won't know that until later in the show.

Stepping under the water, I feel the tension slide off me while excitement takes its place. Yes, I had a mini breakdown last night, but I'm excited about this. It's an unconventional way to choose one's pack, but that's why I love it.

Carter

Riley and I sit in the living room on the first floor, waiting for our date with Bree. Tension and worry radiate off Riley as he sits on the couch with his leg bouncing faster and faster the longer we sit there. He's making it hard for me to keep calm as I push up against him, placing my hand on his knee.

"It's going to be alright, Riley. You need to chill."

"How can you be so sure?" he asks as he turns to meet my eyes.

"Because it's just going to be me, you, and a beautiful omega. No alphas that'll feel like threats. Just the three of us enjoying... whatever Bree came up with for our group date."

Riley grumbles under his breath. "I don't know why she couldn't have just told us what we were going to be doing. What if we're dressed wrong?"

I try to fight back my laughter, but my body is already shaking with it. It's kind of cute how worried he is about this date.

"She told us to dress casually and to plan on being outside. Shorts and a shirt are the right option." I reach over, fixing the collar of his polo shirt. The two of us aren't much for t-shirts, polos being much more our speed. I think it's because we spend so much time in suits, and therefore, collared shirts. It feels weird to not wear a shirt with a collar.

"Gentlemen, are you ready?"

I turn around to find Bree standing there in a pair of shorts that leave little to the imagination. The tank top she wears is two sizes too big, leaving the arm holes open halfway down her side, revealing the sides of her bra. She's tied it at her hip and when she moves, a sliver of stomach peeks out.

She's just as gorgeous now as she was the first time I saw her, dressed to the nines. Honestly, she takes my breath away. A glance at Riley finds my alpha gaping at Bree, and I can't help but smile.

"You look amazing, Bree," I tell her as I stand, offering my hand to Riley. My alpha doesn't even notice as he continues to stare at her. Letting a huff that's half annoyance and half amusement, I flick his ear.

"What the hell, Carter?" Riley's brow is drawn as he turns to me with a smile.

"I believe Bree is ready to go and all you are doing is sitting on the couch, gaping at her. I had to get your attention somehow."

Riley climbs to his feet, stepping into my space. He leans in close, speaking only loud enough that I can hear him. "Don't think you won't be punished for that, beta."

A shiver rocks me from head to toe as Riley grabs my hand and drags me toward Bree, who is watching us in amusement. "I don't know what he just said to you, nor do I want to know, but it must've been something good."

"Uhhh... yep." I nod my head frantically, trying to get my brain back online.

Bree laughs. "I'm glad I'm getting to spend time with just the two of you. Come on."

"Are you going to tell us where we're going and what we're going to be doing?" Riley asks as he trails her, still dragging me along.

"Obviously, I'm taking you off to the middle of nowhere so I can kill you and bathe in your blood."

I freeze, blinking at her as I try to process her words as I frown. "Wait. What?"

Bree laughs as she heads out the front door. "I guess you'll have to trust me and see when we get there."

Riley's looking at me with a raised eyebrow. "Is it bad that I'm a little turned on by that?"

"Fates above, Riley." Ignoring his words, I drag him down the steps to the golf cart Bree is climbing inside. "Do you want to sit in the front or..."

"You can both sit in the back row. You'll still be able to see where we're going and Riley doesn't have to worry about you not being within arm's reach." Bree inclines her head to the row behind her.

"Don't you want one of us to sit with you?" I'm confused. I don't know many omegas but most of them want to be the center of attention. Yet, here's Bree, willingly putting both mine and my alpha's needs above hers. "You're perfect, aren't you?"

Bree snorts. "Not even close. I just want to make sure that you're both comfortable before our date. I want us to relax and enjoy our time together, not have Riley snarling the entire time."

Riley laughs and I can already tell how much more at ease he is with Bree now that we're away from the other alphas. "You should know that I'm usually a snarling asshole, even without mating bonds."

"It's true. You'll see." I climb into the second row and slide over until I'm behind Bree. She turns to look at us as Riley climbs in beside me.

"I'm used to assholes," she says with a shrug. "We'll see if your kind of asshole is the kind I can put up with long-term. Now, hold on."

That's all the warning we get before she floors it and the golf cart bounces across the grass. I grab hold of the bar next to my head with one hand and cling to Riley with the other. This cart goes much faster than any other I've been on before.

Bree swings the cart around and I see the cottages where the crew is staying. She flies past them and keeps going towards what looks like a whole lot of nothing. Maybe she really is taking us out to the middle of nowhere to kill us, I think with a laugh. She seems to know where she's going, so I relax into the seat as best I can with as bumpy as the ride is.

After about ten minutes, I see something in the distance that looks like a body of water, maybe? Five minutes later, it's confirmed as we come to a stop beside a small pond.

"I never would've guessed this was out here," I murmur as I climb from the cart with Riley right behind me.

"No one knows it's here except me, Tessa, and a handful of crew members," she gestures to the cameramen climbing from another golf cart that I realize must've been following us—not that I ever noticed, "and now the two of you. We put in the pond—though I wanted a lake, but Tessa vetoed me. We put it here because there's a hot spring on the other side."

I follow the direction she's pointing, noticing rocks around another water source. It looks like there are a few separate hot spring pools and even though it's already seventy degrees outside, a dip sounds amazing. You have to love California in wintertime, and we're in the desert at that.

Bree moves around to the cart, pulling up the backwards facing third row. She reaches inside and starts pulling things from it. I hurry over and reach in to help her.

"You know, you could just ask and we'd be happy to help you," I tell her, a bit of admonishment in my tone. "You don't have to do everything on your own."

Bree practically glows as she grins up at me. "Thank you, Carter, and I'll try to remember that."

Riley ambles over and starts picking up the things we're pulling from the cart. He loops the picnic basket over his arm before reaching down to pick up the heavy cooler. I grab the backpack and a handful of blankets, leaving Bree to get the pillows.

"Follow me, boys. We're going to set up near the hot springs."

Riley and I fall into step behind her and I can't help the way my eyes immediately zero in on her plump ass as her hips sashay from side to side. I'm definitely an ass man, and damn, does she have a nice one.

Bree giggles and my eyes snap up to find her grinning at me. "Enjoying the view?"

"Immensely." Riley is the one to answer, a growl to the word.

"Next time, the two of you can lead the way then so I can get a nice view too." Bree faces forward again and if I'm not mistaken, she adds more sway to her hips. I bite down on my cheek, trying to fight back the groan that wants to fall from my lips.

"If she keeps this up, I'm going to have to spank that luscious ass." Riley speaks loudly enough that I know Bree heard him. She stumbles for a moment before glaring at him.

"Spankings aren't a punishment for me." Then she's facing forward, marching on and leaving the two of us to gape after her.

I snicker as I turn to Riley. "Not the response you were expecting, was it?"

"I don't think Bree is anything like what I was expecting in general." He shakes his head. "C'mon, I don't want to miss out on any part of this date."

By the time we catch up with Bree, she's standing beside the pond, tapping her foot. "Took you long enough. Trade me, Carter? I need to set up the blankets."

Riley sets the cooler and picnic basket down and takes the pillows from Bree instead. She just shrugs, reaching for the pile of blankets. She lays the largest on the ground first and then sets to work on arranging the others while Riley and I just sit and watch. It's too much like she's building a nest and everyone knows you don't mess with an omega when they're nesting.

"Pillows." Her hand juts out, waving around impatiently until I hand them to her one at a time. She takes a few more minutes to arrange them before sitting back with a satisfied smile. "Perfect."

Turning back to us, she gestures for me to join her. "Riley, will you please put the cooler on the corner of the blanket over there so it's easy for us to reach? And bring the picnic basket in with you?"

"Of course, omega." There's a purr to his voice that's unlike any sound I've ever heard him make. Is that his alpha purr? Damn.

I settle on the blanket beside Bree, handing her the backpack when she holds her hands out for it. "We're having a picnic then?"

"We are. I figured we could eat lunch and get to know one another better. Then we can go for a dip in the pond or hot springs."

"You didn't tell us to bring swimsuits, Bree." There's a warning tone to Riley's words as he settles behind me, his muscular legs straddling my body. One of his legs brush against Bree's and she lays her hand on it as she turns to face him.

"Who said anything about swimsuits?" She flutters her eyelashes at him, the picture of innocence at odds with her words.

Riley shakes his head slowly. "You're a very, very bad girl, aren't you?"

"Sometimes." She's smirking as she turns back to the backpack, pulling out things at random. "I brought sunscreen and some snacks for later."

"What else do you have in there?" I ask as I lean over to sneak a peek.

She snaps it closed and shakes her head at me. "No sneaky peeks."

I laugh, holding up my hands in surrender as she zips it closed after placing various bottles of sunscreen on the blankets beside us. "Am I at least allowed to see what we're having for lunch?"

"I guess."

Riley pops the lid and groans as he checks out the contents. I lean over to pull things from the basket. There's sausage rolls, breads, cheeses, olives, salads, sliced fruits, deviled eggs, and all the makings for sandwiches.

As I lay it all out, I laugh. "How many people were you planning to feed?"

"I may have gone a little overboard. I didn't know what you'd want, so I brought a little of everything," she says with a shrug. "It's better to have too much than not enough. In the cooler there's water, tea, soda, beer, and I might have had Emmett make me some banana daiquiri before we left."

"Is that what you'd like?" I ask her as I stand. I grin when she nods before turning to my alpha. "Riley, what would you like?"

"Dunno. Just grab me something."

I bite back my initial urge to roll my eyes. Whatever I choose will not be what he wants. I hate it when he does this. If I bring one of everything, he'll say I'm being wasteful. I love the man, but sometimes he drives me crazy.

I lift the lid to the cooler and find way more drinks than we need. I shake my head as I pull out a bottle of daiquiri, a beer, a water, and a soda. Whichever he doesn't want, I'll drink. I sit down between Bree and Riley, handing her the daiquiri before holding up the options to Riley.

"No tea?" he asks, eyebrows raised.

I set the drinks down so I can get back up to get him his tea, but Bree's hand slams down on my knee as she shakes her head before facing Riley.

"No, sir. Carter asked you what you wanted, and you said whatever. He was nice enough to bring back options for you. If you knew you wanted tea, then you should've asked for it. He was nicer than I would've been. I wouldn't have brought you back a damn thing. If you want tea, get it your damn self." Bree is livid. "Carter might be your beta, but he isn't your servant or your slave."

"Carter doesn't mind," Riley starts, but trails off at the look on her face.

"You think Carter doesn't mind, but have you bothered asking him? I'm sure you have, of course. Because you want to take care of your beta, right?"

Riley's eyes blaze with annoyance as he turns to look at me. I don't know what he sees on my face, but his face falls instantly. "I'm sorry, Carter. I just..."

"You're a spoiled brat who was raised to have everyone wait on you hand and foot?" Bree cocks an eyebrow at Riley, daring him to dispute her words. "You're a bonded alpha now. You need to grow up. This isn't how the world works and if you think it is, you're in for a rude awakening."

Bree climbs to her feet. "I need to walk off this annoyance. Don't follow me. I'll be back in a few minutes." With that, she sets off back the way we came, practically speed walking around the edge of the pond.

"That went well." I swipe a hand down my face. We haven't even been here twenty minutes and Riley has already set her off. This date isn't off to the best start. Maybe Riley isn't ready for an omega. After all, he's only twenty-four, and he's lived a pampered life. As much as I've tried, I'm not sure I've been able to convince him that his world isn't the world the rest of us live in.

"Which drink did you want, Carter? I'll put back the others." Riley kneels in front of me. "I'm sorry. I never stopped to think about what I was doing. Bree is right. I've been a bad alpha."

"You haven't. You're just... a pampered alpha. I'm the one who never said anything. I don't mind getting you drinks, but I hate it when you say grab whatever and it's never what you seem to want."

Riley nods. "I'll be better about telling you what I want. Now, which drink did you want?"

"Leave the water and the beer. I need a damn drink after this disastrous beginning to our date."

Riley doesn't say anything, just cracks open the beer and hands it to me. He grabs the soda from the blanket and walks over to the cooler, coming back with a beer and a tea. When I frown at him, he just shrugs. "A beer seemed like a good idea."

Neither of us speaks as we wait for Bree to return. We don't touch the food, even though my stomach keeps growling. Bree loops around the pond two or three times before coming to a stop beside the blankets.

"Are you done being a dick, Riley?"

Riley snorts. "I'm not sure that I'm ever done being a dick, but I am sorry for the way I acted."

Bree nods, not saying anything as she settles back on the blanket, though further from us than she'd been previously. "You didn't eat?"

"We were waiting for you. It didn't seem fair to start without you," I tell her.

"That's sweet. Let's eat, finish our drinks, and forget about what happened earlier. I intend to enjoy this date and I'd rather do that with the two of you, but I'll do it on my own if I have to." She piles food on her plate before glancing between us. "Get some food. There's plenty."

Riley and I share a look before we do what she asked. We chat a bit about ourselves as we eat, but it's only surface level shit. I feel like Bree is pulling away even after she said she wanted to forget the first part of the date, and I hate it.

"I'm a little hot," Bree says as she pulls her shirt up and over her head after she's finished eating. I lick my lips at her boobs, barely contained by her bra. I want to get my mouth on her. "Who wants to join me for a dip in the pond?"

My shirt is off before she finishes standing. I strip down to my boxer briefs as she wiggles out of her shorts to reveal a tiny pair of panties that match her bra. It's not until I'm taking her hand in mine that I realize Riley hasn't moved an inch.

"Riley?"

He gives me a half smile. "The two of you go ahead without me. But make sure to put on some sunscreen. We've been out here long enough without it."

I roll my eyes because the chances of me getting sunburned are slim to none—one of the advantages of my dark skin color. Bree, on the other hand, needs all the sunscreen.

"I put some on before we left the house, but I should probably reapply. Help me?"

Riley tosses me a bottle and I quickly cover her lightly tanned skin, trying not to take too long when I'm rubbing it into her boobs or her ass. My hands might linger slightly, but she isn't complaining. Then the two of us are running into the pond, Bree squealing at the coldness.

"How is this so cold?" I ask her as we go deeper into the water.

"We cheat," she says with a grin. "We filter the water in and out of a cooling tank that's underground. We wanted to make sure it was a good temperature year round without being able to shade it."

I lay on my back and float in the water with my eyes closed. I can hear Bree swimming around me, but she doesn't speak. As nice as this is, it's not helping me get to know her.

"I know we haven't got to spend a lot of time together so far because of Riley's reactions to the other alphas, but I need to know—are we wasting our time here?"

Bree jerks her head back like I slapped her. Maybe I'd been a little too blunt with my question. She shakes her head slowly. "I don't think you're wasting your time. Yes, it's been harder to get to know both of you, but that's why I brought us out here today. I may not know you well, but I like what I know so far. Your alpha? He's kind of an entitled dick."

I snicker. "I'm pretty sure you can't say that on television."

"And I'm pretty sure I don't give a shit. Tessa knew what she was getting into putting me on the show. I have the mouth of a sailor." She grins, glancing back at Riley for a moment. "But I notice you didn't disagree with my statement."

"He can be a dick and he's definitely entitled, but once you get to know him, you'll see that there's more to him than that."

She nods. "I don't disagree. I just don't know if he's going to let me get to know him. And more than that, I need to see him interacting with the other alphas to know he can. If he can't, then I can't have him be a part of my pack. I want my alphas and betas to get along. I don't want to have to spend time with anyone separately."

"Of course you don't." I sigh. "We shouldn't have bonded before we came. Don't get me wrong, I don't regret it in the least, but we could've timed it better. I don't know how well he would've gotten along with everyone, even without the bond. He's not the most personable guy out there, is he?"

"Pretty sure he just comes off to the others as an entitled dick most of the time," she supplies unhelpfully.

My stomach drops as I realize we're going to get sent home. "Damn. You're going to send us home."

"Maybe not. Riley has another three days to convince me he can be a part of a pack, and that he can let me get to know him. But if those things don't happen?" She shrugs. "Then yes, I'll be sending the two of you home at the next rose ceremony."

"That sucks." But I can't even blame her. I don't know if Riley can lower his walls enough to let her in with so many other alphas around.

"Let's not worry about that now. Let's enjoy the rest of our date, yeah?" Bree loops her arms around my neck. She grins up at me as she wraps her legs around me and pulls me close to her. "I think I deserve a kiss for not killing your alpha earlier, don't you?"

I grin because how can I say no to this woman? I brush my lips against hers, opening for her when her tongue teases at my lips. But the whole time, I'm wondering what's the point? Our time is limited and do I really want to grow closer to her, only to be sent home?

Maddox

It's almost time for dinner when Bree, Riley, and Carter arrive back from their date. I'm sitting out front on the gazebo when they pull up on the golf cart. There's tension between the three of them that I can feel all the way over where I am. It wasn't there before, and I can't help but wonder what happened on their date.

Carter tries to help Bree grabbing things from the cart, but she just waves him off. His head drops as he follows his alpha back into the house. Bree's shoulders drop and she takes a deep breath as she rubs a hand on her forehead.

I hate seeing her like this, so I make my way over to her. "Everything alright, Bree? You seem a little tense."

Bree spins on her heels, smiling when she sees me. "Hey, Maddox. Yeah, the date didn't go as planned."

"They didn't... do anything you didn't want, did they?" I don't think they would and I'm sure someone was out there with them, at least filming.

"No, nothing like that." She waves away my concerns. "I could use someone to talk to about this, but it might be a little weird since it's about other suitors."

I shake my head. "Nothing weird about it to me. Does any of this need to go inside now?" I gesture to the stuff she'd been pulling from the back of the cart.

She glances around, waving down one of the cameramen who's been filming her since she arrived. "Can you radio someone to come grab this stuff?" At his nod, she turns back to me. "Do you mind if we go inside and talk?"

"Wherever you're most comfortable works for me." We walk side by side up the steps, a camera following us the entire time. It's been interesting getting used to having people following us around twenty-four-seven. Not to mention the cameras that line every room, not that I can pick them out. They've done a great job of camouflaging the cameras, making it easy for us to forget our every action is being filmed.

Bree leads me to the living room, coming to a halt partway into the room. "Oh, I didn't think anyone would be in here."

Finnegan looks up from the book he's reading, smiling at Bree. "I can go if ye would lek me tae."

"No, you were here first. I was just looking for a place to talk with Maddox. We can go somewhere else."

"Or we can all stay," I offer. "Finnegan is probably a good person to talk to. He is a psychologist."

Bree chews on her lip as she considers my suggestion. "I'm fine with you staying, Finnegan, as long as you don't mind. My date with Riley and Carter didn't go as expected, and Maddox offered to talk it over with me."

"I do nae' mind in th' least." Finnegan stands from the armchair he'd been sitting in, moving to the couch, and patting the spot next to him. "C'mere an' talk to Dr. Finnegan and alpha Maddox, omega."

She drops into the middle of the couch, lifting her legs, and wrapping her arms around them while I move to sit on her free side. She doesn't say anything right away and I meet Finnegan's eyes over the top of her head.

"I got frustrated with the way Riley was treating Carter within the first ten minutes of us sitting down. I had to walk off my irritation before I said something I couldn't take back." Bree's eyes stare out the sliding glass door as she speaks. "When I finally calmed down, Riley didn't apologize to me, but I think he'd apologized to Carter while I was gone. Which is all I really wanted.

"We talked while we ate—about nothing, honestly. I decided I needed to cool off, so Carter and I decided to go into the pond. Riley said he was just going to hang out—I think he might've been letting Carter and I have some alone time. Carter asked me if they were wasting their time. I didn't want to lie to him. I told him I liked him well enough, but his alpha is a dick. When he asked if I was going to send them home, I told him that if I didn't see an improvement in Riley's interactions with the other alphas, then yeah, they were probably getting sent home.

"Carter's face fell, and I felt like shit. I hate that I have to hurt people, but I feel like giving them false hope will only make it hurt worse, ya know? But I didn't want him to be sad, so I asked him to kiss me right there in the middle of the pond. He didn't hesitate, and it was a good kiss. Until Riley, who was fully dressed, mind you, came crashing into the water, growling and yanking Carter away from me."

"Did he hurt ye, lass?" I can tell that Finnegan is trying to hide the rage that's shining in his eyes, and maybe Bree doesn't see it, but I do.

She shakes her head. "Not physically. He scared me a bit, but Carter laid into him. It kind of brought the mood down for the rest of the date. I convinced both of them to join me in the hot springs. I was terrified to get too close to Carter and Riley just spent the whole time with his arms crossed over his chest, glaring between the two of us. It was... uncomfortable, to say the least."

"What do you need from us, Bree?" I ask her. "Do you just need us to listen to what you have to say?"

She chews at her lip again, my eyes immediately drawn to the movement. I want to get onto her for chewing on her lip, but now isn't the time. "I'd like to hear both of your thoughts, if you don't mind."

"Of course, lass. Whatever ye need." Finnegan takes one of her hands in his while I follow suit on her free hand. "We all know th' mate bond has been riding Riley hard—honestly, harder than I have ever seen it ride anyone. A'm not sure why that is, but it's not overly important tae th' conversation.

"I willnae speak of their bonding just two weeks afore th' show started because that isn't my business. But th' way ye're being treated is my business. It's all of our business. Nae one should be mistreating ye or making ye feel guilty for yer actions, which is exactly what Riley did today. He's supposed tae be winning ye over because he's supposed tae want tae be a part of yer pack. But he's not acting lek he wants tae be, is he?"

She shakes her head. "No. He makes me feel like I'm in the way of his bond with Carter and I don't like it."

"I don't like it either," I say, shaking my head. "He needs to figure out what he wants, and I think you're going to have to be the one to tell him. I know you told Carter, but maybe he needs to hear it from your mouth."

"He's right, lass." Finnegan squeezes her hand. "It might be hard, but I do nae think ye like tae back down from a challenge. Put it out there so yer expectations are clear. If Riley disnae want tae do what ye need him tae, then he'll have nae one tae blame but himself."

"And none of this is your fault or even something you should try to fix. Finn's right though, you need to tell Riley exactly what you want or need. He seems extremely hardheaded, and I don't think he'll pick up on subtlety. Just lay it out there. Then there's nothing you can do but wait and see if he chooses to listen to you or not."

Bree had allowed her legs to fall after Finnegan and I took hold of her hands and she clamors to her knees. I let go of her hand when she tugs at it before throwing her arms around Finnegan and smacking a kiss to his cheek. "Thank you, Finnegan."

Then she turns to me, hugging me close and kissing my cheek. "And thank you, Maddox. I would've stewed about this for hours if you hadn't asked me to talk about it." She hesitates, glancing over her shoulder at Finnegan. "Also, it's really cute that you called him Finn."

I feel myself flush under her gaze as I shrug. "Finn's easier to say than Finnegan."

She hums. "Uh huh, and it's not because you guys are friends?"

"Nae, lass. We're friends, or I would nae have offered tae let him call me Finn."

"I like it. I'm glad there isn't a bunch of competitiveness between all of you. I want you all to get along. It lets me see how pieces could fit together to form a pack." Now it's Bree's turn to flush.

"Why are you blushing, omega?" I poke her side, fighting a smile as she jerks away from me with a giggle.

"I was just realizing I haven't asked everyone their preferences." She laughs at the look on my face. "Obviously, I know you, Hudson, and Onyx are into both women and men. Same with Riley and Carter. Maverick, Dalton, and Brody are only into women. But I don't know about everyone else."

"An' why is that important tae ye?" Finnegan asks, seeming to be genuinely curious.

Bree's blush deepens. "I like the idea of my pack being involved with one another as well as me—at least the ones that are into it. I would never ask anyone to do something they don't want to do."

"Of course you wouldn't. Well, you know about me and my pack mates. I can tell you that Gabriel and Emmett definitely swing both ways."

Bree giggles. "Because they've been hitting on you and your pack mates. I thought that might be what was happening, but I didn't want to assume."

Finnegan leans forward, waiting for Bree to meet his eyes. "An' me? Do ye wish tae know my preferences?"

"I do."

"I have been with a few men when I was younger an' experimenting. I enjoyed the sex, but there's nae romantic pull for me to be with men. That being said, A'm not against sleeping with men, I just will nae feel for them what I will for a woman."

"That's good to know." Bree nods. "I guess I should ask the others. It just feels awkward to bring it up."

"And why's that?" I can't help but ask her.

She shrugs. "It's just so personal, and what right do I have to ask?"

"You're the omega that they're hoping to be involved with. You have every right to ask." I turn her head with a finger on her chin until she meets my eyes. "You have every right to ask any question you want. The suitors have the choice to not answer, but you can ask anything you want."

"That makes sense. I guess I need to put on my big girl panties and ask."

"Nae one will be offended that ye're trying tae get tae know them, lass. An' as Maddox said, they have th' choice tae not answer th' question." Finnegan scowls. "An' if anyone is offended, ye can send them to me. A'll be happy tae set them straight."

Bree giggles. "Sometimes it takes me a minute to figure out what you're saying with your heavy brogue, but I adore your accent."

"It's a good one, isn't it?"

The three of us laugh together and I'm glad to see some of the weight on Bree's shoulders seems to have lifted. I'm glad that Finnegan and I could give that to her. I hope that soon she'll come to us, or any of the suitors, without us having to coax her to do so.

Until then, I'll be keeping a close eye on her. I'll make sure she knows she can count on me and my pack mates. That we're serious about her and this show. Even though it's only been three days, I just want to make Bree happy. Whatever I can do to make that happen, I will.

Chapter Eighteen

Finnegan

On day four, Bree surprises us at breakfast by showing up with four lavender roses. I know she'd said she planned on having a group date every day for the rest of the week, but she hadn't handed any roses out while we were in the game room after dinner last night. I thought maybe she changed her mind, or needed more time to decide who to invite.

She stops next to Sasha and presents him with a rose. "Sasha, would you do me the honor of attending a group date with me this afternoon?"

"Nothing would make me happier, *zaychik*." He accepts the rose before grabbing her hand and lifting it to his lips.

Bree grins, leaving me to wonder what he'd just called her. I know zero Russian, so I can't even begin to imagine. Next, she walks over to Gabriel and offers him the second rose. "And you Gabriel? Will you join us for a group date?"

"Abso-freaking-lutely." He grins up at her as he takes the rose, and I can see why Bree and some of the other suitors are so enamored with him. He's a very attractive man with a quick smile and knows how to flirt.

Bree walks around the table, stopping next to me. "Finnegan? I'd be honored if you'd join us."

"Of course, lass. Whatever ye want is yer's." When she ducks her head, I lean down until I can meet her eyes again. "It's th' accent again, isn't it? Ye just want me tae come talk tae ye for hours oan end."

This time Bree giggles. "The accent is only part of it. I also appreciate you taking the time to talk with me yesterday. You and Maddox helped me a lot more than you can ever know."

"Good. A'm here anytime ye need tae talk." I take the rose from her, brushing my fingers along hers. Her eyes glaze over slightly, causing my smile to grow. Bree is such a good little omega.

Clearing her throat, Bree makes her way over to Emmett. "And you, my fine sir, will you also join us?"

Emmett's smile lights up the room with how big it is. "It would be my pleasure. Thank you for asking."

After that, we all settle down to eat our breakfast, but my eyes keep finding their way to Bree. Beautiful as always, she seems more at ease today and I love it. I'm glad that mine and Maddox's words helped her. Now, if this breakfast could get over with and the time for our date could roll around—that would be great.

I'm surprised when Bree calls the four of us to her as the other suitors head out. "We're actually going to be leaving the compound for our date. I have a few activities planned for us that I hope you'll enjoy. Dress casually." She glances over what we're wearing and nods. "You're perfect as is. We're leaving at eleven, so feel free to do whatever you'd like for the next hour. I'm planning on grabbing my Kindle and reading on the deck until it's time to go. You're welcome to join me, but there will be no talking. I take my reading time very seriously."

With those words, she leaves us standing around, staring at one another. "I think A'm going tae grab a book an' join her," I tell them.

"I'm going to head up to the game room for a bit. I've barely had a chance to play any of the video games they have stocked here." Emmett grins. "Wanna join me, Gabe?"

"Who would ever turn down spending more time with someone as cute as you?" Gabriel asks. I roll my eyes at his obvious flirting, but Emmett seems to enjoy it. Who am I to judge?

"What about ye, Sasha?" I ask as I turn to the other man.

"I zink I will head to ze gym for my workout. I cannot let myself get out of shape. Ballet waits for no man."

"Alright, A'll see you'se in an hour then." I make my way to the living room and pick up the book I'd been reading the day before. It's a fiction book, which is abnormal for me. Usually I read books on psychology and new methods of dealing with certain diagnoses. The world of psychology is always evolving, and I have to stay on top of it all. But I figure since I'm on vacation—at least of a sort—I can enjoy a book or two just for my pleasure.

I head out to the deck to find that Bree has beat me there. "Ye're a fast wee thing, aren't ye?"

Bree blinks up at me for a moment before her eyes focus on me. She got lost in that book fast. "Oh, you're going to read, too?"

"Aye. Ye were already so lost in that book. It must be a good one."

Bree's cheeks flush. "It's a spicy scene. I was reading it before bed last night, but stopped when I realized it was spicy. Figured I'd read it now."

I just nod, settling onto the lounge chair beside her and break open my book. I want to ask her more about her book, but she had said no talking, so I hold my tongue, quickly losing myself in my book.

I hear Bree moving around on the chair beside me, but don't pay it much attention at first. Not until her scent drifts to me. It's light, telling me she's probably wearing scent canceling panties, but just enough of it leaks out to tell me she's very aroused.

Turning my head slowly to not startle her, I find her with her thighs clenched together as she reads. Occasionally, her hips tilt as if to get some much needed friction. I just watch her, mesmerized by how beautiful she looks with her flushed cheeks while she nibbles at her lip. Her mouth drops open, a pant falling from her lips that has my cock raring to go.

Fucking hell. This omega is out to murder me.

Suddenly her eyes dart up to meet mine as if she'd felt them on her. She snorts as she grimaces. "Well, this is a little awkward."

"What lass? Th' fact that a spicy scene is making ye wet? There's nothing awkward about that. Am happy tae help ye out with that, if ye'd lek."

She looks undecided as she glances between me and the Kindle. "We do nae have to do anything ye do nae wish tae do. If ye just want tae keep reading, then A'll do th' same. But if ye'd like me to help ye feel good while ye're reading—A'm more than willing to help with that."

Bree bites down on her lip before she nods. "Yes, please." Her voice comes out a little high pitched as I smile at her.

"Ye mek sure ye keep reading. I would not want tae distract ye from yer reading time," I tell her as I pull her lounge chair closer to mine. She's made this much easier for me by wearing a dress.

I slide my hands up her legs, beneath her dress, and squeeze her thighs. She slides her legs open for me and yanks her dress up to her waist. "What a helpful omega ye are."

I run my hands up and down her dripping wet panties, realizing this is probably why her scent leaked out. I'm surprised there isn't a puddle of slick beneath her. Though, there will be shortly if I have my way.

Bree whines and wiggles in her seat. My eyes shoot up and find hers on me. "Uh uh, omega. Keep reading. A'll mek sure ye get yer happy ending."

Not wanting to tease her too much, I push her panties to the side. Her scent hits me hard and I somehow hold back my growl of hunger. I want nothing more than to devour her pretty pink pussy, but I don't want to rush things between us.

Yes, I'm aware I'm currently dragging my fingers through her slick covered pussy, but going down on someone differs from fingering them—at least in my book. Plus, I can't leave this omega feeling all needy before our group date. What kind of alpha would that make me?

Bree continues to whine and moan as I trace her slit, but each time I check, her eyes are on her Kindle. Her slick has left my hand drenched as I finally bring my fingers to her clit. Her hips jerk at my touch, but she keeps reading like the good omega she is.

"Good omega," I murmur before sliding my fingers back down to her dripping core. I thrust two fingers inside of her, curling my fingers so I can hit that spot deep inside of her that will make her explode. In and out, I thrust my fingers, paying attention to her reactions. I know she's hit an especially spicy spot in the book when her pussy clamps down on my fingers, slick sliding down my arm.

I want to ask her what has her so aroused, but I also want her to keep reading. I add a third finger and it's a tight fit even with as wet as she is. I lift my other hand to circle her clit. In no time at all, she's abandoned the Kindle. Her hips lift to meet every thrust of my fingers.

"Yes, Finnegan. Don't stop. I'm so close."

"I thought I told ye tae keep reading, lass?"

She's panting, her hands lifting to tug at her nipples over the top of her dress. "I finished the scene."

I guess that's a good reason to stop reading, and that means it's time to have her explode all over my hand. I pick up the pace until she's clinging to my arm as I fuck her on my fingers. Her nails dig into the skin there and her back arches as she lets out a loud scream. I'd put money on everyone not in a soundproofed room, having heard that.

Her walls clamp down on my fingers and a gush of slick comes spilling from her as she comes hard. "Finnegan! Yes! Oh, fates!"

I keep moving my fingers, waiting until she relaxes back onto the lounge chair and her inner muscles relax, before pulling my fingers from her. Lifting them to my lips, I suck them clean while I hum. She tastes even better than she smells.

"Well, that was hot as hell."

My head snaps around to the door while Bree slowly rolls her head to the side. Gabriel and Emmett stand there with very obvious erections.

"Sasha will be sad he missed the show, I'm sure," Emmett adds with a smirk and a wink sent in Bree's direction.

"Fuck," she curses as she tries to sit up, but she's still too limp to do so. "Is it eleven already?"

"Ye have a few more minutes, lass," I tell her as I help her sit up. "We should get ye tae yer suite so ye can change, though. A'm fairly certain ye soaked yer dress, along with yer panties an' th' chair."

Bree laughs as she swings her legs around so she can stand. "You should take that as a compliment. Don't worry about the chair. I'll let Tessa know to have someone come clean it up."

I trail Bree as she heads over to Gabriel and Emmett. "That's two free shows the two of you have gotten." She runs a hand down their chests before nudging them until they allow her to pass. "Why don't the three of you wait in the living room while I run and get changed? Sasha should be along anytime now."

I wait until Bree is out of earshot before glaring at Gabriel and Emmett. "Ye should know better than tae watch her doing something lek that without her permission."

"I feel like doing it on the deck, which is a public area and screaming like a banshee so the entire house can hear, is permission enough." Gabriel shakes his head, smirk firmly in place. "But I'll happily ask Bree for future permission if I come across her in the act again."

I'd like to knock some sense into him, but he isn't wrong. If Bree hadn't wanted others to see us, then she would've asked to move somewhere else.

"I'm beginning to think our little omega has an exhibition kink." Emmett chuckles, stepping back into the living room.

"What is funny?" Sasha asks, as he ambles in.

"Oh, we caught Bree and Finnegan in an intimate position," Gabriel tells him.

I chuckle. "What he means tae say is he an' Emmett spied oan me an' Bree while I was getting her off with my fingers. Speaking of, A'm gonna hit th' bathroom afore we leave. A'll be back shortly"

Without waiting for a response from the three of them, I hurry to the stairs and up to my room. I wash my hands because as much as I'd like to keep her scent on me all day, we'll be out in public and I don't want anyone else to smell her. A quick change of clothes and then I'm sprinting down the stairs to find the three suitors and Bree waiting for me by the front door.

The five of us head down the walkway and find an SUV waiting for us and an older beta man holding the door open for us. He inclines his head to Bree. "Good day, Miss Timmons."

"How many times do I have to tell you to call me Bree, Peter?" she asks as she climbs into the back of the SUV, shaking her head.

The four of us all stand there for a moment until Bree sticks her head out of the door. "What are you waiting for? There's room for all five of us in here. Two of you will sit in the back row with me and two of you will sit in the middle row. Chop chop."

There's another moment of hesitation before we all scramble to make it inside the SUV. Emmett and Gabriel are the first to make it in and they take the seats on either side of Bree, leaving me and Sasha to take the two seats in the middle row. Peter shuts the door behind us and makes his way around to the driver's side. Once he pulls on his seatbelt and starts the car, he turns around to face us.

"Is everyone wearing their seatbelts? There will be no hanky panky in the car and you remain seat belted in your seat at all times. While we're on the road, I'm in charge of Miss—I mean, Bree's safety, and I take that very seriously. Are we clear?"

We all call out our agreement and it makes me respect Peter more. Ordering around alphas isn't something a beta usually does, but he obviously puts Bree's safety above anything else—something I greatly appreciate. The short drive is filled with small talk before we come to a stop outside a building. Ducking down, I see a sign that says Brandini Toffee.

Frowning, I turn back to Bree. "Are we buying ye toffee?"

Bree throws her head back as she laughs. "Not quite. Let's get out of the car and I'll tell you all about it."

Sasha and I glance at one another as the door on Sasha's side opens. We both shrug before climbing out. Gabriel is next and then Emmett. When Bree goes to step out, Peter offers her his hand until she's settled. Behind us, a van has pulled up and a whole camera crew sets out, unloading their equipment and getting it set up.

"I'll be parked just over there." Peter gestures to the parking lot. "Just call when you're done and I'll meet you back here."

"Or we'll just come find you," Bree starts, but she's cut off by Peter.

"Absolutely not. You will call and I will pick you up." Peter shoots her a look, daring her to argue with him further.

Bree throws up her hands in defeat. "Fine, Peter. Thank you. I will call you when we're finished."

A nod to Bree and then he's gone, pulling away from the curb and heading to the parking lot. Bree turns to us with an exasperated sigh.

"Lass, do ye have a phone?"

Bree pulls the phone from her purse. "The omega gets a phone anytime we leave the compound in case of an emergency. It does nothing but make phone calls, so none of us are tempted to troll the internet."

"That meks sense." I don't know why I asked her, but it seems good for us to know she has a phone in case something happens.

"Brandini Toffee has been around since 2006. Yes, over 200 years ago. It's been run by the Brandini family since its founding. They managed to keep it running after the Event. It's also one of my favorite treats. You'll actually find that quite a few businesses here survived the Event, or were rebuilt much the same as they were before the Event. It's one of the reasons Tessa and I wanted to film *Heated* here."

"Wow," I murmur. That's a long time for a company to have been in business. Especially since many businesses failed after the Event. "So, are we here tae buy ye toffee or not? A'm confused."

Bree shakes her head. "Back in their early days, they used to give tours of the facilities regularly. After the Event, they tried to continue with the tours, but there were a lot of issues with the different designations being around one another. They moved to scheduled tours only. They were more than happy to allow us to not only take a tour but also to film it."

The doors to the building open and a group of one female and four males make their way toward us. As soon as they get close enough, I realize they're a pack. The woman is an omega, three of the men are alphas, and the last is a beta.

"Bree," the woman calls, holding her arms out to our omega. Okay, she's not ours yet. Bree sweeps into the woman's arms and they hug like old friends. Her men just smile as they watch the two until they break apart. "Now, who do we have here?"

"Alana, these are four of my suitors. Emmett is one of the three remaining betas. He's a chef at Lyrical in LA. The other three are alphas. We have Gabriel, who's a kindergarten teacher, Sasha, who is my all-time favorite ballet dancer, and Finnegan, who's a psychologist.

Guys, this is Alana Brandini. She's the current owner of Brandini Toffee and a very good friend of mine."

There are quick introductions to her pack, and then they're leading us on the tour. I'll be the first to admit that their process is interesting, and they make some damn good toffee. It's not something I expected to do on our date, but I also kind of love that.

When the tour is done, Bree alerts Peter that we're done before going back to speak with Alana. They hug once more and then Bree's heading back toward us.

"How is it zat you became acquainted with Alana?" Sasha asks.

"We actually met at a business conference for omega business owners. There aren't a lot of us and not all the omegas could afford the trip. Alana and I actually sponsored any omegas that couldn't afford it. Now we have a network that spans the country of omegas like us."

Emmett wraps his arm around Bree's waist, hugging her to his side. "That's actually really cool—all of it. I'm not surprised to know that you sponsored the ones who couldn't afford it. You have a big heart, *gongjunim.*"

Bree tucks her head into Emmett's shoulder before lifting her face to him. He doesn't hesitate to press a kiss to her lips and I find myself smiling. I've always known that if I find an omega, I will be sharing her—there are just too few of them in the world. I hadn't known how I would react to the actual act of sharing, but as I watch Emmett and Bree together, my chest warms.

Out of all the suitors, Emmett is the one I'm absolutely sure Bree will end up picking. I can't decide about Brody. I don't know if she'll want two betas, but she also seems very close to him, so she may end up choosing them both. When it comes to the alphas, I have no idea who she will choose.

Emmett leads her to the SUV and helps her inside before following behind her. I climb in right behind them, and I'm surprised to see Emmett sitting in the middle row. He must see my curious glance because he shrugs. "It's only fair that we take turns. She needs time with all of us."

"Ye're a good man, Emmett," I tell him, slapping a hand on his shoulder as I settle beside Bree. Sasha drops on her other side and Gabriel takes the free seat in the middle row.

"So, what's next?" Gabriel asks as he turns to face us.

"Unless any of you are extremely hungry, I thought we could go work up an appetite."

Gabriel's eyebrows wiggle as he shoots her a smirk. "Oh, yeah?"

Bree leans forward to slap his arm, but she's smiling when she does it. "Get your head out of the gutter. They have a really cool escape room here. It's massive and has like ten different adventures to choose from. It's one of the businesses that was rebuilt after the Event, making it bigger and better than the one it replaced."

"What is escape room?" Sasha's brow is furrowed as he glances between all of us.

"Dae ye not dae anything besides ballet?" I ask. I'm shocked when Sasha shakes his head. "We're most certainly gonna have tae work oan that. Yer passion might be ballet, but ye should have other things in yer life besides yer job."

"An escape room is..." Bree trails off, looking between the rest of us as she tries to figure out how to explain it.

It's Emmett that continues the explanation. "So most escape rooms have more than one room, with each room being themed. A group of people are locked into a room for anywhere between twenty minutes to an hour. You have to discover clues, answer riddles, solve puzzles... things like that. And once you figure it out, you either find a key or something similar that will allow you to escape the room."

"Zat is... interesting. I look forward to escaping ze room with you."

I don't know how Bree pulls it off, but the camera crew is allowed to follow us into the room and record our progress. We manage to break free of the room within forty minutes, and it turns out to be a lot more fun than I thought it would be.

As we're leaving, Bree reveals the reason we were able to bring in the camera crews. "They're retiring that particular room this month, so by the time the show airs, it will already be closed and a new one will have taken its place."

"I enjoyed zis escaping of ze room very much." Sasha grins. "I will need to find a place near my home."

We walk to a Mediterranean restaurant where we're led to a small private room. Bree thanks the hostess as we settle at the table.

"Our waiter has already agreed to be on camera, as have the owners who will pop in at some point, but we decided it would be best to have us separate from the general public so we wouldn't accidentally film anyone who doesn't wish to appear on television."

"You and Tessa put a lot of thought into everything with *Heated* and it really shows," Gabriel says, awe dripping from his words. "I could never do what you two have done between the apps and this show."

I've found myself sitting to Bree's right with Emmett on her left. Gabriel sits beside Emmett and Sasha beside me. The food and conversation are both amazing. I'm sad when Bree announces that it's time to return to the compound.

When we arrive back, the five of us walk leisurely up the path to the door. When Bree goes to open the door, I stop her. "If this is a proper date, then I would lek tae kiss ye afore returning ye home."

Bree grins up at me. "I would like nothing more."

I lean down to kiss her, just a brush of our lips against one another. Sure, I'd helped her to an explosive orgasm earlier in the day, but that doesn't mean I don't still plan to take things slowly.

Bree kisses Sasha, Gabriel, and Emmett in turn. She looks a bit dazed as she turns back to the door, a smile on her lips. I open the door, gesturing for her to enter ahead of me. "Lasses first."

"Thank you, Finnegan. You're very good at wooing a girl." Bree leans up to brush her lips over my cheek before stepping inside. I can't wipe the smile off my face as I watch her walk away. I would love nothing more than for her to choose me as one of her alphas, and I believe I've made a good impression on her. I like my odds.

Bree

I'm exhausted, but I can't seem to sleep. I really enjoyed my date with Emmett, Finnegan, Gabriel, and Sasha. I think it went really well and I can see all four of them as members of my pack in the future. Once we made it back from the date, we had a few hours to kill before dinner. I decided to read in my room this time, just in case. Not that I hadn't enjoyed Finnegan's help, but I can't help worrying that I'm moving too fast with these men.

It's literally only the fourth day and I've been eaten out and fingered twice. Not to mention the blowjob I'd given Roman. I'm going to look like the sluttiest of omegas when the show airs. On the other hand, I regret nothing that's happened. It makes sense to try out the merchandise before buying it, right?

After dinner, I'd sat down with Riley and Carter, spelling out what I needed from Riley for this to work. He'd listened to what I had to say, but hadn't said a word when I finished. Carter apologized for his alpha's behavior, but I can't help wondering just how often he's had to apologize for Riley. It's not his place, but I somehow don't see that changing. Just like I suspect Riley won't be changing anytime soon, which sucks for me and Carter. I will stand by my word, and if he hasn't improved by the rose ceremony, they'll be saying goodbye.

When I'd suggested a movie night, the suitors and I piled into the theater room and watched three movies before I called it a night. I had barely been able to keep my eyes open as I walked back to my suite, but as soon as I laid my head down, I was wide awake.

Rolling my head to the side, I see that it's after three in the morning. I let out an annoyed snarl, pounding my fists on the bed in frustration.

I've been trying to sleep for the last three hours. I'm supposed to be awake in four hours to work out with Maddox, but there's no way that's happening. I'll need to have someone let him know.

Giving up on sleep, I pull on a swimsuit and coverup before heading for the basement. Maybe a soak in the hot tub will be enough to help me fall asleep. I stop at the control room door, pounding on it before waving at the camera. It takes a few minutes for Tom to open the door just enough to peek out at me.

"You shouldn't be here, Bree."

"Hey, Tom. I'm great. Thanks for asking. I hope the family is doing well." I paste a smile on my face, raising my brows as I stare at him.

Tom laughs. "It's good to see you, Bree. Yes, the family is doing very well. I assume you're down here for a reason—besides a dip in the pool. What can I do for you?"

"I'm having trouble sleeping tonight, so I need to cancel my morning workout with Maddox. Could you have someone leave a note on his door or something? I don't want to wake him and his pack just because I couldn't sleep."

Tom's smile is soft as he nods. "I can do that for you. You going for a soak in the hot tub?"

I nod. "I figure if that doesn't work, I'll hit the sauna next. I need some damn sleep."

"Well, I'll take care of your message—"

"You're the best, Tom. Thank you!" I cut him off, rude of me, I know, but I just know he's going to warn me about being alone in the hot tub. The chances of me falling asleep in the hot tub and drowning are slim to none. I could understand if I said I was going for a swim, but I'm not.

I hurry down the hallway and into the lowly lit room that houses the pool and hot tub. There's more than enough light to see, so I don't bother turning on the overhead lights. I head straight for the hot tub, tossing my coverup to the side as I lower myself in the steaming water.

I let out a moan as the water seeps into my skin, and I feel myself relaxing already. I lay my head against the padded headrest, my eyes falling shut. This is exactly what I needed.

I jerk upright at a sound coming from the pool. Someone is climbing up the steps, completely naked. It's too dark for me to tell exactly who it is, but based on their build, it's got to be one of the alphas.

"Who's there?" I demand.

"It's just me, omega." It takes a moment for me to realize it's Gabriel. The closer he gets, the clearer I can make him out—and not just his face. His dick is massive, and I don't think he's fully hard.

I whimper, licking my lips as I'm unable to tear my gaze away from his swinging dick.

"See something you like, omega?" Gabriel asks, amusement painting his words. He stops just before I'd lose sight of his cock—a move that I'm sure he's doing on purpose. "May I join you?"

I force my eyes shut, returning my head to the headrest. "Sure."

I hear him climb into the hot tub and I'm surprised that he doesn't sit beside me. Opening my eyes, I see him sitting directly across from me. "Do you often go swimming in the nude in the middle of the night?"

Gabriel laughs, throwing his head back as his whole body shakes. "I do, actually—almost every night right before bed. It relaxes me. This is the first time anyone's come in while I was here."

"But why naked?" It suddenly occurs to me that Tom might have been warning me I'd find Gabriel in here. My eyes glance down at the water between us as if I could see his beautiful cock. It's then I realize the tension has climbed back into my body.

Damn it.

"I enjoy being naked." Gabriel shrugs, as if his answer is normal. "I regularly walk around my place naked. Since there's a lot of people here, I've refrained from running around in the nude. Any time I'm in my room, my clothes are off, and of course, my nighttime swims. And yes, I swim naked in my apartment pool late at night too."

"You're so weird." I shake my head, laughing despite myself.

Gabriel just grins at me. "So, what brings you down here in the middle of the night?"

"Couldn't sleep. I thought a dip in the hot tub or some time in the sauna would help."

"You know what else helps?" There's a glint in his eyes that makes me not want to ask, but I'm curious.

"What's that?"

"Orgasms." Gabriel stands and I get another peek at his cock, which absolutely has me perfuming. "Which I would be more than happy to help you with. I love watching you fall apart as you come. In fact, it's become one of my favorite things to do since you're apparently an exhibitionist."

"I'm not..." I trail off as my face flushes. I was about to deny his words, but realize that I've enjoyed having oral sex where anyone could walk in on us at any point—starting with the time that all the suitors watched me fall apart in the arms of Dalton and Maverick. Maybe I do have an exhibitionist streak.

Huh. You learn something new every day.

"I'm not sure, I should... I've been intimate with four men in the last few days. When the show airs, everyone is going to be saying what a slut I am."

"Let them say whatever they want. It's none of their business. You're an omega who has been deprived of touch and affection for far too long. Now that it's being offered to you, of course you want it. No one can blame you for that." Gabriel smirks as he makes his way over to me. When he speaks again, his voice is gruffer, hunger painting his words. "But you can be my dirty little whore anytime you'd like."

My mouth falls open, not in shock, but in desire, as a whimper escapes my lips. I have only been spoken to like that by the pack of alphas that wanted to own me. But they hadn't meant it in the same way that Gabriel says it now.

A shiver runs down my body and I *want* to be his dirty little whore. What the hell does that say about me?

Gabriel sits beside me, his eyes never leaving mine. "Is that what you want, omega? Do you want to be my dirty little whore?"

"Yes," I pant as I turn in my seat so I can climb into his lap.

"What a good girl," he purrs as his large hands land on my hips. They're so big that the tips of his fingers touch on my lower back. He pulls me to him so we're touching from chest to crotch. He tilts my hips back and forth so I'm rubbing against his cock.

I link my hands behind his neck, pulling him down to kiss me as I take over the movement of my hips. I grind my still covered pussy along his length, already feeling an orgasm rising. I seem to be constantly turned on around these men, so who can really blame me for my actions? Anyone else in my position would do the same.

My head falls back, breaking the kiss, when Gabriel shoves aside the cups of my swimsuit to capture my boobs in his hands. He lifts one to his mouth, tongue snaking out to circle my pebbled nipple before sucking it between his lips. His tongue flicks back and forth over it, while the palm of his other hand just barely brushes over my other nipple. The dueling sensations have me grinding harder against him and I know it won't be long before I explode.

I want to ride his cock, but I also don't want this to stop. The movement of my hips grows jerkier, more insistent as I climb and climb. Gabriel switches his mouth to my other nipple and his thumb brushes softly against the wet nipple he'd abandoned. When he nips lightly on one, fingers rapidly flicking the other, I explode.

"Alpha," I scream as my hips piston along his length. Slick spills from me into the water as I keep coming and coming before I collapse against his chest.

"So beautiful," he murmurs as he strokes my back. "What happens next is up to you, omega. Are you going to be a dirty little whore and ride my cock right here? Or are you going to be a good little omega and return to your room so you can get yourself off again and again to what just happened?"

I don't answer him, instead lifting my arms to untie my top and dropping it into the water. My hands drop to my bottoms, thankful I'd chosen the string bikini tonight as I untie the sides and lift to allow the bottoms to float away.

"What a dirty little omega whore you are." Gabriel's lips crash down on mine as I lift to my knees and reach between us to grasp his cock in my hands. I can't even close my hand fully around him. If I wasn't an omega, I'd wonder if he'd be able to fit. But my body was built to take alphas and their knots.

I stroke him a few times as he devours my mouth before notching his cock at my entrance. He breaks the kiss as I slowly lower myself on his length.

"Fuck," he grunts as his hands dig into my hips. "You feel so good, omega."

I say nothing until I've taken all of him inside of me. Even though I'm meant to take his big cock, it doesn't mean I don't have to work for it. My eyes meet his as I slide down to his knot.

"I'm so full, alpha. I love your big cock." And then I'm too busy riding him to say anything. I grind my clit against him with each pass, and it's not long until he's lifting his hips to meet me. I drop onto his cock again and again as he thrusts into me, his thumb circling my clit.

I explode around him, going limp in his arms. Slick spills from me onto his cock and his thighs before being washed away by the water. He continues to circle my clit as he fucks me through my orgasm.

"One more, omega. Be a good girl and give me one more, and I promise you'll be able to sleep like a baby."

I can't even lift my head to look at him. I want to agree to his wishes, but I can't even move, let alone speak.

"Hmmmm," he hums. "That one really took it out of you. Looks like I'll be the one doing the work this time around."

Gabriel slides his still hard dick from my pussy as he stands with me in his arms. He spins me around and places me onto another seat. I'm on my knees with my upper body lying along the top of the hot tub. "You've got this, baby. Give me one more and then I'll knot you—do you want me to knot you?"

He slams into me from behind as he asks, and all I can do is scream out his name. He hits differently from this angle and it feels amazing. Once he bottoms out, he pauses. "I need your words, baby. Can I knot you?"

"Yes," I hiss. "Fuck me hard and then knot me."

He presses a kiss to my shoulder and I can feel his smile against my skin. "Good girl."

He pulls out until just the tip remains before slamming back into me. I grasp at the top of the hot tub, trying to find something to hold on to as he pounds into me. Finally, I latch onto the headrest as his hand lands on my lower back so I'm plastered against the seat.

His thrusts pick up in speed and I let out a whine. His knot nudges at my entrance with each thrust and I just want to take it already. Every time he fucks into me, my hard nipples and clit rub against the seat, building me up even more. He doesn't pause or slow down as we pant out each other's name. He fucks me hard and fast until I come hard around him. My walls grasp him with each stroke, not wanting to let go.

"I'm going to knot you now, omega. Gonna knot you so good. Gonna make you come again and again while I fill you with my cum." Gabriel pants as he thrusts into me once more. He grinds against my pussy as it opens to take his knot. I feel it pop inside and let out another scream as he hits me in all the right places.

With his knot inside of me, Gabriel only has so much movement, but he makes it count as he rocks inside of me. "Come again, baby. Squeeze my knot and let me fill you up." His words are enough to push me over the edge once more.

"Yes," he hisses, as he continues to rock into me. He explodes inside of me as he comes, painting my insides. He never stops moving as I milk his knot. I come two more times before he slows.

I collapse forward, fully relaxed and exhausted. Gabriel lifts me carefully, turning us and sits in the seat. He's still knotted inside of me and will remain so for a while, assuming we don't start anything up again. The longer we have sex, the longer he'll stay locked inside of me.

I hope he isn't planning to prolong this because my eyelids are already heavy and I can feel myself beginning to drift off. Gabriel's hands run up and down my arms, lulling me further toward my dreams.

"Bree, where's your keycard?"

"Hmmm?" I don't open my eyes when he speaks to me and I wasn't paying any attention to what he asked me.

"Where's your keycard? You're falling asleep. Once my knot releases, I'll dress us and carry you to your room, but I need to know where your keycard is."

"Cover up," I mumble, hoping he understands because I'm already slipping into sleep.

I wake up later as he lays me on my bed. He presses a kiss to my forehead. "Your keycard is on your nightstand. I'll grab you something to change into that's not sopping wet and then head to my room."

"No," I whine. "Stay."

"What?"

"Get both of us naked and stay. I wanna cuddle."

Gabriel hesitates for a moment before I hear his shorts drop to the floor before he lifts me and strips my swimsuit from me. He climbs in behind me, pulling the sheets over us both before he kisses the back of my head. "Sleep well, omega."

I just hum my agreement as I fall back into the oblivion of sleep.

Chapter Nineteen

Onyx

I sit on the deck, eyes locked on the door that leads inside. Around me, the other suitors eat their lunches, but I'm not hungry. I'm too concerned to be hungry.

Neither Bree nor Gabriel had shown up for breakfast, after someone left a message on our door for Maddox that she wouldn't make their workout session. Tessa had told us that Bree was unavailable and would join us later in the day, but we still haven't heard from her or Gabriel yet.

I know nothing can be seriously wrong or Tessa would be much more upset, but I can't seem to stop worrying. Could she have asked him to bond with her without the rose ceremony? Even as I have the thought, I know she wouldn't have. This show is her baby, and she knows she would need to do this during a ceremony.

But something obviously happened for the two of them to both be missing. I'd tried to ask Tessa for more information, but she hadn't been any more forthcoming with me than she had been with the group, just telling us she would join us later in the day.

"You need to eat," Emmett says as he lays a plate in front of me.

Glancing down, I see that he's made me a sandwich exactly the way I like it, with a pile of cut fruit with no pineapple. I look up at him in shock. "How did you…"

"You eat the same thing every day," he says as he ducks his head, flushing. "I watch you sometimes, so it wasn't hard to figure out what you'd want."

I lift my hand to cup his cheek, butterflies rising in my chest. It was Hudson who'd asked Maddox and I to get to know Emmett and Gabriel in hopes of the two joining our pack—depending on what Bree decides, of course—but it's moments like this, I can't help but wonder if it would have happened even without Hudson's request.

"Thank you, Emmett. I'm not used to having someone around to make sure I eat. Would you like to sit with me while I eat?"

Emmett's smile lights up his face. "I would."

He drops into the seat beside me as I take a big bite of my sandwich, eyes moving back to the door. He sighs. "Worried about Bree and Gabriel?"

I quickly chew my food as I nod. "I can't seem to help myself. Bree seems to thrive on schedules and yet she's already missed two meals."

"I just don't like not knowing what happened." Emmett shrugs. "Technically, it's not my business, but…"

"But you still want to know." I nod because I feel exactly the same. I take another bite, eyes still locked on the door. I sit up straighter when I see two shadows on the other side of the door moments before it opens.

I breathe a sigh of relief when Bree and Gabriel step out, holding hands. Bree looks around the tables and smiles.

"Good afternoon, gentlemen. I apologize for my absence today. I had a bout of insomnia last night and didn't fall asleep until close to four in the morning. Obviously, I needed to sleep." Bree's stomach growls, and she laughs as she lifts her free hand to land on it. "Apparently, now I need food."

"I'll get it for you, Bree." Emmett jumps to his feet and piles food onto a plate for her.

Bree laughs again. "I'm perfectly capable of getting my own food, Emmett."

"I'm aware. You can do anything you want, but isn't that the point of having a pack? Letting them take care of you? I'm just getting a head start so you can see what a good addition I'd be to your pack."

Once Emmett has finished, he sets the plate in front of the chair he's been sitting in and drops into the chair on the other side. Gabriel snickers as he realizes he's being edged out of sitting next to her. He presses a kiss to the top of her head and whispers something in her ear before he heads off to make his own plate.

Bree makes her way over to sit between me and Emmett. "Thank you, Emmett."

"Anything for you, Bree," he murmurs, and I know he really means those words. He's such a good beta—no, a good man.

"If it makes you feel any better," I tell her, nudging her with my elbow as I lean close, "he also made my plate and sat it down in front of me before demanding I eat."

Bree giggles, glancing at Emmett before focusing her attention on me once more. "He did not."

"He absolutely did. I think he enjoys providing for others."

"You can stop talking about me like I'm not right here." Emmett pouts, arms crossed over his chest, and his entire face is pink.

Bree just giggles and the two of us go back to eating. Gabriel sits across from Bree with an overflowing plate and the three of us eat in silence while Emmett watches to make sure we're actually eating. The only thing that breaks the silence is when Bree waits too long between bites and Emmett prods her into eating more. It's adorable.

Finally, Bree sits back as she pushes her plate away from her. "I can't eat anymore or I'll explode."

Emmett looks like he wants to argue, but Gabriel gives a sharp shake of his head and the beta collapses back into his chair. He mumbles under his breath, too quietly for me to hear.

"Emmett, do you have a provider kink?"

Bree turns to me with a frown. "Is that even a thing?"

I shrug because I have no idea, but if it is, it's definitely Emmett's kink. My eyes lock on Emmett's, who's currently shooting me a look of death. I lift my eyebrows, smirking. Let him try to argue—I know he won't because I'm right.

"Alright, let's stop picking on Emmett. He's been so sweet." Bree leans over and presses a kiss to his cheek. "I need some roses. Where did they put the roses?"

"They're on another table. I'll grab them." Emmett is up and gone again before anyone can blink. He's back a moment later, setting the roses down before her.

Bree is grinning, but I can see her teeth digging into her bottom lip—probably in an attempt to not burst out into laughter. Not that I blame her. It's taking everything inside me to not laugh as well. It's adorable, the way Emmett is so determined to provide Bree with everything she wants. And how many times can I call this man adorable this afternoon? What has he done to me?

"Thank you again, Emmett," she finally says without laughing. "Today is day five, so I think it's fairly obvious who I'd like to take on a date today since they're the only ones left. Onyx, would you do me the honor of joining me this evening?"

I take the offered rose, lifting her hand to my lips. "I'd love to join you for whatever you have planned."

"You're just lucky I planned this week's dates. Beginning next week, it is the suitors who will plan dates." She lifts a hand to her lips. "Oops, I wasn't supposed to tell you that yet. Don't tell anyone else, okay?"

"My lips are sealed," I tell her, loving the fact that she continuously makes me smile. I've definitely been told in the past that I don't smile enough. Those people won't recognize me on their television when *Heated* airs.

Bree turns to Gabriel and Emmett, who both mime zipping their lips. "Good. Now, let me go find your pack mates, so I can invite them to dinner too."

She isn't looking at me when she says pack mates, and I wonder if she's counting Gabriel and Emmett as part of my pack. A glance in their direction tells me they're wondering the same thing.

But Bree's gone before I can ask her—not that I was going to ask her. I don't think. This little omega sure has me on edge.

Turning in my chair, I watch as Bree makes her way over to Maddox and Hudson, offering them their roses. Hudson jumps out of his chair and wraps his arms around Bree before spinning her in the air and he yells, "Woo hoo! I'm the luckiest man alive."

The three of us chuckle at his antics. Once he's set her back on her feet, the three of them make their way back to us. Hudson is practically bouncing on his feet. "We're going on a date!"

My eyes fall shut as I shake my head. "I'm aware, Hud. She asked me first."

Hudson's whole body droops for a moment, but you can't keep my pack mate down for long. He perks back up as he turns to Bree. "When do we leave? Where are we going? What should we wear?"

"Hud," Maddox says with a sigh. "Bring it down by like twenty, man. And give her time to answer the question before firing another one at her, yeah?"

Bree just laughs. "It's fine. I love that he's so excited. I can't tell you where we're going, but we'll be leaving here at about six. We'll grab dinner and then we'll be heading somewhere else. I'd say, dress up a little, but not too fancy."

"That's not at all helpful," Hudson murmurs, shaking his head. "We'll figure it out."

"Well, that's still six hours from now. I'm planning on spending my afternoon down here by the pool... maybe in the pool. I haven't decided. I'm going to change into my swimsuit and grab my Kindle."

The five of us watch as she walks inside. Hudson and Maddox take a seat and our attention turns to Gabriel.

"So..." Hudson smirks. "Are you going to tell us what happened last night to cause both you and Bree to miss breakfast and not appear until noon?"

Gabriel grins but shakes his head. "If Bree wants you to know, she'll tell you. I don't want to make her uncomfortable by telling you something she doesn't want you to know."

Hudson and Emmett both pout, leaving me and Maddox to shake our heads. Only six hours until our date. Maybe I'll find Tessa and get her to help me and my pack pick out clothes for the evening. I don't want us to make Bree look bad. Yeah, that's a good idea. In fact, I think I'll do that now.

When I stand, Maddox frowns. "Where are you going?"

"I'm going to go see if Tessa can't help us pick out something appropriate to wear tonight."

"And this is why I love you," Hudson announces as he jumps to his feet, smacking a kiss on my lips. "C'mon, Maddox. All three of us should go."

As often is the case when Hudson sets his mind to something, he drags the two of us behind him.

Maddox

Six comes quicker than I thought it would, but I'm grateful that Onyx thought to ask Tessa with help on what to wear. She wouldn't give us any more information on what we would be doing, but she was more than happy to help us pick out our outfits. We're all dressed in dark jeans and button-down shirts while Hudson has dressed up his outfit a bit more with a fitted vest over his shirt. He looks downright edible. If it weren't for the fact that we're about to take Bree out, I'd throw him down and ravish him for the rest of the night.

Shaking my head, I remind myself that it isn't in the cards for the night. One last glance in the mirror shows my hair pulled back into a bun. Though, as wavy as my hair is, it's a bit on the messy side.

Turning away, I take in my pack mates. Onyx's hair is falling down his back as it usually is. The only time he pulls it back is if he is doing a tattoo. Then there's Hudson with the shortest hair of all of us and I want to laugh at how long he spent getting it ready because it's messy as hell. Why is that even a thing?

"We ready?" As they nod in affirmation, I head to the door. I can't wait to get Bree and take her on this date. We're the last group to take her out, making me wonder what she'll be doing for tomorrow's date. Though, why I'm worrying about that right now, I have no idea.

Stepping into the hallway, I'm surprised to see Emmett and Gabriel waiting for us. Their hungry eyes rove over us and I find myself fighting a blush.

Gabriel groans as he bites down on his fist. "Damn, do I wish I was coming with you all tonight."

"You all look amazing," Emmett adds, his eyes moving between the three of us as if he can't decide who to look at.

"Thanks," Onyx answers, his voice deeper than usual. I think all three of us have been caught off guard by Gabriel and Emmett waiting for us.

I clear my throat, glancing between the two of them. "Did you need us for something? We were just on our—"

I'm cut off by Gabriel's lips, brushing against mine. When he pulls back, all I can do is blink at him. I'm shocked and confused as hell. Gabriel laughs. "Emmett and I wanted to wish you all a good night, that's all."

Then he's gone, and Emmett is standing before me. I lean down to brush my lips across his and when we break apart, he's smiling as he nibbles on his bottom lip. "Have fun tonight, Maddox."

I turn to watch as he pauses to give first Onyx and then Hudson a kiss while Gabriel leans against the wall—apparently he's already given the other two a kiss. I'm slightly surprised by this turn of events, but not upset in the least. We've practically spent any time not spent with Bree with the two of them, and if we'd met them anywhere besides *Heated*, I'm fairly certain we would've already asked them to join our pack.

Yes, I know, it's only been five days, but when you know, you know. But it sucks because we've met them here and we're attempting to keep our feelings from becoming too involved. Bree could choose one of them and none of the others, or all but one... That would suck.

Abruptly, I grab Onyx's hand. I nod to Gabriel and Emmett as I pull Onyx toward the stairs. "Thank you both, but we're going to be late picking up Bree."

"You're going to have a blast. We can't wait to hear about the date later," Emmett calls after us.

We're halfway down the stairs before Onyx and Hudson force me to stop. "What the hell, Maddox?" Hudson demands.

I sigh, rubbing a hand over my face. "I'm sorry. I know that was rude. I just got to thinking about how we have to be careful about how close we get to them and I panicked."

Onyx's hand comes up to wrap around the back of my neck as he yanks me to him. He kisses me quickly, but thoroughly. "That's understandable. Thank you for telling us."

"As much as I love us talking about what we're feeling, we are late." Hudson grins. "How about we push this aside until later and get ready to take out our girl?"

"Not our girl." Exasperation runs through my words.

"Yet," he adds with a grin before rushing down the stairs and heading for Bree's suite.

"You've got to love his optimism." Onyx shakes his head before grabbing my hand and pulling me down the stairs. "We better hurry. We know he won't wait for us to knock."

He's not wrong. When we turn into the hallway, we find Bree has already answered the door while Hudson stares at her awestruck—not that I can blame him. She looks gorgeous.

She wears a slinky black dress that sparkles beneath the lights. It's held up by thin straps that loop around her neck while the dress itself hugs her curves, stopping mid-thigh. She wears silver strappy heels and when she turns around, she reveals that the back of the dress comprises thin straps criss-crossing over her back, stopping just above her ass.

"Damn, Bree. You look good," Hudson finally manages to get out.

"Thank you." Bree grins at him before noticing us over his shoulder. "The three of you look magnificent."

I can tell she's wearing makeup, but since I know nothing about it, I couldn't even begin to say what all she's done. I do know that she's painted her pouty lips fire engine red and now all I can do is think about kissing her.

She laughs when no one says anything else or moves. "Ummm... should we go?"

That kicks us into gear and the three of us all hurry over to her, trying to offer her our arms. Obviously, she can't take all of our arms, causing all of us to laugh before she slides her arm through Onyx's. "The three of you will just have to take turns, I guess."

Hudson and I trail behind them, holding hands. No one will be left out tonight. We're used to having more than one person wanting our attention, or wanting the attention of more than one person.

I'm surprised to find a limo waiting for us on the circular driveway. Bree must see the look on my face because she laughs. "My plan for the night works better when we have a limo. Just trust me."

What else are we going to do? The four of us climb into the limo and a short while later, we're dropped at a fancy restaurant. We're shown to a private room and we spend about two hours there just enjoying the food and conversation.

When we climb back into the limo, Hudson spins on Bree. "Will you tell us where we're going now? It's driving me crazy not knowing."

Bree hums, tapping her chin with her finger. "Maybe I shouldn't tell you then."

"Please, tell me." Hudson drops to his knees on the floor of the limo, crawling to kneel before her. "I need to know."

"So impatient. We'll be there in like ten minutes."

"That's too long." Hudson lays his head on her lap, turning so he can still keep his eyes on her. "Please, tell me."

Bree shakes her head. "Fine, Mr. Impatient. We're going to Eternity."

Hudson sits up and turns to me and Onyx, a frown of confusion on his face. I shrug as I've never heard of it.

"Wow. The three of you need to get out more often. It's only the biggest club in the area. People come here from LA for the weekend just so they can be seen there. And we'll have a VIP area to ourselves."

"We don't go to clubs often." Onyx shrugs. "Hudson would love us to go out every weekend, but me and Maddox are more of a once in a blue moon club goers."

Bree deflates before my eyes, and I know that isn't what Onyx meant, so I need to fix this now. "We haven't been to a club in a while. It'll be a nice change of pace. Especially if we're dancing with you."

"Shit. I didn't mean it like that, Bree." Onyx grabs her hands. "I'm very happy to go to Eternity with you. I enjoy dancing. I promise."

Bree perks back up, eyes moving back to Hudson. "What about you?"

"I'm ecstatic. I couldn't ask for a better date night." Hudson crawls up onto the seat beside Bree, pulling her to his side. "And Onyx and Maddox are especially fun to dance with." He leans over to whisper something in her ear that I don't catch, but Bree's face flushes, eyes dilating as they flash between me and Onyx—giving me an idea of what he might have said to her.

Nights spent at the club with the three of us usually end up with semi-public sex—something I'm becoming very aware that our little omega is quite fond of. Damn it. Not our omega yet, but fates above, I want nothing more than to call her mine.

The limo stops, and I glance out the window. The club appears to have been a warehouse at some point, but it's been updated and now screams elegance and high class. The line is wrapped around the side of the building, and I wonder how far it travels.

I climb out of the limo before reaching in to offer my hand to Bree and my pack mates. Onyx steps out next and then Hudson. When Bree takes hold of my hand, I help her out easily before pulling her against my body with my arm wrapped around her waist.

"I assume we're not waiting in line?" Onyx cocks an eyebrow at Bree, who shakes her head. We wait another moment for the camera crew to climb from their van and take a few external shots before heading toward the door.

Bree and I lead the way, with Onyx on my other side and Hudson on the other side of Bree. When we come to a stop in front of the bouncer, I hear a few people grumbling about us skipping the line, but when I turn my head to shoot them a glare, everyone shuts up real quick.

"Bree baby!" The alpha bouncer stands, moving to sweep Bree into a hug. A growl slips out of my lips before I can stop it, surprising all of us. We stand there for a few seconds in shocked silence before the big alpha lets out a loud laugh. "Don't worry, big boy, I already have an omega of my own, thanks to Bree and her app."

I feel myself relaxing slightly, but I still don't want him touching her. It's a weird sensation for me seeing as I've watched her with others at the house, but the idea of an outsider touching her puts my alpha on edge. It doesn't make sense to me, but that doesn't change my reaction either.

"You good?" Bree whispers as she pats my chest.

I just nod, not trusting myself to speak just yet.

"This is Chad. He's the one who introduced me to Eternity and its owner—who's also his omega."

I offer Chad my hand, feeling properly chastised for my reaction. "It's nice to meet you, Chad. I'm Maddox, and these are my pack mates, Onyx and Hudson. Sorry about the whole growling thing. Not sure where it came from."

"That's okay. I'm glad you're feeling protective of Bree. She can take care of herself, but that doesn't mean it isn't nice to see someone care about her enough to want to take care of her."

I incline my head, appreciating his words as Onyx and Hudson shake his hand before Chad turns his attention back to Bree. "The VIP area is ready for you, and Vivienne is waiting upstairs for you with the rest of the pack."

"Excellent. Thank you, Chad." Bree steps through the door that he opens for us and I hurry to keep up with her, not wanting to let go of her.

I realize I haven't heard any music while we were waiting outside and that I still don't hear it. "Where's the music?"

"They have the club soundproofed, so the noise doesn't make it out. If you go through those doors," she points to the double set of doors we're passing, "it leads to the main level of the club and you'd hear the music."

"But we're not going in there?" Hudson asks from behind us.

"Nope, there's a separate entrance to the VIP area. Usually a bouncer would walk us, but I've been here enough that I don't need anyone to show me to it."

We finally reach the end of the hallway, and it takes me a moment to find the door. It's inset into the wall—a slim break in the wall is the only thing giving it away. I can't see any way to open it from here. "Now what?"

Bree laughs. "Usually, the bouncer would scan their finger to allow us entry, but Vivienne added my fingerprint into the database." Bree lifts her finger and pushes it against the wall—or at least what I thought was the wall. The area lights up, scanning her fingerprint before a low buzz releases and the door pops open. Then the wall goes dark again and I can't see anything to indicate where the fingerprint reader is.

"That's so cool." Hudson shoves between me and Bree so he can examine the wall, causing me to roll my eyes.

"Hudson is quite into tech." Onyx lays his hand on Hudson's shoulder and squeezes. "Come on, babe. We're meant to be on a date with Bree, not inspecting tech, yeah?"

When Hudson turns back to Bree, he gives her a sheepish grin. "Sorry. I've just never seen anything like this. I got a little excited."

"Well, I'll introduce you to Rodrigo. He's one of Vivienne's betas and his company is the one who invented it."

"Seriously?" Hudson rips Bree away from me and swings her around as she giggles. He places her on her feet once more, kissing the tip of her nose. "You're the best."

"How about we go inside now?" Bree smiles, laughter dancing in her eyes as she swings the door open to reveal a set of stairs leading up.

I try to take my spot beside Bree once more, but Hudson gets there first. I shake my head as I watch him lead her up the stairs as he talks excitedly about the fingerprint scanner. Onyx and I chuckle together before following behind them, making sure we pull the door shut.

At the top of the stairs is another door. Bree pushes it open, light and music filtering into the stairwell. It's still not as loud as I expected, but before I can question it, Bree is squealing and throwing herself into another woman's arms. This must be Vivienne.

Me and my pack mates step into the room, my eyes scanning the area. I find two alpha men, one female alpha, a beta man, and a female beta standing near Vivienne. This must be the rest of her pack. I'm surprised by how large her pack is. Including Chad, there are four alphas and two betas. But what's most surprising is that there are three women in the pack, including Vivienne. With the number of women dwindling, most packs don't even have one female, let alone three.

The room we're standing in is large, but nothing in comparison to the overall size of the club. The floor and ceiling are solid, but the three of the four walls are floor to ceiling glass—allowing us a 360 degree view of the club below.

"This is only one of our VIP areas. It's the one our pack uses the most." I startle at the unfamiliar female voice.

Turning, I find the female alpha standing beside me. "We appreciate you allowing us to make use of your VIP area. I think I'd go crazy if we were down there in the masses."

"I'm Lia, one of Vivienne's alphas." She offers her hand, which I'm happy to shake.

"I'm Maddox." I look around and find Onyx and Hudson speaking to other members of the pack. Guess I won't be introducing them then. "Do you allow omegas on the main floor?"

She nods. "We allow omegas to make their choice. They have the option of having a VIP room—we have twenty besides this one—or they can party on the main floor. We want to allow omegas the experience they want. Most single omegas don't wish to be placed into a VIP room because they're here looking for someone. Whether that's for just tonight or whatever they want, that's up to them. Sometimes those omegas will request a VIP room after they've met someone, or multiple someones."

"And they have sex in the rooms?" I ask.

"Sometimes they do and sometimes they don't, but we're not a sex club. That's not the main purpose of the VIP rooms. They're there to keep the omegas safe. If they happen to have sex in them, who are we to tell them what to do or not to do?"

I nod slowly, understanding that they do what they can to cater to an omega's wishes and needs. It makes me wonder if that isn't part of the reason the club has become so popular so quickly.

"I'm sure you've noticed that the music is very quiet in here," Lia says, gesturing for me to follow her as she walks toward the bar. "We have a lot of controls up here, so the experience can be what everyone wants. You can request a bartender, which Bree declined for your visit. All of our bartenders for the VIP rooms are betas in case the omega indulges in one of the rooms. They won't leave the room as they're also there to protect the omega, but they know how to be discreet.

"There are controls behind the bar that allow the occupants to raise or lower the music," she says, pointing to a control pad where each knob or button is clearly labeled. "You can also darken the glass so no one can see inside, but you can see outside, or you can black them out completely."

I watch as she demonstrates each of the controls for me. "Wow, you guys have some seriously high level tech."

She gestures to the man Hudson is speaking to. "Rodrigo is our tech guy. He has his own company and they always have the cutting edge tech. If it weren't for his tech, Eternity wouldn't be half what it is."

"I can definitely see how it's become the place to be." I pause when Vivienne and Bree approach us.

"Having fun?" Bree asks as she cuddles against my side.

"I am. Lia was just showing me the controls for the room." I turn my gaze to Vivienne. "You must be Vivienne. I'm Maddox. It's a pleasure to meet you, and your club is amazing."

Vivienne inclines her head. "Thank you, Maddox. I was just coming to collect Lia. We're going to leave the four of you to your night." She grins as her attention turns to Bree. "Don't do anything I wouldn't do."

Bree laughs. "So, do anything I want is what you're saying."

"Absolutely. Enjoy yourself. No one will disrupt you, but if you need anything, just pick up the phone behind the bar. It'll send you to our head of security and he'll make sure you have whatever you need. Oh, and I left a few bottles of your favorite champagne chilling behind the bar."

"Thanks, Viv."

Onyx and Hudson make their ways over to us as we watch Vivienne and her pack leave. "This place is amazing," Hudson says, awe filling his tone. "And Rodrigo gave me his number so we could discuss his tech after I'm done with *Heated*."

"That's adorable." Bree grins up at Hudson. "Rodrigo doesn't always get along with others, too lost in his inventions to bother dealing with the real world. He must've really liked you and the questions you asked to be willing to give you his number."

Hudson just shrugs. "Did they say something about champagne?"

Bree doesn't bother to answer him, as he's already walking around the bar. He cries out in triumph as he sets a very high end champagne on the bar before reaching back down to grab glasses that he also sets on the bar. He pours each of us a glass.

"Cheers," Bree calls as we each lift our glass and bring them to our lips. The champagne is perfect with just the right amount of bubbles, and it's the best champagne I've tasted in my life.

"Damn, baby girl." Hudson looks at her with appreciation. "You've got great taste."

"And expensive taste," I say as I turn the bottle to look at the label. "These are thousand dollar bottles of champagne, if I'm not mistaken."

Bree shrugs. "I like what I like, and I can afford it, so why not? Not that Viv is letting me pay for a damn thing tonight. She says it's good advertising for the club to appear on *Heated*. She thinks it'll bring her more omega business."

"She's not wrong. *Heated* is ground-breaking and omegas are going to watch for sure. They'll find out about Eternity and know it's a safe place for them." Hudson leans over to take Bree's hand in his. "Your success will mean more business for your friend."

Bree nods slowly and I know she wants to argue that there's no way we can be sure *Heated* will be a success, but she holds herself back. And I've never been prouder. She trusts what we're telling her.

"Enough serious talk. Let's finish this drink and get our asses to dancing." Hudson throws back his glass of champagne, leaving me to shake my head at him. Who just throws back a glass of thousand dollar champagne?

Bree lets out a whoop before downing the rest of her glass, setting it on the bar before throwing her hands up in the air. "Turn the music up and come dance with me!"

Hudson leans down and does just that, the music pounding throughout the space as Bree dances across the room to the open space I assume is considered the dance floor. I glance at Onyx, and we both shrug before throwing back our own glasses.

The three of us stalk toward Bree as one. I can't take my eyes off the sensuous way she moves her hips while she throws back her head, losing herself in the music. Hudson moves in front of her, wrapping an arm around her waist as he pulls her flush against him and sliding his leg between hers. Onyx moves to Hudson's back, hands landing on his hips as Bree's arms loop around Hudson's neck.

I take a moment to watch the three of them grinding against one another, my cock growing harder by the second. When Bree turns to me with pleading eyes, I move behind her until I'm flush with her back. She leans her head against my chest as my hands land on her hips. I roll my hips in time with hers, my hard length rubbing against her back and ass as we move.

I don't know how long we dance for before it turns dirtier, but eventually I notice that Onyx's hand has slipped inside Hudson's pants, stroking his cock as they kiss. Bree sighs, grinding down on Hudson's thigh as she watches the two of them.

"Do you like watching them together?" My voice is husky as I whisper in her ear. She shivers from head to toe before nodding.

"I want to see more."

I grin. "You heard the lady, boys. She wants to see more."

Hudson and Onyx break their kiss to grin at the omega between us.

"Yeah?" Hudson asks, wanting to make sure.

"Yes," she hisses. "I want to see the two of you together."

"Your wish is our command." Onyx's eyes meet mine. "Make sure the windows are set to where no one else can see inside, but we can still see out of them? Then take care of our girl?"

Bree shivers in my arms again, and I don't know which part of his sentence set her off. Was it the part where he called her our girl? Or was it imagining what was about to happen? Or the thrill of someone possibly seeing us together? I don't know, but I'm happy with any of those reasons.

"Why don't the two of you dance with Bree while I take care of the windows?"

Hudson spins Bree as soon as I've stepped away, putting her between the two of them. All three of their hands are roaming as they grind together to the music. I want to keep watching, but I also want to see the show Onyx and Hudson are sure to put on for us. Turning away, I adjust my cock before heading to the bar and clicking the button that will allow no one to see us. I watch the way the windows darken slightly before making my way back to my pack and the woman we're all falling for, even after only a few days.

I grind myself against Hudson's back, and he quickly drops his head back to kiss me. Our tongues duel for dominance as I slide my hand into his still open pants. Pushing beneath his boxer briefs, I take him in my hand and stroke his hard length in my hand a few times before stepping away.

"I think we were promised a show," I say as I grab Bree's hand and pull her from between my pack mates. Spinning her, I yank her to me until my front is flush with her back. I don't know exactly what Onyx has planned, but I know we're in for a damn good show. A show that

I'll make sure she enjoys even more by bringing her to climax again and again with my tongue and fingers—and cock if she wants me to.

Onyx closes the distance between him and Hudson, hands going to the buttons on the front of his vest while they continue to move to the beat. My hands trail up and down Bree's sides as we watch Onyx pull off Hudson's vest and shirt. He leans in to press kisses to Hudson's neck and chest as he slowly leads him backward until he hits the glass.

Onyx gestures for us to follow. "Maddox, wouldn't the omega look good pressed up against the glass beside Hudson?"

Bree lets forth a whine and I grin. "Is that what you want, omega? Do you want to be pressed against the glass while you watch Onyx and Hudson? While I make you feel good."

"Yes. So much, yes." Bree steps forward, but I yank her back against me. She turns to look at me over her shoulder, confusion written all over her face.

"Give me a kiss first."

Bree doesn't hesitate to spin around, throwing her arms around my neck as I lean down to meet her lips. She runs her tongue along the seam of my lips and I open for her, allowing her this moment of control. Because what she doesn't realize is that Onyx and I are about to be running the show.

She pulls away from the kiss, panting against my lips. "Now?"

"Yes, omega, you may go now."

Bree hurries across the room to lean back against the window within arm's length of Hudson. I saunter over to them, realizing that Onyx has completely stripped Hudson already and has lost his own shirt. Bree is biting her lip as she watches Onyx stroke Hudson's fat cock as they kiss.

"What do you want them to do now, omega?" I ask her, a smirk firmly in place as I watch her wiggle about, trying to get some relief. I can't scent her yet, telling me she's once again wearing scent canceling panties. I understand why she feels the need to wear them, but I hate it. I want to smell her at all times, but especially when she's aroused.

She turns to me, blinking. I can see she's trying to fight through the haze of arousal to answer me, but she's struggling. Understanding, I ask her something different. "Would you like to see Onyx with Hudson's fat cock in his mouth?"

"Fates, yes. I want that."

"And I want to scent your arousal. All of us do. May I take off your panties?"

Bree nods rapidly. "Yes. Do that, please."

I haven't even touched her yet, and she's already on edge. She really enjoys watching my pack mates together. Not that I blame her. I also love watching them together.

Onyx breaks their kiss, shooting a wink at Bree before he begins to kiss his way down Hudson's chest and stomach until he's kneeling at his feet. "I expect you to keep your hands to yourself, Hud. If you don't, I'll have to punish you. Do you understand?"

A loud whine spills from Bree as Hudson replies. "Yes, sir. I understand. No touching or you'll punish me."

"Good boy," Onyx purrs, and I see the way Hudson melts against the glass as Onyx lowers his mouth to Hudson's cock.

Kneeling before Bree, I slide my hands up her legs and under her dress. Grasping the sides of her panties, I drag them down, causing her scent to hit me in waves. She always smells like champagne and berries, but with her arousal so high, the berries are becoming dominant. I want to lick her pussy to see if she tastes like she smells, and I will—soon.

Onyx pops off Hudson's cock, stroking him slowly as he turns to Bree. "Your scent is making my cock even harder. It makes me want to rut all three of you right here, right now."

Bree's eyes widen at his words. She's never seen him like this. He's usually quiet and doesn't give off dominant vibes, but in the bedroom, that all changes. It's just one of the many reasons I love him. Given the gush of slick that spills from Bree, she likes it.

Onyx smiles, a ravenous look in his eyes. "I'm going to suck Hudson's cock until he's ready to come, then I'm going to fuck him up against this window while Maddox gets you off again and again. Your arousal is going to make all of us last twice as long—or half as long."

He takes Hudson's cock in his mouth again and I can't help but watch for a moment as he swallows it down like a champ. Hudson's hands clench against the glass as he tries to not sink his hands into Onyx's hair. Hudson and I both know how much Onyx likes it when we thread our hands in his hair while he has our cocks in his mouth, making this harder on him. Hudson doesn't mind being punished, which is what Onyx really wanted when he set up that rule, but I also know Hudson loves being told what a good boy he is.

I turn back to Bree, sliding my hands up her thighs, catching the edge of her dress in my fingers. "How about we get this off you, yeah?"

She just nods, lifting her arms as I stand, pulling the dress up as I go. I yank it up and over her head before tossing it behind me. Bree stands before me in nothing but a pair of heels, mouth open and panting. She's never looked more beautiful.

"Magnificent," Hudson breathes as he rolls his head to the side to take in Bree. Onyx hums his agreement around Hudson's cock and Hudson's hands slap down on Onyx's head as he thrusts forward. I grin, not knowing exactly what Onyx will choose for Hudson's punishment, but knowing we'll all enjoy it.

Onyx pulls off Hudson's cock once more to smirk at him. "Since your hands are already there, I'll allow you to keep them there, but you'll still be punished."

"I don't even care," Hudson murmurs before crying out as Onyx's mouth closes around him once more.

Bree whines, thighs rubbing together as she turns her attention back on my pack mates. I sink back to my knees, more than ready to taste her. Placing my hands on her inner thighs, I press on them until she spreads her legs wide enough for me to dip my head down.

I run my tongue along her from ass to clit, humming as I realize she tastes even better than she smells. I want to take this slowly and savor her, but I know I won't be able to. At least not this time.

I latch my hands on where her thighs and ass meet, squeezing as I bury my face in her. Sliding my tongue inside of her, I stroke her walls again and again as I swallow as much of her slick as I can. I bury myself so deep inside of her that my nose is brushing against her clit as I thrust my tongue in and out of her.

Bree's hands try to wrap in my hair, letting out a frustrated cry when she can't. She makes quick work of the hair tie, keeping my bun in place before burying her fingers. She uses her hands to try to get me closer to her, but I'm already as close as I can get. Her hips cant forward rapidly until she grinds her clit against me instead.

"Touch those pretty nipples for us, omega," Hudson pants out. "Fuck, Onyx. I'm so fucking close."

I hear Bree's head bounce against the glass as it falls back, her fingers digging into my scalp. "Yes, right there. I'm going to come. Please, don't stop. Don't stop."

I feel her walls spasming around my tongue, and I know she's moments from detonating. I circle her clit with my nose as I continue to spear her with my tongue, and then she's falling apart around me. Slick spills from her, soaking my tongue, my beard, and shirt. I continue to lap at her as she shrieks my name, thighs clamping down on my head and body shaking. She slowly relaxes and I lean back enough to not rub against her clit, not wanting to overstimulate her while I continue to lap at her slit.

I could eat her slick all day long and be a happy man. Hell, I'd eat her out until I drowned on her slick if she'd let me. When she pulls at my hair lightly, I ease back to look up at her. She smiles when she sees me covered in her slick.

"You probably should've taken your shirt off before you did that."

Hudson scoffs. "Oh, he's going to proudly wear the scent of you on his face and shirt for as long as we'll let him." He gasps before letting out a long groan. "Onyx, I need you inside of me now."

Onyx and I stand at the same time. Onyx's hands go to his pants as he kicks off his boots. I lick my lips as he slowly lowers the jeans down his legs, revealing that he'd chosen to go commando tonight—a fact I'd already been aware of, but Bree had not. Her mouth is agape as she stares at Onyx's cock and I can't blame her. Long and thick, it's a thing of beauty.

Stepping away from her, I let her watch as Onyx spins Hudson around until he's pressed flat against the window. I make quick work of the buttons on my shirt before tossing it to the side and pulling off the tank top I wear underneath it.

Onyx tears open a package of what I know is lube—we've taken to carrying a couple of them with us at all times. We never know when the mood might strike us. It's better to be prepared, so no one ends up hurt. I watch as he spills some of it on his cock, stroking it up and down a few times before wetting his fingers further.

He slides a finger into Hudson's tight hole while standing far enough back so Bree and I can watch as he stretches Hudson out for his cock. I kick off my own boots before sliding off my own pants and boxers. I turn my attention back to Bree, who's turned sideways as she avidly watches. Her thighs clamp together and I can see her hand snaking its way between her thighs.

"Uh uh, little omega," I purr as I grab her hand and pull it away from where she's circling her clit. "No touching yourself. I know you want to watch Onyx fuck Hudson, but that's something only a good girl gets to watch. Can you be a good girl?"

Bree tears her eyes away from the sight before her to glance at me, whining slightly. "Yes, I can be a good girl. I want to be a good girl. I want to watch."

"Then I have something else to keep your hand busy while you watch." I lead her hand to my cock and she immediately latches on, freezing when she feels my piercings. "It's a Jacob's ladder," I answer the question she hasn't yet voiced. "Have you ever been with someone with a pierced cock?"

She shakes her head as she turns her full attention on me. Her hand is covered in her slick, making it easier as she strokes me from root to tip. She's fascinated by the piercings and I want to tell her how much better they'll feel when I'm inside of her, but Hudson's groan draws our attention.

Onyx is slowly pushing into Hudson's ass, hands tight on Hudson's hips. Once he's fully seated, he smirks. "Your punishment for not listening is that you're not allowed to touch your cock and I won't be touching it either. If you want to come, it'll be from me fucking you."

Onyx pulls out before pushing back inside, oh so slowly. This pace will drive Hudson crazy. Bree's hand tightens around me as she watches, drawing a hiss from me.

Her eyes are wide as she turns toward me. "I'm so sorry, Maddox. I didn't—"

"Do it again, omega," I growl. She shivers from head to toe as she tightens her grasp, continuing to work me over with her hand.

"What happens next is completely up to you," I tell her. "I can get you off on my fingers while you stroke my cock, or I can fuck you against the window, just like Onyx is doing to Hudson."

Her eyes flash from me to my pack mates before returning to me. "The second. I want the second. Fuck me, please. I need you inside me while Onyx fucks Hudson. Fates above, the three of you are so fucking hot."

I smirk as I spin Bree until her back is flat against the window once more. Her hand falls from me as I slide my hands beneath her ass and lift her. "Legs around my waist."

She immediately locks her legs around me. Rolling my hips, my cock slides between her lips. The head of my cock bumps her clit and she squeals as she tilts her hips to meet my thrusts. With just a few more passes, she's whining, her head falling back against the window.

"I need more, alpha. I need you inside me. Please."

And who am I to deny this omega anything? I reach between us until my cock is lined up and sink into her slowly. Our moans are melodic when paired with the sound of skin on skin coming from my pack mates. Turning my head, I find both Onyx's and Hudson's eyes on us as Onyx fucks into Hudson hard and fast.

Fuck, that's hot.

"Yeah, it is." Bree grins at me, eyes hungry as she turns back to watch them. It takes me a moment to realize I spoke out loud. With a smirk, I fuck her in earnest. I want to see how many times I can feel her come around my cock.

"Holy shit." Bree's eyes are wide as she turns back to me. "Your piercings feel amazing. I've never... fuck, you feel amazing. Fuck me hard and fast. Please, alpha."

I pick up my pace, focusing my attention on Bree—not because I don't want to watch my pack mates, but because I don't need the distraction. Her hand slaps against the glass as she reaches for Hudson. He doesn't make her wait long as their fingers intertwine as Onyx and I fuck them without abandon.

The first time Bree comes, her walls clamp down on me and try to milk me. It feels so good that it takes all my willpower not to spill inside of her then and there. Somehow, I manage to fuck her through her first and second orgasms. I know I won't last through a third.

"Fuck," I curse, turning my head to look at my pack mates. Onyx is getting close, and Hudson looks like he's been riding the edge of his own orgasm for more than a few minutes. Looking at Hudson's face, I know he wants to come with Bree. Hell, I think we all do.

"You close, Onyx?" I ask, hips never slowing.

"So fucking close."

I chuckle. "Hudson?"

"I'm just waiting for Bree."

Turning back to Bree, I cock an eyebrow. "And you, my good little girl? Are you close? We all want to come with you."

"Oh, fuck. Yes. I want that." Her hips jerk to meet mine, grinding her clit against me as best she can.

"And do you want my knot?"

Bree's eyes are wide as she nods and her walls clench down on my cock, telling me she really wants that. I grin, picking up my pace and reach between us so I can work her clit with my fingers.

It doesn't take long before I feel her fluttering around me. "She's about to fall apart," I warn the others as I slam back into her, her orgasm slamming into her as my knot pops inside. She screams, back arching as I continue to rock into her, my orgasm hitting me hard and fast.

"Fucking hell," I hear Onyx mutter, turning my head as I continue to rock inside of Bree as much as I can.

Hudson's cock explodes, cum spurting from him and onto the window. Onyx grunts, spilling inside Hudson. He doesn't knot Hudson's ass as that's something we only do occasionally and never in a public place.

"Work your knot," Onyx demands as he lowers his own hand to squeeze his knot. Hudson quickly follows suit and they both groan as they keep coming.

Turning my attention back to Bree, I rock more aggressively against her. She's limp in my arms, but I'm still coming, just like my pack mates. I want her to come at least once more before I'm finished.

Both of Bree's arms wrap around me, nails digging into my back since Hudson had to let go of her hand to work his knot. Her eyes stay locked on the two of them as she clenches down on my cock again.

"Let's see how many times I can get you to come while I'm spilling inside of you." I grin when she whines, her hips rocking against me as we both work to get her off again.

The answer to the question, as we shortly learn, is three. After the third orgasm, Bree whimpers. "No more."

Gathering her more securely against me, I jerk my head to my pack mates and make my way over to the couch. I sit down carefully, not wanting to jostle Bree more than I have to. Onyx settles on one side of us, Hudson on the other as Bree lays her head on my shoulder. Onyx rubs her back while Hudson runs his hand over her hair and I hold her close.

Bree lets out a contented sigh that I echo. "This was not exactly how I thought our date would go," I say with a laugh.

"I was hoping it would." We all laugh at Bree's admission.

"I'm certainly not complaining." Hudson pauses. "Though we should probably clean the window before that shit dries."

Bree twists in my arms, giggling when she sees all the cum and slick clinging to the window. She and Hudson had soaked them. "There's not really anything in here to clean up with. We could call and ask for them to send up some cleaning supplies. They'll clean the room regardless once we're gone, but we can at least get off some of it."

"I'll go call down to security and request stuff to clean up." Onyx leans over to press a kiss to her forehead before moving to the bar.

"I'll need to apologize to Viv for the mess."

I shake my head. "I'm pretty sure she was expecting this, Bree. Her alpha, Lia, made sure I knew everything I needed to know so we could make this happen. And you heard her when they left."

"Oh, I don't doubt that. I just didn't think we'd make such a mess." She shrugs, snuggling back into me.

"I'm going to get dressed and we'll clean up while we're waiting for your knot to release." Hudson kisses both me and Bree before meeting Onyx by their clothes.

"Since you were hoping our date would end like this, have you had other dates end this way?"

Bree flushes, ducking her head. "Not exactly?"

"Oh?" I bend down until she meets my eyes. "Want to elaborate? Does this have something to do with Gabriel staying in your room?"

"How did you... I guess that was pretty obvious, huh?" Bree laughs before regaling me with the tale of her and Gabriel's hot tub adventures.

I love that I'm not even remotely jealous, I just wish I could've watched. The two of them together like that? That would've been fire. Bree relaxes into my arms and she's asleep within seconds. There had been a knock on the door when Bree had been telling me about her night escapades, and I watch Onyx and Hudson clean up the mess before making their way back to us. I repeat Bree's story to the two of them and they're both grinning when I finish.

"This feels right, doesn't it?" Hudson asks as he pushes a stray strand of Bree's hair from her face. "The three of us and her? But more than that, Gabriel and Emmett, too."

Onyx hums as he nods. "It does. Let's just hope she feels the same way. There are still eight other suitors besides the five of us. She could end up choosing any of them."

"Or maybe she'll choose us and some of the others. We don't know how big of a pack she really wants. I don't know if she knows how big of a pack she wants." Glancing down at the woman in my arms, all I can do is hope that she does choose us, because I know deep down that she's the omega for us. She's meant to be ours.

Not that I'm going to admit to Onyx he was right from day one.

Chapter Twenty

Brody

Bree misses breakfast again this morning, while Maddox, Hudson, and Onyx roll in a half hour later. They're being very closed-mouthed about their night, which might seem suspicious to others, but I think they just want Bree to be the one who decides what to tell who—something I can appreciate. But I'm absolutely sure something happened. They're looking a little too smug for it to have been an innocent evening out.

Not that I'm judging. We're all adults here, and Bree is here to find her pack. It's expected that she'll sleep with various suitors, or whatever she decides she wants to do. I'm happy if she's happy and when she finally strolls out to the deck around eleven, she sure looks happy.

"Good morning." I jump to my feet, pulling out a chair so she can join me at my table.

"Morning. Sorry I missed breakfast again. We were out late." Bree swipes a hand down her face and I can tell she's still half asleep.

"It's no problem, Bree. We don't expect you to be with us every second of every day." I hesitate. "Do you want me to go get you something from the kitchen?"

Bree's smile is blinding in its brightness, and mine only grows at the sight. "Thank you, but I stopped in before I headed out here. They'll be bringing me something in a few minutes."

I nod slowly, glancing around the deck to see where everyone is. Most of the suitors are in the pool or hot tub—except Riley and Carter. As usual, the two of them have only joined us for meals. I don't think they're doing themselves any favors by remaining separated from the rest of the suitors as they have been. I get Riley is having a hard time dealing with the mating bond, but this feels excessive to me—almost like he doesn't want to be here.

My eyebrows shoot up when I see Gabriel pinning Emmett to the side of the pool as he kisses the shit out of him. I saw that coming from a million miles away, but I'm a little surprised to see them doing it right here where anyone can see. Good for them, I guess.

Bree sighs happily, and when I glance at her, she's watching them. She's still smiling as she faces me once more. "I love love."

"I don't know if it's love just yet." I laugh. "Probably more like lust."

"That's true, but I think it's headed that way." Bree turns to thank the man setting a plate of food before her.

"What's on the agenda for today?" I ask a few minutes later. I wanted to give her a chance to at least start eating before I bothered her with my questions.

Bree finished chewing the bite she'd just taken. "I was planning to spend some time out here and then maybe go watch a movie." She pauses, grinning at me. "But that's not what you want to know, is it? You want to know about the date tonight because I've taken each of you out on a group date."

My smile never drops from my face, but I wrinkle my nose. She sure has me pegged, doesn't she? "Yeah, maybe…"

Bree doesn't seem offended by my curiosity. "I'm sure you're all wondering the same thing. I have plans and I'll announce them after I've finished eating." When I move to stand, she stops me. "You don't have to go—unless you want to."

"I just didn't want to bother you." I shrug as I drop back into my seat. I scan the deck area again and realize that every suitor is watching Bree—some from the corner of their eyes and some just straight up staring.

Bree hums as she eats, and it's adorable. I just lean back in my chair, watching her eat. A little creepy? Maybe, but she told me I could stay. It doesn't take long for her to finish, and she sets her utensils down on the clean plate and stands.

"I'll be right back." She dashes over to a table beside the door. It's filled with roses in all six colors, causing me to frown for a moment. Until she plucks two lavender roses and makes her way over to the edge of the pool, gesturing for me to join her.

"Hey everyone," she calls, waiting until all attention is on her. If only she realized it had been on her almost from the moment she stepped out the door. "I'm sure you've all realized by now that you've all gone on group dates with me and are wondering what that means for tonight's group date.

"As you can see, I'm holding two roses, so I will be asking two of you to join me tonight. I'm going to be honest with you all. When you arrived, I wasn't prepared for how much of a toll it would be on me to have so many alphas surrounding me. On the one hand, I love it. On the other hand, it can be overwhelming.

"No one has done anything wrong and I've been enjoying my time with each one of you, but I need a break, so tonight, I'm inviting Brody and Emmett to join me on a date." Bree turns and offers me one rose while Emmett launches himself from the pool and hurries over.

"I'd love that," I tell her, honestly. I don't think she only chose us because we're betas—though it was obviously a contributing factor. Even if it is the entire reason, who am I to question another date with her? And I like Emmett, so it's no hardship to have him along with us.

Emmett shakes like a puppy, splattering both me and Bree with water. Bree just giggles, offering him the rose. "And you Emmett?"

"Just tell me where to be and when and I'm yours." He leans in and kisses her cheek.

"If the two of you will pick me up at four, we're going to explore the area. Depending on what sounds good to you, I was planning on a bit of shopping and there's an excellent art gallery. Then I figured we could grab dinner and there's a place called Sip 'n Slide where we can taste a variety of wines while painting."

"That sounds amazing," I tell her, and I mean it. I've always wanted to try one of those sip and paint places, or whatever they're called. I don't know a lot about art, but I like looking at it. Shopping isn't my favorite activity, but if it'll make Bree happy, I'll carry all the bags she wants me to.

"It does," Emmett agrees. "I'm guessing we should dress casually."

Bree nods before shucking off her dress to reveal a swimsuit. "Now, if you'll excuse me, I'm in need of a swim."

Bree doesn't bother walking over to the stairs. She just jumps straight into the water. Emmett rushes over to lay his rose on a table before running after her and cannon balling into the water, absolutely soaking me.

With a sigh, I wave to everyone as I head inside. I hadn't dressed for the pool so I'll need to change now. And maybe I'll take a nap. I'd stayed up way too late last night, waiting for Bree and the guys to come back from their date. Then it took me another two hours to fall asleep. I'm absolutely beat.

I end up sleeping most of the afternoon away, only waking when Bree calls my room around three to make sure I'm alright. I manage to shower and be ready to knock on her door right at four.

Bree wasn't joking about wanting to shop. We spend almost two full hours going from store to store at a mall called The River at Rancho Mirage. I'm fairly sure we hit every store in the place. The art gallery is also there and while it's not big, we spend close to an hour there before heading to dinner at a Korean BBQ place that Emmett agrees is very authentic once we've finished eating.

Now, we're sitting at Sip 'n Slide with our first glass of wine as the owner, Michael. explains the process to it. They have various rooms and teachers, but he's going to be running our private session.

"We have ten different local wines for you to try. You're welcome to a full glass of each if you'd like, or you can just have a sip of each—it's up to you to decide. Bree has arranged to bring home the bottles once the class is done." Michael smiles at us. "You'll find the most used colors on your palettes. Bree requested various colored roses as tonight's painting." He pulls a sheet down, revealing a vase holding multiple roses of each of the six colors used for the show.

Michael continues, "I'll be over here painting in between serving each of the glasses of wine. Bree has booked you for a two-hour session, so I'll be around every ten minutes to bring you a different wine. You'll find a variety of bread products next to your easel. These help you cleanse your palate between tastings. There's also water. If you need any help or have questions, please call me over."

I lift the glass of wine to my lips and take a small sip. Wine is not my drink of choice, but I've found a few that I've really enjoyed. This one is a chardonnay, and it's fairly good. There's a hint of pineapple in it which is interesting. I take another sip and lift my paintbrush, trying to decide where to start.

Bree leans over and whispers, "I plan on making mine very abstract."

I laugh. "Mine will probably end up the same. I've never painted before." I dip my paintbrush into the red, laughing again when I end up with a blob of the color on my canvas. "Yeah, I don't think I'm going to be very good at this."

"That's okay, me neither." Bree glances over at Emmett's canvas and I do the same, seeing that he actually has shapes on his that look like roses. "Emmett's definitely going to put us to shame."

"I've taken painting classes before. I'll never be an expert, but I can definitely do better than blobs." Emmett laughs as he glances between mine and Bree's canvas. He hesitates for a moment, eyes glancing at Michael. "I didn't want to ask and be rude, but I noticed Michael doesn't have a scent. Is he one of the omega business owners you know?"

Bree smiles, glancing over at Michael, who gives her a nod. She turns back to us. "I'd already talked to Michael about this. I knew it could come up tonight. Yes, he's an omega, but that isn't the designation he was born to. He was born a beta. He's still in the process of a medical transition, so he uses the very best scent canceling products there are. Once he finishes with the transition, we're hopeful that his omega scent will come out. Designation transitions are still very new. Michael is one of the first in this area. Fated Industries is sponsoring his transition.

We're considering starting a program to help others transition if it proves successful."

"There's nothing worse than feeling like a stranger in your own body," Michael says as he hands me another glass of wine. "This one is a riesling. And I'm completely open about being in transition, so if you have questions, ask away. Bree and I should be able to answer your questions." I take a sip of the riesling, finding it an interesting blend.

"That's so awesome that you're transitioning," Emmett tells him as he accepts his glass.

"I didn't realize that they'd begun medical transitions. Are they doing a chemical transition or surgical? Or is it a combination?" I grin when all three stare back at me in shock. "I'm an EMT. When it became a possibility, they briefed us on the topic. I guess when I head back after *Heated*, I'll have to go through more training since they're actually happening now."

Michael smiles, but I can see the relief in his eyes that we're not judging him. I can imagine that would be hard for him, and something that probably happens often. "It's a chemical transition. If that doesn't work, they're looking into surgical options. They're hopeful that the medication will affect the body enough for me to transition. It's easier because I'm a beta. They've actually only begun doing beta transitions at this time. Because I'm transitioning to an omega, they don't need to change anything physically... assuming the medicine works."

"That's fascinating. I could honestly talk about this all night, but I'll let you get back to your painting since I'm on a date."

Bree giggles. "I won't be offended if you want to talk to Michael."

"Why would I want to talk to another omega when you're by my side?"

I hear Michael chuckle as he walks away. We fall into a pattern, talking between receiving each wine and attempting to paint the roses. Well, me and Bree attempt it while Emmett is over there creating a masterpiece. He might not think it is, but I'm in awe of his talent.

After two hours, Bree and I are laughing at our attempts, which really are just a bunch of colors spread around the canvas. Emmett gifts his canvas to Bree with a flourish. "Pretty roses for the prettiest lady."

"Smooth, dude. Smooth." I shake my head as I glance at my canvas again. "Yeah, I'm not giving you this. It's terrible."

"Awww, but I want it, Brody." Bree pouts. "It can be a reminder of our date."

I hold up my hands in surrender. "If you want this dumpster fire of a painting, who am I to deny you?"

Michael laughs as he looks between the three of us. "You are adorable," he tells us. "I'll have someone drop the paintings and the wine at the compound sometime tomorrow, Bree."

"Thanks, Michael. It was a blast." Bree stands, wobbling on her feet as she giggles. "Guess I had more than I thought."

Both Emmett and I jump to our feet to help balance Bree, but I'm feeling a little unbalanced myself. "Make that two of us. I didn't drink a full glass all night."

"Make that three." Emmett shakes his head. "That was some damn good wine."

"It was. Now I'm going to need to hold both of your arms to make sure I don't fall over." She takes hold of our arms when we offer them to her, giggling. "What gentlemen."

As we make our wobbly way to the waiting SUV, I realize tonight was exactly what the three of us needed. I hadn't thought that the alpha energy in the house was affecting me, but being away from the house for the night shows me it was. I'm glad that Bree chose me and Emmett for tonight's date. It was just what the doctor ordered.

Sasha

Tonight is the rose ceremony, and we have a free day. Bree joined us for breakfast, but then told us that while she had planned to spend the day with us, she was going to spend the day pampering herself instead. I wonder how much these rose ceremonies are bothering her. It cannot be easy to decide who to send home and who to keep. Most of the guys here are great—excluding Riley, who has been keeping himself and Carter away from the rest of us. I will be surprised if Bree does not send them home tonight.

There has been next to no attempt on their behalf to get to know Bree. That is not one hundred percent accurate. I have seen Carter make the effort, but Riley is always dragging him away. I do not understand why he is here if he does not want an omega—if he does not want Bree.

Shaking my head, I push away my thoughts. I am back in the gym, going through my daily workout and practice. It is the best way to keep myself from worrying about the ceremony tonight. It is hard to get one-on-one time with Bree, with twelve other suitors trying to do the same. I definitely feel a connection with her, but I do not believe that it is on the same level as the ones she has with some of the other suitors. Which is fine. I just hope that she feels it enough to want to keep me here.

I do not believe we have had enough time together to know whether we would be a good match, and I would like the time to determine that. I know some of the suitors have been sexually involved with her, but I have not attempted anything of the sort with her. I want to be sure that there is something real between us before mixing in our hormones. Call me old-fashioned, but I prefer to care for someone before I sleep with them.

I am doing a series of grand jetés when I hear the door open. I do not stop what I am doing, expecting it to be another suitor coming in to work out. I am surprised when I hear a feminine voice clearing their throat. I turn my head, mid jump, to see Tessa standing there.

I finish the jump and bounce in place for a moment to make sure I have my balance and to be sure my legs stay warm before I walk over to her. "Tessa, what can I do for you?"

"I'm sorry to interrupt your training session, Sasha, but this couldn't wait." Tessa frowns, and I cannot help but wonder what is going on.

"What do you mean?"

Tessa takes a deep breath. "I've just gotten off a call with your manager and the owner of the ballet company. They started calling late last night, but I wasn't available and honestly forgot to return the call this morning. They've been blowing up my phone all day."

"Okay..."

"Your understudy was injured in last night's show. There was apparently something on the stage and he caught his foot in it. They're saying his ankle is broken and he won't be able to dance anytime soon. The other understudy is out with a labral tear." Tessa shakes her head. "They wanted to speak with you immediately, but I told them I'd inform you of what's going on and have you call them back."

"Have you told Bree of zis yet?" I ask, mind going crazy, trying to figure out what I need to do.

Tessa shakes her head. "Not yet. Sasha, they're going to try to convince you to leave *Heated*, and I understand completely if you choose to do that. But if you leave, that's it. You're giving up Bree. We could consider you for a future season, but you'd be giving up the last week you've spent with Bree. I won't try to sway your decision either way, but I will suggest a few things."

"*Da?*" I ask, curious what she will ask of me.

"You should go talk to Bree. Tell her what's going on and be honest with her about what you're thinking. With the ceremony tonight, it would be easy enough to send you off tonight. If you can't wait that long, we can just make an announcement. If you choose to stay, it's at the chance of Bree not choosing you. This is your career we're talking about, so it's important that you take the time to think about it and seriously consider all your options."

I nod slowly. "I understand. Zank you for bringing zis to my attention. I believe I will speak with Bree now."

"Once you've spoken with Bree and made your decision, just let me know. You can use the phone in your room to call me. I'll make sure I have my phone on me at all times."

"Zank you, Tessa."

I stare after Tessa as she nods before leaving the room. That is definitely the end of my practice for the day. I need to speak with Bree, but must first do a cool down. I go through it as quickly as I can and then hurry to Bree's suite. I do not knock right away, choosing to pace up and down the hallway instead.

It is not that I do not wish to speak with her, but I do not know where I stand on this. This is my career and choosing to not leave the show could mean the end of it all. I know I am nearing the end of my career due to my age, but I still have a few more years before that really becomes an issue. Then there is the fact that I am meant to buy the company from the current owner when I retire. If I refuse to go back when they need me, will this make her change her mind?

I realize that pacing up and down the hallway is doing nothing but making my head hurt. I need to talk this out with someone and I hope that person can be Bree. I knock sharply on the door, waiting for her to answer. I just hope she is not in the shower or indisposed. If I have to, I guess I can have Tessa call her. Bree has not given me her extension yet, nor do I believe she has given it to any of the suitors.

The door swings open, and I jump back in surprise. I guess I became more lost in my thoughts than I realized. Bree's head tilts to the side, a slight frown on her lips. "Sasha? Did you need something?"

"I do." I nod. "I need to speak with you. It is of great importance. I am sorry for interrupting your pampering time, but it cannot wait."

Bree nods, brow furrowed as she steps back to allow me entry into the suite. "We can talk in my sitting room."

I step inside, letting my eyes roam over the space. Her sitting room is almost as big as my room here. I stand in the middle of the room as Bree shuts the door before moving over to the other door in the room, swinging it shut as well.

"That leads to my bedroom and I don't want it filled with alpha scents." She winces. "Sorry, I'm not sure that came out quite the way I wanted it to."

"It is alright, Bree. You do not want any scents in your room zat are not your own. I understand." Gesturing to the multiple couches, loveseats, and armchairs, I ask, "Should we sit?"

Bree shakes her head. "I swear my brain went offline when I started my pampering. Of course we should sit."

I follow Bree over to the couch. She plops down in one corner, pulling her legs under herself, and when she pats the spot next to her, I sit down carefully.

"Tell me about what has you so upset, Sasha."

I take a moment for myself, closing my eyes and taking a deep breath. It should not be this hard to tell Bree what is going on—it just shows how torn I am over what to do.

"I was in the gym, doing my daily practice when Tessa found me. She said she had just gotten off the phone with my manager and ze owner of the ballet company I work for. My understudy fell last night during ze show and broke his ankle. His understudy is currently out because he has a labral tear. Zey have no one who can dance ze show and wish for me to return.

"Tessa told me it was my decision and that she would not try to sway me, but that I should come talk to you. I do not even know what I want to do. I love dancing—it is my life. I only have so many years left that I will be able to dance at this level. The company owner could choose to release me from my contract if I do not come back. She could also change her mind about selling me the company when I retire from dancing.

"But I have enjoyed my time getting to know you and ze other suitors. It has been a once in a lifetime experience. I feel like we could be good together, but even if I choose to stay, zere is a chance you will not choose me. Zen I will have lost everything—maybe. I just do not know what I should do."

"Oh, Sasha." Bree grabs my hand, squeezing it between both of her smaller hands. "That's a decision no one should ever have to make. You're correct that if you choose to stay, there's no guarantee that I will choose you. I will tell you I have no intention of sending you home anytime soon, but that could change. I wish I could offer you a guarantee, but I can't."

"What would you do if you were in my position?"

She shakes her head. "I can't answer that. It could influence your choice and I won't do that. More than that, I don't know what I would do if forced to choose between my company and being here—luckily, I won't have to find out since my company is producing the show. With that being said, if you choose to leave, there is a chance we could bring you back for a later season. I would be sad to see you go, but this doesn't have to be the end of you finding your omega."

"You have given me much to zink about." I sigh. "I do not know what I will choose. I must call my manager and ze owner to see what zey have to say. I know we are short on time with ze ceremony tonight, but I will give you my decision as soon as I have made it. Zank you, Bree."

"For what?"

"For listening and not being angry. For letting me talk it out with someone before I call my manager. I believe I will speak with her without anger now. She will help me figure out what is best for me, my life, and my career. You are a wonderful, caring woman."

Bree flushes, but smiles at me as I stand. "I look forward to hearing your answer. Why don't you call Tessa from my phone and she'll tell you where to go so you can call? I'll be in my suite for the rest of the day, so please, come see me when you know."

"I will. Zank you." I call Tessa and, with one last thank you to Bree, I make my way to the control room. Talking to Bree did not help me make my decision, but it helped me clear my head. I do not wish to make this decision, and I know it will be a hard one. I do not look forward to making it, or speaking with my manager. I also do not look forward to possibly leaving Bree.

But whatever happens will happen. All I can do now is decide what I want.

Bree

"Welcome back, viewers and suitors," Reginald begins the ceremony. "Bree and her suitors have now been able to spend a week together getting to know one another. After today, there will be a rose ceremony every night, but that doesn't mean Bree will send someone home every night. There are still seven weeks until Bree's heat. How long will she take to find her pack? Only time will tell.

"You'll see there's only one vase tonight with three colors of roses. Bree will not be handing out any date roses tonight, as tomorrow we'll be doing something a little different. Tomorrow, the suitors will compete against one another in a challenge for the first one-on-one date with Bree tomorrow night.

"These challenges will take place about once a week to shake things up. While this one is an individual challenge, the next might be pairs or groups. We're going to keep you on your toes as you all vie for a place in Bree's pack. You'll receive more information on the challenge tomorrow morning at breakfast.

"Now, it's time for Bree to hand out the roses. When I call your name, you will make your way onto the stage. Bree may or may not have something to say to you when she hands you your rose. She will be just as surprised as the suitors about the order you're called in." Reginald laughs. "What can I say? I get my joy where I can? Bree, the stage is yours."

I glare at Reginald as he walks off the stage laughing. I don't care that the camera probably catches every moment. I'm going to kick his ass later. Focusing back on the suitors, I smile as we all await the first name to be called. I try to keep my mind blank, not wanting to give anything away. I don't keep my eyes on any of the suitors for more than a few seconds for the same reason.

"Finnegan Abernathy, you're the first suitor up. Please make your way to the stage."

I'm a mess tonight, not even able to allow myself to watch as he makes his way onto the stage. While I've done two rose ceremonies already, those were easy. I know from here on out, they'll be harder when I have to say goodbye to someone.

Focusing my attention on Finnegan, my smile brightens. "Finnegan, it has been great getting to know you this week. You helped me when I needed someone to talk to. I'm not sure that I could've made that decision if I hadn't talked it over with you... well, you and Maddox."

Finnegan and I both laugh before I continue. "Our group date went well, or at least I believe it did. And when you asked me if you could kiss me goodnight because we were on a proper date, it took everything in me to not swoon on the spot."

I turn to the vase and pluck a rose and offer it to him. "That is why I wish for you to remain on *Heated* so we might continue to get to know more about each other."

"Thanks, lass. I would lek nothing more." Finnegan leans over and kisses my cheek as he plucks the yellow rose from my hand. As he makes his way back to the other suitors, Reginald is already moving onto the next name.

"Dalton Cole."

At least with Reginald calling names back to back, I don't have to switch my gaze back to the suitors. I remain facing the stairs until Dalton is climbing up them. He comes to a stop a few feet from me.

"Dalton, I feel like I've gotten to know you intimately this week." I snicker, unable to resist. Sometimes I have the mind of a teenage boy. What can I say? "But there's still so much more I wish to learn about you."

I reach behind me and grab a rose, offering it to him. "Which is why I'm asking you to remain on the show."

Dalton grins as he takes the rose and pulls me into a hug that has my feet leaving the ground. "I want that too. Thank you, darlin'."

"Hudson Kennedy, Maddox Pierce, and Onyx Holt."

Hudson is grinning as he bounces ahead of his pack mates. Maddox and Onyx are much more controlled in their movement, showing no emotion, as they move to stand on either side of Hudson.

"As one of the two remaining packs, I want to advise you that while you will be called up as a group, that doesn't mean you will all receive the same rose. The only time that it's guaranteed you'll receive the same color rose is if I choose your pack to become my pack, or if you're being asked to leave."

I laugh. "I just wanted to make sure that I mentioned that because I don't know that we did previously. I've had time to get to know each of you as individuals and your pack as a whole this week. It's been fun for sure, but I've also really enjoyed it."

I grab three roses, offering them to the guys. "This week you all receive a yellow rose, as I wish you to remain on the show."

"Thank fuck," Hudson yells and all I can do is shake my head. He takes the yellow rose before leaning down to kiss me square on the lips, surprising the crap out of me. Then he turns to both his pack mates, smacking a kiss on their lips.

"I'd say sorry for the way he acts, but honestly, it's good that you get to see this side of him. Gotta accept the good with the bad, right?" Maddox winks.

"Excuse you." Hudson frowns at Maddox.

Onyx lets out a long-suffering sigh before leaning over to kiss my cheek. "Thank you, Bree. We enjoyed our date and getting to know you. We can't wait to continue getting to know you better."

Hudson looks like he wants to add something, but Maddox and Onyx are already marching him away. I laugh and laugh, and it's just what I needed. The nerves finally fall away, and I know everything happens for a reason. I have seven more weeks of this, and I can do it.

Once I'm done laughing, I find Reginald staring at me with a cocked eyebrow. I just flip him off while he narrows his eyes.

"Carter and Riley Woods."

My amusement sinks when Carter's eyes meet mine. He knows what's coming. I warned them that this is what would happen if Riley couldn't get his act together. Hiding in their suite for most of the week is definitely not what I consider getting his act together.

I grab the two roses as they march their way over to me. "I don't think any of us are surprised by this outcome. Riley, you've been struggling with your mate bond—something I was willing to overlook. Until it became clear to me, you didn't intend to try to fight it. I need to know that those I choose to be a part of my pack will get along, and by refusing to interact with other suitors, I can't judge that. So, tonight is your last night. I'm sorry, Carter. I really enjoyed the time we were able to spend together, but I never got a chance to know Riley well.

"Riley... there was barely any effort made on your part. Sure, there were times I could tell you were trying, but mostly, it's like you didn't care. On the day of our date, you scared me and I don't scare easily. Before you try to add anyone to your pack, make sure your bond with Carter is settled. And be sure that's what you really want, so no one else will be hurt."

Riley snatches the black rose from my hand and stomps off the stage, pausing when he realizes Carter isn't beside him. "Carter," he growls.

Carter shakes his head, fury written along his features as he turns to his alpha. "I'm going to say goodbye. You can wait." He turns back to me. "I'm sorry. If we'd known how hard mating would be on Riley, we would've waited. I still don't regret the choice to bond with him because he is my forever, but I regret what happened here because we came onto *Heated* even though we knew he was having issues. I know there's nothing I can say to make it better, or even okay. But it was a joy getting to know you and being a part of the first season of *Heated*."

"Thank you, Carter. And who knows, maybe we'll meet again if the two of you decide to try out *Heated* again."

Carter presses a kiss to my hand before following his alpha back to where the suitors stand.

"Gabriel Ramirez."

A grin makes its way onto my face as soon as I see Gabriel's smirking face. I kind of want to slap that look off his face, but it looks good on him. "Gabriel, we've had an enjoyable week. Of everyone here, you've been the best at making sure you get to know each of the suitors—though you obviously get along better with some than others." I grin as my eyes find Emmett. He shakes his head but continues to smile.

I grab a rose for Gabriel. "I'd like to continue spending time with you and getting to know you. So, I'm asking you to remain on the show."

Gabriel takes the rose before wrapping his arms around me and dipping me backwards as his lips meet mine. I lose myself in the kiss even with as short as it is. I'm giggling when he finally rights me and I can hear the other suitors hooting and hollering. "Thank you, Bree."

"Things will never be boring with you around," I call after him and he shoots me a wink.

"Sasha Rostova."

Sasha's eyes are haunted as he walks across the stage to me. I grab his hand and pull him into a hug that he so obviously needs. He clings to me for a moment before pulling away.

"Zank you, Bree."

"No, thank you for never bringing up the fact that I was so star-struck when I first saw you that I forgot how words worked." We laugh together. "Obviously, I always knew there was a person behind the persona I saw, but it still surprised me as I got to know you. You don't get to meet one of your idols every day. When I think of ballet, I think of you, and that will never change."

I reach over and grab a rose, offering it to him as I fight against the tears threatening to fall. "When it came down to a choice between the career you love with everything you are and this show, I believe you chose correctly. I'm sad that you're leaving, but I will see you dance again one day and I'll be able to say I know you. You, the amazing man and not just the amazing dancer. Thank you for giving *Heated* and me a chance. But don't think I won't be hitting you up for future seasons. Your omega is out there somewhere, and I hope we can help you find her."

A tear trails down his face as he stares down at me, a hand wrapped around mine that holds the black rose. "You are an amazing woman and an amazing omega. You will make sure zat whomever you choose will treat you as you deserve to be treated, da?"

I nod my head. "I will."

"You will also tell me when you wish to see me dance. I will get you front row seats and behind ze scene access. It is ze least I can do for you. Zank you for being so understanding. It is truly my loss to be leaving here today."

I lift onto my toes to brush a kiss across his cheek. "I wish you the best of luck, Sasha."

As he walks away, I brush my finger beneath my eye to see if any tears leaked out and messed up my makeup. Everything seems fine and when I turn to Reginald, he gives me a thumbs up.

"As you may or may not have noticed, there are only four roses left—two yellow and two white. This means the four remaining suitors no longer need to worry about being sent home, but who will she choose to spend the night with her?

"Brody Sullivan, Emmett Kwon, Maverick Kelley, and Roman Knight. Will the four of you please make your way to the stage?"

I can feel a blush creeping up my neck as I await the four of them. Why I'm so embarrassed about inviting two of these men to my bed, I don't understand. I've had sex with more than one suitor, watched others have sex, given a blowjob, and allowed multiple of them to touch me. It's all been recorded, and obviously, they won't be showing the acts on television, but I know it'll be obvious what happened.

Why is it different to stand up here before the suitors and viewers and announce that I want two of them to spend the night with me? It shouldn't be hard and I shouldn't feel ashamed, but I do. I realize in that moment that I'm afraid of what others will think of me—what they'll say about me.

That isn't me. I've never cared what people thought of me, or what they whispered behind my back. I am who I am, and I'm damn proud of it. Shaking away the worry and the voices in the back of my head, I stand up straighter as the four suitors fan out in front of me, a smile on my face.

"Brody, you never fail to make me smile. You're always smiling and that's contagious. A good kind of contagious," I add, snickers from the suitors, causing me to laugh. "Look, I'm not always good with words, especially when I don't practice them beforehand, but what I'm trying to say is that I've really enjoyed getting to know you. You're not quite what I was expecting when I realized how young you were, and I love that."

Turning to Roman, I smile at his stoic face. "Roman, I know you've worried about the gap in our ages, and I hope I proved to you I don't care. Here you are standing next to the man ten years my junior, the oldest and youngest of the suitors. I don't give a damn how old you are. I care about how you treat me and those around you. And you? You treat everyone with respect. You make me feel safe, cared for, and desired. What more could I ask for?"

"Maverick. You surprised me the day in the pool. You and Dalton both—not that I'm complaining. I feel like I haven't put enough effort into getting to know you as well as I have others, so from here on out, I'm going to make it a point to spend more one-on-one time with you. I want to know more about you, and I want you to know more about me."

"Emmett, my sweet beta. You care so much about everyone around you. You're a true caregiver and I love that. You have a way of making the person you're talking to feel like they're the only person in the world. You care so much, so deeply. Just observing you with others has shown me that. I hope that one day, I can be just like you."

I take a deep breath as I grab the four remaining roses. "Making the decision of who to invite into my bed the first time has been hard. Most of what has happened up until now has just naturally happened. The idea of announcing in front of everyone who I'm taking to my bed has been nerve-wracking because it doesn't feel natural. But I no longer think that's a bad thing. *Heated* is about finding my pack, yes, but also learning to accept my omega side in a way I never have before. Learning things about myself that I've repressed for years."

I shake my head as I laugh. "I'm going to stop talking now because I feel like I'm not making any sense. Tonight, I'd like to ask Roman and Emmett to join me in my suite."

I offer them both their white roses before handing the last two roses to Maverick and Brody. "Just because you weren't invited to my room tonight doesn't mean that I'm not interested in you in that way. It just means I'm not ready for an orgy."

There's a moment of silence as my eyes go wide. Holy shit, Tessa is going to kill me. Then everyone breaks out into laughter and I realize it doesn't fucking matter. I've been honest with these men and shown them the real me.

Reginald waves the men off stage as he moves to stand beside me once more. "Well, tonight's ceremony has been... interesting, to say the least. Nothing about this first season of *Heated* has been dull, has it?"

I snort, amused by Reginald's running commentary. When he turns to me with a glare, I lift my hand to cover my mouth as I try to fight off the giggles threatening to spill from my lips.

"Tune back in next week to *Heated* and find out what the challenge is all about, and who's going to win a date night with Bree. Not to mention all the other fun things she keeps getting up to. Good night!"

I wait a few seconds before swatting Reginald's arm. "What the hell, Reginald?"

"What? Tessa said I should try to incorporate some humor into my speeches. I think it was great."

"And I think you're an asshole. You're lucky I love you." Leaning up, I press a kiss to his cheek and make my way off the stage. Tessa is waiting for me, hand on her hip and foot tapping.

"An orgy, Bree? Really? Do you think we can put that on prime time television? Because if you do, you're sadly mistaken."

I pat Tessa's shoulder. "Don't get so worked up, Tessa. It's bad for your blood pressure. If we have to record a new closing from me later, we can. But let's be real. I'm an omega looking for a pack. Orgies are going to be a part of my life, and the viewers know that."

Tessa shakes her head. "You're going to be the death of me. All this sex and cursing, and now you're talking about orgies. The network will never go for this."

"So they'll put us on the cable station instead. They can show a very edited version on prime time. Stop worrying. They'll figure out a way for the show to air. They want us. They want this. Now, if you'll excuse me, I have two men waiting to take me to bed."

Tessa just gapes at me as I walk away. I'd surprised her—and myself—with my words, but I know they're true. *Heated* is going to be a success.

Chapter Twenty-one

Bree

Leaving the ballroom with Roman and Emmett by my side felt completely normal. For the first time, I don't feel embarrassed or feel like I'm being judged by those around me. It's a pleasant feeling that completely disappears when we make it back to my suite.

The three of us stand in the sitting room, glancing around the room to avoid looking at one another. Not awkward at all. Doubts rush back through me as I worry that this wasn't as good of an idea as I thought it was. I need this to happen. I need to know how well these men can share in the bedroom, and because I'm apparently a horny ass omega.

"This shouldn't be awkward," I murmur, feeling both men's eyes on me.

"And yet... it still somehow is?" Emmett offers with a grin.

Roman laughs. "Yeah, just a little. How is this supposed to work? Or are we just meant to drag you off to the bedroom? That seems... a little barbaric."

I perk up at his words. "Yes, please."

Then the three of us are laughing, the tension slowly leaking from the room. Once I've calmed down, I consider the two of them. "I know the two of you might not know one another as well as you'd like before falling into the same bed with a woman, but I chose the two of you for a reason.

"Emmett, you make people feel comfortable around you at all times. And you're sexy as hell. Roman, I know you'll work well with others—even in the bedroom. By now, you know I've slept with Gabriel and Maddox... and kind of Onyx and Hudson, I guess." I snort. "But this is the first planned night together, and I wanted it to be with the two people who would make me most comfortable. It may have been easier to just ask one of you, but it's important to know that you all can work together, both in and out of the bedroom."

I shrug. "But if either of you isn't feeling up to this, we don't have to do anything. We can just watch a movie, snuggle, and sleep in the same bed. I would never ask anyone to do something they didn't feel comfortable doing."

Emmett snorts. "Bree, I can promise you that both of us want to sleep with you. I'm definitely not passing up this opportunity."

"If this is what you want, Bree, it's what we want. It's just the getting there that's making it awkward." Roman shrugs. "Generally speaking, if I'm taking someone to bed, there's a date or something before it happens. Unless it was someone specifically calling for sex, and even though this is for sex, it's not just sex for any of us."

"Yeah, well..." Unable to think of anything else to do, I start stripping off my shirt as I walk toward the bedroom. "I'll be waiting in my bed, naked. So once you're comfortable—"

I let out a squeal as Roman comes up behind me, scooping me into his arms. "No, omega. You'll allow us the honor of undressing you. Come on, Emmett, we have an omega to take care of."

Roman sets me gently on the end of the bed before stepping back, Emmett appearing at his side as they both just watch me. Their scents deepen, wrapping around me and I perfume—even if they can't tell just yet. I can't wait until I'm naked and my scent is no longer hidden. I want to be covered in their scents and for them to be covered in mine. I lick my lips as my eyes move between them.

Impatient as always, I blurt, "What the hell are you waiting for?"

Roman tsks at me. "Don't be a brat, sweet girl. The anticipation is half the fun."

"For who? Certainly not for me." I reach behind me, ready to get myself naked, when Emmett rushes over. He grabs my arms and pulls me backward until my back is flush with the bed, my arms stretched high above me. My legs dangle over the end of the bed in a way that's not overly comfortable, but when Roman moves up to stand between my legs, I stop squirming.

"Only good omegas get what they want. Bad omegas get punished and teased. Are you going to be a good little omega or a bad little omega?"

My thighs clench, wanting to rub together, but with Roman between them, that's not an option. Roman cocks an eyebrow, and I know he's waiting for an answer. I want to tell him I'll be a good little omega because then I'll get what I want, but I'm more likely to be a bad omega. Sometimes I just can't help but be a brat.

"Do you want me to give you an honest answer or what I want the answer to be?"

Roman's eyes narrow as he stares at me, shaking his head. "So, a bad little omega. Good to know."

Emmett chuckles darkly, and when I roll my head back to look at him, I find a predatory smirk on his face. I bite my lip as slick slips from me. I don't know what it is about that look he's giving me, but I like it a lot.

"Emmett, you'll hold her still for me, won't you?" Roman's words are practically a purr, and my eyes fall back on him. His attention is on Emmett, his gaze heavy with lust and hunger. But is it all for me or is some of that for Emmett? I hope it's for Emmett too.

"I'll keep her still for you, alpha," Emmett replies, not bothering to hide his attraction to the older alpha.

I grin as I look back at Emmett again. "He likes it when I call him daddy. I bet he'd like it if you called him that, too."

"Oh, really?" Emmett looks at Roman with a smirk. "Is she right? Do you want me to call you daddy?"

A shiver runs through me as Roman growls, but I can see the way his cock throbs in his pants. He does like it. He can't hide that from us—I don't know why he would want to.

"I don't need two brats." Roman lifts his eyebrows as he glances between me and Emmett. "Are you going to be a brat or help me punish one?"

"Definitely the second one, daddy." Emmett just continues to smile at Roman, whose eyes fall shut as he shivers. Pairing these two together was definitely a good choice.

"Ummm... Can we get on with the punishing of the omega part of the evening?"

Emmett snorts, shaking his head, but he says nothing as he continues to watch Roman.

Roman sighs, but reaches down to undo my pants. I lift to help him move them over my ass and down my legs. He drops to his knees as soon as he tosses them to the side. He runs his nose up the inside of my left leg from ankle to inner thigh before following the same path on my right leg.

"These scent canceling panties do too good of a job," he groans as he slips a finger on each side of my panties. He grips the fabric and they press into me painfully for a moment as he pulls at them. The sound of my panties ripping is music to my ears as air rushes across my dripping pussy and my scent rolls through the room.

Emmett and Roman both groan and I need to be naked immediately. When I try to pull at my arms so I can get to my bra, which now feels uncomfortable and constricting, Emmett just tightens his grip around my wrists. I whine, needing the offending piece of clothing off my body.

"Please. It's so uncomfortable. I need it gone. Just let me take it off," I beg and plead with my captors.

"Awww, poor omega. Are you uncomfortable?" Roman asks as he stands, leaning over to run his nose down my neck before traveling between my boobs. "Are your boobs suffering and in need of some freedom?"

"Yes. Please. Take it off."

Roman smirks down at me. "If only you'd been a good little omega, then I could do that for you. But since you want to be a brat, you'll just have to suffer."

Roman laughs as he lifts his head to meet my gaze. I bare my teeth to him, letting out a hiss. He thinks he's going to be punishing me, but I'm already plotting my revenge.

Leaning back down, Roman's tongue snakes out as he traces a line down my body until he's hovering over my pussy. I bite down on my lip to keep myself from sassing him again. Maybe I can be a good little omega. Probably not, but maybe. I can at least try.

He runs his nose along my slit, bumping my clit lightly before he lifts his head. The look on his face is one hundred percent predator and I can't hold back the whimper that falls from my lips—not because I'm scared, but because I want him to devour me.

"You smell divine, little omega. I'm meant to be punishing you, not rewarding you, but then I'd be punishing myself." He shakes his head. "Emmett, help her sit up?"

Emmett releases me, and I scramble to sit up while Emmett moves in to settle at my back. I bite my lip as my eyes stay locked on Roman. I want to ask him if Emmett can strip me, but I know better. I'm not in charge right now—Roman is. It takes a lot of effort on my part to be good, and I hope Roman will recognize that and give me a well-earned reward.

"Take her bra off, Emmett. No need for her to be uncomfortable any longer, or to deprive us of seeing those pretty titties."

A combination of a whine and whimper spills from me as I drop my head onto Emmett's shoulder and arch my back to allow him access. Emmett chuckles against my neck, sending a shiver down my spine as his clever fingers quickly pop open the bra and slide it down my arms.

"So beautiful," Emmett murmurs, awe lacing his words as he tosses the bra to the side as I'm completely revealed to them. Now, if they would just fucking touch me, that would be great.

"Touch me, please," I beg as I wiggle back in Emmett's hold, needing to feel his hard cock against my back.

Roman's hands slap down on my ankles and he yanks me back to the edge of the bed. "Who told you that you could move?"

"No one." I drop my eyes, watching him from beneath my lashes. I realize that moving without permission is once again going to get me in trouble, but maybe there's a way to salvage this. "But no one is touching me and I wanted to feel Emmett's cock pressing against me. I'm sorry, daddy alpha. I need you—both of you. I want to touch you and feel your hands on me. Please. Please."

"Do you think rushing this is going to get you what you want?" Roman growls, eyes never leaving me as his hands tighten around my ankle. For just a moment, I can feel his alpha dominance rising between us.

I melt back against Emmett, rolling my head to the side to offer him my neck without looking away. A purr bursts from Roman as he smiles. "Now, there's a good little omega. You can be a good girl, can't you?"

I don't move or answer him, my eyes falling shut. It's already becoming too much for me and nothing has even happened yet. How the hell am I going to make it through this if I'm already losing my mind?

My eyes fly open, a whine forcing its way past my lips when I feel Roman stand and move away from me. I bite the inside of my cheek hard to keep myself from doing anything else. Roman just shakes his head, reaching behind him and pulling his shirt over his head.

Why is that so hot?

"It's because their muscles bunch and relax as they reveal them to us," Emmett murmurs against my ear.

"Do you see what the two of you are doing to me?" I cry out. "That was supposed to be inside my head. I don't know which way is up right now."

Both men chuckle as Roman makes quick work of his pants and underwear until he's standing in all his glory, naked as the day he was born. I lick my lips, leaning forward. I already know what it's like to have that cock inside my mouth and I want it there again.

Though having him naked is so much better. I want to lick more than his cock this time. I want to lick the bulging muscles in his arms, the flat planes of his stomach. He might not have a six-pack like many of the other younger suitors, but the silver hair that runs down his stomach to his proud cock is delicious. His thighs are thick with muscles and I'd kind of like to lick those too. There's not a damn thing I would want to change about the man before me. He's beautiful.

"I want to lick you from head to toe," I blurt, eyes going wide. My omega side has no filter. She just says whatever the hell she's thinking.

Roman smirks as he strokes his cock and I once again find my lip between my teeth. He's so fucking sexy.

"Damn, Roman." Emmett groans into my neck. "So fucking sexy."

At least this time I didn't actually spill my inner thoughts, so that's a win.

Roman's smirk only grows as his eyes flash to Emmett, his hand continuing to stroke his cock. "Get naked, Emmett."

I lean forward as Emmett rushes to listen to Roman's commands. I want to turn and watch him undress, wanting to know what he looks like when he's naked, but I can't tear my eyes off Roman's hand sliding up and down his shaft. It's like I've been hypnotized—no dicknotized. That's totally a thing, isn't it?

"Come here, beta. Let Bree see what she's dealing with." Roman's eyes don't leave me this time as I feel Emmett shuffle off the bed until he's standing beside Roman.

It's the only thing that could get me to look away from Roman. Emmett is lean where Roman is stocky. But both men's muscles ripple over their bodies. Emmett's might not be as defined as Romans, but I love his body nonetheless.

His cock is a thing of beauty. Long enough to guarantee he'll be able to hit me in just the right spot and thick enough that I know I'll feel him after he's wrecked my pussy. He'll be easier to take down my throat than Roman was, but he'll still choke me when I swallow him down.

I'm practically drooling at the idea of his cock between my lips. As much as I'm enjoying watching these men pumping their own lengths, I need to be more involved. I need to suck them. I need them to fuck me. I just need them.

I don't move, having been properly chastised the last time I'd attempted to do just that. "Please," I whimper, not even sure what I'm asking for at this point. All I know is there's two cocks and I'm not being allowed to touch them, and my pussy is soaking wet but oh so empty. Slick spills from me, the bed already soaked beneath me, and I need.

"What's wrong, omega?" Emmett asks.

"Need you. Need you both. Now." I'm panting as I lift my legs so my feet sit on the edge of the bed. I slowly open my legs, revealing my dripping pussy to them. "So empty. So wet."

I want to touch myself like they are, but I don't think they'll like that. Well... they'd like it, but I'd be in trouble. I'm too far gone, I can't deal with the teasing anymore. I will do whatever I need to do for them to touch me, to fuck me the way I need to be fucked.

"What a pretty pink pussy you have, omega." Roman's words hold a growl to them as his eyes latch onto my center. "Such a good girl, showing us how pretty it is."

I preen at his words, hoping it means they'll touch me and soon. Roman turns his attention to Emmett, watching the way he strokes himself as he licks his lips.

Oh.

I sit up straighter. Is Roman interested in my beta too?

I shake my head. No, Emmett isn't mine. Is he? Has my omega already decided on him without me realizing? A humming fills my chest and I realize she has. I squirm in my seat as more slick spills from me. Not only am I turned on by the idea of Roman and Emmett together, but at the idea of making Emmett mine.

Fuck yes.

"You should touch him, daddy," I murmur, licking my lips. "Or let him touch you. I would like that very much, daddy." As if to confirm my statement, more slick spills from me.

"I can see that." Roman shakes his head as he forces himself to look away from me to a wide-eyed Emmett.

"You're into men?" Emmett asks, voice slightly higher pitched than usual.

Roman just laughs. "Don't be so surprised. There are only so many women on the planet. Most of us at least experiment and let's just say I enjoyed my experimentation enough to keep doing it."

"Well, shit," Emmett hisses.

"Do you want to touch me, beta?"

Emmett nods rapidly, hand falling away from his cock as he drops to his knees. "I want my hands and mouth all over you. Can I, daddy?"

Roman's gaze flares as he looks between the two of us. "That's really going to be a thing, isn't it?"

I raise my eyebrows as I lean forward. "If you didn't so obviously like it, we'd stop."

"You're being a brat again. I'll remember this and it won't go unpunished, but you're safe for today. I'm too fucking hard from both of you and I can't leave you both so needy, now can I? What kind of alpha would that make me?"

"A mean one," I snark. "Let Emmett suck your fat dick, daddy. Please."

Emmett has also apparently decided to brat alongside me as he knocks away Roman's hand from his cock so he can circle it with his own smaller hand. Emmett's tongue darts out, lapping at the precum leaking out before taking Roman's cock into his mouth.

Roman's hands twine into the other man's hair as his head falls back on a groan. Not being able to take it anymore, my hand slips between my legs. I run my fingers up my slit, collecting my slick before moving to circle my clit.

Finally.

I touch myself lightly, moving slowly to not draw attention to what I'm doing. I don't know how long that'll last for, but I need some relief. And Emmett is so hot on his knees as he swallows Roman's cock down. Rubbing my clit isn't enough as I slide three of my fingers into my pussy and fuck myself on them as Emmett bobs on Roman's cock.

"Fuck," I moan, long and low—totally giving myself away.

"You just couldn't wait, could you, omega?" Roman laughs as his fingers tighten in Emmett's hair, his hips beginning to move and meeting Emmett's bobs. "That's right, fuck yourself on your little fingers and think about how much better one of our cocks will feel. I want you to come, Bree. Make yourself come."

My walls clamp down on my fingers, ready to follow Roman's demand, but I'm not quite there yet. I roll and pinch my nipple with my free hand and I grind my palm against my clit as I continue to fuck myself with my fingers.

Roman must see that I need something more. He shoots me a wink before looking down at Emmett. "You're being such a good boy, but I need you to open your throat for me so I can fuck it. Our girl needs a good show, so she'll come around those tiny fingers of hers before we take care of her."

Emmett nods the best he can, sitting back on his heels and tilting his head up slightly. Roman hums his approval as he slowly slides his cock in and out of Emmett's mouth.

"I'm going to fuck your throat until I come with our omega, but don't swallow. I want you to keep it in your mouth and share it with our good girl."

A whimper spills from both me and Emmett as I pick up my pace, already so close to the edge, I know it won't take long for me to come. I shuffle around until I'm kneeling on the edge of the bed, making it easier to angle my fingers so I can hit that spot inside me that feels oh so good.

Roman picks up his pace until he's truly fucking Emmett's face, and it's honestly one of the hottest things I've ever seen. I hear Emmett hum around Roman's cock and Roman's head jerks towards me.

"That's it, baby girl. I need you to come. Emmett's mouth feels too good and I want to come with you. Are you close?" He pauses, waiting until I nod. "Good. Then, come omega."

This time, there's a thread of alpha bark to his words, and there's nothing I can do but fall apart. It hits me hard, running all the way up my spine as I arch forward. Both their names are on my lip like a chanted prayer as I come hard, drenching my hand, thighs, and the bed. I collapse onto my side, unable to hold myself up any longer.

Roman roars, hips stuttering as he comes in Emmett's mouth. "Fuck. Be a good boy and share my cum with our omega, Emmett. Don't be stingy."

Emmett crawls across the floor, eyes locked on me. I struggle to my knees as he stands before me. He opens his mouth, showing me the cum pooling on his tongue, and I want it.

"Gimme," I demand, reaching for Emmett, who comes to me easily. He wraps his arms around me, his cock pressing against my stomach as he leans down to kiss me.

Our tongues slide against one another, sharing the cum and spreading it around both of our mouths before we break away and swallow. Once again, I find myself enjoying Roman's taste.

Roman presses against Emmett's back as he stares down at both of us. "You're both so good, listening to daddy."

My eyes meet Emmett's and we share a smile, glad that we've allowed Roman to open himself to something he's obviously into.

"Bree, you made an awful mess on the bed. I think I'll help you clean that up." Roman's hand wraps around the front of Emmett's throat until my beta focuses his attention on Roman. "You can touch Bree as much as you want. Kiss her, make her feel good. But do not touch yourself. And Bree, you're not to touch him either. We want him close to exploding when you wrap your lips around his cock."

Once again, both Emmett and I whimper, because hell yes, I want that. I nod my agreement and Roman releases Emmett as soon as he agrees. "Lay back omega. I want you to open for me." I hurry to follow his request, leaving my ass on the edge of the bed as he had me earlier.

Then Roman is sinking to his knees, licking the slick that soaks my thighs. "Mmmm, you taste so good, omega. With the way you taste, we'll all be begging to eat you for breakfast, lunch, and dinner every day."

Then he's ducking between my thighs as Emmett's lips crash into mine. I wrap my hands in Emmett's silky strands to keep myself from touching him anywhere else.

Roman circles my clit with his finger as he laps at my center, groaning as he tastes more and more of my slick. Emmett attempts to break our kiss a few times, but I refuse to let him go. I want him to kiss me forever. His kisses are perfection.

It doesn't take long for me to fall apart around Roman's hands and tongue. I release my hold on Emmett as the orgasm rips through me, a screech spilling from me as I clamp my thighs around Roman's head.

I grind against his face to draw out the orgasm before collapsing back onto the bed, my limbs feeling like jelly.

"Damn, man." Emmett chuckles. "I thought she was trying to drown you in her slick for a moment there."

Roman's head pops up as he shrugs. Slick soaks his face, his beard glistening with it. "We've all gotta die sometime, am I right?"

I huff at that, but I'm not coherent enough to form sentences just yet. I'm just going to lie here and enjoy the euphoria running through me right now.

"Oh, sweet girl, we're nowhere near done with you yet. You can't give up on us yet." Roman stands as I blink up at him.

"Not giving up," I slur. "Just resting."

Emmett laughs. "I think you broke her."

"Not yet." Roman's grin turns wolfish as he leans down, picking me up easily. He flips me to my stomach, nudging me a little higher on the bed. "On your hands and knees, omega. You're going to suck Emmett's cock while I destroy your pussy."

A shiver rushes through me at his words and I struggle to my hands and knees. I'm oh so ready for this. I blink up at Emmett as I open my mouth, sticking my tongue out in invitation. Emmett only hesitates for a moment, eyes finding Roman before he feeds me his cock.

I hum around it, running my tongue along his length as his precum hits my tastebuds. Chamomile and lavender, just like his scent. I could drink it down all day.

I feel Roman behind me, fingers sliding through my wet center once more. I hear him stroking his cock and I wonder if he's spreading my slick along his shaft. My pussy clamps down at that idea. I want them to cover themselves in my slick so they'll carry my scent. I want them to cover me with their cum so I'll smell like them.

Is that weird? I feel like that's a little weird, but I won't lie—it turns me on. A LOT. I pull off Emmett's cock, glancing over my shoulder to confirm that he is, in fact, stroking himself with my slick.

"Fuck me and cover me with your cum, alpha. I want to be painted in both of your cum."

The two of them groan together as I take Emmett into my mouth once more. I jump a little when Roman rubs his cock against my opening. He chuckles. "Just me, omega. I'm going to fuck you and cover you with my cum, just like you want me to."

With no more preamble, Roman sheathes himself in me with one sharp thrust of his hips. I moan around Emmett when his knot slaps against my pussy. I almost regret asking him to cover me with his cum now that his knot is brushing against me. Oh, well. Maybe he can knot me afterwards.

Roman's hands grip my hips in an almost bruising hold as he pounds into me, forcing me to take Emmett further into my throat. I quickly realize that if I hold still, Roman will not only fuck me, but he'll fuck me onto Emmett's cock.

Hell, yes.

It doesn't take long for us to find our rhythm. Roman fucks me hard from behind, filling me so completely that I don't know if I could take his knot even if I wanted to. He hits that spot deep inside of me with each pass, heating me quickly. One of his hands occasionally snakes down to brush against my clit. Emmett thrusts his hips forward in time with Roman, so his cock rams down my throat and I take him completely. I've never felt so full as the two of them piston into me and it's everything I never knew I wanted.

I can't wait until I choose my pack and then I can have this all the time. Cocks filling all my holes and fucking me into oblivion. Yes, I know a pack is about more than sex, but it's a definite advantage of having a pack. I wonder how many cocks I can take at once, how full they can make me feel. Fates—and the knots. All the cum.

I sigh at the idea. It's everything an omega could ask for. An especially forceful thrust has me coming back to the two men who are currently fucking me. I jolt when Roman's hand comes down on my ass, my walls clamping down on his cock as I whimper around the cock filling my mouth.

"Oh, does our omega like to be spanked?" Roman murmurs as he soothes the area before smacking it again. This time, I jump and keen a high-pitched sound I've never heard before—let alone coming from my own lips. Sure, it's muffled by cock, but I think the two of them understand I like it a lot.

"Something to keep in mind for next time." Emmett struggles to get the words out. He thickens in my mouth and I know it won't be long until he comes. I make a distraught sound around his cock, afraid he's going to come in my mouth. Which isn't terrible, but then how can I rub it into my skin?

Emmett laughs. "Don't worry, Bree. I still plan to come all over that pretty face of yours and those fucking amazing tits." I hum my happiness around him and his hips jerk against me. "Behave, omega, or you won't get what you want."

Obviously, there isn't much I can do, but remain still as they pound into me. I whine when Emmett jerks from my mouth. "Mine," I demand.

"Yes, yours. Don't worry, omega. Fuck." Emmett strokes his cock as he glances over me at Roman. "Can you lift her a little so I can get her face and tits?"

Roman wraps one hand in my hair, pulling it out of the way as he lifts me up a bit, never pausing as he drives into me repeatedly.

"Oh, yes." Emmett's hips thrust forward as he fucks his hand. With no warning, he groans and cum flies toward my face. I let my eyes shut as my mouth falls open. Cum covers my face, some making its way into my mouth, before the stream shifts and hits my breasts and nipples.

I lick my lips as an orgasm hits me out of nowhere. I scream Emmett's name as I grind back on Roman's cock. I whimper when Emmett's hands land on my boobs, spreading his cum over them. "Yes, like that. Rub it in my skin. I want to smell like you for days. Don't forget my face, please. I can't."

I'm still shaking from my orgasm and already building toward another. I've never acted like this in bed before and I'm interested in finding out why, but not just yet. Right now, I want to come again and to feel Emmett rub his cum all over my body.

He does just that before Roman finally lowers me back to my hands, but keeps ahold of my hair. He fucks into me harder, hitting that spot over and over while Emmett sweeps the cum from my eyes. He spreads it down my face and neck and it's just what I wanted.

Roman's hand slaps down on my ass again, pulling a squeak from me as my eyes pop open. "You need to come *right now, omega.*" I can hear the strain in his words, but it doesn't matter because my body is already following his command as I come again.

Roman jerks his cock from my pussy. Slick spurts from me, surprising me. It's supposed to be really easy to make an omega squirt, seeing as we produce so much slick, but this is a first for me.

All thoughts of squirting are erased from my mind as Roman groans seconds before his cum hits my ass and lower back. "So fucking needy, omega. But I'll give you all of my cum. I'm working my knot for you, so I can cover you from head to toe."

I don't know if that sets off another orgasm, or if it's still the same one, but I collapse forward, unable to hold myself up as I shake and moan. Roman is still spilling cum as Emmett leans over and rubs it into my skin.

Another orgasm hits me, white light blinding me as I squeeze my eyes shut. How the hell am I coming from having cum rubbed into my skin? I'm fairly certain I black out, because the next thing I know, I'm cuddled between Roman and Emmett as they tell me what a good omega I am. I nestle back more firmly into Roman's hold, sighing at my scent, still soaking his face. I pull against Emmett until he shuffles closer. I sniff at his chest, realizing he doesn't smell like me.

I reach between my legs, dipping my fingers into my still drenched pussy and soak my hand in my slick.

"What are you doing, omega? There's no way you're still raring to go." Disbelief fills Roman's voice, and I can't blame him. He's right, I couldn't go again just yet. My limbs are heavy and it's taking everything in me to keep my eyes open.

When I slap my slick covered hand onto Emmett's chest, rubbing it in, Roman hums. "Did Emmett not smell like you?"

"No," I retort. "Mine."

Emmett's hand ducks between my legs and I tense for a moment, but it's obvious he isn't trying to do anything but collect my slick onto his hand. "Let me help, baby. We can cover me with as much of your slick as you need to."

Emmett places more slick on his chest, Roman leaning over to help the two of us rub it into his skin. Finally, my hand falls away as I take a deep inhale, and my scent is all over him. I let out a contented sigh.

"I need a nap, but then we need to call down to housekeeping and get the sheets changed while we take a bath. Not that I want to wash away any of our scents, but this is going to get crusty and then it'll bother me." I laugh, finally feeling more like myself. "Then Emmett can fuck me before Roman knots me. Don't let me nap too long. I'm going to be pissed if I wake up in the morning and I haven't been knotted."

I drift off to the sound of the two of them laughing. "Of course, omega. Whatever you need."

Chapter Twenty-two

Dalton

There's a nervous energy in the room while we eat breakfast. We don't know what's coming. Even Bree admitted she doesn't know what this challenge will be. Though she seems to be excited about it. It's obviously going to be something we can do, or they wouldn't have us do it. Will it be a physical challenge? A mental challenge?

That the winner will be the first one to take Bree on a one-on-one date makes the stakes even higher. Every single suitor is dying to be the one to take her on the first individual date. Now that Roman and Emmett have been the first to spend a night with her—kind of, considering Gabriel had stayed the night in her room—the rest of us are determined to be the ones to give her another first on the show.

Speaking of Emmett and Roman, something seems to have changed between the two of them. When they and Bree came in a few minutes after nine, they had no choice but to eat at the other end of the table from Bree. Not that they seemed to mind as their heads ducked close together, sharing smiles and whispered words.

I'm glad they've gotten closer after spending the night with Bree. I'll be the first to admit I've been feeling jealous—not of anyone in particular—but because I don't feel like I've had enough time with Bree. That's obviously on me for not pushing for more time with her. I'm more of a laid-back, go with the flow kind of guy, and that means I'm not always assertive enough in situations like this.

I'm sure that we all feel like we're not getting enough time with her, but I almost feel like she's been avoiding being alone with me or Maverick since that day in the pool. I hate to think that we'd taken advantage of her, though she hasn't really acted like she was upset about it. Maybe it's because she doesn't know us well enough yet and doesn't know how to act around us?

Either way, I have every intention of spending some alone time with her. We're down to ten suitors now and that means more time with each of us—whether that's time together as a group or individually. But I want this first date with Bree. I want her to fall for me, to want to make me a part of her pack.

"You good, Dalton?"

I turn to find Maverick looking on with concern. Glancing down, I realize I've bent the damn fork. Tossing it aside, I run a hand down my face. "I'm fine. I'm just stupidly lettin' the unknown of this challenge get to me. Stress rarely bothers me, but *Heated* seems to have brought it out in me."

The two of us laugh together, not because what I said is funny, but because it's true. I hadn't thought about what it would mean to be constantly surrounded by the scents of so many alphas and betas. Beta scents are never as heavy as an alpha's or an omega's, but that doesn't mean that they can't be overwhelming.

I'm used to the scents of my family, my friends, and the guys who work for me. It's not the number of scents, but the number of *new* scents. Not to mention the dominance and testosterone constantly in the air. I think it'll be easier now that we're down to ten, and now that the toxic alphas are gone. Not that everyone who has left has been toxic.

"Yeah, I'm ready for it to start already." Maverick tears off a piece of his croissant. "Do you think they announced it last night, so we'd psych ourselves out all night and this morning?"

"Absolutely. Tessa is one smart lady. She's makin' sure she gets an interestin' show. Not that I can blame her." I grab a croissant off the plate in the center of the table and tear into it. So freaking good. "It's just a little harder comin' from this side, ya know?"

"Oh, I know, man. I know."

Tessa comes striding into the room, a clipboard in her hand. "Good morning, Bree. Suitors."

Instead of moving to stand beside Bree as I would've expected, she stands behind the chair directly across the table from Bree. Her eyes fall over all of us as she waits to be sure we're all paying attention. Though I guarantee she had our attention from the moment she stepped into the room. She holds the key to the information we're all dying for.

"As Reginald told you all last night, we have a challenge for the suitors today. It might have been cruel of us to not give you any information about it last night, and I'd apologize, except I'm not sorry." Tessa laughs, but no one else joins her. "Touchy crowd this morning."

"Tessa, don't drag this out. You know you're killing them—and me—by not just telling us."

Tessa rolls her eyes. "Fiiiine. The crew spent most of yesterday into last night setting up an obstacle course for the ten of you. Obviously, that means you'll be physically tested, but some obstacles aren't ones you can brawn your way through. There are puzzles that must be completed in order to continue on. There will be a beta positioned at each station who will provide you with water should you need it.

"Since there are ten of you, we decided on ten obstacles. I won't be telling you what the obstacles are, so you'll all be a little in the dark about it. If you don't understand what needs to be done, the crew stationed at the obstacle can explain it. Your prize, also known as Bree, will wait for you at the finish line. She and I will watch the challenge on a screen so we can see how well you're all doing. Are there any questions?"

"What should we wear?"

Tessa smiles, obviously glad that I've asked. "You'll want to wear something you can move in. Something comfortable, but that you don't mind getting dirty. I'd probably recommend pants, but if you'd prefer shorts, that's completely up to you. You'll want sturdy shoes so you don't slip."

I nod, realizing we'll either be dealing with water or mud—or both. That helps set my mind at ease somewhat. At least I have some idea of what I'm dealing with. Finishing my croissant, I toss back my coffee before turning to Bree.

"If you don't mind, I'd like to go get ready."

Bree smiles. "Of course! Once you're done eating, please go get ready. I'm just as excited about this challenge as you are."

I'm the first to stand, but I hear others doing the same. We all head for our rooms and as much as I want a shower, it sounds like it'll be pointless. Instead, I dress in some gym clothes and pull on my tennis shoes. I'm not sure what exactly we'll be doing, but I do a quick warm up before jogging down the stairs.

I find Hector standing there with a few of the suitors. "Where's Bree?"

Maverick laughs as he turns to me. "I asked the same thing when I came down. She and Tessa already left. Hector says our 'prize' is being set up as we speak."

When I turn my narrowed gaze to the beta, he holds up his hands in surrender. "Those are the words Reginald told me to use. If you're gonna get pissed, get pissed at him."

That sounds about right. I do a few more stretches as we wait for the other suitors to arrive. Once everyone makes it downstairs, Hector leads us out front, where three golf carts await us. A beta stands beside two of them while Hector heads towards the third.

"Three or four to a cart, please," he calls out. "I don't care who goes in what cart, but the faster we get this done, the faster we can get you to the challenge."

I grab Maverick and drag him toward Hector's cart. Brody hops on after us. "You two ready to kick my ass?"

"What?" I snort.

Brody shrugs. "Let's be real. In a contest of physical strength, an alpha will win over a beta nine out of ten times. The chances of me or Emmett winning this challenge are slim to none."

"Hmmm... I hadn't even thought of that." Maverick grins as he turns to me. "Guess our odds have just improved."

"Don't be an asshole. You're gonna do great, Brody. You might not be built like an alpha, but that doesn't mean you don't stand a chance to win. I'm sure that was taken into account when they planned the challenge."

Brody shrugs. "Eh, it's fine. I'll do my best, but it's not like it's my only opportunity for a one-on-one date."

"A smart observation, Brody. Now, all three of you hold on. This golf cart goes faster than normal ones." Hector shoots us a grin before taking off.

He isn't lying either. I'm shocked at how quickly we travel across the compound. We pass all the cottages and drive through a patch of desert, leaving me wondering where the hell we're going. I see something in the distance, but it takes a minute to figure out what it is.

Hector pulls to a stop near a banner announcing it to be the starting line. Reginald is waiting beside it and smiles at all of us as the other two golf carts pull up.

"Welcome suitors," Reginald calls, drawing our attention as the golf carts pull off. "I'm sure that Tessa gave you all the information you could ever need about this challenge."

Someone scoffs and Reginald laughs. "That's what I thought. Sadly, I don't know how much more information I have to give you, but, as you can see, we're at the starting line. When we're ready, you'll all line up and wait for the buzzer to sound. This is an obstacle course, but it's also a race. Running is highly recommended.

"Behind me, you'll see your first obstacle is a climbing wall. For safety reasons, we have an inflatable surrounding it on all sides. If you slip and fall, it'll help with impact. If you are injured, we have medics at each obstacle, as well as placed along the trail between obstacles. It might be winter, but we're still in the desert. Please be sure you're drinking the offered water at each obstacle. We don't want anyone to overheat and pass out.

"There are eight physical obstacles and two puzzle obstacles. You must work out the puzzle to proceed. Once your puzzle has been verified, you'll receive something from the crew to carry onto the next obstacle. If you don't have this item at the next obstacle, you'll be sent back to the puzzle. These two items are something you'll present to Bree at the end of the course, regardless of if you're the first or the last person to finish. The trail between the obstacles is clearly marked. Do not stray from the path.

"If you skip an obstacle, you're disqualified. If you sabotage another suitor, you're disqualified. While we believe a little competition is good for our souls, we won't allow you to hurt anyone else's chances. You can assist other suitors if you'd like, but remember, you might slow yourself down by doing so.

"What I know Tessa didn't tell you is that over the next ten days, Bree will have an individual date with all of you. This decides who is the first. From there, Bree will decide the order of your dates. But the catch is that you will plan these dates."

There's muttering around me as I and the other suitors realize what this means. Whoever wins only has the day to plan a date for Bree.

"I can see you've worked out that it means the winner will have to plan a date in a shorter period. Tessa will help you get everything set up, and if you don't have any ideas, you can meet with her. But what Bree wants is for you to plan a date revolving around something you love."

Reginald glances around the group of suitors. "I know that was a lot all at once. Are there any questions?" When no one responds, he nods. "You have ten minutes to warm up and stretch. Remember, while this is an individual challenge, you can work with other suitors. But there can only be one winner. Set the clock to ten minutes."

Glad I'd already thought to warm up, I run through a few stretches just to make sure that I'm good to go. Maverick appears beside me. "What do you say we work together to get through all the obstacles, and then we can let the sprint to the finish line decide who wins?"

I consider the idea. It's not a bad plan, and I believe Maverick and I are evenly matched in physicality. If we can get an early lead, we should be able to keep it. Then it would just come down to whoever saved enough steam to get to the finish line first.

"Let's do it." I extend my hand to Maverick, and he shakes it. "Are you warmed up?"

Maverick scoffs. "I warmed up in my room, which it looks like you did too."

"Great minds think alike and all that." Glancing around at the other suitors, I'm not surprised to see most of them have also grouped together. Hudson, Maddox, Onyx, and Gabriel seem to have grouped off. Then there's Roman and Finnegan, who seem to be trying to convince the betas to join them.

I'm not as concerned about Roman and Finnegan if they're planning to work with the betas. Sure, I'd told Brody he'd be fine, but he wasn't wrong. He and Emmett just aren't built the same way the alphas are. I think Roman on his own would give us a run for our money, but Finnegan has said on more than one occasion that he spends most of his time on his ass, and that's the way he likes it.

The other group is slightly more worrying. All four men are in great shape, but I think if we can just keep ahead of them in the beginning, we'll be fine. It's also easier to only have to worry about yourself and one other person than three other people.

When our ten minutes is up, a buzzer sounds, and all of us make our way to the start line. Reginald is waiting for us again. "That buzzer is the same as the one that will go off when the race starts, so when you hear it, off you'll go. I'll be waiting with Tessa and Bree at the finish line. There are stationary cameras set up along the course, but don't be surprised if you see a crew driving alongside you. Just pretend like they're not there. Good luck, gentlemen, and may the best suitor win."

I'm already readying myself to take off as soon as the buzzer goes off, Maverick doing the same beside me. Everything else fades out as I focus on the course before me and Maverick at my side.

The moment the buzzer goes off, Maverick and I are the first to race forward. The wall is only about thirty feet from us and we make it there quickly. I take a running leap at the wall, grasping a handhold about halfway up the wall with Maverick right behind me. Reaching the top of the wall, I straddle the wall and glance down. It's only about a fifteen-foot drop and with the inflatables, I don't see any reason to climb down. Maverick pulls himself atop the wall and I find the others only a few feet behind us.

"I'm jumping," I tell him.

He laughs. "I'll be right behind you."

I pull my other leg up and around so I'm sitting on top of the wall. A quick prayer to the fates and I launch myself into the air. As soon as my feet hit the inflatable, I tuck and roll forward. That wasn't too bad.

I stand and move to the edge of the inflatable moments before Maverick launches himself off the top of the wall. It looks more terrifying watching someone do that from down here, but he makes it look easy. Then we're taking off down the trail, already being able to see the next obstacle in the distance.

"Welcome, alphas," a beta calls as we near. "Your next obstacle is a mud crawl. Keep low to avoid the barbed wire. Good luck!"

"A mud crawl? I guess it could be worse." I snort, keeping up my pace.

"Now I know why they said to wear something we weren't worried about getting dirty." Maverick's hand slaps down on my shoulder. "We've got this."

As soon as we reach the mud crawl, I throw myself down and begin the crawl through the mud using my elbows. Maverick and I are covered in mud as we crawl out the other side, but we don't let it slow us down as we race toward the third obstacle.

Once again, as we near, a member of the crew announces the next obstacle to us. "Horizontal climb! If you touch the ground, you must go back to the beginning."

"While we're covered in mud?" Maverick scoffs. "That's not dangerous at all."

I glance down at my hands. "And we can't wipe them off on anything since we're surrounded by desert. Oh! Yes, we can! Wipe them on the inside of your shirt. Make sure you drink the water."

We pause to toss back the water before tossing the cups into the trash can. I grab the back of my shirt, finding it mostly clean as I wipe off as much of the mud from my fingers as I can. It makes it much easier to swing from bar to bar. Then we're off and running again.

Our next obstacle is a simple puzzle we're able to do on our own. That's followed by a tire run, a bucket heft—where we have to carry four buckets filled with mud from one side to another—before we have to swing out over a pond of some kind and finish swimming across. Now we're wet and muddy.

Another puzzle that's harder for us to work out, allowing the others to catch up to us. Somehow, we manage to get it done before anyone else and we're off again. We have to clamor our way across four different balance beams for the second to last obstacle. Then we're standing before the last obstacle.

Maverick and I slap hands. "Good luck."

"You too, man."

We take off running and jumping from foam platform to foam platform. Once at the top, I realize we're going to need to jump into the foam pit below. I hesitate for a moment, letting Maverick get ahead of me before I jump down. I fight my way through the pit and climb out a second after Maverick.

It's just us as we're racing to the finish line, our arms and legs moving quickly as we try to be the one who wins the race. We're ten feet from the finish line and it's too close to tell who will win. That is, until I step on a rock, my ankle rolling.

"Fuck," I roar, hitting the ground.

Maverick stops, spinning around as if to help me up, but I shake my head. "Finish it!"

He gives me a pained look before doing as I requested. I may not have won this challenge, but my teammate did, and that feels great. A medic rushes over to me, checking out my ankle before announcing what I already expected—a sprain. He wraps it and someone brings a set of crutches, which I take and head for the finish line with the medic yelling at me to stop.

I ignore him and make my way slowly to Bree and Tessa. She's grinning at me. "You know an injury means you don't have to finish."

"Forget that, darlin'. I like to finish what I've started, even if it means I come in dead last. Plus, I have something for you." I pull the origami rose and bookmark from my pocket and present them to her. Both have seen better days, but I don't think she minds.

"Thank you, Dalton." She leans up to kiss my cheek. "Now that you've finished, get your butt to a golf cart before the medic has a heart attack."

"Your wish is my command, darlin'." I turn toward the closest golf cart and drop into the front seat, waving to Bree as the medic drives us away. A sprained ankle isn't too bad, and I'd endure it repeatedly if Bree would look at me with awe in her eyes and kiss my cheek every time.

Maverick

Planning a date in just a few hours isn't as bad as I thought it would be, though trying to figure out what to do that includes something I love was interesting. As Bree and the suitors know, architecture is my passion, but how to make that a part of a date, I wasn't sure. Not until I went to Tessa, and she allowed me to use her tablet to look up some ideas.

Imagine my surprise when I saw that there was a local company who ran architecture tours. I didn't even know that was a thing until I found their website. The tour will end at a restaurant whose building is from pre-Event days. I'm actually really excited to show Bree what I love and what will hopefully be an amazing restaurant. The reviews online were fantastic, so I'm hopeful.

Tessa had been very helpful, calling the tour company to get us our own tour and calling the restaurant to make sure they had a private room. Which was great and helpful, but left me with way too much time on my hands to worry about my plan. What if she hates it? I don't want to blow this. I know the request was for us to show her something we love, but what happens if it's too boring?

"You a'ight, Mav?"

I turn to find Dalton has somehow made his way into the second floor living area where I've been pacing since I'd left Tessa, crutches and all. I just shrug, having no idea if I'm alright or not.

"Come on, let's grab a beer and talk about why you're pacing the room."

Instead of following Dalton, I keep up my pacing. I don't know if it's actually helping or not, but I know I can't sit still right now. Dalton sighs behind me and I figure he'll give up and leave. Which is why I'm so surprised when he steps in my path, pressing a beer into my hand as he directs me to the couch.

"Sit," he demands as he opens his beer. Once I sit down, he follows suit, setting his crutches to the side. "Tell me what's goin' on. Are you stuck on ideas for y'all's date?"

"Fates, no. If I didn't have a date planned by now, I'd be freaking out a lot more," I tell him as I lean back. "I'm actually picking up Bree in like fifteen minutes."

"So... what's the problem?"

Running my hand over my face, I laugh. "It's stupid."

"It's not if it's botherin' you. Spill it, brother."

"I love architecture, as you well know, so I wanted to work that into the date if possible. Tessa helped me find a walking architecture tour through Rancho Mirage. It ends at a restaurant that was built pre-Event, so we're going to have dinner there afterward."

Dalton nods slowly. "That sounds like exactly what she was askin' for. I'm still not seein' a problem."

"Would you enjoy an architecture tour?"

"No." Dalton shakes his head. "Well, maybe. It just depends, but this ain't about what I would or would not enjoy. It's about what you love and sharin' that with Bree."

"But what if she thinks it's boring?"

"That's why you're shittin' kittens. When she made the request for the dates, I guarantee she knew she would end up havin' to do some things she doesn't enjoy. But that's not what it's about. It's about her gettin' to know us better. She's going to enjoy it because of how happy it's going to make you. You're going to light up like the nerd you are, as they're explainin' the architecture of the buildings. That's what she wants to see."

I consider that for a moment and it makes sense. "You really think so?"

Dalton's eyes narrow as he makes a face. "I've never known you to be so self-conscious. If I'd known you were gonna to act like this, I wouldn't have stepped on that rock. Because I certainly wouldn't be this worried if it were me."

I scoff, shoving at his shoulder. "You say that now. I'm going to laugh my ass off when it's your turn and you're freaking out."

"Maybe." Dalton shrugs. "You should finish your beer and go pick up Bree, who is definitely going to enjoy y'all's date."

I don't argue with him this time, instead lifting my beer and drinking it down. I'm glad Dalton found me. This was what I needed to stop freaking out.

"Thanks, man." I shoot him a grin as I stand up to throw away my empty can. "Do you need any help with anything before I head out?"

"Nawww." He shakes his head. "I'm just gonna stay here and enjoy my beer before headin' upstairs. Enjoy your date."

With a pep in my step, I head downstairs and knock on Bree's door. She opens it within seconds with a smile. As requested, she's wearing pants and tennis shoes. "Good evening, Maverick. I'm really looking forward to seeing what you set up for us."

I offer her my arm. "I just hope it's not going to be super boring for you."

"With you at my side? I somehow doubt it." She pauses. "I asked the suitors to plan these dates because I don't feel like I've gotten to know all of you as well as I would like. What each of you plans might not be something I would've picked to do on my own, but if you're enjoying yourself, I'm going to enjoy myself."

I nod slowly as she repeats the words Dalton has already spoken to me. Deep down, I think I knew that the whole time, but sometimes we just let our doubts get the better of us.

"Do you want to know what I have planned, or would you like it to be a surprise?"

Bree taps her finger against her chin. "A surprise I think. I don't often enjoy surprises, but in this case, I think I will. Lead the way, kind sir."

I laugh at her words, loving how comfortable I always feel around her. She may not have gotten to know me as well as some of the others, but I still feel seen by her. I think this date on our own will be good. We'll be able to delve into getting to know each other beyond the surface level.

Bree is pleasantly surprised when we arrive for our tour and I'm surprised by how many questions she asks as we go from place to place. We're able to tour a couple of houses that are almost two hundred years old and a few buildings that are from the last one hundred years. It's fascinating to see how architecture has changed over the years.

When we arrive at the restaurant, Bree lets out a squeal. "Italian? I love Italian!"

We say a quick goodbye to our tour guide before heading inside the restaurant to find the owner waiting for us. We're led to our private room, where we order a variety of appetizers and entrees to share before settling in with our glasses of wine.

"I don't know if anyone else has been brave enough to ask yet, but they haven't mentioned it, so I'm assuming no one has, but it's something the suitors speak of often."

Bree tilts her head. "I'm a little concerned, but ask away."

"How do you plan to pick your pack from us? Do you know how big of a pack you want?"

"Ahhh, yes. I'm actually surprised no one has asked before now. I was prepared for the question, but no one ever brought it up." Bree sets her glass on the table as she leans toward me. "My answer now differs from what it would have been on the first day."

"Yeah? I'd love to hear both."

"If you'd asked me that first day, I'd have told you I'd choose analytically, keeping my heart out of it—which was a very naïve idea on my part. Number one, emotions have to be involved. I don't want to pick someone just because they look good on paper. I need to choose my pack based on who I feel a connection to—who I could fall in love with. On day one, I would've told you it's impossible to fall in love with someone in just two months.

"I know better than that now. Not that I'm in love with anyone currently, but I can feel the relationships and connections forming. I don't know how I'll choose who will be a part of my pack. Not really. I know I need to learn to listen to my omega side better. I've spent so long repressing that side of myself that I don't know how to listen to my omega's instincts. I'm trying to learn how to do that because I believe that will help me form the pack I'm looking for."

I nod slowly, realizing that she's given me the best non-answer ever. I appreciate that she's been honest with me. It lets me understand where her mind is at.

"As far as how big of a pack? I honestly thought maybe three or four others, but now? I'm not going to limit myself to that number. I could miss out on a potential mate by saying I've picked three or four, I'm done." Bree hesitates. "When I came up with the concept, that's all it was—a concept. It never occurred to me to think about what it would be like for the omega. I don't think I would've ever guessed that this is the way I'd feel or that I would do half the things I've done."

We laugh together. "That's interesting. I'm guessing you're reacting to things differently because you've accepted your omega instead of trying to repress that side of yourself."

"That's the best I can figure. I'm glad that we decided I would be the first omega on *Heated* because I'd feel like an ass if I threw another omega into the position I'm in right now. I already have a million ideas on how to better the show and make things easier on the omega for next season. I think people will enjoy this first season because it's something new, but I think season two will hit better."

"I love that you haven't chosen your pack yet, meaning the season isn't over, and you're already planning next season." I laugh as I lift my wineglass to my lips.

Bree doesn't seem offended by my words as she laughs with me. "I'm a workaholic. I love my job. I love the company that Tessa and I have created. It's our baby, so it's always on my mind. What we can do to make things more efficient or what we can do to make the world a better place for omegas. I can already feel my priorities shifting by being on the show, but I don't think I'll ever lose the drive to make our company the best it can be."

"And you shouldn't. Luckily, I believe the suitors that are left would expect nothing less. You can have it all if that's what you want. You can run your company, have a pack of mates that you love, and have children when you want—if you want them. I shouldn't assume."

Bree's face softens. "I want kids. I don't think I realized how much I wanted them until now, but that's something I want in my life. I don't know how it'll work out, but whoever I choose for my pack… we'll figure it out. That's what it means to be a pack, right?"

"Yeah, I think so."

Bree hums. "Why aren't you a part of a pack?"

"I've never met anyone who I felt like was part of my pack." I pause for a moment, realizing that's not a hundred percent true. "Except maybe Dalton. I feel like Dalton and I could be pack mates if we met outside of *Heated*. All the suitors that are currently on the show, I could see being in a pack together—which surprised me at first. They're not necessarily the men I would've sought to form a pack with, but they're good men."

Bree sighs. "Which is why I have no idea who I'm choosing. Ten is too big of a pack for me, though. So I will have to narrow it down some, I think."

"Yeah… I don't think you'd have time for anything but sex."

"Oh, the horror." Bree snickers, a faint blush rising over her cheeks. "I do have a company to help run, so I guess I can't spend all my time in the bedroom. Though having men involved with one another would help with that."

"You know not all of us swing both ways, don't you?" I raise my eyebrows with a laugh.

"I know that you, Brody, and Dalton don't swing that way. The others? Well, they can at least be persuaded."

I snort as I try to hide my laughter from her. "I'm sorry. I'm not laughing at you, I swear. I was just imagining what your methods of persuasion would be when trying to get men to sleep together."

"Do you think I can't be persuasive?" Bree lifts a hand to her check in mock hurt. "Do I need to show you just how persuasive I can be?"

A smirk slides across her face and I lose my mind for a moment, not being able to form an answer for her. When she pushes back her chair and crawls under the table, my eyes go wide. This is *not* what I thought she'd been talking about. Her small hands land on my thighs before moving toward my crotch.

I glance at the door and the camera crew before tossing up the tablecloth. "You don't need to do this. I believe you."

"What's wrong, Maverick? You weren't afraid to go down on me in the middle of the pool with all the other suitors there, even with all the cameras recording us. What's so different about this?"

"I forgot about the damn cameras," I hiss at her. "We're in the middle of a restaurant."

"No, we're not. We're in a private room with the cameras on us, yes, but they won't show me actually sucking down your cock. And if the waiter comes in, then you'll just have to act normally, won't you? The tablecloth covers all the way to the floor. No one will ever know I'm underneath here." She pauses, tilting her head as she looks up at me. "Unless you don't want this, in which case, I'll go back to my chair right now."

I frown, debating what to do. Getting a blowjob in a restaurant isn't on my must-do before I die list, but I'm not really against it, I don't think. I just don't want Bree to feel like she has to do it or to demean herself.

"That's not... I..." Fuck, I don't know what I'm trying to say. "Of course, I want to feel those pouty lips around my cock, but you don't have to do this—especially not here—if you don't want to."

Bree grins up at me as she slowly unbuttons my pants. "I don't do anything I don't want to do. And haven't you heard? Apparently, I have an exhibitionist kink. Now put down the damn tablecloth in case someone comes in."

I want to argue with her, but she's already pulling me from my pants, stroking up and down my length. I want to watch her as she takes my cock into her mouth, but the door is currently being pushed open. I drop the tablecloth like it's on fire.

"We have your appetizers." Our waiter begins to load the plates onto the table, eyes flashing to Bree's empty seat.

"She's in the restroom," I spit out, my body going tense as Bree sucks my cock into her mouth and takes me deep. "Thank you so much. This all smells amazing. I can't wait to dig in."

The waiter hesitates for a moment, and I turn back to him. "Was there something else?"

"No... I just wanted to make sure you were okay."

I realize I'm currently clutching my fork like I'm going to stab something or someone with it. I laugh, reaching to stab a mozzarella stick with it and setting it on my plate. I can't do anything about how tense my body is, but I smile at him. "There's just so many options and I couldn't decide what I wanted to try first. I'm very intense when it comes to food."

He nods slowly, eyes trailing over to Bree's seat once more. I'm sure he knows exactly what we're doing, and he's about to call us out, but instead, he turns back to me with a smile. "Make sure you save some for the lady. She might stab you if you eat it all before she's back."

"Smart thinking," I tell him, my thighs clenching as Bree continues to work me over with her mouth. Her hand has found its way to my knot, and she's squeezing it lightly as she takes me deep. I can't help but wonder if this guy will ever leave the fucking room. "Thanks again. Looking forward to the entrees."

With that, the waiter finally leaves and I throw up the tablecloth to glare down at Bree. "Really? You did that on purpose, you little minx."

She just shrugs, mouth too full of my cock for her to answer. I assume the waiter won't be back for a while, so I leave the tablecloth where it is as I wrap a hand into her hair. I slowly thrust up into her mouth and she whines around my cock.

"Leave my knot be, minx. You won't be able to swallow that much cum, and I'm not spraying it all over the damn restaurant." Bree grumbles, but releases my knot. "Now, you best hold on. You're in for one hell of a ride."

I lean back in my chair, eyes falling shut as I let myself forget about the cameras and the men running said cameras. I tighten my grip on Bree's hair, shoving her down on my cock until she takes me completely and swallows around me. After that, all bets are off as I fuck up into her mouth while controlling her head to be sure she swallows my entire length on each pass.

It doesn't take long for me to recognize the signs of my upcoming release. I force her down on my cock one last time as I batter her throat with my shallow thrusts until I'm coming. "Fuck, Bree. You're fucking perfect, aren't you?"

I slowly release my hold on her hair. She pulls off my cock and swallows before leaning down to lap at my softening cock. "What are you doing now?"

"Cleaning you up, alpha. I don't want you to get cum all over your underwear when I can just clean you up."

I stare down at her in awe. I don't believe anyone is perfect, but I think Bree is as close as a person can get.

Once she's finished, she makes her way back to her seat while I tuck my cock away. "Mmmm. This looks and smells amazing. Let's eat before it gets any colder."

All I can do is laugh as she piles food on her plate. See what I mean? So perfect.

Chapter Twenty-three

Bree

I can't believe we've been at this for over three weeks. Today begins our fourth week on *Heated*. I've been on an individual date with each of the ten suitors, which have all been a ton of fun.

Dalton had taken me for a tandem bike ride, followed by a picnic. Maddox had surprised me by bringing us to a tattoo shop where he'd gotten the *Heated* logo tattooed on his arm. I decided to get the same design but on the inside of my wrist. My first tattoo is representative of an experience that has changed my life. I can't think of anything else that would've been better for my first tattoo.

Finnegan had found a local park that was doing a showing of the pre-Event movie, *Legally Blonde*. It was so different from the movies that are made today. I don't know if that's really what it was like before the Event, but I loved the movie. Onyx had taken me to a Native American reservation that is about an hour away from Rancho Mirage. We'd spent the entire day there as I learned about how our indigenous people live in modern days.

Roman had taken me to a history museum of the area and a couple of art galleries. Hudson, being Hudson, had taken me to an arcade—which had been a blast. Brody had taken me on a hike and Gabriel had taken us to volunteer at an after-school program in the area where we got to help the kids with their homework and play with them.

Just last night, Emmett and I had prepared a five course meal together for the other suitors, but we ate in the kitchen. It was amazing to watch him in his element and while I didn't help with much; it was nice to have a hand in the making of such an amazing meal. We'd stayed up late under the stars, just talking, and it was... everything.

After spending a week letting my horny omega run the show, I'd pulled back. I haven't done more than make out with anyone since I'd given Maverick a blowjob. There's been no invitations to my suite and I know the suitors are questioning why I haven't chosen anyone else to spend the night with me. They haven't mentioned it directly, but I've overheard them and seen the questioning looks. All of which I've ignored.

I know why I haven't invited anyone to stay with me, but I haven't put it into words yet. The last time I invited someone to my room, my omega side claimed Emmett, and she's a little angry with me that there have been no steps taken to move forward with that. I wanted to go through with the individual dates to be sure because I know that once I make this decision, it's permanent.

I can't help questioning myself and my omega side's insistence on choosing him. I've known him for all of three weeks. How can I be sure? Is that really enough time? But even as I ask myself the question, I recall my conversation with Maverick.

I'd told him I would listen to my omega instincts, and I'd chosen to ignore them instead. This isn't how I want to respond to my instincts. I truly meant what I'd said to Maverick, but it turns out it's harder for me to turn off my brain than I thought it would be.

A knock at my door has me standing. I open it to find Tessa standing there. She takes in my appearance, shaking her head. "You realize we have a rose ceremony in twenty minutes, don't you?"

I shrug, stepping to the side so she can step inside. She heads for my bedroom and I follow her, realizing her destination is actually my closet. "You need to wear these gowns we bought for the show."

"Tessa, I don't want to." I know I'm whining, but I've always despised having to dress up in a gown and pretend to be someone I'm not. I deal with it for work because we need to network, but I don't see the point in wearing them for *Heated*. "Do you really think people care what I'm wearing? They've already seen me in a gown and I dress up for the dates."

Tessa turns to face me, seeing something in my face that has her sighing. She pulls me to the floor and I curl up to her side, already feeling a million times better. "I was afraid something was wrong when you stayed in your room all day instead of spending time with the suitors. I hoped I was wrong, but I'm obviously not. So tell me what's going on."

"I just… I want to follow my omega instincts when choosing my pack because it knows what I need, right?" I don't wait for her to respond as I continue speaking. "But how can I when she wanted me to claim someone for my pack after a week? That's not enough time to know if you want to spend forever with someone, is it?"

"Oh, Bree." Tessa tightens her arm around me. "I wish you would've talked to me instead of holding this in for two weeks. Your omega side has instincts we don't understand. I don't know how it can know after one week, but I wouldn't ignore it. You've spent so long repressing it and I think that makes you feel you can't trust it. But you can. It's a part of you and always has been. Do you really think that something that's a part of you would steer you wrong?"

I shake my head. "No, I guess not."

"Excellent." Tessa jumps to her feet, pulling me up with her. "Now, let's choose a gown. I already told the suitors to wear a suit. We've let you dress down for three weeks. The higher ups at the network said they want to see more gowns, so more gowns they shall have."

"Ugh, and this is why I enjoy working for ourselves. No one else to answer to. Why couldn't we just buy a channel or something?"

Tessa laughs. "Sweet precious child, we don't have that kind of money. Now, which one?"

I choose a gown, but I grumble the whole time Tessa helps me get ready. When Allison shows up to do my makeup, I shut up. It's not her fault I'm annoyed—not that it's Tessa's either, but I know she'll love me no matter what. Plus, Allison works for us and I don't want to make her uncomfortable.

Within twenty minutes, I find myself standing outside the ballroom with Reginald, who is once again dressed in a tux. He laughs when he sees my face. "Bree, it's not the end of the world to wear a fancy dress."

"Says you. You get to wear pants and don't have to wear heels. Torture devices… that's what they are. Be happy you're a man. You'd think that we would've eradicated these fake notions of beauty that are a figment of the male gaze. If you had to wear what we do, you wouldn't think it was so sexy."

Smartly, Reginald keeps his mouth shut as he opens the door to the ballroom, but he can't hide the laughter in his eyes. I allow him to lead me up to the stage because it's so much easier to walk with someone else's support. Damn heels. At least they make my legs look good.

As we come to a stop in the middle of the stage, my eyes moving to the vase of flowers and trying to not freak out over the changes I asked Tessa to make. She was right. I need to listen to my inner omega. It won't steer me wrong. I just have to keep reminding myself of that.

"Welcome back to the *Heated* rose ceremony. Tonight, it's apparently time to shake things up. Bree made some last-minute adjustments to the roses. Are you as interested as I am to find out what's going to happen tonight? I know the suitors are, so let's get started. Suitors, as per usual, your names will be called randomly."

Then Reginald is gone, leaving me alone on the stage as I try not to have a panic attack. I know this is the right decision, but I can't seem to keep it together. It's like my mind is trying to talk me out of the decisions I've made. But I'm made of stronger stuff than that. I lift my chin, straightening my back as I look out over the suitors. I can read the curiosity in their eyes, wondering not only who will receive which rose, but what roses have changed from the original set.

"Roman, you're our first suitor of the night."

I turn away from the suitors so I can meet Roman's eyes as he makes his way onto the stage and over to where I stand.

"Hi, Roman."

"Hello, Bree. A wonderful evening, isn't it?"

I giggle. "Yes. Yes, it is. And thank you for that." Taking a deep breath, I take strength from Roman's presence. "I don't want to draw out tonight's ceremony more than necessary, so there won't be a lot of speeches tonight."

Reaching over, I pluck a rose from the vase and offer it to him. "I'd love it if you would join me and a few of the suitors on a group date tomorrow afternoon."

Roman takes the lavender rose with a nod and a smile. "I'm looking forward to it. Thank you."

"Gabriel."

Gabriel arrives with a smirk as he usually does, taking my hand in his before lifting it to his lips. "You look divine tonight, Bree. And I'm sorry you've been forced into heels again. I'm always willing to cart you around when needed."

I laugh because how can I not? Gabriel always knows how to lighten the mood. "I'll definitely keep that in mind." I grab a yellow rose and offer it to him. "No date for you tomorrow, but I know you won't let that get you down."

Gabriel nods his head as his eyes flash to the vase. I know what he's thinking, but I don't respond to the question in his eyes. "Thank you, Bree." He bends over, giving me a sweeping bow before hurrying off the stage.

"Hudson, Maddox, and Onyx, you're up."

"So I'm mixing things up tonight," I tell them as they stop in front of me. "I know I've been doing things with all three of you besides the individual dates, but I've decided to try having you all with different suitors."

I grab three roses, offering the first to Onyx. "I'd like you to join Roman and I on the group date tomorrow."

Onyx takes the offered lavender rose with a head nod. Before I turn to the other two, offering them a yellow rose each. "Don't fret, you two. You'll be invited on other group dates in the coming days."

Hudson lets out a heavy sigh. "I hate waiting, but I guess I will for you."

Maddox cuffs him upside the head, making me laugh. "I know. I know. You've apologized already, and I knew what I was getting into keeping you here. Thank you, gentlemen."

"Brody, will you please make your way to the stage?"

Brody wears a tux well, especially when paired with that smile of his. "Hey, Bree."

"Hi, Brody." I take a deep breath. "I feel like I got to know you a little better during our hiking date you planned. But I still think we need a little more one-on-one time."

I grab the peach rose, offering it to him. "I was hoping you'd be interested in joining me for a date tomorrow night."

Brody takes the rose as he nods. He leans over and kisses my cheek, bringing a smile to my face. He's always so thoughtful. "I would like that very much. Thank you."

"Finnegan, sir. It's your turn."

I have to fight back a laugh when Finnegan appears on the stage, wearing a kilt with his tux jacket and button-down shirt—no tie in sight. "That is quite the look you have going, Finnegan."

"Well, lass... this is th' traditional Scottish dress attire. I thought I would bring a bit of Scottish flare tae Heated." He spins in a circle. "Do ye approve?"

"I do approve, and I feel like I should tell you that you've been hiding away some nice-looking legs. I think you should let them out more often."

"Lass, ye have seen them when A'm wearing my swim trunks. Do nae act lek this is th' first time ye be seeing them."

This time, I don't bother holding back my laughter. I throw back my head as I laugh before reaching to grab a rose, offering it to him. "Thank you for that. I still want to see you in a kilt again, so I'm going to make that happen. Meanwhile, I'd appreciate it if you'd join Roman, Onyx, and I on our group date tomorrow."

"Lass, ye know A'll go wherever ye want me tae." He takes the lavender rose from me before lifting it to boop me on the nose. "I look forward tae tomorrow."

I hate that Tessa and Reginald decided I shouldn't be privy to the order the suitors are called up. I'm just getting more and more nervous, never knowing when they'll call him to the stage.

"Dalton."

I've already grabbed his rose as he makes his way onto the stage, though I keep it behind my back. I don't know how well they can see what colors are in the vase from where they stand. At least now I know they saved him for last.

"I'm glad to see the crutches are finally gone."

Dalton laughs. "You and me both, darlin'. I just got the all clear this afternoon."

"No more rolling your ankle on rocks," I tell him with a shake of my head as I pull the rose from behind my back. "Because of the plans for tomorrow, you wouldn't have been able to go on the group date with your crutches. I'm sorry that I didn't know you were off of them before now."

"It's no problem." Dalton takes the yellow rose from me. "There's always next time, darlin'." With one last wink, he heads off the stage.

"Our last two suitors are Emmett and Maverick. Will the two of you please make your way to the stage?"

I force myself to take a deep breath. I can do this. Yes, it's a big deal, but it's what I want. I smile when Maverick and Emmett stop before me. Reaching over, I grab the last two roses. "As you can see, I have two roses left… which makes sense since there's two of you. Tonight I'll be inviting one of you onto the group date tomorrow and the other I'll be inviting to become the first member of my pack. Technically, that means you'll both be joining me for the group date.

"I've gone back and forth over the last few weeks, my mind at odds with my instincts. If I would've listened to my instincts, this would've happened sooner. As Maverick knows, I want to choose my pack by leaning on my omega instincts. It's one of the things we discussed on our date. Sadly, I found it harder to do that than I thought it would be. But I'm going to keep trying."

I turn my attention to Emmett. "I know I've said this from day one, but I've always felt comfortable around you. You're one of the most genuine people I've ever met—yes, I'm aware I work in a world where very few people are genuine, but that doesn't change my opinion. You bring brightness to a world that could use more of it and more people like you.

"Maverick. I felt like our date was the first time I allowed myself to really get to know you, and I know you've noticed that I've been making more of an effort to spend time with you. Well, with all of you, but you get my point. You're easy to be around and you make me feel safe."

Taking a deep breath, I hand the lavender rose to Maverick. "We're just not there yet. But know that I'm really enjoying getting to know you. I'd love for you to join me, Roman, Onyx, and Finnegan, on our group date tomorrow."

"We're not, but I look forward to tomorrow's date." He takes the rose from me before turning his attention to Emmett. He squeezes the beta's shoulder. "Congrats, man."

I watch as Maverick heads off the stage before looking back to Emmett, who's staring at me in shock.

"That leaves this one for you." I press the red rose into his hand.

"You're choosing me to be the first person in your pack?" Emmett's words are spoken so quietly, I have to lean closer to hear them. His eyes meet mine and I see the shine of tears there. "Why?"

"Why?" I scoff. "Were you not listening a minute ago? My omega side knew almost from day one that you were just what I needed. I could never say goodbye to you. You are part of my forever... if that's what you want."

"If that's..." Emmett splutters. "What kind of an idiot do you take me for? Of course, it's what I want. Fuck, this is happening, isn't it?"

I laugh. "Well, yeah..."

Emmett laughs, pulling me into his arms and swinging me around the stage. "Yes, yes, yes," he says as he sets me back on my feet, peppering me with kisses. "I want nothing more in this world than to be a part of your pack."

"Thank the fates. I was a little worried there for a moment." Pulling him in for a kiss, I hear the other suitors clapping and yelling. I have to break the kiss as tears fill my eyes. Turning toward them, I can't believe how happy they are for me and Emmett. I wish I could choose them all. They're all such good men.

I startle when Reginald wraps an arm around Emmett's and my shoulders. "Three weeks down and Bree has chosen her first pack mate. With just five more weeks until your heat, how soon can we expect a completed pack?"

I elbow him, shaking my head. "When I decide on one."

Reginald laughs. "As you heard, the suitors are just as happy for the two of you as I am. What comes next is completely up to you, Bree. But for tonight? Enjoy your first member of your pack."

I turn to Emmett with a smile. I'm so glad I made this decision. I can't wait to make Emmett mine.

Emmett

I'm still in shock as I walk back to Bree's suite, her hand in mine. I can't believe that I'm the first one she chose to be a part of her pack. I thought she'd choose an alpha first. After all, alpha knots are what she'll need during her heat. Not that I'll be useless because I will definitely be helping her out through her heat. But I'll also keep an eye on the entire pack, making sure we're all well-fed and clean.

I hadn't even thought that I'd be able to bond with her without an alpha in the pack, because betas can't instigate a mate bond. I recall learning that omegas can instigate one though—that in most cases, they will bite each member of their pack to claim them. But I guess I hadn't really thought about that. I figured I'd join a pack by an alpha's bite at some point.

This is better—so much better.

Bree scans her keycard, pulling me along behind her. "I'd like to do this in my nest, if that's alright with you."

"We can do this wherever you want. I want you to be comfortable. You're sure you want me in your nest?"

Bree laughs, glancing over her shoulder at me. "If I want you to be part of my pack, then I want you to be in my nest."

"That makes sense." Yeah, I'm being awkward as hell. Not exactly how I wanted this to go. "Where exactly is your nest?"

"In my closet." She drags me through the bedroom and I thought she was kidding, but no, she drags me into the closet. Looking around, I don't see a nest and am even more confused. "Over here."

Bree drops on her knees, pressing her thumb against a pad I hadn't even noticed. "We'll get your thumbprint added tomorrow. Tessa will help us with that."

Then the doors to her nest slide open and all I can do is gawk at the room. It's much bigger than I thought it would be, which makes sense considering the dimensions of her closet compared to everything else. It's windowless, and the ceiling isn't as high as the rest of her suite—something I'm sure her omega side appreciates.

"Well, are you coming in?"

She moved without me realizing it as she is already inside the nest, so I take a step toward her, but hesitate before entering. "May I enter your nest, omega?"

A smile lights up her face. "Yes, beta, you may."

I kick off my shoes, leaving them outside the nest before following her inside. "So, how do we shut the door?"

"Just like you'd shut any other door, obviously."

I watch as she leans over and slides the door closed. It's only then that I realize she's turned on some warm hued fairy lights. "Ummm... and if we have to use the bathroom?"

She giggles. "You just hit the button by the door." She points to the green button beside the door.

"Oh, well, guess I should've looked."

"If I'm sleeping, you'll need to make sure you don't shut the door behind you or you won't be able to get back in."

"Got it." I take another moment to take in her nest. "I really like your nest, omega. You've done an excellent job with it."

She ducks her head. "Thank you. I like it. Once I have my pack—well, once we have *our* pack—and we find a house, I want to make my new nest to look a lot like this one." She runs her hands over the material hanging from the walls before laying down amongst the pillows and blankets.

I lay down on my side so I can look at her, resting my head in the palm of my hand. "That sounds like a dream."

"It does, doesn't it?"

I'm definitely feeling awkward, which isn't a feeling I'm used to. So I'm just going to blame what pops out of my mouth next on that. "Any ideas about who else you'll choose?"

Bree blinks up at me before laughing. "Fates! Your face right now! You didn't mean to say that, did you?"

I shake my head frantically. "Not right then, I didn't. I figured I'd ask you about it later. Fates, I'm a mess. Why am I so nervous right now?"

"I am too," Bree admits as she rolls onto her side to face me. "It's this whole planned thing. My omega side is screaming at me to get on with it, but my mind is like, don't you want it to happen naturally? Being on a reality dating show just messes up the entire process, doesn't it?"

"Shit. Are there cameras in here too?" I sit up at her words, eyes scanning the room as if I'd be able to see them.

Bree shakes her head. "No, this, the bathrooms, and the control room are the only rooms free of cameras. No part of our bonding will be recorded."

"I don't know why that freaked me out so badly. I guess it's not really something I want others to see. It should be just for us."

"I agree." Bree reaches for me, so I scoot closer to her as she continues, "It's why I fought so hard against the network about putting a camera in the nest. This is my safe place—the place I go to when everything is too much. I don't want cameras on me then, and I know other omegas would feel the same. If they hadn't relented on this, we would've found another network because an omega's nest is their sacred space. No one is allowed to invade that unless they've been invited."

"Like me?"

Bree grins, looping her arms around my neck and pulling me down to her. "Just like you. Now, kiss me. I want to bond with you."

I don't have to be told twice, brushing my lips gently across her until she's wiggling under me. I pull back with a laugh as she pouts. "What's wrong, baby? I kissed you like you wanted me to."

"You may have kissed me, but not like I wanted you to." Bree surprises me when she launches herself at me, pushing me until my back hits the floor of the nest. "You should know better than to tease an omega."

She drops her weight down on me and kisses me, tongue dragging across my lips until I open to her. I don't fight her when she starts to undress the both of us. I guess I'm kind of a switch—not that I've ever been in the BDSM scene, but it's the closest term I can think of to describe myself—and Bree, really. Sometimes I like to be the one in charge and sometimes I like to lay back and let someone else have the reins.

Since Bree seems to know exactly what she wants, I'll let her have the reins. Less of a chance of it going awkward—especially if she's letting her instincts run the show. No skin off my back.

We're both naked when Bree starts licking and nipping at my neck, grinding her slick soaked pussy along my cock. "Is there anywhere in particular you'd like my bite?"

It's hard to think with her pussy rubbing against me and her lips brushing across my neck. "I... uhh... shit, Bree. I can't think when you're rubbing against me like this."

Bree giggles as she sits up, hips stilling. Her pussy is still pressed up against my cock, but at least she isn't moving anymore. I shake my head, trying to remember what she asked.

Oh, right. Where do I want her bite? I shrug.

"I'm not really sure. But... I do have a question." I rub the back of my neck, not meeting her gaze.

Bree cups my cheek, rubbing her thumb across it until I meet her gaze once more. "What do you need, Emmett?"

"Well, since I can't mark you, I was wondering if you'd consider doing something to mark you as mine… maybe in the same place you bite me?"

She perks up, glancing at her wrist. "Like a tattoo?"

"Yeah, a tattoo is one option. One I like a lot."

"It's almost as permanent as a bite. Though it limits where I can bite you, because I'm not getting a tattoo on my neck." She taps her lips with her index finger. "I mean, I wouldn't mind one on the back of my neck, but I'm not bendy enough to bite the back of your neck during sex."

I can't help but laugh at the way she's trying to work it out. "You're adorable, you know that?"

"Why, thank you, I am aware." Bree glances at her wrist again before picking up mine. "What about here? I can get mine on the opposite wrist, so when we hold hands, they'll be together."

I grin up at her because, of course, she's come up with the perfect solution. "I love that idea."

"Good." She lifts my hand so she can lick my wrist before she rubs the side of her face against it.

"What are you doing?"

Bree shrugs. "I had to taste you and then I thought you could get used to smelling me on your wrist while I ride you."

"Well… okay. Yes, please." I nod, barely even able to get those words out. I yank her down so I can kiss her, needing her now. I'm so ready for her bite, for her to mark me as her own. And who wouldn't want to have sex with Bree? She's fucking sex on a stick. "Ride me, baby."

Bree grins down at me and lifts her hips. Reaching down, she grasps my cock in her hand, giving it one good, long stroke before lining it up at her entrance. My hands shoot down to her hips as she takes me inside of her. She feels like heaven and I want to spend the rest of my life inside of her pussy—which I guess I will be. Thank the fates.

Then she's riding me, head thrown back, her tits bouncing with her movements. I lift enough that I can suck one of her nipples into my mouth, smiling as she whimpers and wraps one of her hands in my hair to keep me there. As if I want to be anywhere else.

I tease her nipple with my tongue. This new angle seems to have me hitting Bree in a new way and she's losing her mind. Her movements are already erratic, her walls squeezing me as her orgasm approaches.

I pop off her nipple to stare up at her. "Are you close already, baby?"

"So close," she pants.

"Let me help you." It takes a little wrangling, but I finally get my hand between us. I stroke her clit as I thrust into her from below. I don't know if she plans to bite me when she comes the first time, or if she plans to wait. But just in case she plans to bite me now, I plan to make it an out of this world orgasm.

She shrieks as I hit that spot inside of her that's going to send her flying. Who knows, maybe I can even get her to squirt like Roman did. The image of her squirting all over Roman just before he came has me fucking into her harder. Fates, that night had been so hot.

I'd been so surprised when I realized Roman was not only into men, but me. I've definitely jerked off to that memory more than once since that night. It's pushing me closer and closer to my orgasm. I pinch Bree's clit and she goes rim rod straight just before she falls apart.

A keening moan spills from her lips as she grinds down on my cock, her pussy squeezing me so tight. "Fates, Bree. Your tight pussy is going to make me come early. You feel so fucking good as you fall apart on my cock."

"Yes," she hisses, reaching for my wrist. "You must come."

I get a flash of her elongated canines before she bites down on my wrist. My body's reaction is immediate as my back arches off the ground and I explode inside of my mate. I'm overwhelmed by the new sensations running through me and I know that's the bond snapping into place.

For a moment, all I see is white light and there's no sound. When I come back to myself, I hear the sound that falls from my lips and it isn't anything I've ever heard before—half pain, half pleasure and so fucking happy as I fill her with my cum.

It's the longest orgasm I've ever had, ending only when Bree releases my wrist from her teeth. Then she licks it, sending aftershocks running through my body.

"Holy shit," I pant. "Do that again."

She lets out a giggle before her tongue is scraping across the bite marks again, sending another aftershock through me. She lays my wrist on the floor of the nest before leaning down to kiss me.

"Mine," she growls against my lips.

"Yours. Definitely yours."

I don't know how this became my life, but damn am I glad it is. As she kisses me, I feel my cock growing hard inside of her again. That hasn't happened before.

I roll us until she's on her back with me hovering over her with my cock still inside her. "My turn," I tell her before I slam into her. I hope she doesn't plan on getting much sleep tonight. I may not be able to claim her as mine, but I can feel her through our bond now and I want to give her as many orgasms I can to thank her for choosing me.

Brody

I'm not going to lie. I spent most of last night and today dreading our date. Not because I don't want to spend time with Bree. I love spending time with her. But I knew I needed to have a serious conversation with her and I'm still not sure how she's going to react.

Bree booked a planetarium for our date and we're currently laying side by side as we stare up at the ceiling filled with stars. It's beautiful, as is the woman beside me. But something is missing between us and I've denied it as long as I can. She's mated to Emmett now, so I don't have to worry about her being beta-less. Now it's time to be honest with her.

I sit up slowly, and she follows me with a frown. "What's wrong, Brody? Something's been off since you picked me up for our date, but I didn't want to say anything and ruin the night."

I take her hand in mine, rubbing my thumb across her knuckles. "Did you have fun on your group date today?"

Bree looks confused, but nods. "I did. We went and rode dune buggies through the desert. I've always wanted to do it and it was a blast. I only drove once, though, before trading out with someone else. I don't think they liked the way I drove it."

I laugh as I picture it. I wonder who all she'd had in her buggie. Not everyone is an adrenaline junkie, but I can see how much Bree enjoyed it—telling me she is one. "I'm glad you guys had fun. Emmett was grinning all day long, happily showing off his bond mark."

"Is that what this is about? You're concerned because I chose Emmett? That doesn't mean I won't choose you. There are plenty of packs that have more than one beta—"

"But what if I don't want to be chosen?" I ask, cutting her off.

Her shoulders drop as she tilts her head, considering me. "Do you not want to be in my pack?"

"We get along well, right?" I wait until she nods before continuing, "Is there anyone else in the house you haven't slept with or had some kind of sexual encounter with?"

Bree frowns, and I can see her going through the guys in her mind. Just like I can see when the realization hits her. "No."

"Do you think of me like you do the others?"

She frowns, and I know she doesn't like the questions I'm asking, but they need to be asked. "Maybe not? I just thought it was taking us longer to click. Except we do click... just not like that."

"Exactly, and that's okay. I've been thinking about it recently, but I didn't know if you and Emmett were there. I didn't want to leave you without a beta... though I wouldn't have bonded with you. I want more than friendship with the woman I bond with... or the woman I marry if it ends up being another beta. I want love and I know you do too."

"I do, and I want that for you, too. I should've noticed this sooner."

I shake my head. "You're still juggling ten men. The fact that you didn't notice that we make better friends isn't that surprising. I could've said something sooner, but I wanted to wait. But now, you have a beta, who if you don't love him now, you will. I can see it. I'm so happy for both of you, but I want to find that for myself. I can't do that here. I think you should let me go at the next rose ceremony."

"Of course." Bree laughs, and I can see tears in her eyes. "It's still going to suck to see you go. You're the puppy—yes, Tessa told me. You're the one who always brings sunshine to any room you're in. I won't hog that or keep you from finding the person or people you're meant to be with. But you better give Tessa your number so we can get together after this is done. Assuming you want to be friends with me."

"You're a dumbass," I tell her with a laugh. "We just had a conversation about how good of friends we make. Of course, I want to be friends after this is all said and done."

Bree nods. "Yeah. I can do that." She pauses, looking around the room. "Do you want to head home, or are you cool with having a friend date?"

"A friend date sounds like just what I need." I pull her to lean against me before laying us both back down. "I love looking at the stars. It makes everything else seem so inconsequential."

"It really does, doesn't it?" Bree sighs as she settles her head against my shoulder.

I'm glad I finally brought this up to her. Now, we can both enjoy the evening as two friends. It feels like I'm finally being truthful with her, and that makes me feel more at ease. This might be the end of my *Heated* journey, but it's not the end of my friendship with Bree, nor the end of my journey for love. I know there's a woman out there who will love me just as much as I love her.

Chapter Twenty-four

Bree

Another week has come and gone. We said goodbye to Brody the day after our date. The other suitors had been shocked, but Brody and I told them we'd talked about it and decided it was what needed to happen.

Emmett hadn't even needed an explanation, as our bond was already growing between us even after only two days. Now, after a week, I can feel his emotions and he can feel mine. I even felt it when he stubbed his toe in the middle of the night. It's been nice to have him in my bed every night, even if it's only to cuddle.

He's mine and I'm his. And it's the best thing in the world. I don't know what it'll be like to bond with an alpha whose mark I will also wear, but I'm looking forward to finding out. Hopefully soon. I know the others are getting antsy now that I've chosen one member for my pack. I'll need to choose someone else soon. And while I have an idea, I'm still not sure. I also want to talk to Emmett about it before I make a decision.

Speaking of which, I need to find him. I want to decide before tonight's ceremony, and that's only a few hours away. I'd checked out by the pool, but Roman said he'd left the pool about an hour ago. There was no sign of him on the first floor or in the second floor living room. I'd knocked on his door, but there hadn't been an answer. No one had been in the theater, so I'm hoping that he's in the game room. Maybe he's hanging out with some of the guys up there.

I hesitate at the top of the stairs when I hear a moan—more than one moan, actually. I bite my lip, not wanting to interrupt anything, but Emmett's arousal hits me out of nowhere. It hits so hard that I have to bite back my moan as I struggle to remain standing. Which means at least one of those moans is coming from my mate.

I step onto the landing to find Emmett sitting in Onyx's lap, the alpha's hand wrapped around both of their cocks as he jerks them off. Hudson and Maddox stand on either side of them, eyes locked on the show before them as they stroke their own cocks.

Don't get me wrong, it's hot as hell and I definitely wouldn't mind getting myself off to the sight, but this isn't something Emmett and I have discussed. And it's definitely something we should've discussed. I clear my throat, surprised they didn't hear me step into the room. It's not like I was trying to be stealthy.

Emmett's head falls back as he moans, coming all over Onyx moments before the other man comes. Hudson and Maddox's eyes are wide as they stare at me before hurrying to tuck away their cocks.

"What—" Emmett breaks off as he turns on Onyx's lap. He visibly pales as his eyes lock on mine. "Bree…"

"I think we need to talk," I say, keeping my face neutral. "Why don't you meet me in the suite after you clean up?"

They all try to speak at once, but I just hold up my hand. "I need to speak with my mate. The rest of you can wait."

Turning on my heel, I make my way back down the stairs. My emotions are a mess, as are Emmett's. I can't even figure out what I'm feeling with his emotions pulsing inside of me. We're still learning how our bond works and it's turning out to be harder than I thought it would be—especially right now.

So rather than try to untangle them, I shove them down deep. It's harder to do now after weeks of letting my omega side out and with my bond with Emmett. I knew that being on *Heated* would change me, but I don't think I truly understood how much.

Finally, making it back to my suite, I push open the door and kick off my shoes. I'm climbing into my nest before I even realize it was my destination. Wrapping myself in blankets that smell of me and Emmett, I lay down and bury myself in my nest.

I don't know how much time passes as I lay there, but one moment I'm alone and the next Emmett is laying across from me, tears streaming down his face. "I'm so sorry, baby... I..."

I shake my head. "Shhhh. Just hold me for a minute. I need a little longer before we talk about it."

It's clear that Emmett wants to argue, but he sits up and pulls me into his lap. I allow my eyes to fall shut and revel in his closeness. Am I stalling? Absolutely, but it doesn't mean that I don't need this. I also know that this conversation needs to be held in my suite where there are cameras, but I need just a few moments of silence in my mate's arms.

Finally, I push off the blankets and pull myself from Emmett's hold. Leaning over, I press a kiss to his cheek before standing. "Come, mate. We need to have a conversation and we can't have it here."

Not just because of the lack of cameras, but because I don't want my nest tainted by the coming conversation. Emmett doesn't stand with me and I wonder if he might need some time to himself. I can give him that, if that's what he needs.

I make my way to my bedroom, plopping onto the bed to wait for Emmett. It doesn't take him long to follow me, and he looks like shit. His guilt drips from head to toe. His eyes are red and puffy, showing he continued crying after I left the nest. I hate to see him hurt.

I pat the bed beside me. "Come here, Emmett. I'm not mad. We just need to discuss some things."

I turn to the side so I can face Emmett as he settles onto the bed. The look of confusion on his face is kind of adorable.

"What do you mean, you're not mad?"

I take Emmett's hands and lift them to my lips. "I love you, Emmett."

"I love you too, Bree." His eyes are wide and I can see tears threatening to spill over once more.

"Good. I was hoping you'd say that. The reason I'm not mad is that we never discussed this. We never discussed how things would go for the rest of our time on the show." A mistake, obviously. "I knew you were interested in Hudson, Onyx, Maddox, and Gabriel. You never kept that from me. I'm not even remotely against the idea.

"I would love nothing more than for my pack to be with one another as well as me. That's what I've always wanted. It's good that you've shown interest in the other suitors. The problem is, what happens if you're emotionally attached to someone I don't choose? I don't want my pack to be involved with people outside of the pack."

"Of course you don't." Emmett shakes his head. "That's the first time anything has happened between me and any of the guys since we bonded. I just... I have no excuse for it."

I snort. "I think you're missing the point here. You don't need an excuse. I understand and support what happened, but we need to talk about what happens if I don't choose them. I need to decide who I want to join the pack. As much as I love you, you cannot help me through my heat on your own. We need alphas."

"Yes, we do." Emmett sighs. "I just don't know where to begin this conversation."

"Let's start with the simple part. You're attracted to... all the men who are also attracted to men?"

Emmett snorts. "Well, I'm attracted to all the guys because Tessa sent you a plethora of insanely attractive men. But yes, I would be involved with any of them."

"Good. That's helpful. Now, if I ask Maverick and Dalton into the pack, would you have a problem with it?"

"No. It's not the first time I've been attracted to straight men. I'm not going to try to force them to do something they don't want to do."

I frown. "Did I say that?" When he shakes his head, I continue, "How emotionally attached are you to the others?"

He shrugs as he ducks his eyes, telling me it's worse than I thought. He's already formed emotional connections. Fates above. I don't want to hurt this man by not choosing those that he's fallen for, but I can't let him dictate who I choose for my pack, either. I value his opinion, but the decision will always fall to me in the end.

"What's going to happen if I don't choose them, Em? What is that going to do to you? Are you going to be able to handle it?"

Emmett nods. "Will it suck? One hundred percent yes. Being in your pack is what matters. Being by your side is what matters. I would rip my heart to shreds daily if it made you happy. You're who I choose. I will always choose you, and the pack that you choose."

"Okay. Then we need to figure out who the hell I'm choosing next. Because right now, I don't know. Choosing Maddox, Hudson, and Onyx would be the easiest choice. You're already attached and I'm assuming it's the same for them. But the same could be said for Gabriel. Hell, even Roman—though, he's also close with Finnegan. I think Dalton and Maverick are close to forming a pack of their own. It doesn't matter who I choose next—someone is going to be hurt."

"Hey, hey." Emmett wraps his arms around me. "You don't need to worry about everyone else's feelings. They're all grown ass men and they can deal with some hurt feelings. This needs to be about who you can see being a part of our pack."

I let myself melt into Emmett's touch. "But what if I could see them all as part of our pack? I don't want that big of a pack, though. Why is this so hard?"

"Because love isn't easy? I have no idea, baby. I just know I wouldn't give it up for anything." He pulls back and I lift my head up to meet his eyes. "How did you say you wanted to choose our pack?"

"By following my omega side's instincts."

"Exactly. So what are they telling you right now?"

And just like that, I know who I'll be choosing next.

Hudson

I'm stressing out. Hell, I've been stressing out since Bree walked in on us. We didn't mean for things to get to that point. It's not like we're trying to steal Bree's mate. The worst part of her catching us is that I couldn't get a read on what she was thinking as she stared at us.

"We've ruined this. She's going to send us home. There's no way she'll choose us now," I murmur for what I'm sure in the hundredth time in the last hour. Both Onyx and Maddox have tried to distract me, to keep my mind off of it, but I keep spiraling.

The last thing I want is to end up in a depressive spiral, but I can feel it tugging at me—demanding that I give up and crawl into bed. Of course, Bree is pissed at us. How could she not be? We'd done the unthinkable with her mate. She's going to kick us off the show and that'll be it. No more Bree. No more Emmett.

We'll return home with broken hearts and memories of our own stupidity to keep us warm at night. Why hadn't I stopped it? Why hadn't any of us stopped it? What had we been thinking?

Oh, right. We weren't thinking. I squeeze my eyes shut, rubbing the palms of my hands against them to keep the tears at bay. This isn't how I wanted this to end. I don't want it to end. I want her. I want them. I just want.

"Hudson, you have to calm down. She's going to be here any minute now. You're spiraling." Maddox's words are quiet as he wraps his arms around me. I can feel the eyes of the other suitors on us, and I hate it. I don't want them to see me like this—I don't want anyone to see me like this. But what choice do I have? I'm about to lose everything... okay, not everything. I know I'll still have both Maddox and Onyx at my side.

"C'mon, Hud." Onyx wraps around me from behind. "You've gotta push through this. You're strong and you have me and Mad to help you through this. But we don't even know what's going to happen. We don't know what she's going to say."

"Do you think you can keep it together through the ceremony?" Maddox asks as he leans back to look down at me.

I drop my hands and look up at him, still fighting tears. "I can try."

Onyx's lips brush against the back of my neck. "That's all we can ask of you."

The doors to the ballroom open and I have to bite my lip to keep the tears from falling. I'm so afraid of what I'll see on their faces. Will they hate us? Of course, they'll hate us.

Fuck.

Onyx and Maddox move to stand on each side of me, gripping my hands in theirs. It helps to ground me, but the only person who can keep me from spiraling further is walking onto the stage with Reginald and Emmett. I can't look at their faces, too lost in my embarrassment and fear of what I'll see.

My eyes lock on the vase of roses, realizing for the first time that there aren't any roses inside of it. What the hell is going on right now? My eyes flash to Reginald when he speaks.

"Good evening suitors and viewers alike. Tonight, we're shaking things up with the rose ceremony once again. We've gathered the roses Bree requested, but instead of placing them in the vase for all to see, we're keeping them hidden from view. One will be revealed at random and given to Emmett, who will in turn present it to Bree. She will then call forth the suitor who the rose is for. Who doesn't love a bit of mystery? Let's get this party started, shall we?"

Reginald steps off the stage and grabs a box, setting it on the side of the stage. Emmett walks over and takes a peach rose from him, walking back and handing it to Bree.

Bree looks out at the suitors, but I duck my head down. I'm so afraid of what I'll see in her eyes that I just can't meet her gaze. I'd rather keep my head buried in the sand. Deny what's coming for as long as I can.

"Dalton." My shoulder slump as she calls his name. Of course, she wants to go on another date with him. He's perfect. He isn't a fuckup like me.

I lose track of the roses as she calls on Gabe, Finnegan, Maverick, and Roman. Now, it's just the three of us. I squeeze my eyes shut, ready for her to announce that she's sending us home.

"Before you give me the last three roses, I'd like Hudson, Maddox, and Onyx to come on stage."

My body is frozen in place. I'm not ready for this. I don't want to say goodbye.

"Come on, Hud. We have to go on stage. Please don't make us drag you up there," Onyx begs me.

I can feel every set of eyes on me, but I can't lift my head. I hate that I'm this way, but I also know there isn't anything I can do to change it. I force myself to take a step forward as the loves of my life hold on to my hands, being my life vests as I bounce around in the dark waters, threatening to pull me down into its depth.

You'll always be a fuckup. Everything you touch crumbles. You don't deserve to be happy. You'll never be enough. One day, even Maddox and Onyx will leave you. You're weak and unloveable.

Each whispered sentence in my head is another weight on my shoulders, trying to push me down until I can't get back up again. If it wasn't for Onyx and Maddox, I would've succumbed a long time ago. They lend me their strength when I have none of my own.

Too soon, we're stopping in front of Bree and Emmett, but I keep my eyes locked on their shoes. One look at their faces and I'll be lost. It's too much.

"Hudson, are you okay?" Bree asks, worry lacing her words. I don't answer her because I can't. When she takes a step toward me, Onyx and Maddox take a step back and I can see the way Bree freezes.

Onyx clears his throat. "I don't think you should touch him. He's... not doing well."

"Not doing well? I don't understand." I can hear the frown in her voice and I bite the inside of my cheek, hating myself for not being brave enough to tell her about the depression I suffer from. She doesn't understand because I've never shared it with her. Like an idiot. Just another thing I've done wrong.

I hear Emmett whispering in Bree's ear, but I can't make out the words. She gasps and then she's moving across the stage toward me. When my pack mates try to shuffle us back further, she growls at them, causing all of us to freeze. That was an omega growl—usually reserved for when someone is threatening their pack... which doesn't make any sense.

Bree's small hands land on my cheeks as she forces me to look at her. "Why didn't you tell me?"

"Afraid. Embarrassed. Hate." I'm shaking now, not even able to form sentences as I stare into Bree's beautiful amber eyes. There's fear and worry in her eyes, but no hate, and I almost slump to the floor with relief. She doesn't hate me. I don't know how I got this lucky, but fates above, she doesn't hate me.

"There's no reason to be embarrassed about something you can't control, Hudson. I understand the fear and hate, but never be embarrassed that you have to deal with depression. So what if it looks different from others? We're all different and how we react to things is always going to differ."

Bree shakes her head. "There was a lot I wanted to say, but there's no way I'm going to leave you like this. Emmett, get the roses."

She might not hate me, but she is about to send us home, isn't she? I don't even blame her. Why would she ever choose me? Onyx and Maddox, sure. But not me. I'm not worth it.

"I choose you, Hudson. I choose you and your pack mates. For now and forever. Do you hear me? I choose you. Emmett chooses you. You're ours."

It takes me a moment to wrap my head around her words and the roses she's offering me. They're red, not black. That doesn't make sense.

I'm suddenly surrounded by four bodies, each whispering to me, "I choose you."

Tears roll down my cheeks and as hard as I try to keep them at bay, sobs rack my body. "You choose me?"

"Yes."

"Always."

Their hands stroke over my body, through my hair as they offer me their words and comfort. I can't believe they choose me. But I'll be damned if I ruin this again.

Somewhere beyond my pack, I can hear Reginald ending the ceremony. I've probably ruined their plans, but I can't seem to find it in me to care. I just need my pack to help me, to pull me free from the thoughts threatening to drown me. With their help, I'll make it through it.

Onyx

It takes longer than I would like to calm Hudson down. Thankfully, Reginald had closed out the show and Tessa had escorted the other suitors from the room. I was so afraid that we'd finally lose Hudson. He'd been so sure that Bree was sending us home, and if I'm honest, I thought the same damn thing. I was so sure that *Heated* was going to be our ruin.

But Bree is always full of surprises, isn't she? Instead of sending us home, she asked us to join her pack. I can barely believe it myself, but I know it's what will bring Hudson back from the edge. It'll still take him time to get back to himself, but we'll be there for him and help him in any way we can.

We've finally made it back to Bree's suite and Hudson is passed out with his head in Bree's lap as she strokes her hand through his hair. Emmett sits on the floor in front of the couch they're laying on, clinging to Hudson's arm and one of Bree's legs. He looks absolutely shattered.

"Obviously, this isn't how I thought tonight would go," Bree murmurs, finally lifting her eyes from Hudson to look between me and Maddox. "I understand why he didn't tell me, but why didn't either of you tell me?

I needed to know this. I would've handled things so differently. I didn't like seeing him like this."

"Me neither," Emmett adds.

I shake my head, finally sitting on the couch across from them. "It wasn't our place to tell you. He kept saying he'd tell you, but I should've known better."

"We're not keeping anything else from you." Maddox runs a hand over his face as he finally stops his pacing. "You're right, we should've told you. We provided the information to Tessa, and I figured she'd tell you, but that's what I get for making assumptions."

"It's in the past. All we can do now is move forward." Bree glances back down at Hudson. "We need to have a conversation and he needs to be awake for it."

"I'm awake." Hudson shifts until he's looking up at Bree. "I'm sorry I didn't tell you. I'm sorry you had to find out this way, and I'm sorry about earlier—"

Bree places her fingers on his lips. "No more apologies. It's all in the past. Just don't keep things from me in the future. That goes for all of you." Her eyes move over all of us, waiting for each of us to nod. "Can you sit up, Hudson?"

Hudson sits up, but remains at Bree's side. He's going to be extra clingy for the next few days, but I somehow doubt our little omega is going to mind. I can't help but smile as I realize we have an omega. Sure, we haven't bonded yet, but I'm assuming that's at least part of what Bree wants to discuss.

Bree cuddles against Hudson before gesturing for Emmett to do the same on his other side. "First and foremost, I was never angry at any of you for what I walked in on earlier. I was annoyed with myself for various reasons, including that I hadn't spoken with Emmett about sleeping with anyone else after we mated.

"I didn't care that he was involved in the scene upstairs. In fact, it was hot as hell and we can recreate it any time. I'm concerned about him becoming emotionally attached to someone that I might not choose for the pack. I already have to worry about the fact that *I'm* emotionally attached to all the suitors. I can't worry about him at the same time.

"He is part of the reason I chose your pack tonight, but not the whole reason. I believe the five of us will be good together, but I also don't think our pack is complete yet. All four of you can do whatever you want with the other suitors, whether I'm involved or not. You have my permission. I won't go all possessive omega on you, I promise. Just know that I can't worry about any of you becoming attached to someone else."

"We understand, Bree." Hudson presses a kiss to her hair. "If you say the pack isn't complete, then it isn't complete. You're the boss... literally, in this case."

Bree laughs. "On a more serious note, I know that I've asked you to join my pack, but I don't want to be marked until our pack is complete."

It's so quiet, we would be able to hear a pin drop. I'm trying to make sure I'm understanding her correctly while my alpha is roaring at me to let him out. He's demanding that we mark her as ours immediately.

"What the hell are you talking about?" Maddox's voice is quiet, but I can hear the growl beneath it. Neither he nor his alpha are happy with Bree's remark.

"We all saw first hand how Riley was with Carter. Do you think it's going to be better or worse when you bite me—an omega? Because I can guarantee you, it's going to be worse. I want you to mark me, but I need to be able to choose who else belongs in our pack. I'm not doing this to hurt you. I'm doing this to make sure no one is hurt."

"But you claimed, Emmett." Hudson's voice is small, reeking of dejection. I want to pull him into my arms and tell him it'll all be alright, but I can't. This is something that only Bree can make right.

She turns to face Hudson, lifting her hands to cup his cheeks. "Omegas are possessive whether we've bonded you or not. Once we've decided you're ours, that's it. And I'm not against biting and claiming the three of you. We can do that right now. You just can't bite me. Please tell me you understand?"

"You'll claim me as yours now, and then when you decide our pack is complete, all the alphas will mark you—claim you?"

"Yes. Exactly that. You're mine. They're mine. I'm yours. This doesn't change any of that. It's just what I need to make this work."

I clear my throat. "I just want to make sure you're aware of what you're getting with this. Our alphas want to claim you, make you ours right now. This could make us irritable and huge pains in your ass."

Bree nods. "I'm hoping that if I claim you, it will calm your alphas some, but I understand that you're still going to be possessive. But am I wrong to assume it'll be easier to control your alpha now than when I wear your marks?"

"Yes." Maddox is the one who answers. "This will be easier. Especially with your marks on us."

Bree grins. "Good. Which leads me to my next question... I assume each of you will want to claim one another as well as Emmett?"

"You need us to wait for that too," I say slowly, fairly sure I can see where she's going with this.

"Yes. I can't have you going all alphahole over any of us for this to work on the show. But I know Emmett has a request for his marks and you might already know where you want to mark one another. We should talk through that now before I bite somewhere that someone else wants to. Emmett?"

Emmett chews on his lip for a moment while Hudson runs a hand through his hair. He looks between the three of us before nodding.

"I want to carry all three of your bites, just like I do Bree's. Betas can't mark like omegas and alphas, so Bree already agreed to mark me where she'd be willing to get a tattoo to act as my mark. I'm hoping that the three of you will do the same."

"Ahhhh, that's why she marked your wrist." Hudson lifts the beta's arm, staring at the bite mark that is now completely healed, but will remain for all of Emmett's days. "What tattoo are you thinking?"

Bree's the one to answer. "We actually decided that we'd wait until after the show was over to come up with a design. There's just too much going on here to deal with that now."

"Well," I drawl. "The good news is you just added three tattoo artists to your pack. We can help with both the design and the tattooing itself.

I'll gladly wear a tattoo for you, Emmett. Though you'll have a harder time finding blank skin on us versus Bree."

"I have some space on my legs. Pretty sure there's some room on my thigh," Hudson offers and Emmett's face flushes. "How does that sound to you?"

"Good," Emmett squeaks, and I smile.

"We can do the back for my bite and your tattoo," I tell him and he just nods before his eyes move onto Maddox.

"I'm running out of room for places I want to have tattoos." Maddox laughs as he tugs down the waistband of his pants, pointing to a spot on his hip. "We could do here."

"Uhh... yes, please." Emmett is nodding so hard I'm almost afraid his head's going to fall off. And he's blushing so hard he's bright red. We should probably change the subject.

"This is something that Maddox, Hudson, and I have discussed. We'd like to bite one another's neck, but if that's a spot you'd prefer..." I trail off when Bree shakes her head.

"No, I'd like to mark you here." She slaps a hand over her heart and I melt a little. Our little omega wants to mark us over our hearts.

"Sounds great." Hudson scoops her up, throwing her over his shoulder. "Come on guys, we have marks to receive."

All I can do is laugh as I watch Emmett hurry behind him to the bedroom. Turning to Maddox, I grin. "Are you ready to be marked by our omega?"

"Hell, yes."

By the time we make it into the bedroom, Hudson has stripped himself, Emmett and Bree out of their clothes. What a lovely picture the three of them make. Bree and Emmett lie on their backs while Hudson hovers over both of them. His hands stroke along both of their bodies as he kisses one and then the other. As hot as it is to watch them, there's no way I'm sitting this one out.

I pull my shirt over my head, dropping my hands to undo my pants as I kick my shoes off. Beside me, Maddox does the same. We move to the bed as one, but Bree's the only one who notices us stalking across the room.

We each grab one of Hudson's ankles, dragging him down the bed. "Fates, damn it! What the hell are you doing? Let me go."

Emmett and Bree sit up, leaning against one another as they laugh. They say nothing, content to wait and watch to find out what we have planned. Hudson is fighting mine and Maddox's hold, but we get him flipped onto his back and pin him there.

"Someone seems to be feeling a little greedy. You took off with our omega, our beta running after you. Then we come in here to find both of them beneath you as you teased them," I tell him and he stops struggling.

"To think you selfishly wanted to please them on your own, just leaving your pack mates in the cold." Maddox shakes his head.

Hudson makes a face. "Let's be real. This is not how it was going. I was keeping them company until you slowpokes came in."

"Mmmm... I'm not sure I believe him. What about you, Mad?"

Maddox shakes his head. "I don't know... What do the two of you think?"

"I think there's four hot naked men in my bedroom while I'm soaking the bed with my slick and not a damn one of you is doing anything about it right now."

I grin at our omega, and she quickly returns it. "Looks like our omega has a job for you, Hudson. Go take care of her."

Maddox and I release him, but I smack his ass when he turns around to hurry back up the bed. Hudson yelps before turning back to us with a glare. He shakes his head before throwing himself at Bree.

When she opens her mouth to yell at him, he kisses her. She moans into the kiss, wrapping her arms around his neck. It won't be long until he's inside of her. Maddox and I turn our attention to Emmett.

"I think our beta needs us to take care of him," Maddox says as we slowly make our way to where he sits, eyes flickering from where Hudson is already thrusting inside of Bree to the two of us as we stalk toward him.

He looks like he wants to dart away, but it's too late as we climb onto the bed and pull him between us. His back is against my chest, with Maddox pressed to his front as he kisses him. A feminine hand lands on my thigh and I turn my head to find Bree and Hudson have paused to watch us.

It takes me a moment to realize there's something in Bree's hand. "Lube?" I ask with a smile.

She nods. "Well, I assume you're going to fuck Emmett while Hudson takes care of me. You're gonna need lube for that. Afterward, we can take a quick bath. Then I want you and Maddox to take me together so I can mate you at the same time."

"Fuck," all four of us curse.

"I guess you're all on board with that idea. Great. Now, the three of you better make sure you do this where I can watch." She turns back to Hudson. "Back to work. Get those hips moving."

"Bossy ass omega," Emmett murmurs, but he's smiling at her with love in his eyes.

"You ready for this, Em?" I ask, grinding my cock between his ass cheeks.

He groans as Maddox sucks at his neck. "Yes. So ready."

I meet Maddox's eyes over Emmett's shoulder. It'll be up to him to keep Emmett occupied while I ready him for my cock. Popping open the bottle of lube, I pour some of it over Emmet's ass, watching as the beta shivers at the cold. Then I use it to wet my fingers. There's a momentary resistance as I press into him with one finger before he lets me in.

I want to make sure he's ready for me, but I also need to be balls deep in his ass as soon as possible. I work my finger in and out of him as Maddox kisses him, stroking their cocks together as he does so. Memories from earlier in the day rush through me as I remember how much Emmett had loved it as I stroked our cocks together. It had felt fucking amazing.

I take as much time as I can to prep Emmett, working up to three fingers as he continues to clamp down on me. I can't wait any longer, grabbing the lube to pour over my straining dick. Once it's as slick as it's going to get, I press the head to Emmett's puckered hole.

"I'm going to fuck you hard, Em. Are you ready for that?"

Emmett whimpers, trying to push back onto my cock. "Yes. Please. Now."

I laugh, loving that he's already losing his mind and we haven't even begun to fuck him. "I want you to suck Maddox's cock while I take you from behind. Will you be a good boy and do that for us?"

"Fuck. Yes." Emmett pushes on Maddox's chest, trying to get him to back up.

Bree whimpers. "Get on your back, Hudson, head toward them. I need to see it all."

"What about me seeing it?" Hudson asks, but he's already moving as she requested.

"You can look at my damn boobs while I ride you."

Hudson considers that. "Yeah, that's a fair trade. Come on, omega. Get back on my dick."

I shake my head at their antics before focusing back on Emmett and Maddox. Emmett is on his hands and knees, mouth already wrapped around Maddox's cock.

So fucking hot.

I line myself up with Emmett again before slowly pressing forward. I can hear Emmett groaning around Maddox's cock, causing Maddox to thrust into his mouth.

"Let's give our beta the ride of his life, yeah, Maddox?" I ask as I sink all the way to my knot. I wonder for a moment if Emmett can take my knot in his ass. We'll have to work up to that, but if he wants it, I definitely want it.

Maddox just grins at me as he links his hands in Emmett's hair. We start off slowly, one of us sliding out as the other slides in, but it doesn't take long for Emmett to start wiggling between the two of us.

I brush my hand against the spot between his shoulder blades with a smile. "This is where I'll mark you, beta. But for now, we'll both just have to deal with me fucking you so hard you'll be feeling me all week."

I grab his hips and plow into him over and over as Maddox fucks his face in time with me. I can just barely hear Emmett's keening moans around Maddox's cock, but it tells me he's enjoying himself just as much as we are.

Turning my head, I find Bree bouncing on Hudson's dick while he plays with her tits. Her eyes lock on where I'm fucking into Emmett and it makes me smile. "You really do like watching us together, don't you, omega?"

"More than anything." Her pace picks up. "Fates. I'm going to come." She screams out her release before she bends to bite Hudson over his heart. Hudson drags her down onto his dick, his knot popping inside of her as he roars his own release.

They'll be at that awhile, so I focus my attention on the men before me. "You close?"

Maddox nods, arms straining, telling me just how close he is. I think Bree and Hudson falling apart beside us is adding to our own arousal. Emmett suddenly yanks off Maddox's length as he screams out, fingers digging into Maddox's thick thighs. His cock pulses before he comes all over the bed.

I chuckle. "I guess our beta was really close, too."

"It's Bree. I can feel her coming over and over again. I even feel Hudson through our bond. Jesus. Fucking as a pack is going to be amazing." Emmett groans as he comes again.

"Well, fuck. I want to feel what he is," I say with a laugh. "Beta, you need to take care of your alpha. Make him come while I fill you up."

Emmett sucks Maddox's cock back into his mouth as I fuck into him with short, hard bursts. There's so much going on around me, and my orgasm is just out of reach. My eyes pop open when I hear Maddox curse as he spills into Emmett's mouth, setting off our beta again.

When Emmett clamps down on me, there's no holding back my orgasm. I grind against his ass as I spill inside of him. The three of us collapse onto the bed to find Hudson and Bree locked together, watching us.

"That was hot as hell," Bree says, eyes hazy with lust. "As soon as Hudson's knot releases, we're heading into the bath. No point in having the sheets changed until we're done for the night. We made an awful mess."

"And we're going to make an even bigger one soon." I lean over to kiss Bree and then Hudson before moving over to Maddox and Emmett.

This is what pack life is supposed to be like, and while our pack may still not be complete, I can't wait until it is.

Chapter Twenty-five

Gabriel

After we're dismissed from the ballroom, I know I won't be good company for anyone. While the other suitors head up the stairs, I make my way to the deck and pour myself a drink. Bree has now chosen the four men I've allowed myself to fall for. I might not be in love with them, but it's heading that way.

What the hell am I supposed to do? What if she doesn't choose me? We've grown close and I know she and I share a connection, but what if it isn't enough? There are still five suitors for her to choose from. Her pack is already bigger than she thought it would be, so how many men is she really going to be willing to add to her pack?

I don't want to leave the show. I want to remain here and fight for a spot by her side. But none of this guarantees that she'll choose me. This could turn out to be a complete waste of time. I could leave here missing not just Bree, but Emmett, Maddox, Onyx, and Hudson.

Fuck.

I pour myself a shot and throw it back, but it's not enough. Another five shots later, things are feeling a little hazy around the edges. I collapse onto a lounge chair and try to figure out what to do.

I'd been the first suitor that had spent the night with Bree. The first to have sex with her, but it feels like she's pulled back from me since then. Though, until she bonded with Emmett, she had invited no one to her bed. And since bonding with Emmett, there's been no one else.

Though, I'm sure that's going to change tonight. There's no way that she's chosen to take those men into her pack and not sleep with them. I wonder if she'll allow them to mark her. That would certainly make the rest of the show interesting. Bree didn't act like they were the last suitors she would add to her pack, so at least there's that.

And watching Hudson fall apart on the stage had almost brought me to my knees. I wanted to know why he was falling apart—hell, I still want to know. I wanted to pull him into my arms and hold him until I could make everything better for him. But that's not my place. I'm not a member of his pack.

He has three pack mates and an omega who will take care of him. The knowledge pierces my heart, hitting me in a way I didn't expect. I don't know if I can survive losing not just Bree, but the four of them. But what choice do I have?

I need to stay away from them—the guys, not Bree. I need to focus all of my attention on her. She's the reason I'm here and I keep forgetting that. I need to give my all to winning Bree over so she'll choose me. Will I still want the guys? Yes.

I need to protect myself, to protect my heart. If Bree doesn't choose me, then I'm going home alone. I can't allow myself to fall any harder for these men. Maybe with some time and space, it won't hurt as badly if I have to leave. My heart will still break for what I'd be losing, but maybe it would be survivable.

"Gabe?"

I roll my head to the side and it takes longer than it should for my eyes to focus on Roman as he makes his way over to me. I sigh, knowing how pathetic it must sound, but unable to keep it in any longer. "I'm not especially good company right now."

"I didn't think you would be. I wanted to come check on you. I'm sure you're hurting right now and you don't need to be alone."

I scoff. "Why not? It seems like that's how I'm going to end up. Alone with just me, myself, and I."

"You can't think like that." Roman sits in the chair beside me but turns to face me. "Bree doesn't even know how big she wants her pack to be. She doesn't know how many of us she'll choose. All you can do is keep trying. You wouldn't be here if she wasn't interested in you."

"Yeah, but it's not just her. I let myself fall for them, and now they're her pack. And I might never be."

"Or you could be the next one she chooses. If you give up now, then she won't. Maybe they'll be able to put in a good word for you. I'm sure they don't want to lose you either. So keep on fighting—for yourself, for Bree, for them."

"I need to stay away from them." My words are slurring together and I realize I had a few too many shots. "I have to protect my heart. I don't want it to break and I will.. I just... can't."

Roman sighs as he kneels beside me, throwing my arm around his shoulder. "I get it, but don't make any decisions tonight. Wait until it doesn't hurt so bad, until you're sober. You're going to come stay in my room with me. I don't trust you on your own tonight."

I try to help Roman as he lifts me to my feet, but I'm sure I'm more of a hindrance than anything else. Once we're both standing, I slap my hand on Roman's chest. "You're a good man, Roman. Bree needs an alpha like you. She should choose you."

"Thanks, Gabe." Roman chuckles as he helps me to the house. "We're in this together, bud. If you need someone to lean on, come lean on me. We'll make it through this the best way we can."

His words warm my heart, but I can't seem to get my mouth to work. It's taking all of my focus to keep on my two feet. Too many shots in a short period. Never a good idea. Thank goodness for Roman coming to my rescue, or I might've ended up dead in the pool.

I should spend more time with him and the remaining suitors because he's right. We're all in this together.

Finnegan

I don't think this damn week could get any worse, and it's nowhere near being over. Tessa has been fielding calls for me for the last few days, and I have no choice but to bring it to Bree.

Which is why I'm currently sitting in the dining room in the middle of the day, waiting for Tessa to pull Bree away from her new mates. I was happy for the guys last night, but I was also sad that she hadn't chosen me.

Today's phone call was the last straw. I honestly don't think Bree will choose me and that means there's no reason for me to stay. I could be wrong, but I don't think I am. If it wasn't for my life falling apart around me, I wouldn't even have questioned staying until the end. But this phone call? I can't ignore it.

The door opens, and Bree yawns loudly as she steps inside. "I'm sorry, Finnegan. I'm a little tired today. Tessa went to go get me some coffee so I can be coherent for this."

I can't help but check her for new mating bites, but I don't see any on her neck or arms. Unless they're somewhere hidden, I don't believe her new alphas bit her, which is interesting. But it's none of my business.

Bree settles across the table from me just as Tessa carries in a carafe of steaming coffee and two mugs. "I brought two in case you need some too, Finnegan."

"Thank ye, Tessa."

"It's my pleasure. I'll be in the control room if either of you needs me."

Bree frowns as she pours her coffee, adding cream and sugar left on the table from breakfast. "You're not joining us?"

"A've already made Tessa aware of the situation." I tell her with a tight smile. "She does nae have tae be here. Unless ye would lek her tae join us."

Bree shakes her head as she lifts her cup to her lips, taking a long drink of it before sighing. "It's just that she's usually here. No worries. Thanks, Tessa."

We both watch Tessa leave the room before I focus my attention back on Bree. She gives me a small smile as she reaches for my hand. "What's going on?"

"A'm sure that Tessa has nae been bothering ye with all that's been going oan. My ma is sick. It came oan suddenly. They're saying she willnae mek it long."

"Fates above, I'm so sorry, Finnegan. What can I do?"

I drop my head, hating what I'm about to do, but I need to know. "I need tae return tae Scotland. There is nae way I can remain, but Tessa said that if ye wanted to make me part of yer pack, that it can be done before I leave. I know that ye've just added to your pack, but this shall be th' last chance for me to be a part of your pack."

"Oh... I..." Bree shakes her head, and I already know her answer. She might not be able to say it right now, but if she'd wanted me to be a part of her pack, the first word out of her mouth would've been yes.

"It's okay, lass. I did nae think that ye would say yes, but I needed to ask before I left. A've enjoyed my time with ye and getting to know all th' suitors, but I have tae leave. I cannae wait for the ceremony. It will take a lot of time for me to mek it to Scotland an' I need to be with my ma."

"Of course you do. I'm sorry, Finnegan. It's really hard to say goodbye to all of you now. You mean a lot to me and I'm sorry that I can't choose you for my pack. You've been amazing and one day you'll find the omega for you. She'll be the luckiest omega because she'll have you."

"Thank ye, lass. Thank ye for giving me a chance an' for understanding why I have tae leave. You're choosing well for yourself. I cannae wait tae see who else ye choose. Good luck."

Without waiting for a response, I leave the room and head up the stairs. I need to get packed, and I can call Tessa from my room. I need to find the fastest way to get to my ma, so I can tell her how much I love her and how much she'll be missed.

While it hurts, I'm glad to know where I stand with Bree and I can leave *Heated* with a little less weighing on my heart. There's nothing that can take away this pain, but I will survive everything that life is throwing my way.

Bree

Saying goodbye to Finnegan was hard. With each person who leaves, it just gets harder. While we're supposed to have a rose ceremony every night, I'd asked Tessa if we could cancel tonight's, as well as my date with Dalton. I feel bad about canceling our date, but I do plan to reschedule it as soon as I can.

But this is more important. I need to speak with the remaining suitors with my pack by my side. I need to make sure that their expectations are where they should be. I don't expect this to be an easy conversation, but it's one that has to happen.

"Are you okay, Bree?" Emmett wraps his arms around me, setting his chin on my shoulder. "It's understandable if you're not."

"Are you trying to get me to talk about the emotions you feel through our bond without coming right out and asking?" I roll my eyes in the mirror and he just grins.

"Maybe. But that doesn't change my statement. It's okay if you're not alright. And we're all here if you want to talk about it."

I nod once I've finished applying my lipstick. "I know you are, and no, I'm not okay. I just had to say goodbye to an amazing man who just wasn't the right fit for us. A man whose mom is dying, and he didn't want to leave without being sure that he didn't have a chance at being in my pack. It hurts that he's hurting and that I made it worse.

"But there's only so much I can do about that. There's no way I can keep all the suitors that are remaining. I know that, but it doesn't make things any easier. I don't want to hurt anyone, but at this point, there's no way to avoid it. We're all attached. That's why I need to have this conversation with all of them, and I need my pack beside me."

"And that's where we'll be, angel." Hudson's smile holds an edge of sadness as he leans against the doorframe. "The suitors are all in the living room, along with Maddox and Onyx."

I nod again as I glance in the mirror once more. Allison had stopped by earlier and tried to cover up my puffy eyes and the dark circles that ran beneath them, but there's only so much makeup can do. "Let's do this."

Emmett and Hudson trail after me as I walk through the suite and into the hallway. I take a moment to calm myself, helped out by each of my mates taking one of my hands. This time, my smile isn't as forced. Putting this kind of pressure on an omega is asking a lot of them. There will definitely be changes made to the next season to lessen the load for the omega.

I allow my mates to escort me to the living room, giving their hands one last squeeze before stepping away from them. I'd had the crew rearrange the furniture, so I'd be able to see each suitor, as well as my pack, while I had this conversation.

I sit in the armchair that now faces the rest of the room. Directly across from me on a couch are the four members of my pack, each shooting me smiles of encouragement. Emmett and Hudson are half sitting on Onyx and Maddox, so there's enough room for all four of them on the couch, which is enough to bring another smile to my face.

Turning to my right, I find Dalton and Maverick sitting on the other couch. "Before we start, I want to apologize for canceling our date tonight, but this felt like it was more important. There won't be a rose ceremony tonight and after we're done with this, I'd like it if we could all go watch a movie together or something. I think we need time with all of us together."

I shift to face Gabriel and Roman, who sit on a loveseat to my left. "Thank you all for coming on such short notice. This isn't a bad meeting or whatever. No one is being sent home. I'm not angry with anyone, or whatever the worst-case scenario you've all built in your heads.

"I don't know if Finnegan was able to say goodbye to all of you before he left, but he is gone." I have to blink against the tears already threatening to spill. "His mom is in the hospital and they don't expect her to make it. Of course, he went home, but before he did, he spoke with me. He'd already spoken with Tessa and she told him that if it was what I wanted, we could bond before he left. When he asked me, I froze. I couldn't give him the answer he wanted right then, because while I know my pack isn't complete yet, I don't know who else will be a part of it.

"I hurt Finnegan today and that hurts me." I swipe at my tears because I hadn't been able to hold them in. "So, I wanted to bring you together to tell you that. I feel a connection to all of you, but I don't know who I will choose. I can't choose all of you. I can't handle a pack that big. There are still four weeks left until my heat. I'm telling you now, I won't be rushed into a decision.

"There's a chance I might not choose anyone until right before my heat. I need to know that I'm making the right decisions for me and my pack. You'll notice that none of my alphas are going batshit crazy like Riley was. While I've marked and claimed them, I've asked them to wait until our pack is complete. That's to make sure that this remains fair to all of you. If they are a little more abrasive than usual, that's my fault."

"Or it's just Maddox being Maddox," Hudson supplies.

Maverick leans forward, my eyes moving to him. "While I appreciate you bringing us together and telling us this, you didn't need to. You don't owe any of us an explanation. We knew what we were signing up for when we joined *Heated*. I'm sure the other suitors feel the same way."

All three of them pipe up their agreement and it makes me smile. "I know I don't owe you anything, but I needed to do this. I need all of us on the same page for my own sanity. But thank you for saying that."

I hear a throat clear from the doorway and look up to find Tessa standing there, eyebrows raised. "Oh, right. There was another reason I wanted us to get together. Tessa has an announcement to make, and I'm pretty excited about it myself."

Tessa comes to stand next to me, laying her hand on my shoulder and squeezing. I lay my hand on top of hers, appreciating her support as always. My attention falls to my mates to find all four of their eyes locked on where me and my best friends are touching. None of them say a word, but I can tell it bothers them.

That's too fucking bad. Tessa is my best friend, and she's been there for me more times than I can count. I know our relationship isn't the typical one between an omega and an alpha, but I love our relationship. They'll need to get used to it.

No, that's not the kind of omega I want to be. I'm letting my frustration bleed into everything. We'll need to discuss this between the five of us and decide what they can deal with, along with what I will always need from Tessa. But that's a problem for another day.

"As you know, Bree and I are co-founders of Fated Industries. We support a lot of charities—especially those surrounding omegas and females. With the way our world is now, there are less and less of both every year, and that means some people will take what isn't offered to them. That's especially true for omegas.

"One of the biggest charities we donate to is Keeping Omegas Safe. We throw an event for them three or four times a year to help raise awareness and money. We had nothing planned because of *Heated* but I received a call from their board of directors this afternoon and the company that was supposed to host a gala for them in a few days went under, so they're floundering on where to hold it."

I stand, drawing the attention from Tessa to me. "These events are huge fundraisers for them, so when they asked if we could host a last-minute gala, we didn't hesitate to say yes. What that means for us is that Tessa and I will pull some strings over the next few days to get this prepared. It will cut into our time, unfortunately, but we've decided to include *Heated* in the event. That means in two days we'll leave for

LA. That'll be the day before the event. You'll be able to go wherever you'd like and enjoy your time until the gala the next day. Where you'll all attend as my dates.

"We'll have each of you fitted for tuxedos or suits to match whatever dress we can find for me. Then after the gala, we'll stay a few days in LA. I want to see your lives. I want to see where you live, where you work, whatever you want to show me. Hector is in charge of setting that all up, so tomorrow you'll want to get with him to let him know what you'd like to do. We might not do everything, as we'll only be there for two days after the gala.

"Dalton, I know you're the only one who isn't from LA, but if there's anywhere you've wanted to go, let Hector know. We can make sure it gets added to the schedule. And maybe we can plan a trip home for you at some point."

"Thank you. That means a lot that y'all would think of that. I'm sure I can add somethin' to Hector's list." Dalton smiles and I'm glad that he can be involved—though I have some things planned that he'll be thrilled about—assuming it doesn't fall apart. That's the only reason I'm not mentioning it now. Plus, who doesn't love a surprise?

Tessa glances around the room. "Does anyone have any questions? No? Well, that was easy. If you think of questions, feel free to ask Bree tonight. If you think of any tomorrow, ask Hector. He'll find out the answer if he doesn't already know it. Enjoy your night."

I watch Tessa walk away before turning back to the men who all sit watching me. "This is also why I suggested that we all spend the night together. I'm going to be busy until the gala. Though, Dalton, we will still have our date tomorrow night. When I have a free moment, I'll come find you guys, but I don't know how much free time I'll have."

"Well, then I suggest we all go watch a movie," Roman says as he stands. "I'm sure we can all find one to agree on... maybe."

I laugh and watch as the men head for the stairs, already debating which movie we should watch. Did I need the added stress of planning a gala in just three days? Definitely not, but we couldn't have turned them away. I know a few companies had already said no when they called us. They knew we were busy filming *Heated*, which is why we hadn't planned on attending the gala in the first place.

For tonight, I'm not going to worry about any of that. I'm going to enjoy spending the evening with my pack and my suitors. I feel better knowing that we're all on the same page. I'm no longer dreading moving forward with the show.

"Are you coming, Bree?"

I shake my head to find Gabriel waiting for me. "Yes, I am."

When he offers me his arm, I take it without hesitation. I know I should be freaking out about the next few days, but instead, I feel calmer than I have in a long time. It's all thanks to these men surrounding me. I can't imagine saying goodbye to any of them, but that's not a worry for today. Today's only worry is how to convince these men to watch a movie I want to watch.

Chapter Twenty-six

Dalton

The three-hour drive to LA is kind of nice when you get to ride in the back of a limo. This has to be the longest limo I've ever seen, not that I've seen many before arriving in California, but it manages to fit Bree, the four men she's already chosen for her pack, myself, and the other three remaining suitors. Plus Tessa, Hector, and the other producer—Lydia.

I'm going to be honest, there's so many crew members we've been introduced to, but rarely see that I haven't bothered to remember their names. Is that terrible of me? Maybe, but there's only so many names I can keep straight and this last month or so has been a lot of new faces and names.

I didn't spend too much time in LA before heading to Rancho Mirage for *Heated* but I didn't have the best impression. People were rude and always in a hurry, rushing off to do fates know what. And there are so many people crammed together like sardines. It's hard to believe that there were even more people here before the Event. I can't even imagine it.

"Why are we going to the airport?" Emmett asks with a frown, head craning to look out the closed window.

Bree just grins. "It's a surprise. You'll just need to wait to find out."

A surprise? For who? I guess we'll find out soon.

It's not even a little surprising that even the traffic at the airport is heavy, but at least I'm not the one driving. When the limo pulls to a stop beneath the arrivals sign, I wonder who we're picking up. Until I see them.

I jump out of the car and run toward them. "Mama! Pop!"

I pull my mom into my arms, hugging her close. Tears stream down my cheeks as Pop's arms wrap around the both of us. I've missed them so much. Not being able to talk to them or see them every day has hurt more than I ever thought it could. But they're here now.

Wait. Why are they here?

"Not that I'm not so happy to see y'all, but what in the world are you doin' here?" I ask as I pull away to look between my parents.

"That would be the sweet little omega you're courting," Mama replies, gesturing behind me.

I release my hold on my mom to turn to find Bree standing beside the limo, grinning wildly. "You did this for me? Why?"

"Because the others get to show me their life here in LA and since you're the only one not from here, I thought we could bring a little piece of your home here. I was also listening every time you mentioned how much you missed your family. I'm sorry, I could only get your parents out here."

I shake my head because she has nothing to apologize for. I sweep her up into my arms, smacking a kiss on her lips before hugging her to me. "You just made me the happiest man alive right now. I don't know how y'all managed this, but thank you. It's the sweetest thing anyone has ever done for me."

When I set her on her feet once more, I'm smiling so hard it's almost painful. "Let me introduce you to Mama and Pop."

"I'd love that."

I take her hand and lead her back the short distance to my parents. "Mama, Pop, this is Bree Timmons. She's the co-founder and CEO of Fated Industries, one of the creators of *Heated*, and the woman that I'm hopin' will be my omega one day here soon."

Mama throws herself into Bree's arms. "Thank you so much for bringing us out here to see our boy. We've missed him."

"And he's missed you as well." Bree smiles as she returns Mama's hug, letting out a squeak when Pop grabs her from Mama's arms, lifting her off the ground as he squeezes her tight.

"It's so nice to meet you, Bree," Pop says.

"Old man, will you please set the omega down before her alphas notice?" I shake my head. I know Pop hasn't been around many omegas, but he should know better.

Pop chuckles as he sets her down. "Sorry, I guess I just plumb wasn't thinkin'."

"That's okay, Mr. Cole."

"Oh, no, peach." Pop laughs. "We don't go for any of that fancy stuff. You can call me Pop or Cash. The love of my life goes by Mama or Magnolia."

"Or Maggie," Mama adds. "That's what I let people I like call me."

"Of course, Cash. Maggie. It's nice to meet you both. We should probably go ahead and get to the hotel. I still have so much work to get done for the gala tomorrow night."

The four of us climb into the limo—which is definitely full now—before I introduce Mama and Pop to everyone. Bree is sitting next to me now and I lean over to whisper in her ear, "Thank you for this. It really does mean the world to me."

"You're welcome."

I can't believe she's done this for me. I feel like the Grinch when his heart grew three sizes. This totally makes up for the gala we'll have to attend tomorrow night.

The last day and a half has rushed by as I spent time with the guys and my parents. We haven't seen neither hide nor hair of Bree since arriving at the hotel. Apparently, she and Tessa were able to get the rooms and the hotel's ballroom that the other company had reserved for the gala at a deep discount. So we've all got rooms of our own again, though Emmett, Onyx, Hudson, and Maddox are sharing a room with Bree.

I'd be jealous, but they said they haven't seen her much either. She apparently rolled into bed at one in the morning and was gone again before the sun was up. She's working herself too hard, which I hate, but I know this is something she feels passionate about. I just hope it turns out the way they want it to with all the work they've been putting into it.

There's a knock on the door and I already know it'll be my parents. Bree hadn't just flown them out. She'd gotten them a super nice suite and had a personal shopper bring dresses for Mama to try on and pick out one to wear tonight. The same shopper had suit options for Pop to go with whichever she picked. I don't know what she's going to be wearing, as she said she wanted it to be a surprise.

"Just a minute," I call out as I straighten my tie once more. Bree has obviously gone with red again, if my vest and tie are anything to go off of. I can't wait to see what dress she's chosen. Not that she won't look amazing either way.

Opening the door, I find Mama and Pop dressed to the nines. "Wow, Mama. You look amazing."

And she really does. She looks radiant in a sky blue dress. Leaning down, I press a kiss to her cheek. When I pull back, I let out a whistle as I take in Pop's tux. "Lookin' sharp, old man."

"You look so handsome, Dalton." Mama grabs my cheeks, squeezing them like I'm still a five-year-old. "If that omega doesn't choose you, she's plumb out of her mind."

"Thanks, Mama, but all the suitors are amazing."

Mama clucks her tongue. "That may be, but none of them are the amazing son I raised."

I duck my head, feeling a blush creep across my face. "You have to say that, Mama."

"That doesn't make it any less true." She boops me on the nose as if to prove her point and I have to bite back a laugh. Fates, I've missed this woman.

"Alright, Maggie, leave the boy be. He needs to go pick up his date." Pop nods down the hallway where I see the others waiting outside of the room Bree's been staying in.

I offer my arm to Mama. "Shall we?"

Mama grins up at me as she nods. "We shall."

When we make it to the end of the hall where the others are, Mama drops my arm and goes around fussing with each of the men's ties.

"You boys all look so handsome. Bree is one lucky lady. Oh, lemme retie this for you." Mama doesn't even wait for Maddox to reply as she undoes his tie and goes to work retying it. His eyes meet mine and he raises his eyebrows.

"Mama likes to keep her hands busy when she's nervous," I tell him, earning me a slap on my arm from Mama.

"I just want to make sure you all look your best for Bree. Since none of your mamas are here, I'm just fillin' in."

Maddox inclines his head. "Thank you, ma'am. These two," he nods to Onyx and Hudson, "are always getting onto me about how bad I am at tying a tie."

"I guess it's a good thing you don't have to wear one often, huh?" Hudson wiggles his eyebrows at his pack mate. "Because you really suck at it."

Before Maddox can bite back at that comment, the door to Bree's room opens and all eyes turn to her. I'm stunned speechless. I've seen her most every day for the last few weeks and I'd thought that I'd seen her at her most beautiful, but I was mistaken.

I was correct in assuming the dress is red and her lips are painted the same vibrant color. The dress is sleeveless and fitted against her curves until it hits her knees and then it drapes out, dragging along the floor. I know little about dresses, but I know this one looks damn good on her.

I have to lift a hand to my mouth, biting my knuckle to keep myself from groaning with my mama by my side when Bree takes a step forward, revealing a slit up the front of the dress that stops mid-thigh. She does a spin, revealing that the dress leaves her back bare all the way to the top of her biteable ass.

And now I have an erection with my mama right next to me. Fucking hell.

We all quickly swarm Bree, who lets out a laugh. "One at a time, please. I can't listen to you all at the same time."

I step back and let the others go to her before me. It gives me more time to stare at her. Her long hair is curled and styled so that it lays over one of her shoulders. She practically glitters as she moves with all the jewelry she wears and they've done something, I'm assuming, with her makeup, to make her amber eyes pop.

Then it's my turn to greet her, and all I can do is stare at her a little more. "You're the most beautiful woman I've ever seen." I pause. "Besides my Mama, of course."

Bree giggles, leaning around me to see Mama. "You look exquisite, Maggie."

"Nowhere near as good as you look, doll." Mama comes over to run her eyes over Bree. "There's no way I could have ever pulled off a dress like that, but you? It's like it was made for you."

Bree's grin just grows. "Thank you, Maggie. Now, is everyone done complimenting me because we have a gala to get to."

We all pile into the elevator, though it's a tight fit with this many alphas. The elevator stops on a couple of floors, but obviously no one gets on since we're so crammed in here. The doors to the lobby finally open and my eyes go wide. The lobby has been completely changed from the last time I was down here a few hours ago.

Black, red, and silver decor is spread throughout the area and a red carpet leads from outside, straight through the lobby before veering off to where I assume the ballroom is.

"There you are. I was beginning to think you'd never make it down here. The guests have all arrived and they're ready to announce our arrivals," Tessa says as she hurries over.

"Announce our arrivals?" I ask, confused.

Tessa turns to me, a ghost of a smile on her lips. "As the hosts of the event, we're the last to arrive so we can be announced. The board of Keeping Omegas Safe will be announced before us, and then it's our turn. You'll all be announced as Bree's pack and suitors. This is great PR for *Heated*."

"Okay." I just nod because this is so far from the world that I grew up in.

"Emmett will escort Bree down, then Onyx, Maddox, and Hudson will enter. Dalton, you and your dad will escort your mom. Then it'll be Roman, Maverick, and Gabriel. Any questions?" We all shake our heads. "Don't worry if you forget the order. You'll be able to hear your names called."

Tessa leads us over to the red carpet and we follow it to the closed ballroom doors manned by two men in uniform. An older man rushes over to speak to Tessa and Bree, hugging them and speaking quickly before making his way back to what I'm assuming are the other members of the board.

I hear names being announced, and people begin to enter. Tessa shuffles us around until we're in the order we'll be called and then she's walking into the ballroom herself.

"*Co-founder and CEO of Fated Industries, Bree Timmons. She is escorted by her newly bonded beta, Emmett Kwon. Bree met Emmett on* Heated, *the new reality dating show that Fated Industries is currently filming. Emmett is a highly sought after chef who is currently the head chef at Lyrical.*"

Bree and Emmett disappear between the doors.

"*Following Bree and Emmett are Onyx Holt, Hudson Kennedy, and Maddox Pierce, owners of Infinite Ink and Bree's new alphas.*"

The three of them disappear and then it's our turn.

Mama squeezes my hand. "No reason to be nervous, Dalton. If you're to become Bree's alpha, you'll have to get used to these kinds of events."

Isn't that a scary thought?

"*Next we have* Heated *suitor Dalton Cole, owner of Cole Construction in Georgia, along with his parents Magnolia and Cash Cole.*"

We step into the ballroom and I hesitate for a moment, not knowing what to do next. But Mama is already following the red carpet to where Tessa, Bree, and her pack wait for us.

"Our last group are the other three remaining suitors on Heated, *Maverick Kelley, Roman Knight, and Gabriel Ramirez. Maverick is one of the top architects at Powerhouse Designs. Roman is a history professor at Hartfield University, and Gabriel is a kindergarten teacher at a local elementary school."*

Around us, applause fills the room, and I have no idea why we're being applauded. I'm so out of my league here. But soon I'm surrounded by familiar faces and we're being led to the front of the room to a large table set up in front of the stage.

"So, I have a question," Emmett says as he leans toward Bree.

"Yes?"

"They just announced us as your pack mates and suitors, so they know who you've chosen and who's still in the running. Won't they tell others and ruin the surprise of the show?"

Tessa is the one that answers with a grin. "Every person who walked in this door had to sign an NDA. If they speak about anything to do with *Heated*, they'll be sued for everything they're worth and some of them are worth billions. They're also used to NDAs and things like this. It's why we weren't worried about having you announced."

"Huh," I say, shaking my head. I know what an NDA is—we had to sign one when we agreed to be on *Heated*—but before this show, I've never had to sign one. And this ballroom full of people is used to signing NDAs to go to parties. This couldn't be any different from my life in Georgia.

"Now, welcome Tessa Hanson and Bree Timmons to the stage for the opening remarks."

We all sit around the table while Tessa and Bree climb onto the stage. Bree takes the offered microphone.

"Welcome, each and every one of you, to the KOS gala. As you know, we're here today in support of the Keeping Omegas Safe organization—one that is near and dear to my heart. KOS helps omegas that don't have the money for everything they need—those who need a little help along the way. They provide bodyguards to omegas who need them. They offer temporary housing for omegas who find themselves without a roof over their head. They help omegas find jobs and homes in good neighborhoods. They offer so many services, I'd be here all night listing them.

"What KOS does is right there in their name. They keep omegas safe—in whatever way they can. Many of you may not be aware of this, but I reached out to KOS when I was eighteen. I'd been accepted to Hartfield University, but some of my parents weren't supportive of that. Along with support from my dads and KOS, we were able to set up safe living arrangements for me.

"I didn't know what to expect as I'd never left the town I grew up in, so when I expressed my fears of the unknown, they assigned me a bodyguard without me even asking. There were three of them who alternated going everywhere with me for a few months before I felt comfortable. Only then did they stop guarding me. I don't know if I would've made it through those first few months of college without the support of KOS. It's a big reason why I'm such a supporter of theirs. It might not seem like much to those of you who aren't omegas, but it can be a scary world out there for us. Especially with the decrease in female births. Some people believe that they can take what isn't offered to them because they feel it's owed to them. It's because of this that we need organizations like KOS. I hope you all will keep that in mind when you're making your donations."

Tessa takes the microphone from Bree and smiles as she looks around the room. "Many of you might be aware that we weren't the original hosts for this gala. The company that was the host had to back out at the last minute and we stepped in to fill their shoes, knowing that KOS needs these funds. Dinner will be served in just a few moments. We will follow that up by opening up the dance floor for a few hours. The silent auction will begin at the top of the hour. If you don't have the auction app on your phone, you'll find information at your table on how to download it.

"The auction will end at ten o'clock tonight when we'll announce the winners. Also at your tables, you'll find information about how to make your donations online. You can do so anonymously if you'd like, but we appreciate anything you can give to KOS so they can keep doing what they do best—keeping our omegas safe. Thank you."

Tessa and Bree make their way back to the table. Once they're seated, I turn to them. "I'm in awe of both of you. What you've put together in just a few days and for such a good cause. I hadn't heard of KOS before finding out about this event. I don't know how much of a footprint they have in Georgia, but I'd like to make sure it's bigger."

"That's really sweet, Dalton. Thank you." Bree stands to come around the table to press a kiss to my cheek while Mama squeezes my hand. "It's men like you who make me realize that this world isn't a terrible place."

Her words put a smile on my face for the rest of the night.

Maddox

Today's our last day in LA. The gala was two days ago and yesterday we'd spent a good portion of the day showing Dalton and his parents the sights of the city. We'd made a stop at Hartfield University, where Roman had shown us around. We even ended up interrupting one of the classes he'd usually be teaching. It was an upper level class and many of the students had called out to their professor.

We visited Gabe's classroom and were mobbed by thirty five-year-olds. Though, if I'm being honest, it was the highlight of my day. We spent way longer there than we needed to, playing and reading to the kids. They all had to have time with Mr. Gabe. It's obvious his students love him and have missed him when he's been away.

We'd even visited Powerhouse Designs and met some of Maverick's co-workers. He'd pointed out various buildings he either designed or helped design throughout the city as we traveled around it. That was pretty cool. Knowing someone who designed the surrounding buildings? It's unreal.

Today, we spent the morning at the beach before heading to Fated Industries, where Bree and Tessa gave us a tour of the building. They explained what all they were working on and surprisingly, I wasn't bored. I think it's because it's my omega's company and she's very passionate about the things they're doing. It's very clear that they're a very pro-omega company and I love that.

We're currently on our way to Infinite Ink to show everyone around. There's been talk of some of the guys wanting to get a tattoo, so that should be fun. The limo comes to a stop outside our storefront, and I smile as soon as I see it. Being on *Heated* has been amazing, but I've missed the shop and our employees. We believe in a family-like workplace, so they're all more than our employees—they're our friends, our family.

"This is it," I say as I open the door and climb out. "Infinite Ink."

Everyone climbs onto the sidewalk when the door to the shop flies open. "Thank the fates you're here. I'm so over these people."

I spin around to find Val standing there with her bright blue hair all over the place as usual and her hands on her hips as she grins. "Bullshit. You love bossing around those assholes."

"Yeah, yeah, yeah." Val comes over to hug me, but stops when a growl sounds behind me.

Val and I both turn to find the source of the sound, only to find Bree staring at Val with narrowed eyes. "Mine," she barks as she moves to stand in front of me.

Val's eyes are wide as she takes a step back and I can tell she's trying her hardest—and failing, might I add—to fight the grin threatening to overtake her face. "Of course, omega. I'm sorry, I wasn't aware."

Bree shakes her head as she flushes. "Shit, I'm sorry. That was rude."

Pulling Bree back against me, smiling like an idiot. "Val, I'd like you to meet our new omega, Bree. Bree, this is our manager, Val. She's the one running the show while we're gone. And don't worry, she's just like an annoying little sister to us."

"And you're like annoying, overbearing older brothers that I never wanted," Val spits back.

"I really am sorry. I don't know what came over me." Bree pauses. "No, that's not true. I know what came over me, but I'm still sorry. It's very nice to meet you."

Val shakes Bree's hand with a smile. "It's no worries. If someone had warned me that you'd bonded them, I wouldn't even have thought about touching them. But enough about these assholes. Introduce me to everyone else?"

There's a quick round of introductions, and then we're heading inside. "How booked are we today?"

"This afternoon? Not at all. Hector called to give me the heads up that you all were coming and that some of you might want tattoos, so we went ahead and pushed back all the appointments to tonight."

"And this is why we left you in charge," Onyx says as everyone piles into the shop, looking around. A few of our artists filter out of the backroom and more introductions are made.

Bree tugs at my hand until I glance down at her. "Yes?"

"I want to get my tattoo for Emmett while we're here, but we haven't had time to design it."

"You're in luck, omega," Hudson purrs. "I've actually been working on some ideas while you were busy planning the gala. Why don't the five of us go to the office and we can go over my ideas?"

"Really?" Bree bounces on her toes. "I'm so excited."

"One of you assholes is doing my tattoo since I couldn't get an appointment before," Tessa warns, and I nod.

"Of course, Tessa. Let us do this with Bree real quick and then one of us will come see you." I look around at the others. "If anyone else wants a tattoo, it's on the house. It looks like we have three artists and a piercer here right now. Plus, Val and then us. As long as it's nothing too in depth, we should be able to get it done."

"I've always wanted a tattoo," Dalton's mom says with a grin, turning to our artists. "Which one of you young men is gonna help me figure out what I want?"

I hear Dalton groan behind me and I shoot him a grin. "They'll take good care of her, I promise. We'll be back in a minute. Emmett?"

Emmett's head spins in our direction. "Yes?"

"We're going into the office to discuss options for the tattoo?"

"Hell, yes!" He practically runs over before I lead them to our office. There's plenty of room for all five of us as we settle on the couch and loveseat in the corner.

"I've drawn up some rough sketches and ideas. Since it's for Emmett, I think he and Bree should choose which one we go with." Hudson glances between me and Onyx, and we nod our agreement. Hudson grabs the tablet off the coffee table and messes with it for a few moments before handing it over to Bree and Emmett. "If you don't like any of these, it's no problem. We can totally come up with—"

"This one," Bree and Emmett say at the same time, their fingers jabbing at the screen.

"Well, okay then." Hudson laughs, leaning over to see which one they've chosen. "I do like that one. Hang on, let me get it on a screen by itself. We can individualize it for each person, using different colors, etc."

"Hurry the fuck up, Hud. I wanna see it too," I say. Onyx grunts his agreement.

"It's the Korean word for family with a lotus flower behind it." Emmett's eyes are locked on Hudson as he works, a look of awe and love filling them. "Did you look it up? The meaning of the lotus flower, I mean."

"Of course. It symbolizes creation and birth." Hudson shrugs. "I thought it made sense since we're creating something new together, and one day we'll have a family, if that's what Bree wants."

"It is," she says and warmth fills me. She wants to have our children. Thank fuck. I would've dealt with it if she didn't want kids, but I've always wanted to have a big family. I don't know how many kids Bree is willing to have, but even one would be a blessing.

Hudson finally hands over the tablet. I smile because it's beautiful—as is everything Hudson designs—but I can see why both Emmett and Bree were drawn to it. "This is amazing, Hudson. It'll work in black and white or color. We'll do the word family in black and then the flower can be whatever colors we want them to be. Hudson, since you came up with the idea, why don't you tattoo our pretty little omega?"

"I know we're doing the tattoo to take the place of the marks I can't leave, but I'd like to get it today too, if you don't mind." Emmett's request is timid as he looks around the room.

"Mind?" Onyx chuckles. "Nothing would make me happier than to tattoo that pretty skin."

I narrow my eyes. "And who says you're the one who gets to do it?"

"Because when the time comes, we're going to have you do mine and Hud's and one of us will do yours."

I enjoy tattooing Hudson and Onyx, so it's hard for me to argue. "Fiiiine," I finally say, just like a petulant child. "I guess I'll tattoo Tessa."

We filter back out to the main part of the shop again and get to work. A few hours later, we're leaving with a slew of new tattoos as we head to Lyrical for dinner.

As we have with all restaurants, we find ourselves in a private room. When the host attempts to give us menus, Emmett halts him. "What do you say to letting me order for the table? I know what's best here since I came up with most of the plates myself. We can get a lot and share so everyone can taste a bit of everything?"

Everyone agrees, and Emmett takes the time to turn to Dalton's parents. "Do either of you have any allergies or anything you won't eat?"

Dalton's mom reaches out to pinch Emmett's cheeks and I barely manage to cover my laughter with a cough. "You're such a sweet boy for asking, but no. We'll eat anything you put in front of us."

"Lito here will take your drink orders while I go put in the food order." With that, Emmett disappears out the door and we all fall into a quiet conversation.

The evening is actually very relaxed, and the food is amazing. The owner, a middle-aged beta named Jun-seo, comes in to introduce himself. He brings in bottles of pricey champagne as a celebration gift for Bree choosing Emmett as hers.

I would've been content to stay there all night, but eventually, we have to drop Dalton's parents off at the airport and begin the drive back to the compound. As we're all settled into the limo with Bree snuggled up against me on one side and Hudson on the other, I'm glad we got to do this. It was a nice break from the day to day at the compound. And after all the stress Bree dealt with, she deserved the couple of days' break.

Not too much longer now and it'll be time for Bree's heat. We'll be a fully formed pack as we help her through it. I can't wait.

Chapter Twenty-seven

Emmett

We've finally hit the end of the sixth week. Bree hasn't chosen between the remaining four suitors, but we all know her time is running out. I don't know if she plans on delaying the decision all the way until her heat hits or not, but I know it's stressing everyone out. Bree still doesn't seem sure of who she should choose, which is, of course, stressing her out.

Maverick, Dalton, Gabriel, and Roman are all going crazy the longer she goes without choosing anyone. I've tried to talk to Gabriel about it, but he's kept his distance from me and the guys. I get it; I do. He's trying to protect himself in case Bree doesn't choose him, but that doesn't make it any easier to watch him from afar. He and Roman seem to have grown closer over the last few weeks, so it's nice that he isn't alone.

It's been killing me and the rest of my pack mates not being able to be near Gabriel. We've all grown rather attached to him—though, no one quite as much as me—and we keep hoping that Bree will choose him, but we're trying not to pressure her.

After all, she'd chosen the three of them, at least in part because of me. I won't do that to her again. This needs to be her decision completely.

To say I'm surprised to find Gabriel sitting in the second floor living room is putting it lightly. I thought everyone was out by the pool, enjoying the weather. I needed a break so I decided to grab the last of my things from my room so I can move it into Bree's suite—no, *our* suite.

"Gabe?"

Gabriel's head shoots up as he tries to wipe away the tears he obviously didn't want me to see. I drop my bag onto the floor and hurry over to sit beside him. I grab his hands, which he promptly tries to pull from grasp, but I refuse to loosen my grip.

"Talk to me, Gabe. What's going on?"

He shakes his head. "I'm not supposed to be near you. I'm supposed to be keeping my distance, but it's breaking my fucking heart."

"Then stop," I urge him because he's hurting all of us with his distance.

His head drops, tears streaking down his face again. "I can't. Bree isn't going to choose me and then I'll have five holes in my heart. It's already going to be broken when she sends me home, but I need to save what parts of me I can. Don't you see?"

"Why are you so adamant that she won't choose you?"

"If she was going to choose me, she would've done it when she chose the rest of your pack. She knew we were all involved in some way and yet she didn't choose me. I've tried to keep my head up and Roman keeps reminding me that there's always hope until she hands us that black rose. But I can't keep doing that. The more I let myself hope, the harder I'm going to crash. Why doesn't she just send me home instead of letting me fall for her more and more every day?"

I sigh, wishing he would talk to Bree about this—not that she needs any more stress about choosing, but it's only her words that are going to make this right. "I don't think she's going to choose anyone until the last minute. I think she's torn about who to choose because she feels something for all of you. So she keeps pushing off the decision. There's only two weeks left until her heat, Gabe. You can make it. You can do this. You've just got to be strong a little longer."

"I don't want to be strong," he explodes as he leaps up from the couch. "I want to be chosen. I want her to love me as much as I love her. I know it's stupid to fall in love with someone this quickly, but how can I not? Bree is everything I could ever want in a mate."

He pauses, scrubbing at his face. "And then there's you, Onyx, Maddox, and Hudson. Do you know how close I am to falling in love with all of you as well? It's why I've had to stay away—why I had to protect myself."

"And what if she chooses you, Gabe? Then what?"

He shakes his head. "No, I can't think about that. I can't."

"Gabe..."

A sudden noise by the stairs startles both of us and when I turn, I find Bree standing there with tears in her eyes. "I'm so fucking sorry," she manages to get out before she bursts into tears and sinks to the floor.

What the hell?

I rush across the room, Gabriel right behind me. I drop beside her and gather her into my arms. "Bree, baby, what's wrong? Why are you crying? Are you hurt?"

Bree buries her head in the crook of my neck as she cries, shaking her head. She doesn't answer right away, but eventually manages to croak out, "I hurt Gabe. I'm a terrible omega. Why would anyone want me as an omega? I just keep hurting people and they keep wanting to leave me. I'm a bad omega."

All I can do is blink down at her, wondering where the hell this has come from. I've never seen her behave this way. But it's also not the first time I've noticed her acting oddly over the last few days. She's been crying more, and she yelled at Hudson this morning for being too cheerful. Then there are the clothes that keep disappearing while we're showering.

There's no way... her heat isn't supposed to start for two more weeks. Symptoms rarely start before the few days leading up to their heat. I lay my head on her forehead and she's burning up.

"Well, fuck..."

Bree lifts her eyes to meet mine. She's stopped crying, but she looks terrified. "My heat's coming early, isn't it?"

"Yeah, baby, I think it is."

"Fuck," Gabriel curses as he jumps to his feet. "I'll go call Tessa from my room. Should you go to your suite?"

I shake my head. "No, we'll come with you while you call Tessa. She'll know what to do."

I try to stand with Bree in my arms, but I'm not exactly as ripped as these alphas. Rather than watch me struggle, Gabriel leans down and easily takes her from my arms. "Grab my keycard from my back pocket so you can open my room," he tells me as I stand.

Grabbing it, I hurry down the hall and open the door for us. Bree's head is buried in Gabriel's neck as she runs her nose along it. When he tries to set her on the bed, she lets out a whimper.

"Just keep holding her and I'll call Tessa." I'm worried about Bree, but the fact that she's clinging to Gabriel while she's closing in on her heat gives me hope that she'll choose him.

Bree

It turns out that if an omega claims alphas and they don't claim the omega in return, it can cause the omega's heat cycle to begin early. Something I would've loved to know before I bit my alpha mates. My heat cycle is beginning two weeks early—something that should never happen.

I don't feel ready to make this decision yet. I planned to use the next two weeks to think about my decision and stall as long as possible. Is that fair of me? No, probably not. I guess my heat has taken that chance away from me either way.

Tessa had the top omega doctor flown in by helicopter from LA—which is definitely overkill. It's not like I'm dying or anything. Dr. Olga was an older beta woman, and she was so sweet that I immediately felt comfortable with her. She confirmed that I am going into heat. She's also the one who told me that claiming the alphas probably tripped my heat cycle early. It'll be good information for future seasons, but I wish I would've known before today.

Dr. Olga warned me she can't pinpoint exactly when my heat will kick in. It could be in a few hours or a few days. Knowing that I need to make a final decision, I asked Tessa to set up a final rose ceremony. I didn't even argue with her—much—about putting on a fancy dress. At least we found one that didn't make me feel like ants crawling across my skin.

It's made of crushed velvet, which is way too hot, especially since I'm about to go into heat, but Tessa assured me she'll have the AC blowing at max power the entire time. Poor Allison. She's had to apply and reapply my makeup three times already with the way I'm sweating. A portable AC unit was brought into my suite so I could stay cool enough to not melt off my makeup.

Reginald is waiting for me outside the ballroom. I'm annoyed that I'm wearing a dress I don't want to wear with heels that are uncomfortable as hell. I don't know why I can't just be barefoot.

"Hey, Bree. How are you feeling?"

"How the fuck do you think I'm feeling? I'm hot and I'm not ready to make this decision. I don't want to wear this fucking dress and these shoes are cutting off my circulation. Obviously, I'm perfectly fucking grand right now."

"Oh, omega. I'm sorry." Reginald drops to his knees in front of me. "I can help you with at least one of those problems."

I'm confused until he taps my foot. When I lift it, he slides the offending shoe off and throws it down the hallway. I gratefully put down my now bare foot and lift the other. Reginald pulls it off and tosses it to land with the other before righting himself.

"Is that better?"

I sigh my pleasure. "So much better."

"Why didn't you tell Tessa they were hurting your feet? She would've let you go without."

"We're already having to scramble because of my heat coming on early. I didn't want to be extra needy." I shrug. It's really just that I was worried about biting Tessa's head off after she demanded that I wear a gown for the ceremony. It could've gone one of two ways, ending in tears or violence. Neither were options I wanted to deal with, so I bit my tongue.

"Fine. I'll let you get away with it this time, but if anything else is making you uncomfortable, you'll tell me and I'll take care of it, yeah?"

"Okay," I say quietly as I wrap my arm in his. "Thank you, Reginald. You're the best friend a girl could ask for."

He laughs. "I know it. You ready to do this?"

"No, but we need to anyway."

Reginald leads me into the ballroom, and I just want to turn around and run back out. Today, there's no stage. Today, the four current members of my pack stand across from the four remaining suitors. A vase of roses filled with well over four dozen roses of all colors sits on a pedestal that Reginald leads me over to.

"Welcome back to our suitors and viewers. As you know by now, Bree's heat is coming early. We've learned that an omega claiming their alphas without them claiming the omega will eventually send the omega into heat regardless of their cycle. It's their body's way of forcing the mating mark from the alphas.

"Bree could go into heat at any moment, so she's chosen to move forward the final rose ceremony. Bree has spent six weeks getting to know these men and now it's time for her to make her final decisions about who will become part of her pack. Good luck, suitors."

I take a deep breath as I meet each of their eyes—Maverick, Dalton, Gabriel, and Roman. I care about all of them deeply, but I know they're not all meant to be a part of my pack. That won't make it easier to say goodbye to them today—especially with my emotions all over the place from my impending heat.

"Maverick, the first thing I noticed about you—besides how hot you are—" he snorts and I hear laughter from some of the others, "is your passion for architecture. It's not just a job for you. It's something you love, and you shared that with me repeatedly. Some things you said went straight over my head, but I still enjoyed the conversation. It also made me realize I wanted someone to be as passionate about me as you are about architecture.

"Dalton, the moment you opened your mouth, and that accent came out? Instant swoon, especially when paired with those boy next door looks and easy smile. And your parents? Oh, how I wish they were my parents. Growing up in your house must have been amazing."

"It was, and I know Mama will be happy to hear that." Dalton grins.

"But you're more than your good looks. You care about people with everything you are. When you do something, you don't do it halfway. Like reaching out to KOS about their footprint in Georgia. When you found out they only had one small office near Atlanta, you found local companies to become sponsors, so more centers could be built there. Because of you, they have ten new state-of-the-art centers being built as we speak. That wouldn't have happened without you."

I bite my lip, already fighting tears. "You're both wonderful men who will one day make an omega so happy, but that omega isn't me. As much as I hate to say goodbye, I have to make a decision. Thank you for taking a chance on me and on *Heated*, but this is the end of your journey."

They both step forward as I take two black roses from the vase to offer to them.

Maverick leans down to press a kiss to my cheek. "I was pretty sure I was going home today, but I don't feel like this was a waste of time for me. Being on *Heated* showed me what I was missing. I want a pack. I want an omega. I want a family. Yeah, it sucks that this didn't work out with us, but I've already started to build my pack."

I glance between him and Dalton. "The two of you? You're forming a pack?" A smile overtakes my face.

"We are and it's all thanks to you, darlin'." Dalton leans down to kiss me as well. "If it weren't for *Heated* I never would've met Maverick. Then you keepin' us on for as long as you did solidified our friendship. This may be the end of our *Heated* journey, but it's the beginning of another one."

Their words make it easier to say goodbye to them. They might not have found their omega on the show, but they found each other. They're leaving here with plans to form a pack. I can't wait to see the amazing things they do together.

I turn my attention to Gabriel and Roman. "That leaves you two. Gabriel, from the first moment you opened your flirty mouth, I fell under your spell. You have such a big heart and it's obvious you were meant to love more than one person. When I walked in on yours and Emmett's conversation earlier, I felt like my heart was being torn apart. I didn't like that you were hurting and that I was the cause.

"Roman, I'll admit, I wasn't sure about you at first, and it's not because of your age—so don't start getting any ideas about being too old for me again. It just takes you longer to warm up to others and open up. Unless you're talking about history and then you can talk anyone's ear off." Laughter follows because he's done it to all of us at least once over the last six weeks. "You're kind and you look after the people around you. Don't think I didn't notice how you've been helping Gabriel out over the last few weeks after most of his friends were chosen for the pack while he still wasn't.

"I thought for sure I'd only be adding one more person to my pack, but the idea of saying goodbye to either of you feels like I'm ripping my heart to shreds. So, instead, I'm asking both of you to join my pack."

There's yelling, hooting, and hollering all around me, but I hear none of it as Gabriel scoops me into his arms and kisses me. It's not a gentle, chaste kiss. No, this man kisses me like he's trying to fuck my mouth.

My head is spinning, and I can already feel the slick spilling from me as he sets me back on my feet. Roman is there to sweep me into his arms, kissing me just as deeply as Gabriel.

"Damn it, you didn't even let me give you your roses," I whine, which causes all of them to laugh. I grab the damn red roses and stomp back over to where Maverick and Dalton are congratulating Gabriel and Roman. I thrust the roses into their hands. "Here, assholes."

"Don't mind her," Emmett says, wrapping his arms around me from behind as he sets his chin on my shoulder. "Apparently upcoming heats make Bree a grumpy girl."

"Shut up. You're an asshole too." I try to stamp on his toes with my heel, but he's too fast.

"Now, now, baby. Is that any way to treat the men who are going to take care of you during your heat?" Emmett dances away from me as I try to smack his hand. He makes his way over to the rest of the pack as they welcome Roman and Gabriel to the fold.

"Don't forget what Dr. Olga said," Tessa says as she comes to stand on one side with Reginald on my other side.

"I know. I know. Taking their bite will send me immediately into heat. Guess I'm going into heat then."

Roman's eyes narrow and I realize he heard at least my response. "What's this about you going into heat?"

I shrug. "If I take any of your bites, it's going to send me into heat. Which I intend to take all of your bites now, soooo... I'm going into heat."

"Then what the hell are we waiting for?" Hudson throws me over his shoulder and rushes from the room.

Roman

I can't believe she chose me.

It's the thought that has been running through my head since she announced that she wanted both me and Gabriel. I figured Gabriel was a shoo-in, which is why I fought so hard to keep him from losing all hope. I also figured that if she was going to choose to take another suitor, it would be one of the other two.

But no. She chose me. It blows my mind.

"Come on, Rome," Emmett stands in the doorway to Bree's suite. "You don't want to miss this... and you don't know where the nest is, so hurry."

He looks adorable standing there and I'm grateful that we'll be able to explore what we started the night we shared Bree. If I'm not mistaken, all the alphas are interested in our beta. I'm not as close with Onyx, Maddox, and Hudson, but I'm not blind. They're all hot and who knows what'll happen between all of us as we figure out this whole pack thing.

I wrap my arm around Emmett's shoulders after he makes sure the suite door shuts behind us. "So I guess you'll be getting some bites, too?"

Emmett shrugs. "I'm not worried about that right now. This is about Bree. She has to take five bites, and it's going to send her into heat. Any or all of you could end up in rut. I've got to worry about making sure we're all fed and hydrated… and somewhat clean."

"How about you don't worry about that just yet?" I stop us, placing my hands on Emmett's shoulders. "Let's just worry about enjoying ourselves for now. It's doubtful that all five of us will end up being thrown into rut. We'll help you the best we can during her heat."

Emmett nods. "I know. You're right. Plus, Tessa already told me all I had to do was call the kitchen and deliver food to the suite—leaving it outside the door, of course."

"What are you two doing?" Bree stands in the doorway leading into her closet. "Roman, I need to add your thumbprint to the door."

"Huh?"

Emmett laughs, grabbing my hand as Bree disappears back into her closet. "She has this real high-tech nest hidden in her closet. The only way in is by scanning your thumb. She wants to make sure no one gets locked out during her heat."

I nod, not really understanding what he's talking about, but willing to follow his lead to find out. When we step into the closet, I realize a wall is standing open to reveal a nest. I'm thankful it seems to be big enough for all of us.

"Come on, Roman!" Bree waves me over, grabbing my right hand and lifting it to a scanner. It scans my thumb before letting out a long, low beep. "Okay, now you're all added. If you have to leave during my heat—which obviously you will—you can shut the door behind you and scan your thumb to be let back inside."

"That's... really cool," I say. It makes me feel better about her having her heat in this house. There's just so many people here and you never know when someone might snap. I'm aware they're unfounded fears, but this soothes most of them.

Bree drags me through the door, and I realize everyone else is already in here. She shuts the door behind us and the room dims, lit only by warm fairy lights. I can see why Bree would like this for her nest.

"So, here's the thing," Bree starts. "As soon as one of you bites me, my heat is going to kick in. I want to be conscious of what's happening while we're mating, and things get a little hazy during heats. So I figured we'd have a big orgy with everyone fucking everyone, and when it's time, you can all bite me at the same time."

"I guess that's one way to do it." Gabriel laughs.

"That's actually going to require some planning, baby," Emmett says with a grin. "Why don't we set everyone up where you want them during sex and we'll make sure they can all bite you, yeah?"

Bree nods. "That sounds like a fun game. Let's do it."

"I guess we should start with you," Emmett begins, but Bree shakes her head.

"Hell, no. Someone is going to be fucking you, too. I don't have enough holes for all six of you." She laughs. "I think you should let Gabe fuck you. He's the only one you haven't been with yet."

The heads of all four of the other alphas snap to me. "Don't worry, I'm into men as well. I just don't broadcast it like all you do."

"Huh." Gabriel licks his lips as he runs his eyes over me. "That is good to know. Oof. What was that for?"

Bree shakes her head. "Just hush, all of you, while Emmett and I figure this out. This is going to be harder in the nest. If we had the height of the bed, there could be a nice train going on."

Emmett bursts into laughter. "You did not just say that."

"I sure the fuck did." She laughs. "Okay, so Gabe fucks you next to me. He'll need to be close enough to bite me, maybe my wrist."

"It should be the one with my tattoo."

Bree nods. "Done. That means the two of you will be on my right side. That leaves four men and three holes. One of you is going to have to fuck someone else."

"So, someone takes your ass…"

"Fates above. Will the two of you stop?" I ask. "You're quickly turning this into a puzzle instead of the sexy experience it should be. Why don't we all get naked and go from there? Though I do like your idea of Gabe and Emmett together."

Bree nods excitedly. "It's going to be fun to watch, but you're right."

When Bree starts pulling off her dress, everyone starts ripping off their clothes until we're left with seven very hot, very naked, very horny people. I crawl behind Bree, kissing her neck when she jumps from my arms.

"Shit! I forgot the lube. How could I forget the lube?"

Onyx pulls her back down to her knees, shuffling her back towards me. "Don't worry, little omega, we grabbed more than enough. Now, kiss your new alpha."

Bree backs up until her ass is rubbing against my aching cock, twisting to kiss me over her shoulder. I quickly lose myself in the kiss, completely forgetting about the others until someone slaps a bottle of lube in my hand. I break the kiss, blinking at Hudson blankly.

"You're the lucky alpha who gets to fuck her ass since you're already behind her, but you're gonna have to prep her. It shouldn't take too much. We've been working on plugs with her every night."

"O-okay," I agree, hard to believe I'm having this conversation right now. Taking the bottle, I glance around to see what I missed while I was lost in Bree. Onyx's head is buried between Bree's thighs while Maddox is fucking Onyx on his fingers. Bree and Emmett are kissing while Gabriel is working the beta on his fingers. "There's a lot of asshole stretching going on right now."

Bree breaks her kiss to laugh, glancing at me over her shoulder. "That's because there are more dicks than I have holes. You all better get used to fucking one another."

"I don't think that's going to be a problem for our pack," Emmett says with a laugh of his own.

"Don't be a brat." My hand comes down on Bree's ass and she explodes around Onyx's tongue and fingers.

"Bree likes spankings. Good to know." Gabriel hums.

I smirk, meeting his eyes around Bree. "So does Emmett."

"Oh, really? I might just test that out if you keep being a brat."

Hudson is still kneeling beside me as I pour the lube over my fingers. He bites his lip as he watches me slide my finger inside of her puckered hole. "You have been working with her, haven't you?"

She's still tight as hell, but she relaxes into it and it takes a lot less time for me to work a second finger into her.

"Can I kiss you?"

My head snaps up to Hudson, realizing he's asking me. "Yeah, sure."

It feels kind of weird to have him ask if he can kiss me, but let's be real—this whole situation is a little weird. We're a new pack and we're all going to mark our omega at the same time. We're literally having an orgy the day the pack is fully formed.

Bree's heat will help us get over anything that might be holding us back as we work together to help her through it. But we're doing this because our bites are going to force her into heat. We can't wait for her heat to ease us all into this. Our omega wants all our bites at once, so that's what she's going to get.

Hudson's lips ghost over mine, and it's not enough. When he tries to pull away, I chase him with my lips, my fingers never stopping their movement. Hudson grins and slams his lips down on mine. He's a damn good kisser, too. Just like with Bree earlier, I lose myself in Hudson's kiss. My fingers never stop their movements and I even add a third finger, but everything else is lost to me.

When Bree clamps down on my fingers, coming again, I realize that Onyx is already fucking her while Maddox fucks him. Even Gabriel is sliding in and out of Emmett while the beta clings to Bree's hand. Seems like Hudson and I are the odd men out right now.

"Finally decide to get involved?" Gabriel asks with a laugh.

"Fuck off, we were... experimenting." Hudson sticks his tongue out at Gabriel, causing me to shake my head.

"You ready for me, baby girl?" I ask Bree as I stroke my cock, covering it in lube.

"Yes. Fates above, fuck me, daddy!"

A flush creeps up my neck as I realize the other alphas are watching me with interest. Hudson leans close, licking a stripe up my neck. "He does have daddy energy, doesn't he? I like it."

Ignoring the other man, I nudge my cock against Bree's ass and slowly begin pressing in. By the time I've bottomed out, Hudson is on his feet and slowly fucking Bree's mouth.

It takes us a few moments to work out a rhythm between all of us, but soon Bree is screaming around Hudson's cock as we pound in and out of her. She feels amazing as she pulses around my cock. I wonder for a moment how many times we can make her come before we all follow her.

Too bad we won't be finding out just yet as Bree pulls off Hudson's cock and twists in mine and Onyx's arms to bite down on my shoulder. My entire body freezes up as I come harder than I ever have before. She almost immediately releases me, and I bite down on her shoulder in return.

That just starts a whole chain reaction of orgasms and bites as Bree comes with my bite. Hudson drops to his knees, stroking his own cock as Onyx falls apart, biting down on Bree's neck. I see Bree grab Gabriel's arm so she can bite him, and he bites her wrist in return as he falls apart. Onyx's orgasm sets off Maddox's, and he bites down on Bree's ankle.

I reach around, though my arm doesn't want to work, and take over stroking Hudson's dick so he can pick his spot to bite her. His hot cum spills over my hand as he bites down on her nipple. The scream that pours from Bree's lips as she tightens around me and Onyx has another orgasm rushing through me.

We all collapse together in the nest, piling together around Bree. I can barely feel my limbs as the bond forms and through Bree I can already pick up on some of the others' emotions. It's crazy.

Within ten minutes of us all falling apart, Bree starts whimpering.

"What's wrong, Bree?"

"I need a knot, alpha. No one knotted me. Will you knot me?"

A glance at her eyes confirms that Bre's heat has started. I sigh, still trying to get the feeling back in my body so I can crawl between Bree's legs.

"I've got it, alphas," Emmett says as he lays a hand on my arm. "Let me get her ready for your knots. That's what I'm here for."

Then he's dropping between her legs, Bree mewling at his attention. Being part of a pack definitely comes with its advantages.

Epilogue

Bree
Four Months Later

Looking around, I can't help but smile.

We're finally done. We're finally moved into our new pack home.

Emmett, Hudson, and Roman have crashed down onto one of our couches. Roman has his arms around Emmett and Hudson as they cuddle into his side. Maddox and Onyx are leaning back on another couch, eyes closed as their feet rest on the coffee table.

The only one missing is Gabriel, and I know he's around here somewhere. Probably causing some kind of mischief while no one has eyes on him. I need to talk to all six of them, but I don't want to interrupt their resting. It's been a long day of making sure everything made it into the new house and arranged just the way I wanted it.

Two arms snake around me, causing me to jump as Gabriel nuzzles my neck. "What has you thinking so hard, little omega?"

I hum, turning my head to kiss him. "I'm really glad that we're all moved in."

"That might be true," Roman calls from the couch with a stern look, "but it's not the only thing you're thinking about. Talk to us, Bree."

Chewing on my lip, I know I'm giving away just how nervous I am to talk to them, but I can't seem to help myself. It's not like what I need to talk to them about is bad news. It's just a lot.

"Can we talk in my nest?"

I watch as my pack exchanges nervous glances and I want to reassure them that everything's okay, but I keep my mouth shut.

"Of course, sweet girl," Roman says as he climbs off to the couch, moving to me and sweeping me into his arms.

Gabriel grunts when Roman takes me from him, but says nothing. I lay my head on my alpha's chest as he walks us down the hallway, his purr settling me in a way nothing else can.

My nest is off the main bedroom that we've dubbed the pack bedroom. It's huge and we had the bed custom built so we can share whenever we want. Everyone also has their own bedroom in case they want to have a night alone, or if I want a night alone with one of my guys. I plan on us being in the pack bedroom more often than not and I turned my bedroom into an office, knowing that I'll never sleep alone.

Plus, I have my nest. If I need some alone time, I can always find it in my nest. No one would dare enter without my explicit permission.

Roman drops to the floor of the nest with me still in his arms and my stomach drops for a moment. I hold my breath, afraid that I'm going to lose my lunch, but it slowly settles as the rest of my pack sits around us.

As much as I love being held by any of my men, I need to see all of them to have this conversation. So I struggle out of Roman's arms and settle beside him.

"Is everything okay, *gongjunim*?" Emmett scoots closer until he's flush against my side.

I lay my head on his shoulder, taking in his eucalyptus, lavender, and chamomile scent. Just a sniff of my beta has everything settling inside of me. "Yes, I'm sorry for worrying you all. This isn't bad news. I'm just a little anxious and we all know I feel better in my nest. There's been so many changes lately. I need to be here for this conversation."

Emmett smiles when I lift my head to meet his gaze. He gives me a kiss, but thankfully doesn't attempt to deepen it. As soon as any of them touch me, I'm putty in their hands. And I really have things I need to talk to them about.

"What's going on, Bree?" Onyx asks, watching me carefully.

I smile as I glance around at each of them, my heart filling with love. "Well, first, the network is calling *Heated* a hit. It had the best ratings of their prime-time shows this year and it's been everywhere on social media—as you're well aware."

Most of us had a social media presence before the show, but once *Heated* aired, we all blew up. Fans wanted to interact with myself and all the suitors. Most people were supportive, but of course there were a few trolls.

"So, we've been picked up for a second season." I laugh. "Actually, they went ahead and green-lit us for four more seasons. They wanted to do the show twice a year, and I said no, absolutely not. Tessa and I put the call out for omegas and we've been overwhelmed with applicants. Not all of them fit the criteria we've set, but that's fine. That's what interns are for. But Tessa and I have already begun discussing the changes I think need to be made to the show."

"That's great, omega." Maddox reaches across the nest to squeeze my hand. "But I don't think that's everything you have to tell us."

I shake my head with a laugh. They can all read me so well and after so little time. "It's not. We plan to have the second season happen around the same time of year, depending on our chosen omega's heat cycle. That means I'm going to have to go back to Rancho Mirage in seven or eight months, for about three months. Obviously, you can't all come with me because of jobs and stuff. But I hope you'll all be willing to come out as often as possible. It's going to suck not having you all there all the time, but by then..."

I trail off for a moment. I hadn't meant to tell them this right now. I'd wanted to wait until after we'd finished talking about *Heated*, but it slipped out. And now they're all looking at me expectantly.

"By then... what?" Hudson finally asks.

"I'm pregnant."

Silence surrounds me as my eyes flit from face to face. I'm not worried about their reaction, not really. I know they'll all be excited about a baby—or babies—but for just a moment, worry seeps in at their silence.

"A baby?" Gabriel murmurs, and that seems to break everyone out of their stupor.

Roman pulls me into his lap, hands going to my still flat stomach. "We're having a baby? Really?"

I nod. "We are. I wanted to be sure before I told you all. The doctor confirmed it yesterday. We apparently conceived during my first heat."

"So, that's why you didn't really have a heat cycle last month," Roman murmurs.

"It's what made me book the doctor's appointment. One day of heat isn't normal." I shrug. "I'm surprised none of you guessed it, honestly."

"We're having a fucking baby," Hudson crows behind me as Roman's lips descend on mine.

We spent the next few minutes with me being passed from man to man, each kissing me, telling me how much they love me, and just how excited they are for a baby.

"Wait, a second." Emmett's voice breaks through the celebration. "So that makes the baby due when?"

I grimace. "In about five and a half months... right before I have to go back to Rancho Mirage for *Heated*." This was the part I was worried about.

There's another moment of silence before everyone starts talking at once, trying to figure out how we're going to make this work.

Emmett puts his fingers in his mouth, letting out a loud whistle that draws everyone's attention. "Talking all at once will help no one. Plus, I already have a solution if you'd let me talk."

He waits to make sure everyone is done before he pulls me into his lap. "I'm sure you've been worrying about this since you found out, but you don't have to. None of us expect you to stop working. We know how important your company and *Heated* are to you. It just means that my timetable needs to be slightly accelerated. I'll need to make sure the new chef is trained before you have the baby. That way, I have at least a month with you and the baby before you have to go back to work. Then I'll watch him or her while you're working."

"What are you talking about?" I frown, arms looped around his neck. "I would never expect you to give up your job."

"I know that, baby. But this is what I want. I've already talked to Jun-seo. I talked to him as soon as I went back to work to let him know what I was planning. I was planning to talk to you about it tonight, but he wants me to buy into Lyrical and be a partial owner. I'll still be able to go in occasionally to cook, or fill in when they need me to, but he knows I want to stay at home with the kids so you can work. We'll probably schedule me as a celebrity chef once or twice a month. But I'll help with the running of the day-to-day business, which will help him."

I hear the others murmuring behind us, but I can't tear my eyes away from my beta. "This is what you want?"

"This is what I want more than anything. I want to take care of our baby—of our children if we're blessed with more. I'm sure there will still be some juggling that has to be done, but I want to be the one to stay at home with our kids. I want to be the one here for everything. Even if that means I go to Rancho Mirage with you for three months every year for the next however many years."

My heart feels like it's going to burst as I lean down to kiss him. I love that he wants to do this and went about putting a plan in place for it without ever being asked. I just love him.

"I love you, Em," I whisper against his lips.

"We all love you, Emmett." Gabriel's hand wraps in Emmett's hair, turning him away from me. "Thank you for taking care of this for our girl."

Emmett flushes, but nods. "Like I said, it's what I want. It's what will work best for our pack."

"Oh!" I squeal, jumping up from Emmett's lap and rushing into the bedroom. I grab the envelope I'd set on the bedside table earlier. Running back to my nest, I find all six of them blinking up at me. "This came today!"

"And what is this?" Maddox asks, already reaching for the envelope, but I lift it from his reach and give it to Roman.

Roman takes it from me, brow furrowed. "What is this?"

"It's a surprise we've been working on for you." I glance at the others and they return my smile as they realize what it is. "Open it."

Roman shakes his head before tearing into the envelope and pulling out the paper. His eyes skim over it for a moment before popping up to glance at each of us. "Is this... Are you... I..."

"Yes, it's real, Rome." Onyx pulls the alpha into his arms. "We want you to be our head alpha, and we're taking your name."

"We're officially Pack Knight from today on," I cry out with glee as tears stream down Roman's face. "Are you happy with your surprise, alpha?"

Roman nods. "Of course I am, omega. I wasn't expecting this. We hadn't even talked about it."

"Sure we did. Just not with you." Gabriel kisses the still shocked Roman. "We all knew what it would mean to you and we wanted your name. And now we're officially a pack in the eyes of the government."

As I watch each of my men kiss Roman, I place a hand on my stomach. Our family is growing and I couldn't be more excited. *Heated* changed my life in so many ways, but I know I've never been happier than I am at this moment.

Author's note

What did you think? I'd love to hear what you thought!

First and foremost, thank you for picking up this book and giving me a chance. Without readers, I'd have a very short career. And to my ARC and alpha/beta teams. All of y'all make sure I get out the best book I can.

This book turned out to be about 30k longer than I thought it would be. It was definitely a journey writing it. Both Bree and I learned better ways for the omegas to meet their alphas in the writing of this book, so expect things to be changed up some if you join us for Knot Their Reality. It's set to release in the summer of 2023, so ignore the date listed. I've already introduced the omega and some of the suitors in my story, A Very Knotty Christmas. You can find that story in the Jingle My Balls antho—which is also available on KU. Once it's unpublished, I'll make sure to get it uploaded again for all of you to read!

Thank you again for giving this author a chance!

Thanks y'all, Miranda May

About the Author

Miranda is a new author who has been writing since high school, but never considered being published until now. When she discovered reverse harem books, she knew it was time to share her stories. She has plans to write paranormal romance, urban fantasy, omegaverse, and contemporary—all reverse harem/why choose/polyam stories.

Growing up a Navy brat, Miranda has lived in many places. She currently makes her home in Piney Flats, TN with her husband and adorable corgi, Luna. Don't worry if you've never heard of it, it's a teeny tiny town less than an hour from the Tennessee/Virginia border. When not writing, Miranda spends most of her time reading or playing Dungeons and Dragons like a true geek. She also has an almost unhealthy obsession with corgis—so don't be surprised if she brings them up.

Follow Me

Please follow me! It's the best way to keep up to date on what I have going on!

Also By Miranda May

SECRETS OF SORLPHI
A Fae Realms Series.
Paranormal RH Romance.

Silent Secrets | Book One
Sinful Secret | Book Two
Sinister Secrets | Book Three (Spring 2023)

HEATED
Series of RH Omegaverse Intertwined Standalones.

Knot My Reality | Book One
Knot Their Reality | Book Two (Summer 2023)

STANDALONES

The Music That We Make (Spring 2023)
A PNR Rockstar second chance story.

ANTHOLOGIES

A Whale of a Time
Eleven spicy RH whale shifter short stories.
featuring The Music That We Make

Jingle My Balls
A Gay & Merry LGBTQ Charity Anthology
featuring A Very Knotty Christmas

Printed in Great Britain
by Amazon